LION
OF
JUDAH

THE ANOINTED, BOOK II

JACOB A. WELDON

Printed in the United States of America
Anointed Book, LLC
Paperback ISBN: 979-8-9926555-2-0
Ebook ISBN: 979-8-9926555-3-7

AUTHOR'S NOTE

Thank you for taking the time to read this book, the second installment in the *Anointed* series. While these books should stand alone, the reader will find that certain chapters or excerpts introduce characters that do not appear again until later installments in the series. Please keep in mind that the entire series covers an eighty-year period of history. As in life, it will be difficult to see how or why certain events play out until revealed in the grand scheme of the completed work. I appreciate your patience and continued interest.

This series is based on the stories of 1 and 2 Samuel from the Hebrew Bible / Old Testament. While the author has made every attempt to ensure that the storyline is true to the Word, fictional backstories, characters, and dialogue have been added to the biblical framework. Any and all artistic license has been taken with the goal of supporting and bringing to life the biblical stories from scripture. Readers are encouraged to read the corresponding scriptures which are provided at the beginning of many chapters. I hope you enjoy this book and that it leaves you with a deeper understanding of God's Word.

ACKNOWLEDGMENTS

I want to thank my wife, Sarah, and daughters, Seanna and Scout, for the countless hours they have sacrificed for this book.

Many thanks to my editor, Susan Hendricks, my father and mother, Michael and Mickie Weldon, who gave their time to review multiple revisions of this work.

I could not fail to mention the influence of my brothers, both in blood and in service, which influenced many of the stories that fill the pages of this work.

So many of the positive influences in my life have come through Rock Springs Church and my Pastor, Benny Tate. Thank you, Benny, for your guidance and influence during our trip to Israel in June of 2023. Thank you, Rock Springs staff and members, for your support, friendship, encouragement, and sharpening.

Thank you, Christopher Young, for pointing me to God's word when the going got tough.

Thank you, Jonathan Sexton, for your mentorship, coaching, support, and faith.

I thank God for this calling, His patience, His gentle correction, and the numerous affirmations He has provided throughout the process.

CONTENTS

OPPORTUNITY

1069 BC, Gibeah, Benjamin, Israel

Two years had passed since the overwhelming Israelite victory over the Philistines at Michmash. Prince Jonathan, Saul's oldest son and heir to the throne, had shown great promise in the battle that had driven the Philistine forces from their lands. Prior to the battle, the Israelite forces had dwindled to merely 600 fighting men. Whether by audacity, courage, lunacy, or divine protection, Jonathan, along with his armor-bearer and closest confidant, had turned the tide against a vastly larger enemy force. The Philistines had suffered a substantial loss of their domestic forces and, for a time, had been driven back to their strongholds near the Mediterranean Sea from whence their ancestors came.

The interior of Israel enjoyed a period of safety and prosperity. It was now a rare occurrence to spot a Philistine anywhere near the royal city of Gibeah, located in the heart of Israel and the tribal lands of Benjamin. Free from the threat of attack, its walls were raised and strengthened. Its fortifications began to rival the Jebusite and Philistine strongholds of Jebus and Gath.

Capitalizing on the victory at Michmash, the once reluctant King Saul set his mind to building up the Israelite military, using every opportunity to add to their numbers. In only two short years, Israel had amassed a force of two hundred "elephs" consisting of roughly one thousand men each.

Jonathan's younger brothers, Abinadab and Machishua, were already following in their older brother's footsteps and showing promise as military leaders.

Still, Saul had learned better than to bask in their victory and searched for ways to secure Israel's borders from those who would threaten it. Never again would he allow his people to become so weakened or vulnerable. In his zeal for Israel, Saul sought to secure Israel's borders with the neighboring kingdoms.

"Ein breira!" he would say. "No alternative." It had become the rallying cry of the Israelites. It exemplified a mindset - be prepared for war at all times. What their neighbors had to offer, slavery or extermination, was not an alternative they were willing to accept. "We grow, we strengthen, we fortify, or we die. That is no alternative," Saul was often quoted as saying.

Finally relieved of Philistine garrisons within the kingdom, King Saul turned his attention to other threats. Moab, south of Reuben and east of the Dead Sea, had formed a loose alliance with Ammon following the defeat at Jabesh Gilead. Together, these two groups had begun to build more and more settlements along their borders with Reuben and Gad near the fertile soil of the Jordan River valley. South of the Dead Sea, the king of Edom encouraged his people to move north along the western shores of the Dead Sea toward Hebron of Judah. In the north, far from the palace, the kings of Zobah had gone completely unchecked for many years and, like the Amalekites in the south, sent raiding parties every harvest season into Israelite territories, occasionally taking women and children with them.

Equipped with newly acquired Philistine armor and iron weaponry, the growing Israelite army was stronger than it had ever been. Everywhere King Saul and his army went, young men from the Israelite tribes joined the ranks, eager to dole out vengeance on their enemies who'd gone unchallenged for decades. For a time, Saul's forces enjoyed a period of small but unfettered victories.

***

The men raised their cups for another toast to their king before downing the contents. The wine wasn't the best, but the company was what mattered. The king's hall was filled to the brim with officers, leaders of elephs and me'ahs[1]. Before another toast could be given, Abner stood. The room began to grow quiet as the more attentive among them hushed those who'd already partaken too liberally from the wine.

"Years ago, our people were threatened to be brought once more into subjugation. Our people cried out to God and one man was chosen to lead our people. He led us to victory over the Ammonites and ransomed our people. Since then, we prevailed over the Philistines despite overwhelming odds. No longer will the outsiders rule over our people as in times past. We are stronger now than we have ever been," Abner said loud enough for everyone in the room to hear. "But only if we maintain the standards we have since instilled. Only if we hold tight to the discipline which each of you has embraced."

The men shouted their affirmations and rapped their knuckles on the table. As Abner resumed speaking, the room quickly grew quiet.

"You have trained day and night, endured every hardship, bled and sweated. You've been broken to bits, reshaped, and remolded. Some of you quite literally," Abner remarked as the men laughed. "You've pushed past your own limitations and accomplished that which you never thought possible. You have worked hard. King Saul and I could not be more proud of you all," Abner continued as he scanned the crowd.

"Look to your right and your left. You men have come from different backgrounds, rich and poor, large families and small, some fatherless, some orphans. You were stone masons, carpenters, merchants, farmers, and clerks, but in a short time, all those differences faded away. It is for the man to your right and left that you train and fight. It is for the man under your command. It is for his family, for his wife and child that you have trained. Remember that when the time for battle comes! And make no mistake, it will come!

"Our land has never been long without war, but with your effort and hard work and the blessings of Almighty God, we will secure victory for our people so that we will at last know peace. There is but one way that

---

[1] A company or unit of roughly one hundred men.

we obtain this peace. Discipline in all things. There is no alternative!" Abner raised his cup high into the air.

The officers raised their cups and shouted in unison, "EIN BREIRA!" They downed the contents again and when Abner had returned to his seat, resumed the boisterous laughter and retellings of the events that inevitably occur during long periods of training.

Saul was listening to the men and enjoying the crude, but good-hearted banter of men who endured constant hardships together when an unmistakable sound caught his attention.

THUMP, THUMP, THUMP, echoed through the hall. He stood and looked over the heads of the men to see the end of a large wooden staff protruding above them and purposefully ambling its way towards him. Just below it was a shiny bald head rimmed with silvery gray hair. The clamor of the men grew quiet as the old prophet waded through them.

Remembering their last encounter, Saul moved to intercept Samuel and greeted the prophet without drawing attention. He would not be publicly scorned and embarrassed in front of the men a second time if he could help it. Saul invited the old prophet into a private chamber away from the crowded main hall, shouting "As you were" to the men as he and Samuel exited.

When the royal guard started to follow them, Saul motioned sternly for them to remain in the hall. No sooner than they'd entered the chamber, Abner joined them.

"It's good to see you, Samuel," Saul lied. "To what do we owe this visit?"

"It seems you have finally embraced your anointing. It is a shame that it has come so late. Still, I am the one the Lord sent to anoint you King over His people Israel; so listen now to the message from the Lord," Samuel said, letting his words take effect. "The Lord has a job for you."

Saul nodded as he listened intently.

Abner summoned a scribe and a moment later the man returned with writing materials.

"Go on," Abner said.

"This is what the Lord Almighty says," Samuel began. "'I will punish the Amalekites for what they did to Israel when they waylaid them as they came up from Egypt. Now go, attack the Amalekites and totally destroy all that belongs to them. Do not spare them; put to death men and women, children and infants, cattle and sheep, camels and donkeys.'"

Saul looked to Abner, then back to Samuel.

"It will be as He has commanded," Saul said with a bow.

"Does the Lord have any guidance as to where or how we should attack them?" Abner inquired.

"Only that he will give you the victory if you do exactly as he commands," Samuel replied. "You shall devote everyone and everything to destruction."

"Very well," said Saul. "We will be the implement of the Lord's wrath for what was done to our people."

Samuel nodded approvingly, then turned to leave. Saul thought he'd seen the slightest sign of a smile on the prophet's face. It had been years since he'd enjoyed the company of old man, the only man who'd believed in him when no one had.

"Samuel," Saul called after him. "Will you not stay? It would do the men good to have you break bread with us."

The old prophet stood silent for a moment. For a moment, Saul thought that his offer would be accepted. Then, just as quickly, the prophet shook his head and the wall of silence was back up. He proceeded out of the chamber to the courtyard where he would not have to pass by the joyful and celebrating men. He knew his presence would likely only dampen their fellowship. Ahijah followed him out, along with the prophet's ever-present apprentice who'd been all but completely unnoticed during the entire encounter.

Saul longed for the relationship he'd once enjoyed with Samuel. He remembered the sorrow and emptiness he'd felt at Gilgal when Samuel had left them there, but resolved to not let the emotion take hold.

"Good!" Saul exclaimed, turning to Abner. "Should we tell the men?"

"If we don't, they will have questions about why he came and left so quickly," Abner mused.

"Doesn't he always?" Saul said defensively. "Very well, you tell them we have a new mission, ordained by the Eternal and that we will begin preparations immediately. Leave the details out until we've briefed the officers. We don't want word to reach the Amalekites before we step off."

"Agreed," Abner replied. "Word travels fast. That will be enough to assuage their concerns for now I think."

*****

The next morning the army of Israel gathered into their elephs to receive instructions. The army had grown to two-hundred elephs consisting of roughly twenty companies or groups of one-hundred. Reviewing the vast array of his forces, Saul mused about how they had multiplied from so few at Michmash to the great and powerful army which stood before him. So much for Samuel's prediction, he thought to himself. He supposed that the Lord had once again found favor with him. Indeed, the Eternal has forgiven me, he said to himself as he looked on.

After receiving the report, Abner released the men to their captains and called for his most trusted commanders. There was Jehoiada, a Levite priest who'd been instrumental in garnering support for an Israelite king prior to Saul's anointing, along with Dodo, an Ahohite of Benjamin who'd fought with Jonathan at Geba and Michmash, and Hotham, a Gadite from Aroerite who, like many others of his tribe, bore a scar in place of where his right eye had once been. There was also Shimri the Tizrite and Agee the Hararite, from the hills country of Judah.

"Gather around," Abner called to the men, pointing to the terrain model laid out before him. He wanted a small enough audience so that each man could see, hear, and ask questions. They would each later return to use the model to go over their specific mission with the men under their command.

"The Lord has instructed us to lay waste to the Amalekites for what they did to our ancestors years ago when they came up out of Egypt. Their yearly festival has already begun when they make sacrifices and engage in general debauchery and drunkenness. Our spies tell us they will be gathering to worship Baal, or whatever other god they've constructed, on a mountain south of the spring at Avdat. They've congregated near its base there, calling the place the city of Amalek," he said, pointing to the dirt mound replica between himself and the men.

"If we seize the high ground, taking them by surprise, we can push them into an ambush here," he said as he followed a trough-like feature leading down to a shallow depression in the dirt. "This represents a large wadi in the Zin Valley. I want to stage an ambush there. The main body of our forces is going to make a wide sweeping movement around the Amalekite camp west and south to cut off their escape. We want them to think they're being enveloped, but before we close the gap, we'll let them escape through the wadi where the ambush will be lying in wait. Once the ambush is sprung, sealing off their escape route, the rest of the army will close in through the ravine to sweep up."

Abner paused, examining the faces of the men around him as they studied the earthen diagram. Several nodded their assent and looked back to Abner to continue. Taking on a more somber tone, he continued.

"Everything must perish. We spare nothing and no one. This is the command of the Eternal. I don't like the idea of killing women and children, but we must trust that God is good. Remember that this life is not the end. God knows their fate and will see to them as He alone sees fit. We must follow His commands," Abner said in a somber voice. He let the men reflect on this for a moment before continuing.

"Jehoiada, I want your division to move ahead of the rest. You are the main effort. You will move under cover of darkness to the ravine and stage the ambush along the valley. Use your best judgment on the location and how to array your forces there. If you need additional bowmen or other equipment, you will have them," Abner said, scanning the rest of the leaders. They all nodded their understanding.

"Dodo, you will take the lead maneuver element to encircle Amalek and take the high ground. We must sweep wide enough to the west that we don't cut off any stragglers from the lot of them. The same is true when we hook around the southern side. You need to move fast enough that they don't all escape to the south. I want you to take up positions Southwest to South of the city."

"Agee, you will fall in behind Dodo, making up the south to south-east. Hotham, you'll have the western portion of the cordon, and Shimri will take the northern section," Abner concluded.

Jehoiada briefed the others on what signals would be used in the event reinforcements were needed or certain maneuvers were called for after the battle had commenced. Signaling predominantly consisted of various easily distinguishable calls from the shofar or a standard trumpet. Standard bearers carried with them various colored flags which could be waved for visual confirmation. Dodo then addressed other practicalities, such as water, where the men could find additional armor and weaponry, caring for the wounded, and so on. There was no need to address quarter for the enemy, for none would be given.

"Because we will not be partaking of the enemy's livestock or other provisions, we will have extra rations. We will not be killing and eating anything that belongs to the Amalekites. Provisions will be brought up and available near the staging area."

"This isn't going to be another Michmash scenario, is it?" Agee asked sarcastically.

"Which part? If you mean fasting, not if I can help it," Abner responded.

The men laughed nervously.

"Thank God for that," Dodo exclaimed.

"You all know the succession of command. Does anyone have any questions?" Abner asked.

Following a few brief inquiries centered around the length and speed of travel, the commanders dispersed to their divisions and saw to the finer details as they prepared for the long march, sobered by the grave task ahead of them.

AMALEK

1069 BC, Amalek, Negev Desert,
South of Israelite Controlled Territories

"What then is this bleating of the sheep in my ears
and the lowing of the oxen that I hear?"
I Samuel 15:14

From within his tent, Agag, king of the Amalekites, awoke to a strange sound. Still groggy from the night before, he pushed the women aside which lay about him and staggered outside to relieve himself just outside the tent. Realizing for the first time that the noise had risen from the camp below him, his eyes focused as he tried to determine the source of the sound. He still strained to see in the light as his eyes adjusted. He blinked several times, then rubbed his eyes before looking again. Spanning his view from one side to the other, he could see that the camp was almost completely surrounded. Turning eastward, he saw a great number of the camp fleeing towards the wadi to the east, which extended towards the great salt sea. He looked behind, further up the mountain, trying hastily to determine the safest course of action. The line of troops surrounding the camp was quickly closing in. It seemed their numbers were increasing the closer they approached. He started in the direction where the others were fleeing and hurried to catch up and disappear into the mass of commoners.

His lungs and throat burned. His head ached as he sprinted with all his might towards the ravine. Hundreds poured in and crowded around him, running and shouting. Suddenly, there was a great commotion ahead of them and he found himself crushed against a wall of people. From atop the ravine, artillerymen appeared from hidden positions and began raining arrows, javelins, and stones down upon the great mass of fleeing Amalekites. Agag could see the priest Shoshak up ahead of him in his unmistakable priestly garb as he turned and ran back towards the mouth of the ravine. Bodies fell to either side of him as the mass of commoners fled the onslaught from above on the ridge. Instinctively, he fell to the ground and pulled a writhing body atop his own. Others rushed past, knocking him to the ground. He cursed them as they fled, kicking and stepping on him as they ran.

Shoshak, too, was knocked to the ground among the mass of fleeing men and women. From the ground, he saw a horizontal crevasse in the southern slope of the ravine. When he managed to get to his feet, he was scraped and bloody but surging with adrenaline. Arrows seemed to rain down all around him when he suddenly realized the conspicuousness of his cloak. Without slowing down, he shed the outer garment and staggered to the crevasse. He found a young woman already concealed inside, leaving little space for him to occupy. Seizing her by the arm, he snatched her from her hiding place. Several arrows struck the ground around them as he threw himself into the crease and squeezed his overindulged belly into the small opening in the rocks. The woman screamed in terror and tried to crawl back into the space. Shoshak pressed his hand to her face and pushed her away. He'd managed to get deep enough into the crevasse that he could hide and avoid detection, but it was not big enough for two, and now she was surely drawing attention. She struggled against him, trying to reach the safety of the rocks when an arrow pierced her back. She screamed and writhed in pain, surely calling more attention to the place where he was now safely concealed. He reached about him and drew in several rocks into position near his body, further concealing himself.

Time seemed to slow for Shoshak as the seconds inched by, watching the life fade from the young woman. As he watched her, the effects of the herbs and mushrooms he'd consumed the night prior began to subside. His mind began to clear and he came to the realization that he'd seen this woman before. Recalling her from the encampment, he remembered that she'd had two small children with her when he'd seen her last, twins he recalled. He did not need to ponder where they were.

As he listened to the screams from camp and watched the carnage unfold in the ravine, he couldn't help thinking, "So much for Baal's deliverance." All the same though, he thought. He'd never really believed in the deity anyway. His father had been a priest and it had provided a luxurious and prestigious lifestyle. So what if the sacrifices had been in vain? They hadn't had enough food in the camp to feed all those extra mouths anyway, he rationalized.

The thought made him think about food. He'd not eaten since early in the prior evening. Who knows how long he'd have to hide here in this crevasse before it would be safe to emerge. His plump belly was becoming more and more raw as he shifted around on the rough stone, trying to make himself comfortable. In an effort to take his mind off of his own discomfort, he decided to focus on the scene that played out before him.

He'd surmised earlier that the attackers were Israelites. Now that he could see them up close, he was sure of it. He watched as bearded men mercilessly dispatched the remaining survivors. Suddenly, a raucous sound could be heard from below. A Hebrew was shouting to his comrades and standing over an Amalekite corpse with his spear cocked to strike. Shoshak listened intently, trying to determine the cause of the commotion.

A few other Hebrews quickly joined him, including one who Shoshak took to be their captain. He could see now that the body the Hebrew was standing over was no corpse at all, but King Agag. He'd been discovered among the dead and was somehow unharmed thus far.

Shoshak heard the Israelite captain shouting at Agag to get up, then had him searched for weapons. The king was dressed in only his evening gown, a long purple coat trimmed in gold, and a vast array of jewelry. Fool, Shoshak thought to himself. King Agag stood out like a peacock among pigeons. Shoshak applauded himself for having the wherewithal to disrobe despite the chaos surrounding him earlier. The men seized Agag by either arm and followed the captain out of the ravine. Several Hebrews followed along with spear points nearly touching the king's back.

If Agag receives quarter, perhaps his chief priest would also, Shoshak thought. His thirst made surrendering seem like a decent alternative to dying of dehydration in this hole. His head ached from the libations of the previous evening. He saw another Hebrew officer address the one escorting Agag. Their words appeared heated, and while Shoshak could not make out the details of the debate, it clearly pertained to the Amalekite King. The officer drew his sword as if to slay Agag, but was stopped by the captain. More arguments ensued. A moment later, the officer returned his sword to its sheath as the captain proceeded on with King Agag and his escorts in tow. The offended officer shook his head as he watched them leave the ravine.

The interaction was enough to discourage Shoshak's thoughts of surrender. He wiggled his way further into the crevasse and tried to get comfortable. One thing was clear. He wasn't going anywhere anytime soon.

***

Joash came to the center of the Amalekite camp where a single tent still stood erect, nearly everything else had been reduced to ash.

"Shalom, Raanan!"

"Shalom!" Raanan replied to the captain.

"I have a gift for Saul," he pronounced. "We've located King Agag. I've brought him here to present to King Saul to do as he sees fit."

Raanan was surprised. There'd been no discussion about taking prisoners, but the captain outranked him. Perhaps as king, this man deserved some special, or more public, demise. Raanan turned and ducked into the tent.

"General Abner, King Agag has been captured. Joash has him under guard just outside," Raanan reported.

Hearing the news, Saul and Abner both exited the tent. As they approached, the defeated king knelt and stretched forth his hands, with his palms raised.

"King Saul, anointed of the Most High God, leader of the chosen people of the Eternal God of heaven. You have wrought a great victory over us this day. I have led my people for over forty years and now am old, yet you, in your youth, have overtaken my great and powerful nation and have utterly defeated us. Surely, the Eternal is with you, for he has stripped me of my kingdom and my people."

Abner placed his hand on the hilt of his sword but was stopped by Saul.

"Surely, I may be of greater service to you as a captive and advisor than just that much more dust of the earth. If you will see fit to spare my life, I pledge my allegiance to you and to your God. Alas, I am prepared to die if it suits you, for what is a king without a people? Let not your heart be troubled by taking my life though I am disarmed and naked before you."

"Truly," Saul said as he thought momentarily. He had not considered this scenario. Now that his army had been defeated, King Agag was as good as dead if God so desired.

Seeing a group of Israelites approaching the corals where his stock was kept, Agag watched as the men began hacking the animals down.

"Forgive me, King Saul, but why do your men destroy such fine animals so unceremoniously? I assure you there are no finer animals anywhere. Would they not be better as rewards to your captains?" Agag suggested. "Or sacrifices to your God?"

Just then, shouting could be heard from the corals from several Israelite soldiers.

"What's that about?" Saul asked.

"I'll take a look," Raanan answered and approached the men.

After several minutes, Raanan returned.

"It appears these fine animals he boasts of were taken from Israelite farms," Raanan reported, staring down at the defeated king. "Several of the men recognized familiar brands and claim that the animals were stolen from their families. Some of them insist that the animals be restored and are preventing the others from carrying out your orders."

"Look around King Saul, since your Lord gave your people this land, we've been left with nothing. We've scraped by on what we could.

Recently, some of people reported finding some lost animals in a ravine and brought them here. We thought it an answer to our prayers. If they were stolen, it was without my knowledge or consent, I assure you," Agag insisted.

"Let me put an end to this forked-tongued idolater here and now," Abner insisted.

"King Saul, I have heard rumors you are also a prophet, greater in splendor and stature than the whole of your people, but I confess, the rumors of your majesty were wholly inadequate. Surely, surely, a man as endowed as yourself must know the ways of the great kingdoms of the East. The Chaldeans, for instance! Whenever they defeat a kingdom, they take its leaders and bring them into the service of their king, and thus, his greatness is magnified. It is one thing to be served by advisors from one's own people. It is another entirely to have a king at your right hand. If you slay me now, what of the decades of knowledge I possess? What of the languages I have mastered and the experiences which I might add to your learned counsel? Who else among your counsel is able to understand the burden of the crown upon your brow?"

His appeal had struck a chord. Truly, there were questions Saul had. This was indeed the only other king Saul had ever interacted with. Certainly, it would do no harm to allow him a couple days more during the trek to Benjamin. Perhaps something could be learned from him. He might even reveal the location of other Amalekite settlements or hideouts, Saul considered.

"I will not take your life today. It seems that the Lord may have spared you for some purpose yet. You will come with us," Saul said. "This is one of my captains," he said, pointing to Joash. "He will see to it that you accompany us on the journey back. You are to pay him the same deference you would to me."

"What of the animals sir?" Raanan asked.

"Bring the aggrieved men to me. I will hear what they have to say."

Saul returned to King Agag's tent as the men were summoned and a guard was posted to ensure the animals were not harmed until their fate was decided. Minutes later, a large group of men poured into the tent and formed a semi-circle so that the eldest among them sat in front nearest Saul.

Recognizing a wealthy elder before him, Saul asked the man to speak.

"My King, we were instructed to devote all Amalekite animals to destruction. We would never stop the hand of the Lord from exercising this judgment on the uncircumcised, but these, these animals are not Amalekite property. They belong to the tribes of Israel, specifically Simeon and Judah. Many of them were stolen not long ago and have been missing for less than a week, perhaps less! Judging by the conditions of the Amalekites, surely these animals would have been slaughtered and eaten if this were not so. Shall we dispossess our brothers a second time by slaughtering them here? Surely the Lord meant to return them to His people."

"I take it some of these animals are your own?" Saul asked.

"Indeed, my King, many of them bear my brand. Some of them I did not even know had been taken. I believe the thieves must have stolen them during our march."

"Who else believes these animals rightfully belong to them?" Saul asked.

Nearly every hand went up from those sitting inside the tent.

"The Lord requires that everything belonging to the Amalekites be devoted to destruction. You men would have me ignore the instruction of the Eternal? Do you realize what you ask?" Saul asked.

"Surely Samuel said to devote the Amalekite animals to destruction, but these are not Amalekite animals we're talking about," one wealthy Simeonite commander shouted vehemently. "These are animals I have taken great pains to raise! Consider what we found here. There is no food in the camp. The Amalekites, save their priests and king, were thin and weak. These animals must have been taken only days ago. Surely they must have just returned from raiding our land while we trained with you in Benjamin!"

"Perhaps there is a middle ground," an elder injected. "All of these men would offer sacrifices to the Lord for the great victory we have had today. Each of these animals, so far as I have seen, is fit for such purpose. Why not offer them to the Lord at Gilgal instead of spilling their blood here? Has not the Lord restored them to these men? Would they not be expected to make sacrifices from their heards and flocks?"

Most of those in attendance nodded their heads in affirmation of the suggestion.

Saul instantly recognized the strength of the elder's argument. These men, if given credit for the sacrifices, would be spared the same requirement from their remaining flocks and herds.

"Are you all in favor of this suggestion?" Saul inquired.

A chorus of yeses was repeated around the audience.

"Very well," said Saul. "I don't suppose it matters where they are slaughtered. We will take them to Gilgal, but only those fit for sacrificing. Only the best and those completely without blemish."

The matter concluded, the audience exited the tent.

"May I have a word?" Abner asked.

Saul ordered the rest of his staff to exit the tent.

"I think we should not trouble ourselves with this man. Why bring Agag back with us, or these animals for that matter? The command was to destroy them all; as you said, why should it matter where they are slaughtered? God is capable of restoring what the Amalekites took. Remember, 'obedience is greater than sacrifice.'"

The words of the prophet's rebuke stung, especially when repeated from the lips of his most trusted friend and ally. Saul gritted his teeth. He hated being questioned after an order was given.

"The difference is the sacrifice," Saul replied. "We have rituals that the Lord requires. Certainly, slaughtering an animal in the field is not the same as presenting it as a sacrifice by a Levite priest, something I know all too well. I do not need to be reminded," Saul said.

Abner thought momentarily, unable to put his finger on the problem.

"It is a long way to Gilgal. What if some of the men try to keep the animals? We'll be passing through their lands en route. Any one of these oxen would fetch a year's pay and a lot can happen between here and Gilgal. Our ranks have grown so quickly, not all of these men have been vetted. I am afraid the temptation may be too great for some of them."

"Then put your most trusted men in charge of escorting Agag and the animals back to Gilgal. Get a thorough inventory of everything before we step off. I've made my decision. Make it happen." Saul then turned and exited the tent.

Frustrated, Abner knew there was no sense in trying to change his mind once it was made up. Saul would rather be wrong than retract an order already given.

"Raanan!" Abner called out. The impressive guard entered a moment later. "I need our best men to escort the animals back to Gilgal. Only the best animals. If they've got any, even the slightest blemishes, you personally strike them down on the spot. I only want the absolute best, do you understand?" Abner said. Pausing for emphasis, he reiterated, "only the very best."

"Understood!" Raanan said.

"Take whoever you need. Men you trust," Abner said.

"And Agag?" Raanan asked.

"Keep him under watch at all times, and for heaven's sake, keep him quiet and as far away from Saul as possible."

***

By the time the army was formed and ready to march north, Raanan could hardly lift his arm. It seemed as if every soldier of Judah or Simeon claimed at least one animal had been stolen from him and considered it the most praiseworthy beast to ever walk on four legs. Many were displeased with him and considered it a personal affront when the animals they'd selected were cut down at one glance.

The animals that remained were closely guarded by picked men. Raanan felt he had culled the herd sufficiently according to Abner's instructions and those that remained had no discernible blemishes that he could identify.

Finally, the order came to march and the procession started north towards Carmel in formation. Raanan caught up with Abner and reported the number of livestock that were being escorted back with the army.

Pleased with the young soldier he'd seen numerous times around the palace grounds, Abner thanked him and instructed Raanan to accompany him for a while.

The general spoke cordially with him and inquired of Raanan's upbringing and family. Such conversations made a long march pass quickly. Apart from the princes, Raanan had never actually conversed about non-military matters with anyone of such high rank and the general seemed genuinely interested in what he had to say as they walked alongside the general's impressive stallion. A short ways ahead of them, Saul rode atop Samson, his beautiful and powerful warhorse. Near him were the young princes, Abinadab and Malchishua, mounted on equally impressive horses.

Raanan looked around them, wondering where Prince Jonathan could be in the procession. He remembered how the prince had often appeared out of nowhere, walking as the rest and talking with the soldiers around him as if they were his own blood. Raanan noticed a solitary horse several columns to his rear being escorted by a large broad figure he recognized instantly as Yuval. Judging by this, he knew Jonathan was somewhere within the ranks of that division. A standard with a seafaring ship flew above the guide at the head of the column, signifying the tribe of Zebulon.

The tribe of Benjamin was at the foremost of the procession, enjoying the place of honor as the tribe of the royal family. Benjamin's wolf head standard flew high above them near the front of the column. Next was the Lion, representing Judah, then Isachar, Zebulon, Reuben, Simeon, Gad, Levi, Ephraim, Manasseh, Dan, Asher, and finally, Naphtali.

Jonathan would, as in times past, make his way among the various tribes where he enjoyed the unadulterated respect of men young and old. His mere presence lifted the spirits of those around him. It was astonishing to see how the men responded to him. Raanan knew the same could not be said of Malchishua, Abinadab, or even Saul. Apart from Jonathan, it seemed Abner was the most highly favored by the men. Stoic as he was, the man was genuine and honest. He had a fatherly air about him and though he was technically part of the royal family, he was regarded as having risen through the ranks since he was still a young man when Saul began his reign so many years ago. Thus, it was perceived that his position was earned rather than given. Abner had proven himself in combat on numerous occasions beginning with the defeat of the Ammonites at Jabesh Gilead when he was merely fifteen years old.

"Do you have any children?" Abner asked.

"Not yet. I don't have a wife yet," Raanan replied.

"Ah," Abner replied. "Yes, that should come first."

Ranaan smiled at the general's comment, then realized it had never occurred to him that Abner had any life outside of the military. He had a hard time thinking this man existed apart from the army. "And you? Do you have a wife and children?"

"I do. My wife's name is Sarah, and we have a seven-year-old son, Jaasiel."

Surprised, Raanan tried to picture the man holding an infant or small child and laughed.

"What is it?" the general asked.

"Oh, it's just, I've never heard anyone talk about you being married or having a child."

Abner smiled. "I've found it's like that many times. We think we know someone because we see them every day. We may interact or talk with them even, but who can know all that another human has experienced, accomplished, or may be enduring."

"I suppose it's rarely a good idea to make assumptions about people," Raanan replied.

"At least not about things you can learn by asking or observing," he said with a smile, "but generally it's a good rule for life. It's better to be curious, than to assume."

"As a youth, I assumed everyone was all good or all bad. I've come to learn that there can be good in the worst people and even the best of men are capable of terrible things. We rarely know until we're tested."

"If I might inquire sir, Saul is the first anointed king of Israel. I know how he was chosen by God for this task. You grew up farming, like the king. You were not raised in a royal family or formally educated. If a man wanted to gain the wisdom and understanding you possess, what should he do? I suppose what I am asking is, how did you do it?" Raanan asked.

Abner laughed. "Well, I'm happy you think me wise, but the truth is I've learned more from my mistakes and failures than I have from my successes. I did not come about my understanding on my own. I had a great mentor, many great mentors in fact, but one in particular greatly influenced me, a man named Nuri. He was a brilliant tactician and educated in the histories of many peoples. I spent a great deal of time with him."

"What happened to him?" Raanan asked, surprised he'd never heard the man's name.

"He was killed in battle with the Philistines many years ago. I suppose it's been nearly eleven years now. I was trained by him for almost nine years. I suppose you've probably never heard of him since you would have been very young when he died."

"He's the one who trained you then?"

"One of many," Abner replied. "You can always learn from others. Even those you don't necessarily respect can teach you a great deal if you will humble yourself. Nuri taught me to think. He opened my eyes and for that I am forever in his debt. One does not need to be exceptionally gifted to become exceptional at something. Not all of us are gifted with Samson's strength or Joseph's wisdom. I don't rely on someone or something to deliver divine insight before a battle. If I did, I probably wouldn't be a very good leader. A leader must be curious. He must prepare, study the terrain, and he must learn everything possible about the enemy, even things most men would consider trivial matters. He must consider how far they've come, what they are fighting for, what they believe, their logistics. Just as importantly, he must consider his own men, how much they've had to eat, to drink, how far they have traveled, what effect the weather will have on all of these things. It's not enough to know the enemy, one must know himself and his own tendencies, strengths, and weaknesses."

Raanan considered these things. "The way they're told, to hear the stories of the old battles, it just seems like God worked everything out for our people in times past."

"I believe God helps those who help themselves. He gave you a brain so that you could use it. Just believing isn't enough; that's lazy. You have to own the consequences of your actions. And inactions!" He added with special emphasis. "Sometimes God intervenes, but I don't believe it is His intention that we should rely on Him to dig us out of messes that we put ourselves into. He is a God of action. He favors those like Himself. He gave us sense enough to think. We might as well use what He's given us before we go asking Him to do a miracle, don't you think? If I gave you an axe and told you to cut down a tree, would you then ask me to do it for you?" Abner asked rhetorically. "Of course not. And so it is with God. We must use the tools He gives us for His glory."

This was not the first time Raanan had heard similar things from the general. He was beloved by the men, especially those like Raanan who enjoyed the privilege of being close enough to him to enjoy regular exposure. The more Raanan observed him, the more respect he'd gained for the man. Abner was the first to rise in the mornings and could regularly be seen training with the men, especially when training under the severest of conditions. At thirty-nine, Abner was far from being the oldest man in Saul's army, but he was almost universally respected. Raanan tried to think of all the questions he'd wanted to ask the general.

"What is the most important thing that you would tell those of us just beginning to serve?" Raanan asked.

Abner thought for a moment before responding. "I think the most important thing I've learned about leading is that you can't do everything. You have to find and put the right people around you. Sometimes the men I put on my staff are at the top of their game, but that's not necessary. Often, I will put men in positions they have no experience with. I select men with the right mindset. The kind of man that has to be pulled back rather than prodded. Many times, they can't do the job as well as I could, but given enough time, they quickly gain the skills necessary. The point is, if someone can do a job anywhere close to as well as I can, it's better to let them. I can't be two places at once. I've learned to give men the freedom to decide how to accomplish the things I need from them."

Raanan considered Abner's words, recognizing them as simple but important truths.

"I'd better get back there and make sure everything is carrying on well with the animals," Raanan said. Though he wished he could spend the entire march talking with and learning from the general, he desired more to ensure that the task he'd been assigned was carried out.

"It was a pleasure Raanan. Let me know if you need any more help back there," Abner said.

"The pleasure was mine sir! You've given me a lot to think about. Thank you," Raanan responded before heading back towards the rear of the column.

***

The first leg of their journey was a nearly forty-five-mile march to Carmel, the first large town they'd reach en route to Gilgal. It was a long way to drive animals while keeping up with the army and Raanan didn't want to be the cause for delay in reaching their destination.

It was mid-afternoon the second day when Raanan lifted his eyes to see Carmel in the distance. Nearly halfway there, he thought to himself. As they drew closer to the town, he could see men stopping up ahead and setting down their rucks and weapons. As the line compressed with the escorts bringing the animals up closer to the rest of the army, men unburdened themselves for what was likely to be a short rest.

Raanan turned and designated several men to obtain food and water from the city for the beasts.

"What's that?" One of the men said, pointing towards Carmel.

Raanan turned to see a group of men already headed in their direction with wagons loaded down with straw and buckets of water.

"Looks like it's already taken care of," Raanan replied.

When the men arrived and began feeding and watering the animals, Raanan inquired of the soldier escorting them. "What's the word? How long do we have before we step off again?"

"Maybe a day or two," one man responded to Raanan's surprise. "The city elders informed Saul that several of the surrounding villages were raided days ago. When they learned about these animals, they sent a party to feed and water them. They've insisted that the army stay here for the night while they erect a monument in honor of the king. Looks like another night on the road," the soldier informed them.

"A monument?" Raanan asked.

"Yeah, they've got the stone masons working on it already. I don't know what you can expect from something that takes a day to erect," the man said sarcastically. "But maybe they will surprise me. Did I hear right? Is the Amalekite King Agag back here somewhere?"

"He was, but the king sent for him and now he's up there with the rest of the royalty."

The soldier cursed. "I was hoping to get a look at him. I'd love to spit in his eye after hearing what they did to these Carmelites. What are they planning on doing with him anyway?" The soldier asked.

"I have no idea. I don't know why we'd bring him this far only to execute him. I've heard of other nations subordinating foreign Kings to advisory roles," Raanan mused. "Hell if I know what that man is capable of advising anyone. Did you see the condition most of the Amalekites were in? It almost makes you pity them. Like we were putting them out of their misery."

"I don't feel sorry one bit. Didn't you see the altar?"

"Up on the high place, you mean?"

The soldier nodded.

"Someone told me about it yesterday. I guess it's still hard to believe," Raanan said somberly.

"Sickening is what it was," the soldier replied. "I'd heard that certain Canaanites sacrificed their children in times of drought, trying to get their gods to send rain, but I thought it was just a story, a myth. To be honest, I didn't really believe it. For the rest of my life, I'll never get that out of my head. We shouldn't waste one more second on that filth. I'd do the deed right now if they'd let me."

"I think nearly everyone here is in agreement on that," Raanan replied.

The soldier shook his head. "You're Raanan?"

"How'd you know?"

The man laughed. "Royal guard armor, big biceps. You're the king's pet," the man said with a smile.

Raanan shook his head and smiled. "I guess position has its privileges," he acknowledged. "What's your name?"

"Elika," the solider responded.

"Where are you from Elika?" Raanan asked.

"Harod, it's in the Jezreel Valley," Elika explained. "Not much up there."

"I get it, I'm from a small village as well. One benefit to serving is that we get to see a lot more of the world though, right?"

"Agreed. It's just too bad Joshua didn't build more altars. Always having to go back to Gilgal for these ceremonies…. I suppose it could be worse. At least the altar isn't in Dan."

"Yes, that would be a long trip," Raanan replied. "It was good talking to you Elika the Harodite," Raanan said. "I hope to see you around."

"Likewise," Elika said as they parted ways.

***

The ceremony honoring King Saul had been brief. Raanan surmised that Abner could be thanked for this. The general rarely tolerated delays, but the village elders insisted and Saul was not impervious to flattery. Raanan couldn't recall seeing Abner more agitated. Agag was permitted to dine with Saul and was given his own tent near the king that night. Though a prisoner, he'd enjoyed better treatment and accommodations than most of the men in the Israelite army.

Raanan was happy to be back on the march. It seemed nearly everyone was on edge. Members of the other tribes with no interest in the spared livestock were more than a little irritated with the delay caused by bringing them along. The men could easily cover far more ground without livestock in tow and many were eager to return to their farms and families now that the excitement of battle had passed. Not a few fights had broken out in camp over the matter.

The long column of soldiers moved steadily north through the hill country of Judah. As the land began steadily sloping downward towards the Jordan River, Raanan knew they were on the final approach to Gilgal.

Leaving a senior in charge of the cursed livestock, Raanan jogged ahead, passing the main body of troops to determine where they would need to collect the animals. The column was several miles long, and by the time he'd reached the front, those in the Benjamin division had just begun setting up on the outskirts of the city. The valley ran from the city in a slowly descending slope down to the Jordan where Raanan could see several small groups of livestock grazing in the fertile fields between the city and the river below. An irrigation canal ran west from the Jordan toward the hills then south, before forking into several parallel canals flanked by lush green crops.

Men were settling into bivouacs on whatever flat piece of ground they could find. Raanan heard several men cursing about another night in the field. Many among them were not happy about another night spent away from their wives, children, and farms. Raanan hadn't spoken with a single man who cared anything for this victory parade through the countryside and apart from the men of Judah and Simeon, no one thought it worth the trouble of sparing the cattle and sheep.

Raanan studied the landscape, looking for a suitable place to keep the doomed animals separate from those of Gilgal's residents when a figure passed close behind him at a brisk pace. When Raanan turned to see the man, he recognized the unmistakable figure. It was a bald man with a long staff and maroon mantle draped over broad shoulders, walking at an incredible pace.

Raanan followed, wondering why the prophet had come from the South. He was headed from the same direction they'd just come. The road from Benjamin and Ramah to the west was still north of their location, but judging by the way the prophet was walking, Raanan chose not to interrupt him or delay the man, but kept close behind.

Samuel could be seen scanning the troops as he went. Raanan knew the prophet's quarry. Samuel strode up a small embankment, giving him an elevated view of the throngs of men before them. He looked to Raanan like a hawk searching for a field mouse with his keen and fierce-looking eyes and curved nose. Finally, gazing over Raanan's head to the east, Samuel's eyes locked upon their target. Using his staff, he hopped off of the embankment with the agility of a much younger man and resumed his rapid pace. The prophet's brief pause had lasted just long enough for Raanan to see two others following the prophet at a short distance on the trail that paralleled his own. Samuel's apprentice, Nathan, and another younger man were in tow.

Raanan hastened to keep up as Samuel made his way through the camps towards the elevated knoll where men were erecting the king's tent near the center of the assembly. By now, Nathan's and Raanan's paths had converged.

"Good afternoon. Have you all come for the sacrifice?" Raanan asked the young men of God, though judging by their faces, Raanan knew their arrival would not be a welcomed one.

"Raanan," Nathan acknowledged, nodding to him. "Nothing good, I'm afraid."

The younger man remained silent.

A discerning guard outside Saul's tent announced, "Samuel the seer," but offered no resistance as the prophet approached and entered.

"Saul," the three men heard the prophet shout from within, sounding like an irritated father.

Raanan and the two others entered the tent to see the king's entourage, including the most affluent men of Gilgal, open like the Red Sea parting before Samuel, leaving a direct path to where Saul was seated.

"Everyone clear out," Abner ordered in a tone Raanan had rarely heard from the general.

Everyone, including Raanan and the Samuel's apprentices, poured out of the tent.

"Samuel!" Saul said with a raised cup, spilling wine as he stood hastily. "Blessed are you of the Lord! I have performed the commandment of the Lord."

Samuel approached Saul, ambling slowly and deliberately, his head cocked with his bushy gray eyebrow raised, and his right hand cupped to his ear. "What then is this bleating of the sheep in my ears, and the lowing of the oxen which I hear?"

Saul could hear Raanan's men bringing up the sheep and oxen.

"Ah, yes. The people brought them," Saul explained. "They have brought them from the Amalekites; for the people spared the best of the sheep and the oxen, to sacrifice to the Lord your God and the rest we have utterly destroyed. Just like you instructed!"

"Be quiet! And I will tell you what the Lord said to me last night."

Saul's face paled. "Speak on," he replied.

"When you *were* little in your own eyes, *were* you not head of the tribes of Israel? And did not the Lord anoint you King over Israel? Now the Lord sent you on a mission, and said, 'Go, and utterly destroy the sinners, the Amalekites, and fight against them until they are consumed.' Why then did you not obey the voice of the Lord?" Samuel demanded as he slammed the end of his staff into the dirt as his feet. "Why did you swoop down on the spoil, and do evil in the sight of the Lord?"

"But I *have* obeyed the voice of the Lord, and gone on the mission on which the Lord sent me, and brought back Agag, King of Amalek! I have utterly destroyed the Amalekites."

They heard the long soft lowing of cattle just down the hill. Samuel tilted his ear toward the sound and turned his fierce eyes back towards the king.

Saul struggled to find a response. "But, but the people took of the plunder, sheep and oxen, the best of the things which should have been utterly destroyed, to sacrifice to the Lord your God in Gilgal," Saul explained with his hands held open to the prophet.

"Has the Lord *as great* delight in burnt offerings and sacrifices, as in obeying the voice of the Lord?"

Saul stood silent.

"Behold, to obey is better than sacrifice, and to heed than the fat of rams. For rebellion is as the sin of witchcraft, and stubbornness is as iniquity and idolatry. Because you have rejected the word of the Lord, He also has rejected you from *being* king," they heard the prophet say.

Saul approached Samuel, lowering his voice so the men outside would not hear.

"Please understand, what does it matter whether they die in the desert or here as an offering to the Lord?"

"You were given an opportunity to redeem yourself and still, like one of those oxen, you must be prodded into doing the will of the Lord. What does it mean to be God's anointed? What do you think it means to be chosen by the Lord who sees the hearts of men to lead His people? It would have been better if the Lord had to rein you in, but *you*, you choose the goad and must be provoked to action. The Lord appointed you King. YOU! No one else! Not any of *the people* you constantly blame for your own shortcomings. *You* have taken His great name in vain, for you fail to act with the authority He has entrusted to you, sparing even Agag, the leader, the king of that wretched and loathsome people," Samuel declared. "Did you not see? Did you not witness their evil abominations?" Samuel shouted.

Saul stood silent, unable to respond.

Samuel shook his head, then turned and exited the large tent. Saul quickly ran after him.

"I have sinned," Saul confessed, hoping to stop the prophet, "for I have transgressed the commandment of the Lord and your words, because I feared the people and obeyed their voice. Now, therefore, please pardon my sin, and return with me, that I may worship the Lord. Help me to make amends."

"I will not return with you," Samuel responded as he turned to address Saul face to face. "For you have rejected the word of the Lord, and the Lord has rejected you from being King over Israel."

Samuel turned again to leave, but Saul seized the edge of his robe to stop him, when a piece of the tattered and worn robe tore from his sleeve and hung limp in the king's hand.

Samuel turned back to the king and looked down at his garment, then back at the piece still dangling in the king's hand. "The Lord has torn the kingdom of Israel from you today, and has given it to a neighbor of yours, who is better than you. And also the Strength of Israel will not lie nor relent. For He is not a man, that He should relent."

Saul again pleaded and fell to his knees at the prophet's feet, "I have sinned! I have sinned, *yet* honor me now, please, before the elders of my people and before Israel, and return with me, that I may worship the Lord your God."

Samuel gazed down at the dejected King at his feet, weeping with his head hung low.

"For the sake of your sons and for the sake of Israel, I will go with you," Samuel conceded.

Abner had ordered the men outside far enough away from the tent that few could see and hear the words exchanged between the prophet and the king.

Samuel turned to Abner.

"Have the men assemble at the altar of the twelve stones," Samuel instructed, referring to the ancient altar that the tribes had assembled so many years before from the dry riverbed of the Jordan. "Then bring me all the beasts taken from Amalek," Samuel commanded.

Nathan and the second young apprentice went to work building a fire on the altar of twelve large river stones. Samuel commanded the men to bring more fuel for the fire.

By the time the army had assembled around the altar, the flames had reached twice the height of a man. Samuel then prayed for Saul before the assembly, for the army and the leaders of the army, and for the people. The prophet then went to work, sacrificing the animals brought from Amalek until the sun set on the ridge to the west and well into the night. Saul stood watch throughout the entire ceremony, his mind filled with regret as each new sacrifice reminded him of his failed opportunity.

Samuel and the two apprentices were filthy with blood and soot by the time the last sacrifice was bled and burned. The old prophet's arms trembled with fatigue.

Raanan had been present for the entire proceeding and was thankful that it now seemed at an end. Many of the men present were nearly asleep on their feet.

As his Levite apprentices burned the final ox upon the altar, Samuel turned to Abner.

"Bring me Agag, King of the Amalekites," he said, his voice exhausted, but resolute.

Two of Raanan's men went to the nearby tent where Agag was sleeping peacefully. The men seized Agag under the arms, lifted him to his feet, and escorted him to where Samuel stood before the still raging fire.

Upon seeing the bloody prophet before the raging fire at the altar, Agag's demeanor shifted from confusion to horror.

"Surely the bitterness of death is past," he said extending his empty palms toward the prophet. "What am I but a worm in your hands," Agag asked as Samuel seized the hilt of a sword from one of the guards and unsheathed it.

The guards shoved Agag forward towards the prophet. He fell to his knees and scanned the faces around him before his eyes locked up on King Saul.

"Please," he shouted with his arms stretched out toward the king.

The panicked Agag, took several steps and fell to his knees at Saul's feet, grasping the hem of his robe. "What does it profit you to slay me," he pleaded. "My people have paid in full for the deeds of our ancestors, have they not?"

He buried his face in Saul's garment and wrapped his hands around Saul's ankle.

Samuel seized the Amalekite by the hair and wrenched him backwards.

Agag cried out as he fell upon his back into the dirt and began cursing the prophet in his native tongue.

"As your sword has made women childless, so shall your mother be childless among women," Samuel pronounced as he lifted the sword with both hands and brought it down upon the prisoner.

Agag screamed as the sword cut deep into his outstretched arm. "King Saul, my King! Save me!" he shouted as the prophet brought the sword down again, severing several fingers.

Agag screamed and kicked at the prophet, trying in vain to defend himself as the sword came down again and again, slicing his feet and legs. Agag rolled onto his stomach and crawled towards Saul, pleading for salvation. "I don't want to die! Save me, please! Make him stop my King," he cried, reaching for Saul's feet. The old prophet severed Agag's outstretched arm, spattering Saul's face with blood.

The fading cries of the wretched King Agag fell silent as Samuel struck him several more times, cleaving his skull with the sword as Saul watched in disgust. When Samuel finally relented, the ghastly dismembered figure of the Amalekite King lay sprawled out in the dirt at Saul's feet.

Samuel breathed heavily from the exertion. His work finally at an end, Samuel let the sword drop from his hand. Turning his face upwards, Samuel raised his arms which were coated with dried blood, then closed his eyes.

"It is done, My Lord," Samuel declared.

As the somber assembly slowly dispersed, Samuel's young apprentices brought several buckets of water over to the prophet. Nathan poured the water out as Samuel washed the blood from his arms and hands. Sufficiently cleansed, Samuel straightened and took one last sorrowful look upon King Saul. Then, without a word, the prophet turned and proceeded toward the hills to the west, disappearing into the darkness.

Saul stared out at where the seer had departed. A cold chill swept over him and with it, a wave of sorrow. He looked about him. No one save Abner remained.

"Where does this leave us, cousin?" Saul asked.

TORMENTED

1069 BC, Gibeah, Benjamin, Israel

Now the Spirit of the Lord departed from Saul,
and a harmful spirit from the Lord tormented him.
I Samuel 16:14

S tanding alone atop the mountain, Saul somehow recognized the place, though he'd never seen it from this view. All was dark about him except for the fire blazing at the base of an altar, the carved stone statue of Baal with its arms outstretched and blackened by the fire licking up around its upturned palms. Saul turned from the statue as something was handed to him in the darkness by a hooded figure. Saul placed the small bundle upon the stone palms of the idol.

Saul watched as the fire engulfed the bundle, when suddenly a child's screams could be heard from within, terrifying and heart-wrenching. The bundle began to thrash about as Saul tried to reach for it, but the flames grew and prevented him, nearly burning his exposed skin and threatening to swallow him up as well. The hot blaze flared up at him, causing him to fall to his back on the ground. He placed his hands upon the earth to lift himself. The ground was wet and sticky. On his knees, he raised his hands to examine them as the light from the fire revealed the dark red blood that covered them. His stomach began to turn when a familiar voice caught his attention. It was comforting, reassuring.

"Come Saul! Sit and dine with me," Agag beckoned as he moved to Saul's side. "This is no place for a King of Israel," he said comfortingly as he helped Saul to his feet.

Agag walked him over to a table lavishly arrayed with fruit, meats, and several vases of wine. In the candlelight, Saul recognized Agag's tent, which now surrounded them. The Amalekite King poured a cup of wine and handed it to Saul. Parched by the heat of the fire, Saul turned the cup upward, guzzling the contents. Saul sat as Agag invited him to recline at the table, though Saul could not understand why he was doing as the man asked. Why was he here, he thought? Why was he breaking bread with this man, he wondered, before the thought was disrupted by a rush of servants flooding into the tent and surrounding the table.

They were all scantily clad apart from their faces, which were veiled. Saul could see the beautiful, tanned skin of their long, smooth legs as they crooned around him, touching him as they moved. Several crowded around him and knelt beside him, gently caressing his shoulders and legs. Saul looked into the eyes of the one whose face was nearest his, mesmerized by her bright teal-green irises.

"More wine?" The beautiful woman asked as she filled his cup.

Saul thanked her as he sipped from the cup before noticing the taste of iron in his mouth.

He peered down into the cup. It was filled with the thick red blood that coated his hands. He spat and nearly vomited as Agag and the servants roared with laughter. Infuriated, Saul turned back to the green-eyed servant. He seized her by the neck. Her skin felt strange. It was cool to the touch. He moved to strike her when he suddenly noticed the shape of her eyes; they were slitted, like the eyes of a viper. Her neck writhed like a snake in his grasp. Reeling in terror, he drew his hand away, catching and tearing the veil, revealing the grotesque demon underneath. There were elongated nostrils where a nose should have been and a wide mouth full of menacing sharp teeth instead of the soft lips and cheeks he'd expected. Their true identity exposed, the demons seized upon Saul as their veils seemed to melt away. A terrifying sound of piercing hisses and raspy, sinister laughter filled his ears. Saul fell rearward as he was pulled away from the table and into the darkness. He screamed in terror as claws gripped his legs, thrashing about as he struck the floor hard on his back. Struggling and kicking against his attackers, he suddenly realized they no longer held him.

Breathing hard, he was awoken by his own flailing on the floor next to his bed. Seeing a dark silhouette on the bed above him, Saul scurried rearwards till his head and back struck the wall of his bed chamber. He was drenched in sweat, his heart still racing. In the dim candlelight, he could see Ahinoam on the bed speaking to him. He stood silently against the wall as his mind finally began to process her words.

"A nightmare, it was just a nightmare," he finally heard her say as she cautiously approached him. Saul's arms shot up defensively, his mind still trying to grasp reality as Ahinoam reached to take his hands in her own.

Remembering the blood, Saul withdrew his outstretched hands and frantically wiped them on his robe. He spat and wiped his face with his forearm. He trembled as his mind recovered from the terrifying dream, trying to separate the delusion from reality. The blood on his hands. It had all felt so real. Looking at his hands, the king sank to the floor against the wall and buried his face as he began to sob uncontrollably.

ANOINTED

1069 BC, Bethlehem, Judah, Israel

Reports of the prophet's coming had already reached the elders of Bethlehem from those who'd passed him on the road. Uncertain what the seer's visit could mean for the small, quiet town, the elders assembled and went out to meet him. What was more certain were the reports of the enmity between Samuel and the king.

"Shalom," one of the elders said as the older yet nimbler prophet approached, pulling a young sand-colored heifer alongside him.

"Shalom," Samuel replied.

"Do you come in peace?" The head elder asked, getting straight to the point.

Samuel examined the faces of the men in front of him before responding.

"Yes, in peace. I have come to sacrifice to the Eternal One," Samuel said, motioning towards the heifer. "Sanctify yourselves and come with me to the sacrifice," he invited as he began walking again.

The small group of elders parted as Samuel walked towards them along the path. They began following alongside the prophet, eyeing one another suspiciously.

"Is there a Jesse, son of Obed, son of Boaz among you?" Samuel asked as they walked.

"Jesse is not here," one of them responded. "Would you like for us to send for him? Do you have some business with him?"

"I was acquainted with Obed, his father, and Boaz his father's father. I offered many sacrifices on their behalf in my youth. They were humble and righteous men, always caring for the poor. Bessed is the son of these men and blessed are his sons," Samuel said as he stopped and turned to the elder who'd addressed him earlier. "I should very much like for Jesse and his sons to join us."

"I shall send for him," said a feeble man whose servant had accompanied them. "Their land is not far from here," he added before sending the young servant to go with Jesse and his sons.

When they reached the city, the elders led Samuel to the altar where the ceremonial sacrifices were offered, then sat and attempted to engage in small talk while they awaited Jesse's arrival.

"How was your journey?" one of the men asked.

"Purposeful," Samuel replied.

"And Ramah, is it faring well?" the man asked.

"Yes," Samuel responded.

Nervously, the elders waited in silence for Jesse to arrive.

"Ah, your apprentice, aren't you typically accompanied by a young man under your tutelage?"

"Yes," Samuel responded.

"And he was unable to make the journey with you?" the elder asked sheepishly, feeling as if he were beginning to pry, given the prophet's terse responses.

"No," Samuel replied.

"Ah," the elder remarked, determining that any further inquiry was not only useless, but clearly unwanted.

The others present kept to themselves, the unspoken consensus being that it would be imprudent to appear too friendly with any man not in good standing with the king. Furthermore, it appeared quite clear from the prophet's demeanor that their presence was neither necessary or even desired at present. As the time passed without word or incident while waiting on Jesse and his sons to arrive, several of the elders in attendance found opportunity to slip away from the small gathering.

Hours later, when Samuel could see a middle-aged man along with an entourage of younger men approaching, there were still several men of influence present who hadn't been in any hurry to find some other business to tend to. Samuel studied the young men as they approached. One was clearly the eldest. He walked alongside his father, his steps sure and confident. He had a muscular build and was taller than the rest. Samuel thought of Saul in that moment, a thought accompanied regret and despair over his shortcomings. He'd been so hopeful for the young man when he'd anointed him all those years ago, but the word from God was clear. The time to grieve Saul had passed, Samuel reminded himself as he stood to greet the new arrivals.

"Shalom, I am Jesse, son of Obed, son of Boaz," Jesse said with the customary greetings.

"Shalom, I knew your father and your father's father," Samuel said. "I trust you have raised them in like manner after them."

"Indeed," Jesse responded. "This is Eliab, my eldest son," Jesse said as he placed his right hand on the impressive young man's shoulder.

As Samuel looked into the young man's eyes, he anticipated the familiar confirmation he'd received upon meeting Saul near the gates of Ramah all those years ago. Instead, the inaudible but unmistakable words of God materialized in his mind.

"He is not the one."

Samuel acknowledged the young man as Jesse presented the next.

"This is Abinadab," he said. Then, using the more formal pronunciation, "This is Shammah," Jesse continued, presenting each of his sons to the prophet.

Curious, Samuel greeted the young men as Jesse presented four more sons. Samuel had felt the presence of the Lord when he'd anointed Saul; he knew the quiet but unmistakable voice of the Lord in his innermost being and how clearly the Lord had presented His anointed one. There was no guesswork, no room for human speculation. Finally, the old prophet threw up his hands.

"The Lord has not chosen these," he exclaimed to their father. "Are all your sons here?"

Somewhat confused, Jesse eyed his sons, then turned back to Samuel.

"All but the youngest," he admitted hesitatingly, "but he is off keeping the sheep."

A shepherd, Samuel thought to himself. "Send for him and bring him here. We will not sit down until he arrives," Samuel concluded.

"Ah, uh, certainly," Jesse replied before calling for Raddai and Ozem, the swiftest of those present. Pulling the young men aside, he instructed them in a low voice. "Go get your brother. Make sure he's presentable and for heaven's sake, tell him to leave the harp and just get him back here quickly. This distraction has taken long enough. Go, and hurry."

***

Unsure as to why the prophet was giving such special treatment to Jesse and his sons, the remaining elders had returned to their business about the city. They'd already waited for Jesse's first seven sons to arrive; now the prophet was insisting that everyone wait for the youngest. They'd come back when the sacrifice was ready to begin.

Samuel watched with anticipation as the three young men approached. The boy was only about thirteen years old, but he looked strong and healthy. He was confident. Samuel felt a peace come over him. This boy was the Lord's chosen. Samuel welcomed David, placing his hands on the youth's bare shoulders.

"The Lord told our people that when we came to this land that the Lord God gave us to possess and dwell in, when the people said 'I will set a king over me, like all the nations that are around me,' we may indeed set a king over us whom the Lord God chose. One from among our brothers shall set as king over us. This day, the Eternal has chosen a new King in Israel, one after his own heart," Samuel said, looking at Jesse and each of his sons, before turning back to David. "You are God's anointed King." With these words, Samuel took the oil and poured it over the young man's head. Samuel looked David in the eyes. "I know this is a great deal to take in, but as the Lord's anointed, you needn't worry. Until you have fulfilled the purpose for which you have been called, no harm may come to you. You shall enjoy His divine protection so long as you walk in His ways. As in the words of Joshua, son of Nun, be strong and courageous, for the Lord your God is with you wherever you go. Conduct yourself accordingly."

Still speechless, David let these words sink in. His father and brothers around him stared in silence.

"Ah," he said, raising his hand and tapping the edge of his forefinger to his brow. "I think it comes as no surprise that King Saul would not be pleased about this. You would do well to keep this amongst yourselves for now. God will see that this young man becomes King of Israel, but, as for the rest of you... I can't make any promises."

Samuel surveyed them each. They seemed reluctant to accept the prophet's words. Annoyed by the blank stares of the men, he shouted at them, "Well? Is this how you acknowledge the Lord's anointed? I should think not!"

Samuel scowled at Jesse. Finally, Jesse moved solemnly to David and took his hands, kissing each of them.

"My King," Jesse said, then moved aside and looked at Eliab, indicating his eldest son should do the same. One by one, each of his brothers repeated the ritual without so much as a word being spoken.

"Well, that's a bit more appropriate, I suppose," Samuel said. "To whom much is given, much is required, however, as King, the Lord has placed but a few restrictions. You must not acquire many horses for yourself or cause the people to return to Egypt in order to acquire many horses, since the Lord has said that the people 'shall never return that way again.' You shall not acquire many wives for yourself, lest your heart turn away from God, nor shall you acquire for yourself excessive silver and gold," Samuel continued.

"And when you sit on the throne of the kingdom, you shall be required to write for yourself a copy of the law of Moses, approved by the priests, which you must keep with you. You shall read in it every day, all the days of your life, that you may learn to fear the Lord God and keep all the words of His law and statutes, and do them, so that your heart may not be lifted up above your brothers, and that you may not turn aside from the commandments, either to the right hand or to the left, so that you may continue long in the kingdom, both you and your children," the prophet instructed.

Samuel then turned to the altar he'd kept fueled over the preceding hours and the heifer tied near to it. Taking the lead rope in one hand, he skillfully administered the cut with flawless precision, which quickly drained her of life. He butchered the heifer and offered the meat upon the altar, periodically offering prayers for the young, newly anointed King as the sun began to sink in the western sky. When no one remained save Jesse and his sons, the prophet turned to his audience.

"The Lord bless you and keep you. The Lord make His face shine upon you and be gracious to you. The Lord turn His face toward you and give you peace." The old prophet concluded his blessing upon David before turning his attention to all of the men present. "I won't burden you by raising further suspicion and staying any longer. I will be going back to Ramah now," Samuel said.

"Wait," Jesse said, "how do we, how do *you* know that the Lord has chosen him?"

"I expect the Lord will present some opportunity for him to prove himself. Until the appointed time, Saul will want him dead if he hears about this."

"But when will that be?" Jesse asked. "Can you give us a sign?"

"Soon I expect," Samuel responded.

"Soon?" Jesse asked. "When Saul was anointed, you gave him signs, confirmations, did you not?"

"And much good it did him," Samuel replied, somewhat irritated. "Gideon prayed for a sign from the Lord and God gave it to him. If you need a sign, ask it of Him," the prophet concluded before turning back to David. "I expect to see great things from you young man. The spirit of the Lord is upon you. You bear his name. Do not bear your anointing in vain."

"I won't," David responded.

"If you need me, I'm not hard to find," the old man said as he turned and departed.

Sure the prophet was out of hearing, Abinadab spoke for the first time since David arrived.

"Has he lost it? He said Saul was God's anointed. Is Saul not still living and breathing? Is he trying to get us all killed?"

The others looked at Eliab and Jesse uneasily.

"We had better not breathe a word of this to anyone or we will all be branded as traitors," Eliab said. "Saul will have our land for sure."

"Don't you mean our heads?" Abinadab replied.

David looked to Jesse for some show of support. None came.

"Come on," Jesse said. "We've wasted nearly a whole day for this," he said as he headed toward the gates.

One by one, they followed after him.

"I can't believe that's what we were called all the way here for," David heard Nethanel say as his brothers departed after their father.

Only one of them remained with David. Shimea looked at his youngest brother as David stood motionless, still contemplating the prophet's words.

"David," Shimea said. David continued staring off into the distance, watching the prophet with his long, quick strides. "David," Shimea said louder.

When David did not respond, Shimea too followed after the others, leaving the young shepherd alone. As the fire from the altar burned brightly in the fading light of day, within him, a new flame was kindled.

BEAR

1068 BC, near Bethlehem, Judah, Israel

The four young shepherds lay quietly sleeping under the stars as the light of the moon cast a blue hue on their tanned faces. Their breath could be seen with each exhale as it dissipated into the cool night air. One of the youngest stirred and shifted in his sleep. A strange rustle in the nearby brush caused him to open his eyes. He sat up, eyes wide, looking to the direction in which the noise had come. The fire was nearly out.

The sheep slept soundly below them as Abishai examined them from atop their rock perch. On hearing his nephew stir, David opened his eyes and listened as he lay still. Suddenly Gideon rose to all fours and sniffed at the breeze. His head lowered as his neck stiffened between his shoulders. A low growl rumbled up from deep in the dog's chest. David sat up and placed a hand on the black shepherd dog.

"What is it?" he whispered to Abishai.

"I don't know," the boy responded. "Maybe another fox," he suggested optimistically.

The quiet of the night was instantly broken by the sound of a screaming lamb. Joab and Asahel jolted upright out of their sleep, trying to make sense of the sudden commotion. The boys could see the sheep below, worriedly pushing into a tight group as the nearly blind animals sought safety in their numbers. Gideon darted off, barking frantically as he disappeared in the direction of the crying sheep.

David's eyes strained as he struggled to see in the moonlight.

"What is it? Do you see anything?" Joab asked.

"There!" Abishai said, pointing to a dark figure near the edge of the flock.

David could see a massive, obscure figure in the darkness. It lifted one of the sheep, screaming from pain and terror, then turned and fled into the darkness with Gideon in pursuit.

The sight sent a shiver down David's spine. He leapt to his feet, grabbing his staff and sling from the ground and slid down the rock onto the dirt. They could still hear the lamb screaming as it was being carried away.

"Where are you going?" Asahel asked worriedly.

"I'm going after the sheep!" David replied. "You three stay here and guard the flock," he shouted before disappearing into the darkness.

Abishai was already on the ground and running after David.

Joab's heart pounded in his chest as he watched his uncle and younger brother disappear into the darkness after the monster. Asahel started after them. Joab went to seize him by the belt, but wasn't fast enough.

"What do you think you're doing?" he called after the six-year-old.

"I'm going to help," the boy shouted.

"You'll do more harm than good. Stay here and watch the sheep!" It was too late. The boy was gone.

Joab slid off the rock and grabbed the extra wood they'd piled nearby, tossing it onto the fire before running after his younger brother, leaving the flock unattended.

David ran as fast as he could to the sound of the crying lamb and Gideon's barking. In the moonlight, he saw the shrouded thicket ahead and hoped the dog would slow the fleeing beast.

Gideon's barking grew louder with every step as he sprinted through the knee-high grass. Finally, he could see the dark figure of the bear standing tall above its prey. It roared menacingly at the comparably tiny figure of Gideon bouncing and lunging threateningly at its feet. The bear swiped at and charged the dog, who narrowly avoided each potentially fatal blow from the predator's huge claws.

David whirled his loaded sling and flung a fist-size stone at the bear's head. Fractions of a second later, he heard the muffled crack of fur-covered bone as the stone collided with the bear's jaw.

The beast growled in pain, then charged menacingly at Gideon, striking him with a heavy blow and sending him spinning through the air. Turning its attention to David, the beast charged again. The boy froze in his tracks. Raising the base of his shepherd's staff towards the attacker, he braced it with both hands as the animal's massive weight struck him and sent him flying rearward onto his back, snapping the staff in two. He could see the bear raise up high above him, its silhouette briefly outlined by the starry sky. David planted the end of the staff as the bear came down hard on top of the splintered end. It let out another cry of pain as it reeled backwards, the broken staff protruding from its chest.

David looked for another weapon, something, anything to defend himself. Realizing he still held the leather sling in his right hand, he scanned the ground for a rock. Gideon had rejoined the fray and was tearing wildly at the bear's heel, momentarily occupying the beast's attention. David fumbled on the ground, scanning it quickly in the moonlight when he located an oblong rock just small enough to fit into the leather cup of the sling. He wrapped it and cinched a knot down on the stone as the bear pinned Gideon to the ground. The dog cried out as the bear attempted to bite down on his skull. From out of the darkness, Abishai appeared, running to the dog's aid when he was struck rearward with the back of the animal's paw, sending him sprawling into the dirt before it turned its attention back to the wounded dog.

David, now armed with the knotted sling, ran and leapt onto the bear's back. Straddling the bear, David seized a handful of thick fur in his left hand. The bear reared and turned its head in an attempt to take hold of David's calf when the boy brought the heavy loaded sling down like a mace onto the top of the bear's skull. The bear spun, trying to dislodge its attacker. David clamped his heals down around the bear and swung the heavy stone again. The bear slumped to the ground, sending David rolling headlong into the dirt. It rose shakily onto all fours and started toward the shepherd boy as he scrambled backwards. Blood streamed from its head and mouth as it stumbled towards him. The bear raised up again for another attack before falling hard on its side to the rocky ground. David stood and rushed the bear, bringing the stone down hard on top of the animal's head before it could recover.

Droplets of blood spattered David's face and chest as the force of the stone caved in the top of the bear's thick skull.

"DAVID! DAVID!" Abishai called several times before his uncle finally relented.

The animal's skull was now smashed beyond recognition.

The night was suddenly quiet. David stood over the massive beast, his chest heaving and his heart pounding. He strained to hear above the sound of his own heartbeat pounding in his ears. He scanned the ground around him until his eyes locked on a lightly colored lump on the ground nearby. He rushed over to it. The sheep lay in the dirt where the battle had begun, wet with blood and saliva. It was weak and in shock, moaning as he lifted it. David heard movement from behind and spun around to see Asahel kneeling over the crumpled body of Gideon. Abishai stood over Asahel, looking in David's direction.

"Gideon," Asahel said as he sat in the dirt and cradled the beloved pet's head. The dog whimpered softly as the small boy stroked its fur.

David carried the wounded lamb over to them. Setting the lamb beside its guardian, David began stroking the bloody fur of his broken and battered companion. A soft whine and shallow breath were the only signs of life in the old shepherd. Joab reached them a moment later, panting and out of breath.

"Oh no," he said as he looked down at the two injured animals.

"Come on, we have to get back to the flock," David said, lifting and handing the sheep to Abishai. Together David and Joab lifted their wounded companion and started back to the flock. Asahel struggled along, trying his best to lift the dog's head as the older boys cradled Gideon's body. Carrying the heavy dog made for a difficult trek, though there was no problem finding their way, even in the darkness. The cries of a single sheep calling for its lamb and the fire that Joab had the foresight to fuel led their way. None of them had realized how far they'd run in pursuit of the bear.

Joab prayed the fire would ward off any other predators in their absence.

When they finally reached their small camp, David and Joab nursed the huge dog as best they could, tearing strips of cloth from their own garments to bandage its wounds, while Abishai and Asahel ran to get help. By the time their mother, Zeruiah, and uncles Raddai and Shimea arrived, Gideon had taken his last breath. The two boys sat beside him on the ground, teary-eyed and trying to restrain their emotions.

"Father will not be pleased about this," Raddai said. "That was his best sheepdog and you let him go after a bear for one measly lamb. That thing will be lucky to survive," he said looking at the injured sheep. "What were you thinking?"

Shimea looked at Raddai incredulously as David stared at the ground between his knees.

"Quiet Raddai," Shimea responded. "What's the matter with you?"

"Come on now Raddai," Zeruiah chided. "These boys defended the flock from a bear and all you have is condemnation for them!"

She knelt beside her youngest brother in the dirt. "Are you ok David? Are you injured?"

David had been too consumed with tending to the dog's wounds to consider whether or not he'd been injured. Checking himself, he realized he'd had a dull pain in his calf during the trek back from the battle with the bear. Examining himself now more closely in the firelight, he observed the torn skin and blood running down his arms and calf till it became indiscernible from Gideon's dried blood, which covered both his hands.

"I'm fine," David croaked as he tried to steady his shaking hands.

Zeruiah took the bottle of turpentine from the medicinal satchel she'd grabbed from the cupboard and poured it carefully onto a clean piece of wool before pressing it to his elbow, soaking the wound in the antiseptic. David winced at the burning sensation and held the cloth in place while Zeruiah cleaned his calf where the bear had attempted to bite down at some point during the melee.

"Abishai and Asahel said you killed the bear."

David nodded.

"Ha! Take me to it then!" Raddai said jeeringly. "Let's see this great big bear."

Still holding the gauze to his elbow, David lifted his right hand and pointed in the direction from which they'd returned from the fight with the bear.

"It's that way."

"Ha, yeah. I bet," Raddai said nervously.

"Well, go ahead and see for yourself!" Asahel growled. "Abishai knows the way. He can show you."

As much as he enjoyed the apparent fear he read on their uncle's face, Abishai's desire to return and examine the kill was even greater. He began making a torch to light their way, using a dry limb and some of the strips of cloth his mother had brought for bandages in her medicine bag.

"We should skin it!" Asahel said excitedly, wiping the tears from his face. Joab and Abishai were elated at the idea.

Abishai brandished the flint knife he always carried and had honed to perfection. Its handle wrapped tightly in dried sinew.

"Uncle Raddai, do you have a knife I can use?" Asahel asked.

Raddai was beginning to realize this was no tall tale.

"Let's find the bear first," was his only reply.

"Here," said Shimea as he produced a large blade tucked inside his belt.

The small boy took the blade instantly as a smile spread across his reddened face.

Abishai took the torch he'd prepared and lit it, then started off into the darkness, Asahel and Joab at his side. Raddai fashioned his own torch and followed after.

Shimea looked at David once more.

"Are you ok if I go with them?" he asked Zeruiah.

Zeruiah placed her arm around David.

"David killed a bear. I think I'm safe with him," she responded.

Shimea smiled, nodded, and turned to follow after his three nephews.

Alone in the darkness, Zeruiah squeezed David tight to her side.

"Don't listen to Raddai. I think what you did is amazing. Who else would have been brave enough to rescue the ewe?"

"Or dumb enough," David said regretfully. "It was reckless. Raddai is right. Father will be so angry with me. I shouldn't have taken the risk and left the flock. The ewe might not even survive and now Gideon is dead." David said as he buried his head in his knees. "It's my fault he's dead."

"And what if you hadn't gone after the bear. Who's to say it wouldn't have come back and killed ten more sheep? Who is to say it wouldn't have killed you or one of my boys?" She asked.

David lifted his eyes and watched the flames dance above the fire. He turned and could see Abishai's torch growing smaller in the distance.

"They were right there with me. Abishai, Asahel, Joab. They all followed me. They were very brave. Joab even had the foresight to fuel the fire before he left," David told his sister.

"You know David, most mothers would never allow their sons to be out here night after night, subjected to bears, lions, wolves, and whatever else might be out there. Do you know why I let them?"

"To get them out of the house?" David said jokingly.

"It's because you're here with them," she said, placing her hands on each side of his face. "I know that there is nothing to fear so long as they are with you. I know that you will teach them to be men, better men than any of our brothers would. Even Shimea," she said, watching David's eyes. "I know your heart David and I know that it is good. There is no greed in you, no selfishness. You care about these sheep, my boys, and the rest of your family despite how our brothers have treated you. And," she paused, "despite how Father has treated you."

David nodded and laid his head back down on his knees between his folded arms as his body began to quake. He'd never spoken with anyone about the disparate treatment he received from his father and brothers. Having it acknowledged by another somehow intensified the pain.

"I know how you feel David," she whispered. "Mother and I are so proud of you. I want you to know that."

David nodded, keeping his face hidden.

"Why don't you get some sleep?" she suggested. "I'll keep the fire going until the boys get back."

Zeruiah stood and added some dried limbs to the fire. It was a long while before the three boys returned with their uncle Shimea holding the heavy rolled bearskin draped over his shoulder. The three boys all proudly flaunted long claws liberated from the bear's paw. Raddai had already returned home with no interest in "defiling himself" with the unclean animal.

"You sure did a number on that bear David," Shimea said, shaking his head. "I don't know how. You're lucky to be alive is all I have to say."

David beamed as he examined one of the long claws in his hand.

"I'm going to head back. I've got to get cleaned up. I probably won't get any more sleep tonight before we head to the fields in the morning, but I'm going to try. Zeruiah, do you want me to walk you back?"

"No," she responded. "I think I'm going to stay out here tonight."

The three young boys smiled. It had been a long time since they'd spent the night in the presence of their mother.

"I think you're in safe company," Shimea responded. "Nice work," he said before bumping David's shoulder with his fist. "Good night."

"Thank you," David responded. "Good night."

David laid back on the ground next to the warmth of the fire and placed his hands behind his head.

Abishai and Asahel laid their heads on their mother's lap as she sat with her back pressed against the large rock. Joab moved his mat near to the fire, added several limbs, then laid down to sleep.

Zeruiah realized that David had already drifted off to sleep. She always marveled at this. He was so much like the man she'd loved so many years ago. He, too, could fall asleep at a moment's notice during the early years of their relationship. Now, thinking of her sons's actions just hours earlier, it appeared that they too possessed some of their father's more admirable qualities.

There alone with her thoughts, her mind slipped back to happier days when the father of her sons had been a respectable and caring man. He'd been so brave, so kind and loving early in their marriage. By all accounts, he'd served with valor and distinction in the battles with the Philistines. Over time, however, he'd descended into malaise and despair. It had started with him waking in the middle of the night, screaming or fighting some unseen attacker. He'd sought relief in strong drink. She'd hoped the birth of their second son, Abishai, and later, Asahel, would bring him back from the darkness she saw him steadily slipping into.

She shook her head, considering her own foolishness. Having more children had been like adding weight on an already drowning man. She remembered how elated David had been when they'd come to live with her mother and Jesse. It wasn't long after that when Zeruiah had returned to their home in the city and found him, the father of their three sons, slumped over the one possession he hadn't sold or traded in exchange for wine. Since then, David had been a godsend to her and the boys.

Zeruiah looked at her sleeping young brother, then repeated a prayer she'd said every night for years now, a prayer for his safety and the safety of her boys.

"Thank God for you David," she whispered to the sleeping boy.

WEAPONS OF WAR

1068 BC, Gath, Philistia (Modern Day Israel)

Standing at six cubits tall, Goliath looked as if he were made of bronze. Covered in armor from head to toe and dwarfing the men around him, he was an impressive and intimidating spectacle. Despite having claimed the lives of countless enemies, he had suffered no serious injuries and most of his scars were reminders of bygone days training with Ishbibenob. He'd long ago lost count of the men he'd sent to the underworld. To those he served with, he was a demigod, like Achilles and Hercules before him. At twice the size of most men fit for military service, he'd come to believe that he was indeed a god.

After three years of honing his skills at sea, a requirement for any Philistine who would be considered a warrior, he'd returned to Gath. As they entered the gates, Goliath was greeted by a great tumult of applause and celebration. Everywhere were awkwardly smiling, gawking faces. Despite the smiles, Goliath sensed the underlying fear that their happy façade belied. He'd seen the fear on too many faces in too many places to be fooled by those now before him. To them, he was a freak, a menace, a champion for sure, but not "one of them." He was something different. He was a weapon, not to be loved or adored, but maintained until he could serve his purpose and be used as an implement of destruction. Despite the best efforts of the men in his platoon, even though each of them had shown courage fighting alongside him at one time or another, Goliath knew that their allegiance to him was based in fear. None of these men would be inviting him to join their families at the dinner table. Rightfully so, Goliath considered. He was a man who took what he wanted and was unaccustomed to restraint.

The long procession marched through the streets of Gath. Men and women showered flower petals on them as they walked through the crowded streets. Beautiful women seized and kissed the faces of the men on their flanks as they looked sternly on. They seemed to shout even more vehemently when Goliath turned a corner. They looked at him with awe and adulation.

"OUR HERO! OUR CHAMPION!" He heard them call. As they approached the amphitheater in the heart of Gath, the chant slowly began to rise, "GOLIATH! GOLIATH! GOLIATH!"

General Aphek proceeded on his impressive stallion at the head of the procession straight into the amphitheater, the columns of the division filing in behind him amidst the pomp. As they poured into the amphitheater, they marched into formation and stood erect while the rest of the division moved to their positions and the audience grew quiet. Goliath began to wonder how long they would have to wait here and endure this. He could feel every eye upon him.

The rest of the division in their places, the division's senior enlisted called the men to attention and the companies sounded their report. The General stepped forward to the center ahead of the division and addressed them loud enough for all to hear.

"Today, we return from a triumphant campaign at sea. All of you showed yourselves men of valor, worthy to be called warriors of Philistia! Warriors of Gath!" The crowd let out a great cry of applause at this. As the roar began to subside, the General resumed speaking. "Because of your efforts, our borders are increased and our people secure. Because of your sacrifice and the sacrifice of those valiant men we lost along the way, our people prosper. You earned the respect and admiration of our Greek ancestors."

"We are a tribe of warriors! Our forefathers carved out a place for us here in this most fertile of lands. They fought the Pharaohs of Egypt. They fought the Canaanites who possessed this land. They struggled and bled so that we might possess a land capable of sustaining our progeny. Time and time again, our small place among these coasts has been challenged. Those around us would push us into the sea. The

Habiru have tested us, time and time again. Their leaders have massa-cred our people and set our crops ablaze. Some say 'peace, peace!' It was offerings of peace that brought them here when our forefathers showed kindness to their patriarch and in return they have soaked the ground with the blood of our people! I say NO MORE!" the general shouted. "In our prolonged absence, the Habiru has taken some of the land we once possessed and slain many of our brethren. The reign of the Habiru Saul must come to an end!"

Angry cries and shouts of "NO MORE, NO MORE" echoed through the city. The roar of the crowd was deafening. The general motioned for them to quiet down and a hush came over the crowd, anxious to hear his message.

"Many years ago, Dagon the conquerer, Dagon the mighty promised our forefathers a champion. The prophesies of old have come true. Our champion stands before you today!"

More cries and hoorahs went out from the people.

"He requires no introduction. He has shown himself worthy of our praise and admiration. Through countless engagements in the south-ern continent, the isle of Mediterranean, and Hattii, he subjected him-self to great danger and inflicted devastating wounds upon the enemies of Gath. I believe he has much greater things to accomplish still. He was raised and trained here among you. He is a son of Gath. The King of Gath, this great city as well as those of Ekron, Ashdod, Ashkelon, and Gaza join in our praise. Goliath! Step forward."

Goliath took a great step forward at the front line of columns, then turned and proceeded towards the general, stopping abruptly in front of him. To onlookers, the sight was nearly comical. The General turned and removed an ornate sheet from atop the table behind him. Till this point, few had even noticed its presence. Beneath it was concealed a huge sheathed sword. The general slid his upturned hands under it and lifted it horizontally. He then turned and spoke again.

"In recognition of your accomplishments thus far and the battles still to come, the five kings had a weapon forged in your honor. This is not just any weapon. Forged of Cretan steel from the best blacksmiths in all of Hellas, the same whose forefathers crafted the sword of Peleus which he gave to Achilles, we present to you, the theristikí michaní. There is none like it in all the world."

The general lifted the massive weapon towards Goliath.

Taking the hilt in his right hand and the sheath in his left, Goliath drew the sword and examined it. "Theristiki michani," Goliath said aloud, the Greek words for harvester or reaper.

"Now show them," the general said, speaking so that only Goliath could hear.

Goliath turned to the crowd and raised the weapon high above his head.

A deafening roar filled the air. Goliath was intoxicated by their praises. As he looked at the faces around him, whichever place he looked, they grew louder and more intense with their celebration.

The general stepped forward and Goliath sheathed the sword. As the general quieted the people, Goliath returned to his place among the men. The captains called their men to attention and grew silent as the men were dismissed to their barracks and homes for leave. As they marched through the streets and out of the city, they were showered with praises and small pieces of papyrus on which names and addresses were written. Each man, save Goliath, did his best to grab two or three as inconspicuously as possible.

On entering the garrison compound, the men quickly dispersed to the recently vacated barracks, where they shed their armor and weapons. After thoroughly drying and polishing their breastplates, greaves, armlets, feathered helmets, shields, swords, and spearheads, they took to cleansing their belts, sheaths, and other leather items, caked with grime and lines of dried salt from being long at sea, followed by the march inland to Gath.

On seeing one of the general's staff enter, several of Goliath's men looked up and began to stand.

"At ease! At ease," he said before most could come to attention. "It's been a long five years. The general knows you are eager to see your families. He wants to remind you that you are representatives of Gath.

You are representatives of this unit. Don't do anything that would bring dishonor on those men to your right and left that have served you so faithfully over the past several years. General Aphek has authorized four days of liberty," the captain said. The men were silent despite their elation, a further display of their discipline. "Everyone is being called back by noon on the fifth day. Enjoy yourselves, love your families, and get some rest. Unless your captain says otherwise," he said, turning to Goliath, "you are released until then."

Goliath nodded to the captain as he turned and exited the barracks.

"You're free to do as you please. Be back here on the fifth day, or the gods help the man who fails to do so," Goliath announced. Turning to his bed, he removed the new sword from its sheath and examined it again. The general had not exaggerated in his boasting.

It was nearly twice as long as the standard xiphos. The grip was large enough for Goliath to spread his fingers broadly, unlike his previous sword, which provided barely sufficient room for him to grip it tightly. The quillions were broad and turned upward towards the point, designed to protect the hands and forearm of the man wielding it, a feature its owner deemed hardly necessary. Despite its size and the thickness of the blade, it was perfectly balanced.

He'd long pondered what his return to their homeland would bring when he could no longer act with impunity on enemy soil. He would have to learn to behave himself, he considered, if he were to continue to enjoy the fruits of his might. Though he'd seen many and frequent battles over the past five years, wielding his new armament, Goliath felt a strong desire to put it to use.

Sheathing the weapon, he laid it down on the massive rack and peered down at it.

"Soon," he said with a smile.

LION

1067 BC, Gibeah, Benjamin, Israel

The Lord is my shepherd; I shall not want.
Psalm 23:1

Raanan was startled by the scream from within the king's chamber. A chill went down his spine as he moved to peek inside, checking in on the king to be sure he was alone. In the dim light, he could see Saul lying in his bed alone, his skin glistening with beads of sweat. Suddenly, the sleeping man writhed as if fighting off some unseen enemy, screaming out in pain or terror.

"No! No! Don't do that!" the sleeping King shouted. "Stop!"

Raanan backed away from the doorway and returned to his post alongside the second sentry.

"Nightmares again," he said. Over the past few months, the men had become familiar with these almost nightly episodes. At first, it had nearly scared them out of their wits – fearing King Saul was under attack by some unseen assassin. Now, they rarely even checked in on him when they heard the frightened cries and shouts from within his bed chamber.

"Going to be another long night," said the other sentry.

King Saul's nightly terrors, followed by his heightened aggressive attitude during his waking hours, left everyone in his service on edge, but none more than the Royal Guard. The king's face displayed his fatigue and anguish. It appeared as if he had aged a decade since the siege of the Amalekites. His hair, previously untouched by age had begun to show signs of gray. How much longer could the king go on like this? They wondered.

It was indeed a long night. By the time of the changing of the guard, Raanan wondered how the king could have slept at all. He briefed their replacements on the details of the night's events, warning them to be especially vigilant this morning since Saul would likely be in an extremely foul mood. During the exchange, General Abner approached and stood nearby, waiting patiently for the men to finish their debriefing before the morning's changing of the guard. Once complete, Raanan walked wearily over to the waiting general. Abner motioned for the sergeant of the guard to accompany them as they departed toward the general's planning room.

"Can I get you anything Raanan?" Abner asked.

"No. Thank you. I intend to go straight to sleep if I'm able. That is, unless you have something else intended for me this morning."

"No, I won't take much of your time. I wanted to speak with you two about Saul's condition. He can't go on like this. Music seems to be the only thing that gives him any relief. Even that is beginning to lose its effect. Saul is becoming annoyed with their repetition. The same melodies played over and over aren't working anymore. We need some fresh lyrics, new songs, new instruments. Something to occupy and distract his weary mind," Abner said as they entered the room.

"I don't want just anyone." Abner continued. "We need musicians we can trust to be left alone with the king. Someone that he won't despise or become annoyed with. You know how he despises certain characteristics in men. The last thing he wants is to be perceived as some sort of pederast like our neighboring kings. They can't have any effeminate characteristics. We don't need rumors spreading that the King of Israel spends his evenings in the company of pansies and you know this task is not for the faint of heart. He must be able to perform at a moment's notice under intense pressure from the king."

Abner shook his head. He knew how difficult it would be to find musicians of the caliber he was seeking.

"Just spread the word, but do it discretely. I don't want word spreading that Saul is unwell, understood?" asked the general.

When the men gave their assent, he bid them good evening and departed.

"Do you know any musicians?" asked the on-duty sentry.

The other sentry shook his head. "I wish."

Raanan thought momentarily, trying to recall. Apart from his sisters, he couldn't name any, other than those who played at the tabernacle for worship and the ones Abner was seeking to replace.

"Can't think of any off the top of my head," Raanan responded. "My sisters play instruments, but that doesn't do us any good. I won't be the one to incur Ahinoam's wrath by suggesting a woman put the king to bed. What about you?"

"No one I'd recommend to the king. We've been fighting since our people crossed the Jordan. Who has time to learn music?" the sentry responded. "My grandfather tells me that our people had very skilled musicians back then. Guess they had a lot of time on their hands wandering the wilderness, eating manna, and all for forty years," he said with a chuckle. "What do your sisters play?"

"Well, most of them play the flute, but a couple of them can play the harp as well," Raanan said.

"Are they any good?"

Raanan thought for a moment. He felt as though he'd had this conversation before, but with whom, he wondered. For a long moment, he thought, silently staring at the ground.

"I didn't think it was that hard of a question," the other said jokingly.

"No, they're good, but it just reminded me of something." Suddenly, the distant memory of a young shepherd perched on a rock flooded his mind. "That's it!" he exclaimed. Thinking momentarily about the qualifications Abner had mentioned, he realized the young man was the perfect candidate. He wouldn't have any children, his music was all his own and therefore would certainly not be redundant. He certainly had very masculine qualities for such a young man.

"What's it?"

Raanan seized the sentry's shoulder.

"There is a family in Judah, eight brothers I've grown very close to over the years."

"So?"

"The youngest brother, he played the harp as if he were trained in heaven. He's a shepherd, a warrior too! He's killed beasts that have come after his sheep and defended them from thieves and raiders. He's surprisingly well-spoken."

"Sounds promising, what family?"

"Jesse of Bethlehem, son of Obed. The oldest brother's name is Eliab. I trained with him back when Saul recruited the three thousand before Jonathan took Geba," Raanan continued excitedly.

"Well, you better let the captain know. The sooner you get him here, the better for all of us."

"Right, see you tonight," said Raanan as he took off in the direction of their captain's quarters.

Minutes later, Raanan had found Ribai, Captain of the Royal Guard. To Raanan's delight, his sergeant was with him.

"What have you got for me?" Ribai asked, seeing Raanan waiting anxiously.

"It was another long night," Raanan reported. "Abner stopped by and brought us up to speed on his intentions to find new skilled musicians."

Ribai nodded. "Go on."

"I have seen a son of Jesse the Bethlehemite who is skillful in playing, a man of valor. He would be a good man of war, even prudent in speech, and a man of good presence, and one can tell the Lord is with him," Raanan said enthusiastically, recalling his time with David. "Are you familiar with him?" Raanan asked the sergeant, who was also a man of Judah.

"I recall a Jesse of Bethlehem," the sergeant replied. "He has a lot of sons."

"You know where to find him?" Ribai inquired.

"I do. I tell you, David is the best I've ever heard."

"What's that?" The men heard from behind.

Raanan turned and was surprised to see King Saul standing just behind them.

"Who is the best you ever heard?" Saul asked.

"Ah, sir, I was just telling the captain that there is a young man I know who plays the harp," Raanan responded cautiously.

"Oh? He is a professional musician?"

"No sir."

Saul cocked his head and stared at Raanan. His eyes were glassy and streaked with red veins.

"He tends his father's sheep," Raanan offered.

Saul continued to stare questioningly at Raanan.

"I was just thinking that because he creates all his own lyrics and tunes, it might be worth having him come and play the harp for you," Raanan suggested nervously.

"David, you say?" Saul asked.

"Yes, son of Jesse, son of Obed, a Judahite of Bethlehem."

"Very well," Saul said. "Go and tell this Jesse, send me David your son, who is with the sheep," Saul instructed before turning to leave.

"Understood," Raanan said, as Saul departed.

Turning back to the captain, Raanan knew Ribai was thinking. However disconcerting, it was not unusual for Saul to show up unexpectedly. He had a way of doing so despite the armed guards assigned to escort him everywhere. It was as if he were spying on them, trying to catch someone doing or saying something they weren't supposed to. He'd become noticeably paranoid in his sleepless state.

"I'm sending Ira, Gereb, Ittai, and Yoshi with you," Ribai said. "How does that sound?"

"They are some of our best riders," Raanan responded.

"Then you've got it. I'll let their sergeants know. Why don't you meet them at the stables at noon. Does that give you enough time to catch some shut-eye?"

"I'd prefer to step off earlier if that's alright. I doubt I'd get much sleep and since we'll be on the move anyway, I'll be fine without it."

"Very well, I'll tell them to meet you at the stables as soon as they're ready. Safe journeys," the captain said as he stood. "The sooner he's able to get some rest, the better," Ribai said, glancing over Raanan's shoulder in the direction the king had departed. "Ein Breira!"

"Ein Breira!" Raanan responded as the two men hammered their fists on each other's breastplates.

Within the hour, the five men were headed southwest towards the town of Bethlehem. Being of the Royal Guard, they were all familiar with each other and in good spirits to be relieved, albeit for a short while, from the monotony of their daily guard duties.

"So you say this shepherd boy is pretty good with the harp?" one of the men asked.

"That's right. Like nothing I've heard anywhere else. He makes his own songs as well."

"You remember that Amalekite shepherd we caught by surprise down in the Negev?" Another asked.

One of the men erupted with laughter, recalling the thought. After hearing the story recited in detail, Raanan was thoroughly disgusted. The child sacrifices they'd discovered at the city of Amalek had cost him some sleep and left his mind reeling for the past several months since the attack, but he hadn't yet heard any stories like the one just told. The depravity of man never ceased to amaze him.

"Where did you think we got the term 'sheep lover' from?" one of the men asked as the others laughed hysterically.

"I just thought it was funny. I didn't realize there was any substance behind it," replied Raanan.

"Well, now you do. Say, what's the name of the kid's brother again?"

"Eliab," Raanan responded.

"I think I do remember him; he's a big guy, right? About your size?" asked Ira.

"Yes, that's why we were paired together in training."

"Yeah, I remember him. Strong, good soldier. Handsome guy, very clean if I remember correctly."

The other men laughed. "Sounds like he made an impression," they jeered.

"Hey, Gereb, you remember him, right?"

"Nope," was his only reply.

"Well, if it's the same guy I remember, his younger brother ought to be decent enough," Ira suggested.

"Brothers can be very different, my friend," Gereb responded.

That's the truth, Raanan thought to himself. He'd always gotten the feeling David's brothers didn't care for David very much. Recalling the last time he'd visited, the brothers were especially contemptuous towards the young redheaded shepherd. Raanan never could wrap his head around how they could be so welcoming towards himself, an outsider, and still treat their younger brother with such contempt. Raanan had grown to love all of them and had spent a good deal of time with them over the past several years. He'd felt sorry for David, but always assumed in the back of his mind that David had done something to deserve their disdain. Apart from David's mother and sisters, one of whom Raanan had grown especially fond of, the rest of the family acted as if David didn't exist when he was absent and were relentless when he was around, always trying to provoke him in some way.

"I take it you have brothers," Raanan inquired.

"Look, I come from a big farming family. I've got a lot of brothers and sisters and we're all very different. Sure, some of us resemble each other, but that's where the similarities end. Don't get me wrong, I love them, we're just... different," he exclaimed.

"Do you get along all right?"

"Well, sure we do now, we're grown. Growing up though, we fought like cats and dogs."

"Over what?"

"You name it. With brothers, there doesn't have to be much of a reason. I used to aggravate my younger brother constantly. I don't know if it was out of boredom or what, but it was bad. Cruel even. He'd get mad and we'd start fighting. My older brother was more mature and didn't really want anything to do with us in public, but back home we'd inevitably get into it over something. I remember one time we were just playing a marbles game and the competition got so heated that we started duking it out." He said with a laugh. "There's a lot of competition among siblings. Don't you have any?"

"Sure, I've got five sisters. Being the youngest and the only son, they all fawned over me," Raanan answered. "I could just about get away with anything. I don't remember them fighting that much. Usually when one was upset they'd go and seclude themselves from the rest until the offending sister went and apologized. My father got me out of the house as often and as long as possible. We worked late everyday. Every day for as long as I can remember, he took me to work with him. I think he spared me a lot of the drama."

"What kind of work was that?"

"He's a carpenter."

Ira nodded as the men silently observed their surroundings. While this was mostly undisputed Hebrew territory since the last victory against the Philistines, an encounter with a Philistine contingent was not outside the realm of possibility. While it was unlikely they would be engaged on the road with only five men in their party, small skirmishes did occur. With the current climate between the two nations, it was better to be cautious. After several miles, Raanan found the landmark he was looking for. They were getting close to Bethlehem.

"Alright, so their land is over to the south there, southwest of the city. Their home isn't much farther."

As they approached Jesse's home, Raanan smelled the familiar fragrance in the air. It was always a pleasure to visit this place. It had become like a second home to him since he visited it as frequently as he returned to his own home. They crossed the final hill before the home came into view. Raanan raised the standard of King Saul to ensure they did not raise any undue alarm among the occupants as they approached. Raanan saw several children playing outside from the distance. One of them ran inside as the others stood and stared at the approaching formation.

The men dismounted and walked the horses slowly until they reached the exterior wall around the family dwellings. Raanan recognized the oldest boy they'd seen playing in the yard.

"Asahel, how are you friend?"

"Raanan! I thought that was you. We were playing soldier. Did you see our sword fight? Can I hold your sword?" Asahel asked, mounting the horse as Raanan held the reins. The boy immediately began curiously touching and fiddling with the guard's armor.

Raanan hardly had time to answer the first of the boy's questions when they were greeted by Zeruiah as she stepped out of the gate.

Acknowledging Raanan's new rank, she bowed. He nodded and tried to conceal the large smile and reddening of his face from the others.

"Greetings," he said.

"Well, to what do we owe the pleasure of having such fine company?" Zeruiah said.

The other men now beamed as well.

"We're on a mission from General Abner. King Saul requires your family's service."

"Does he?" Zeruiah said with an air of sarcasm. "Does the king wish to leave us women here alone to defend our father's land and tend his crops? Are Eliab, Abinadab, and Shimea not sufficient enough?"

"I'm sure the king is grateful for their service. We have not come to ask for additional soldiers. King Saul requires someone with a different skillset presently."

Nitzevet exited the dwelling at about the same time that the words left his lips.

"Raanan! So good to see you! Come inside, come inside! Look how impressive you look in your armor!" She exclaimed as she turned to the other men. "All of you. I'm sure you've had a long ride. The boys will see to your horses while you come rest yourselves inside. Jesse should be here in a moment."

Raanan had hoped to meet with Jesse and avoid Nitzevet altogether for this task. He felt a tinge of guilt asking a mother for yet another one of her sons. He turned to one of the men and instructed him to post a watch outside the exterior wall of the residence.

"Send one of the boys to alert us if you see any sign of trouble."

Zeruiah instructed Asahel and one of the other youngsters to see to the horses as the men followed Nitzevet inside.

As Raanan had come to expect, the guests were treated with the utmost hospitality as they were ushered into the home. Tea, bread, cheese, fruits, and nuts were placed before them as they sat at the family table and awaited Jesse's arrival.

"How are my boys? Have you seen them?" Nitzevet asked.

"Unfortunately, no. They have been assigned to the Legion of Judah.

I am currently under Ribai, Captain of the King's Guard. His son Ittai has accompanied us here," said Raanan, indicating the young man with him. Ittai turned and bowed his head slightly.

"Congratulations," she said, "that sounds like a great honor."

"Yes," replied Raanan.

Raanan noticed the darkening of the doorway and turned to meet Jesse as he entered the home.

"Raanan," Jesse said, apparently relieved. "It's good to see you." Comforted by the lighthearted mood of the guests, Jesse surmised that they did not come bearing bad news. The patriarch greeted Raanan with a warm embrace. "How is your family?"

"They are well. Though it has been quite a while since I've been home, they write often."

"You know you can count on us to check on them if you like. It's not all that far for us."

"I sincerely appreciate the offer. During times like this, it is easy to be concerned for the well-being of your family when you're miles from home," Raanan confessed.

"You shouldn't have to worry about your family's safety while serving our people. We will make it a priority to check in with them often," Jesse assured.

"Thank you. I can't express how much that means to me."

"Now tell me, what brings you here today?"

"The king is in need of your service," Raanan paused, he'd rehearsed the conversation in his mind several times on the journey. "This may seem an odd request in times such as this, but Saul asks that you send him David. You see, I told him of how skilled David is with the harp. Very much so in fact. I have heard the musicians that play at the palace and I assure you that there has been no one equal to David in ability. It is for this reason I have been sent here to request your leave of him to come and serve King Saul."

Jesse sat, silently staring at Raanan. His expression stoic and indiscernible.

Jesse thought to himself as he considered the men before him. Had someone, perhaps one of his older sons, leaked information about Samuel's visit? While he'd been content to forget the matter until now, this was too odd of a request not to raise his suspicion. Perhaps from anyone else, Jesse would have disbelieved the men, but this was Raanan. Jesse turned to the other men present, then back to Raanan. Each of them bore a pleasant, nonchalant demeanor without the slightest trace of ulterior motives. Jesse cleared his throat, then leaned forward.

"The Philistines are reinforcing at the border of blood. Rumor has it, they've been patrolling the Jezreel Valley, but you've been tasked with a special mission, with five of King Saul's own guard in fact, to come here and collect a shepherd boy, whose audience has been largely limited to the four-legged variety, so that he may go and play the harp for the king?"

"That is one way to put it. Yes, sir." Raanan responded sheepishly.

"And you were the one to suggest David?" Jesse asked.

Raanan lowered his head apologetically, then raised his eyes to meet Jesse's again.

"Forgive me. I meant to pay you and your family an honor when I suggested him to the king. At the time, I did not consider the trouble that his absence might cause."

"Do not trouble yourself. If the most pressing business for the kingdom is the recruiting of musicians, then perhaps things are not as bad as I supposed," Jesse said as he stood. He looked over to see Raddai and Ozem eavesdropping from the doorway. "Go and get David. Tell him to bring whatever he needs. He may be gone a while," Jesse instructed. "And tell him to bring his harp!" Jesse added before turning back to his guests. "Be sure you have a good meal and fill up on plenty of water before returning to Gibeah. To the extent that you can, please instruct David on the proper customs in the presence of the king." Jesse paused momentarily. "Does the king understand what he is getting?"

"Absolutely. We would not be here if I did not have the utmost confidence in David's ability."

Jesse let out a long breath. "Very well," he said. "Please excuse me. I have much to tend to with three of my eldest and most capable sons away. I trust you have no other requests?"

"None, sir. Thank you," Raanan replied. "Rest assured, you will be compensated for your service to the kingdom."

For the first time since the initial pleasantries, Jesse's mood appeared to lighten.

"Very good. Send the king my respects and warmest regards. The house of Jesse is always at his service. You men may wait here while we prepare something for the king."

The men continued eating from the table as Jesse went and took a donkey and loaded it with their finest bread and a skin of his best wine.

***

Several fields and hilltops southwest of the city, a red-haired youth watched his father's flock from his perch overlooking the field, the best vantage point available in this portion of his father's land. On lower ground, two of his nephews kept the sheep from straying too far from the rest of the flock. They looked to their uncle not just to direct them to wandering sheep, but for protection. Unknown to them at that moment, concealed in the swaying yellow grass, another watched close by.

David searched the perimeter of the flock, his eyes moving slowly right to left then back. He scanned the grass for any break, any movement not caused by the wind, focusing on small groups of shrubs that scattered the field, anything that might conceal an intruding predator. Back and forth, his eyes moved when suddenly something caught his attention. There, not thirty cubits from his eldest nephew, Joab, something caused the grass to bend towards the flock. The grass swayed with the wind around it. His eyes focused in, the hair on his neck stood. His right hand went to the swing on his side, his left clinching the nearly fist-sized rock he'd selected for just such an occasion. As he peered at the gap in the tall grass he saw the dark mane of the lion as it raised its head just slightly.

Joab walked along, calling to the sheep, prodding them back to the flock when necessary, and ignorant of the danger that lurked nearby. He looked to his brother, Abishai, on the other side of the flock. Abishai glanced upwards towards David's position on the rock. Suddenly Abishai froze, his eyes towards David quickly shifted to Joab. Startled by the sudden shift in his brother's demeanor, Joab's stomach sank. From the corner of his eye, he saw a flash of movement to his left where David had been. He turned to see David sprinting towards him, his right hand moving in an arch behind then over and above his head, the sling following behind it. Joab instinctively closed his eyes as the projectile flew past him, then heard it strike with a loud "CRACK."

Opening his eyes, Joab spun around to see what the target had been. There, not fifteen cubits from him, was a large male lion now kicking and struggling in the tall grass.

David ran straight past him, dipping to grab a large rock from the dirt as he sprinted towards the beast, still writhing in pain and confusion, smearing blood in the pale grass around it. David leaped atop the struggling predator, straddling its body. Clinching a fistful of its thick tawny mane in his left hand, David repeatedly brought down the stone with his right, striking the lion's skull until finally, it cleaved in. Its kicking and struggling stopped.

Joab's heart pounding, he wearily approached. Abishai was already at his side. They gazed down at the beast as David stood above the bloody animal. Blood spattered David's face and arms. Joab's eyes turned to his brother. Abishai was beaming with the largest smile Joab had ever seen on his brother's face.

"That was amazing!" Abishai shouted. Joab, not yet convinced that the predator had been alone, scanned the nearby grass and shrubs, then back to his uncle, still speechless, his hands shaking.

David, breathing heavily from the exertion, turned from the beast as if noticing his nephews for the first time. Joab was pale with terror. David stepped over the beast and touched his nephew's shoulder.

"Next time, it could be one of us. We must not get complacent."

David placed his other hand on Abishai's shoulder and bowed his head. Abishai followed suit.

"Eternal Lord, thank you for this victory. Surely without your hand on us today, it would not be the blood of this beast which soaks the ground, but one of our own."

Joab, still scanning the land around them, glanced back at his uncle and brother with bowed heads.

David continued, "We ask that your hand of protection be continually on us and bless us as we watch over my father's flock. We, your servants, praise you. We are forever in your debt. Amen."

David turned to Joab, who was still clearly shaken. He needed something to take his mind off of the fact that he was nearly a meal.

"Let's work on your slinging," David suggested. Kneeling and selecting a fist-sized rock from the ground, he handed it to Joab. "Abishai, you take watch for now."

Taking a hysup branch, David dipped it into the lion's still-warm blood and painted a small crude image resembling a lion's head on the face of a large, flat rock. Comforted by the distraction, Joab went to work, hurling stones as David observed and corrected his technique. With each successive throw, the rocks struck more consistently nearer and nearer to the lion's head.

"Remember, you're not just aiming for its head," David instructed. "You want to hit him right between the eyes, or here," David said, raising his finger to Joab's temple, "depending on which way he's looking." Joab's next shot struck the lion right in the teeth, shattering the projectile into a thousand pieces. "That's it!" David shouted. "Great job!"

Joab had long lost track of how many rocks he'd slung at the target. He was searching the ground for more ammunition as David washed the blood from his face and arms when they heard Abishai call out to them from the overlook.

"David! Uncle Raddai and Ozem are headed this way," he shouted, raising his outstretched hand towards the home.

"Let me see what this is about," he said before jolting off to meet his elder brothers.

Joab joined Abishai on the rock and watched the brief encounter. David turned to see both boys now perched on the rock.

Running back to the base of the rock, David looked up to his nephews. He seemed momentarily at a loss for words.

"I have to go. You two are in charge now," David said. "Raddai and Ozem said there are men from the palace here to take me to play for the king."

"What?" Joab exclaimed. "Are you serious?"

"Father said to hurry!" Raddai shouted impatiently from where he and Ozem stood, waiting.

"We… well, David, just killed a lion!" Abishai shouted.

The two older youths exchanged glances and then turned back to their nephews.

"So what! Father is waiting!" Ozem shouted.

David ran over and searched the flock until his eye locked upon the kid he was seeking. Taking it under one arm, he ran to the spot where they'd slept the previous evening and grabbed the harp from where he'd hung it on a tree.

"Don't let the mother follow me," David said to Abishai and Joab. "I'm taking the best of the flock as a gift for King Saul. I will send word as soon as I am able." Sensing the growing apprehension, David shook his head. "You two are ready for this. You will be in my prayers. Remember, be strong and courageous! Do not be terrified nor dismayed, for the Lord your God is with you…'"

"Wherever you go," the brothers said simultaneously.

David nodded. "You are ready."

"Come on!" Raddai shouted.

David turned and ran toward his brothers, the kid under one arm and his harp under the other.

***

David met Jesse in the courtyard.

"I thought you might want to present an offering on behalf of the king. This is the best of your flock," David said.

Jesse took the animal and examined it. It was pure white and unblemished. Its new skin and hair were soft to the touch and clean. "I've never seen one so white. I didn't know I had any solid white goats."

"You didn't until this one," David explained excitedly.

"Beautiful," Jesse said aloud, then looking to his youngest son who bore no resemblance to himself, he noticed for the first time the keen likeness David bore to his own father and grandmother. For a moment, Jesse stared as David stroked the animal's pure white hair.

"It will be difficult not having you around," Jesse managed to say.

"Don't worry, Father," David reassured, "Joab is very capable. He's prepared to take care of the flock while I'm away. Abishai and Asahel will help him as well."

"Very well," Jesse said. They tied the young goat in a satchel with its head protruding alongside the donkey.

Raanan, who'd been watching from the doorway, thought he saw the slightest hint of sadness come over the stoic patriarch's demeanor. He turned his attention back inside to be sure the old man was not offended, giving the father and son a moment to bid their farewells.

Jesse pulled David's head close to his own.

"Be careful David. If this had come from anyone other than Raanan, I would be suspicious. I trust Raanan, but the circumstances are strange. If the king ever hears what Samuel did, he will kill you. Keep it to yourself and tell no one," Jesse cautioned. "Do you understand?"

"Yes, Father," David responded.

Raanan and the others waited inside while Zeruiah and Nitzevet served each of them a bowl of herb-seasoned lentils with some barley bread. Ittai finished and went to relieve the sentry outside, thanking the women for their hospitality as he left.

A few moments later, David entered, holding his harp under his right arm.

"Raanan!" David exclaimed. "I didn't realize you were here!"

"It's good to see you," Raanan responded as he stood. "Is there anything we can help you collect? I'm not sure how long it will be, but I'm sure your needs will be attended to. You shouldn't need much."

"Then I'm ready now. Raddai told me to bring the harp."

"That's right. That's why you're needed," Raanan said.

David turned to his mother. Seeing the mix of pride and emotion in her strained face, he put the harp on the table and embraced her.

"Don't be upset Mother. I'll send you letters as often as I can till I can come home. I will be with Raanan, so you needn't worry."

Nitzevet did not attempt to speak. It was all she could do not to let the tears escape from her burning eyes. She motioned for them not to leave as she disappeared into her room. A moment later, she emerged with a leather package tied with string at the top.

"This was for your birthday," she said, her voice cracking as she strained to say the words.

David untied the string at the top, which held the leather folded around its contents. A clean ephod was folded neatly within.

"You'll need something nice to wear in the king's presence."

David smiled. "Thank you Mother," he said as she nodded and embraced him again. Nitzevet turned and began packing provisions for him and his escorts, busying herself to distract her worried mind. David rewrapped the clothes and tied the package securely.

Moments later, the men and David saddled their horses and the donkey with the abundance of provisions gathered by Nitzevet and Zeruiah. David bade farewell to his mother, sister, nieces, and nephews. As Raanan turned their horse to leave, David scanned momentarily for a face he hoped but fully expected not to see. There were none present to see him off but women and small children. Raanan kicked the horse and the six men departed.

None present knew or saw the pitiful sight perched in a nearby tree as Asahel wept bitterly over the parting of his beloved uncle.

COMFORTER

1067 BC, Gibeah, Benjamin, Israel

The ride to Gibeah had been uneventful. Raanan assumed his young shepherd friend was anxious, perhaps even fearful, being so far from home with no family nearby.

"I know you've got to be anxious," he said at they approached Gibeah. "I would be, but I've heard you play before. Just pretend you're out in the field playing for your sheep," Raanan said with a smile.

"What's that?" David asked, as if waking from a dream.

"I said I figure you've got to be nervous, being this far from home and having to play for the king."

"No, I'm just taking it all in," David said. "I want to be sure I can find my way back if I need to by myself."

Raanan looked at Ira, his expression revealing that he was impressed with the young man's answer.

"Is this the farthest you've ever been from home? Ira asked.

"So far, yes. Every step."

When they arrived at the palace gate in Gibeah, Raanan and Ira dismounted. David and the others followed suit as the gatekeeper opened the large, heavy wood and bronze door. The men proceeded inside. One of the men took Raanan's and Ira's horses and departed with them. Raanan and Ira instructed David to follow as they proceeded down the path towards the palace courtyard.

As they approached the palace, David was awestruck by the structure. It dwarfed all he'd previously seen in Bethlehem and the outlying areas. He'd never been to a city the size of Gibeah before. As they entered the interior gates which surrounded the palace, David saw King Saul's guard of approximately fifty well-armed and strongly built men training within the courtyard.

David had stopped and was staring at the men. In the center of the various groups, there were three men, two struggling on the ground and one standing next to them. After a short time, their instructor would call "Go" and the man standing would join the fray, attacking the man in the inferior position on the ground. After a brief period of having to defend himself from two attackers, the instructor would relieve the man by calling "out," in which the defender would be released, while the other two men squared off and locked arms.

They all looked extremely exhausted, David thought, as their sweat soaked the ground around them.

"David," Raanan said, directing his attention towards the palace. "This way."

As they entered, David familiarized himself with the layout. There was a large dining hall and various adjacent corridors. They proceeded to the very end and through a corridor to the left, then finally arrived at the barracks that would be David's living quarters for the indeterminate future, assuming Saul approved of his playing.

"This is where you'll be staying. I figure since you'll want to practice, it makes sense you stay here where the day shift guards sleep. They'll be gone when you're here and sleeping while you're out in the evenings. Go ahead and settle in. I'll be back," Raanan said as he disappeared from the doorway. A moment later, he returned with a pumice rock, oil, and a strigil and handed the items to David. "There are baths on the roof if you want to get cleaned up while I see about getting you some fresh clothes. I'll probably be racked out for a while, so you'll have some time to kill before this evening if or when the king calls for you. I'll be in the next barracks if you need anything." Raanan paused, considering for the first time how out of place David must have felt. "Do you need anything?"

"Just some time to practice," David replied. "You've heard me play before. Is there anything you think he'd like? Any idea if he has any sort of preference?"

"My recommendation?" Raanan thought for a moment. "Your songs typically express a certain feeling, something that you're going through or have been through, yes?

"Sure," David responded.

"Then just play something you think applies to his current state of mind. If he's in a good mood, play something cheerful. If he's feeling low, play something more somber," Raanan suggested. "My father always tells me, 'use the bait that suits the fish.'"

David smiled. "That's good advice. I'll have to remember that."

"You're going to do great David. See you this evening," Raanan said before disappearing from the doorway.

David was left alone in the empty barracks. He laid the lyre on a table in the center of the open room and uncovered it, remembering the first time he'd seen it. His grandfather had presented it to him as a gift one year. He'd had the discernment to present it to David in the field when it was just the two of them. David recalled how he'd wanted to show it to everyone right away, but Obed wisely intervened, convincing him it was best to wait until he'd learned a song to play before revealing the instrument to his family.

So wait he did until he'd mastered a complete tune. Obed had attempted once again to dissuade David, but his excitement could not be contained. He'd wanted to show everyone, especially his father, who David was sure would be impressed. That evening, when David had run to the house with the instrument in hand, he was never more sure of anything than the hope that his father and brothers would be moved by his talent and hard work.

David stood alone, still staring at the instrument, the hurtful words his brothers and father had spoken so many years ago still ringing in his head as if it were yesterday. David forced the painful memories from his mind.

"You *are* the Lord's anointed," he whispered to himself. "You *are* the Lord's anointed. Do not be afraid for the Lord thy God is with you wherever you go. Do not be afraid for the Lord thy God is with you wherever you go." David continued praying and repeating the verse Obed taught him from the scroll of Joshua so many years ago.

David went to the baths on the roof and found clean, warm water heated by the sun. He smiled. The last time he'd bathed was in a shallow creek well over a week ago. He'd had none of these luxuries then. He took the oil and rubbed his arms and legs, letting it saturate his skin to pull the filth and grime to the surface. Using the strigil, he scraped his skin free of the oil, then stepped into the bath. The water was hotter than any he'd ever enjoyed before. Despite the desire to soak, David began scrubbing himself clean with the pumice and combed his hair free of the dirt that had accumulated there for months. When he emerged from the bath, he was cleaner than he'd been in years.

As he dressed himself in the kethoneth laid out for him by one of the palace servants, he recited the lines of the song he intended to play. There were many songs he'd sung over the years to sheep in the fields, but like any musician, he had his favorites.

During the ride, he'd considered many of them, but knew from Raanan's input that the king was in a state of agitation or sadness, or both. He'd settled on a particular song that had been a personal comfort to him during times alone in the wilderness. He sat and played and sang the tune until it came without thought, making slight improvements to the chords and melody while he waited to be summoned.

As mid afternoon approached, a servant came to check on him and invited David to join the palace staff for dinner. Too nervous to eat, David thanked the servant and declined. He continued his practice, and a short while later, he was brought a plate of fruit and nuts, along with a cup of wine offered graciously by the servant to help ease his spirit.

As evening approached, the guards who occupied David's barracks flooded in.

Most of the men ignored David as they passed him on the way to their spaces within the barracks, but as David watched each of the impressive figures pass him, one man stopped and turned towards him.

"What are you doing on my rack?" the man inquired.

David looked at the neatly made sleeping mat and empty shelf, then over to the other racks, each containing their owner's clean folded ephods and kethoneths. Turning back to the guard, David simply replied, "This isn't your rack."

"Like hell it isn't. You're squatting on my rack sweetheart. The musicians sleep with the cooks and palace servants. You're in the wrong place," the man said, glaring down at David.

David set the lyre down on the bed beside him and stood to address the man when another huge guard seized the fellow by the arm.

"Give it a rest, will you?"

"I was just sizing him up," the guard replied. "And look! He's got some sand," the man declared, slapping David on the arm.

"My name is Adriel," the second said as the large guard extended his arm. "Raanan told me you'd fit in well here. Don't worry about Hezro. He is almost tolerable when you get to know him."

Hezro extended his arm and shook David's arm violently. "Pleasure!" he said with a sly smile.

"Don't let any of these guys give you too hard of a time. If you need anything, let us know. Raanan will be along shortly to take you to the king's chamber." Leaning in close, he lowered his voice. "Did Raanan fill you in on what to expect this evening?"

"He told me about it on the ride here," David responded.

"Good, it can't be any worse than guarding sheep, right?" he said, slapping David on the shoulder before proceeding to his space within the barracks.

A short while later, darkness had settled in on the mid-summer evening, and Raanan appeared in the doorway.

"You ready?"

David nodded and stood with the lyre under his arm.

Raanan took David across a large manicured garden to the palace entrance flanked by several guards. They proceeded through the corridor to a wide stairway that led to the royal family's chambers on the second floor of the large building. They proceeded down the lamp-lit hall to the king's chambers where several guards stood watch. Raanan rapped on the door three times and waited for an answer.

"Enter," David heard from within.

Raanan opened the door and gave David the nod to enter. "Good luck," Raanan said quietly as David entered King Saul's room.

David stepped in and introduced himself as instructed.

"David, son of Jesse the Bethlehemite, reporting as ordered My King."

Saul stood over a table at the opposite end of the room to David's right. He slowly turned around and looked at his guest.

"You must be a very good musician to have been selected for this task."

"Someone seems to think so," David responded. "I hope that my skills will be pleasing to Your Highness."

"What lies have they told you about why you're here?"

"That Your Highness requires a skilled musician," David responded.

"What else? What of my condition?" Saul demanded, much louder than his prior inquiry.

"I gathered that you are having trouble sleeping My King. I don't recall what specifically was said that gave me that impression."

"That's a profound understatement," Saul said as he poured himself a cup of wine and turned it up, emptying its contents. "How long have you been playing music for a living?"

"I wouldn't call it my occupation, Your Highness."

"Ah, yes, you're a shepherd," Saul exclaimed.

"Perhaps I should play something, Your Highness, so that you may discern whether I am suited for the task."

"Yes," Saul conceded. "I suppose so. I am going to lie down. You can sit anywhere over there. Don't bother me if you must leave to relieve yourself. If I am able to fall asleep, don't wake me for any reason. Do you understand?"

"Yes My King."

"Well then, let's see what you've got," Saul said as he moved behind the curtain of his bed and sat on the side opposite David, concealed from view.

David sat on a cushion on the floor and positioned the lyre. He quietly cleared his throat, then began plucking the strings. A soft melody filled the room, slowly increasing in volume till it reached a pleasant and soothing pitch. Several minutes into the melody, David began to sing.

The Lord is my shepherd; I shall not want.
He makes me lie down in green pastures.
He leads me beside still waters.
He restores my soul.

Saul listened to the soothing words and tunes. Amazed and delighted by the young shepherd's skill, he laid down and closed his eyes, focusing on the young musician's words.

He leads me in paths of righteousness
for his name's sake.
Even though I walk through the valley
of the shadow of death,
I will fear no evil,
for you are with me;
your rod and your staff,
they comfort me.

A moment later, Saul was asleep. The young shepherd continued his melody late into the evening. After several hours of playing, David had finally gotten to the end of the long list of songs he'd been prepared to play. He paused and listened briefly. Hearing nothing, he sat the instrument down and proceeded quietly to the door.

Exiting the room, David was met by Raanan and the other sentry.

"Where did you learn to play like that?" The sentry asked once the door was firmly closed behind them.

"My grandfather taught me many of them and many I've come up with on my own."

"And he's asleep?" the sentry asked.

"As far as I can tell," David responded. "I really need to relieve myself," David confessed. He'd been straining for at least an hour, but had been too worried that the king would awaken when he stopped playing.

The sentry escorted David to the toilets.

"How is it that you know so many songs? I've never heard any of the ones you've been playing."

"As a shepherd, you have a lot of time to yourself. I tried to make the most of it and keep myself busy by writing songs or practicing other useful skills."

"Like what?" the sentry inquired.

"Mostly slinging," David replied.

"Very smart of you kid," the sentry said, considered the practicality of the weapon. "Did your grandfather teach you that as well?"

"Yes, but there's really not much to teach. Practice is the only thing that will make someone a better slinger."

On their return, David was given some bread and water.

"You might as well get some rest," Raanan advised. "You never know when he might awaken. You can sleep on those cushions on the floor. If you hear him begin to stir or he awakens, just start playing again. We turn over to the next shift before morning. One of them will come and get you at first light."

David thanked the sentries for the bread and quietly reentered Saul's chamber. Making himself as comfortable as possible on the cushions provided, he laid his head to sleep. He lay there considering the turn of events that had brought him to this place. In less than twenty-four hours, he'd gone from sleeping in the wilderness with only sheep about him, to passing the night in a palace with the King of Israel as his sole company.

***

As promised, one of the sentries had roused David just before the light of a new day could be seen on the horizon. He was permitted to return to the barracks and rest at his leisure. As the process repeated itself for several nights without incident, David was able to move freely about the common areas of the palace grounds during his waking hours. He quickly familiarized himself with its layout and occupants. While King Saul rarely engaged in much talk with the new musician, he was slowly growing more and more comfortable with David's presence. As the king's once sleepless nights gave way to several nights of uninterrupted slumber, he came to appreciate the young musician's skill.

As days passed, David taught other musicians the songs that Saul preferred the most. The king grew fond of the exuberant young shepherd who, apart from his singing, never spoke unless provoked to do so by the king.

By day, David's familiarity with the men of the royal guard had grown rapidly. As the king's mood steadily improved after several weeks of peaceful rest, David won the respect and appreciation of the men who benefited most from it. He was awakened one morning by the soldier he'd met on his first day in the palace.

"David," Adriel said, touching his shoulder and lightly shaking him. "I've got some news for you."

David sat up on the rack and blinked his eyes open, squinting as his eyes adjusted to the light. By now, he was accustomed to the broken sleep.

"Saul wants you to be one of his armor bearers. You're to start training right away."

David smiled and stood to stretch.

"Where do we begin?"

***

David prayed that the night would pass without incident as he bathed and rinsed the grime from his body. The day's training had been grueling, beyond anything he'd previously experienced. Though tired, he felt elated. Reflecting on the day, he recognized a feeling he'd not had since his grandfather's passing. He couldn't recall any time since the death of Obed that he'd been taught or trained by an older man.

He'd done all he could to pass on that knowledge to Joab, Abishai, and Asahel, but . It was clear that they were genuinely interested in helping him. The camaraderie, the training, the food, the comparatively lavish treatment, it was as if he'd died and gone to heaven.

He looked down at his arms and thighs to see fresh bruises and was reminded of the training that produced them. He thought back on the times he'd fought with his older brothers. If only he'd had this training back then. He smiled at the thought.

Once clean, he returned to his rack and dressed for the evening. The barrack was busy as the other men prepared for whatever festivities the night had in store. David, on the other hand, lay on his rack, exhausted, hoping to get some rest before being summoned to play for the king. Despite the loud banter of the men around him, sleep came quickly.

When he was roused several hours later by Raanan, he awoke to find a cup next to his bed covered with a small note. David took the note and read it.

"Drink. It will help with the soreness, Hezro."

David looked into the cup and noticed the liquid was orangish in color. It tasted awful, but he guzzled it down nevertheless. David stood and stretched, preparing himself for a long night. Taking the lyre, he strummed a few cords and tuned the instrument then headed to the king's room. While no one outside of the royal family or interior guard was allowed to roam the castle unescorted, David had been granted the privilege, reasoning that if he could be trusted in the sleeping king's chamber, he could be trusted anywhere.

By now he knew the route most likely to guarantee a brief encounter with the king's youngest daughter, Michal. The same was chosen this night. Conveniently, the princess was exiting the library at approximately the same time that he passed by. He bowed and greeted her as he'd been instructed. The princess returned his greeting coupled with a warm smile and the two continued on their separate ways. The princess's female escort turned her nose up as she passed.

After a brief update from the guard, David entered Saul's room.

The king was at his table as usual when David arrived. He turned and greeted David.

"How was your training today?"

"Excellent Your Highness," David responded. "Thank you for the opportunity."

"It is I who should be thanking you my son," Saul said as he approached. "You have brought peace and rest to my weary mind. Now that I have been restored, I'm ready to begin the Lord's work anew. Come and see," Saul said as he turned back to the table.

David placed the lyre against the wall and walked over to the king's side.

There were pieces in place representing Philistine garrisons and units, updated daily by Saul's staff of military advisors.

"God has commissioned me to fulfill His work in purging our lands of the uncircumcised and I will do just that. I will cleanse our lands of these filthy wretches if it's the last thing I do. Work hard at your training David. Pretty soon, you will be called upon to use it."

"I look forward to the opportunity to serve my Lord in battle," David said.

Saul laughed. He was encouraged by the young man's courage, though he'd seen men full of courage crumble in battle.

"Once trained, my armor bearers go where I go. As king, I try to be where the battle is the fiercest. Philistine kings do not do this you see? They hide behind their high walls at Gath, Ekron, Ashkelon, Gaza, and Ashdod as their raiding parties destroy and burn our villages to the north."

"Will we be going soon?"

"I will. The army will. You are not ready yet. You are far too young to accompany us yet. Train while you can, your time will come."

Saul removed his cloak and hung it on the wall near his bed. David took this as a sign to take up his post near the opposite wall. He did so and settled into position with the lyre and began to play.

Saul dimmed the lamp to the smallest flicker and laid to rest as David forced himself to focus on the task at hand, rather than indulge his mind in thoughts of future battles. Still, he felt rejuvenated by the prospect and played heartily into the night despite his bodily fatigue. Saul listened to the words as he slowly drifted off to sleep.

You prepare a table before me
in the presence of my enemies;
you anoint my head with oil;
my cup overflows.
Surely goodness and mercy shall follow me
all the days of my life,
and I shall dwell in the house of the Lord
for-e-ver.

SONS OF ZERUIAH

1067 BC, Bethlehem, Judah, Israel

Months had passed since David's departure, though it seemed like years to the trio of nephews he left behind. Joab had assumed the role of shepherding the flocks in David's absence, with Abishai serving as his assistant. Asahel, the youngest still had no real responsibilities, which was the source of constant chiding and aggravation from his older brothers. Still, they watched over him like a mother bear guards her cubs. Today, however, presented a reprieve from the monotony. Their mother claimed that she required their assistance with a load of provisions from the market. Joab knew that in truth, she preferred to have him as an escort on the journey and would never hear the end of it if she left the other two at home. The presence of the three boys had the desired effect of discouraging would be suitors.

As the small caravan walked the dusty road to Bethlehem, Joab plodded along thinking of the last time they'd been to the market. David was with them then and had introduced him to one of the breadmaker's daughters, whom Joab had become very fond of. She was the most beautiful girl Joab had ever seen and he was excited about the opportunity to see her again, but disappointed that his uncle wasn't there to help facilitate the conversation. Her older sister was clearly enamored with David like most of the girls they encountered. Joab admired David's way with the girls. He wondered how David was doing in the palace, what pretty girls he was likely to be wooing there. There were rumors that Saul had a beautiful young daughter that was somewhere between Joab and David in age.

Joab's thoughts were interrupted by the annoying sound of his younger brothers. Abishai had been irritating Asahel the entire way and now Asahel was chasing Abishai with a stick, attempting to retaliate.

These two certainly wouldn't be any help with the girls. It seemed they would never grow up. All they did was fight. It made him long for his uncle's company all the more. They tended to behave better in his presence.

Finally, Zeruiah put a stop to Abishai's pestering and Asahel's whining. Goodness, Joab thought looking back at them, they can't even walk in a straight line. They were constantly running back and forth, side to side along the dusty road. Why had his mother even brought them, he thought? He settled on the answer that it was probably to get them out of the way of the men back home. Though she said it was to help carry provisions so she and their grandmother didn't have to, he suspected he'd be doing the lion's share of the work carrying their provisions.

As they approached the village, his brothers noticed a group of boys in a cow pasture playing stick-ball. He recognized some of the boys and knew them to be the sons of the husbandman of the land.

"Mother, can we go play while you shop? We'll stay out of trouble," said Abishai.

Zeruiah stopped and looked at the boys playing in the nearby field, then to her mother.

"They could play while we shop," said Nitzevet. "It will be good for them. After all, they seldom get to see other children."

Joab was happy to hear his brothers would be occupied for a time.

"Ok," Zeruiah said to her middle child. "But I want Joab to go with you." Turning her attention to him, she said the last words Joab wanted to hear. "Watch over your brothers Joab." Then turning to Abishai and Asahel, she instructed them sternly, "now, you two behave and don't get into trouble. Listen to Joab. Do you understand?"

The boys nodded impatiently before their mother released them to join the game. Abishai and Asahel sprinted off towards the group of boys playing the pasture. Joab looked at his mother again.

"You know where to find me if you need me, right?" she asked.

"Yes Mother," he replied and began walking towards the other boys.

As they joined the group, one of the farmer's sons called out.

"Hey! We've got two more. We need to pick."

Another of the sons shouted in reply, "we've got Abishai!"

"Alright Asahel, you're with us."

"Our brother is with us, his name is Joab," Abishai said.

"Good, you guys already have Zacchaeus," the boy said pointing to a large older boy on his brother's team. "We get Joab. That will even things out." The large boy looked at Joab and snuffed. He apparently took the statement as a challenge.

"Alright, let's play," said the older brother and threw the ball into the fray.

The boys chased after the leather ball, kicking and pushing as they went. Joab momentarily forgot the girls he was missing out on seeing in the village. As one of the oldest boys present, Joab set his mind on outperforming his younger brothers, despite their innate athletic prowess. Focused on the ball, Joab ran right into the large boy who stiffened as he saw Joab approaching. Joab bounced off of him and toppled to the ground.

"Watch where you're going you little maggot," shouted the large boy. The other boys stopped their playing as Joab stared back up at the large boy. Seeing all eyes were on them, he insulted Joab again. "Say, you're one of those bastard kids, aren't you?" One or two of the other boys oohed and jeered at the statement. Encouraged by the instigators, the chunky boy smiled.

Joab was silent. He began to stand up and was immediately pushed back down by the large boy.

"I'm talking to you, bastard," shouted the large boy. "Didn't your father teach you to respect your elders?"

Joab stared back at his tormentor from the ground. The boy kicked dirt at his face.

"Answer me bast.."

The boy's word was cut short as his head snapped to one side, his body jerking the other direction as he was struck waist level by a blurred figure. As the two boys toppled to the ground in front of him, Joab realized the bully had been tackled by Abishai who'd struck Zaccheus at a full sprint. Joab was already on his feet before the large boy could recover. As the boy struggled free from Abishai, Joab landed several punches to the boy's sides as he tried to stand. Zaccheus shouted as he pulled free of Abishai. He turned to face Joab just as Abishai jumped onto his back, wrapping his arms around the bully's neck and wrenching him rearward. Zaccheus fell flat on his back, pinning Abishai underneath him next to a fresh pile of manure. He squirmed and wrestled to get free of Abishai's grip around his neck as they both writhed in the manure. He tried to stand again as Joab punched at the boy's ribs and back. Finally freeing himself, he again turned to face Joab, who punched him squarely in the nose. As he stumbled backwards, Abishai grabbed both of the boy's ankles and squeezed them together. Joab seized the opportunity and tackled the boy to the ground.

The bully rolled Joab onto his back and mounted him, using his superior weight to pin Joab to the ground. Joab anticipated the bully's fists and covered his head as he suddenly felt the weight lifted from him. Again, the large boy was wrenched rearward by Abishai's arms around his neck and again the two boys toppled back onto the ground.

Before Joab could rejoin the fight, Asahel dove onto the boy. He grabbed one of the large boy's plump legs and bit down hard on the meat of his calf. Zacheus cried out in pain. Joab grabbed ahold of one of the boy's flailing feet and began to twist, trying to get the downed assailant to roll onto his stomach. Suddenly, he saw a large figure reaching to grab Asahel. Asahel turned to bite at the new assailant, but quickly recognized the adult. Joab released the boy's ankle as his mother reached for him. Looking down at the boy, Joab noticed for the first time that he was gasping for air, his face nearly purple as his mother shouted at Abishai to release his grip around the boy's neck. Abishai reluctantly complied, then wriggled out from underneath the larger boy.

Regaining his breath, Zaccheus began to sob, then quickly stood and ran away from the field before anyone could stop him. He'd clearly gotten more than he'd bargained for.

Joab looked down at the grassy turf knowing his mother's gaze was upon him. The three of them stood motionless as their mother glared at them.

"Come on boys," was all she said.

Asahel looked as if he were beginning to cry now. Zeruiah picked him up and held him as he buried his face in her shoulder. She motioned Abishai and Joab to her side. Joab looked at his manure covered younger brother. Red faced and breathing hard, Abishai looked back at him. They stood silent for a moment. Neither said a word; none were necessary. Joab nodded. Abishai returned the gesture and smiled as they both turned and joined their mother's side. As the boys walked away from the field with their shoulders back and chests out, they looked a little taller than when they'd arrived.

CALL TO ARMS

1067 BC, Bethlehem, Judah, Israel

And Saul sent to Jesse, saying, "Let David remain in my service,
for he has found favor in my sight."
I Samuel 16:22

J esse stood and wiped the dirt from his hands. Surveying his sons'
hard at work, he stretched as his back. His shoulders popped and
cracked. Most men his age had stopped this sort of work long ago.

"Why don't you leave it to us, Father? There's no sense aggravating
your back again," Nethanel suggested as he worked.

"I'm fine son," Jesse replied. "A rolling stone collects no moss," he
said with a wink.

Nethanel smiled and shook his head. He searched the field for one
of his younger brothers.

"Elihu," he called.

Elihu straightened from his work. Nethanel nodded towards his
father and motioned for the water. The younger brother made his way
to the water pail at the end of the field and carried it over to Jesse.

Jesse took the ladle and drew several long sips from the pail.

"Thank you, son," he said before returning the ladle to the pail and
resuming his work.

Elihu visited each of his elder brothers with the bucket before returning it to the edge of the field.

The sound of shouting caught his attention before he could resume
his work. He turned toward the house from where the noise originated
to see his nephew sprinting in their direction with one hand held high
above his head.

"Grandfather!" he shouted. "Grandfather! A message from Gibeah. It's from the king's guard," Asahel shouted as he ran.

"Stop there!" Raddai shouted as Abishai reached the edge of the field. "We just planted those rows you donkey. Watch what you're doing!"

Asahel stopped his sprint and looked down at the soft dirt he was now standing in, then began slowly and carefully stepping over the rows of newly planted seeds.

Still panting from his sprint, Asahel reached Jesse, who finally stopped his work and stood straight. The boy held the sealed letter in his outstretched arm, more eager to know its contents than its intended recipient.

Abinadab walked over to where Eliab worked, turning over fresh dirt with his hoe. Eliab paused as they both watched their father wipe his hands clean before taking the letter.

He examined the royal seal briefly before breaking it. It was a wolf's head with a crown above it and leafy vines running down either side. Jesse unrolled the missive and read it to himself. When he finished, he rolled the letter up and returned it to Asahel.

"Go give this to your grandmother for safe keeping, be careful not to lose the seal."

Asahel sprinted off in the direction he'd come from as Jesse returned to the spot in the field where he'd been planting.

Eliab and Abinadab exchanged curious glances. Their father was smiling as he returned to his work. The two young men likewise returned to their work. They wouldn't learn anything about the letter until their father was good and ready to tell them.

"What do you think it was?" Abinadab finally asked in a low voice.

"Some report concerning David," Eliab mused. "I can't imagine what else it could be."

Abinadab considered this as he pressed his fingers into the dirt to make a small hole before planting another seed and covering it up.

"Can you imagine David playing his harp for the king? Can you see him singing one of his little ditties?" he asked, laughing at the very thought.

Eliab, too, laughed at the thought of their bawdy and tempestuous younger brother playing his harp before the royal family in his shepherd's ezor.

The men carried on planting as the sun beat down on their tan necks and backs. Elihu periodically brought water to his older brothers as they stood and stretched their backs and legs. When he'd made his final round with the water, his father called for him.

"I want you to get a fatted calf and bring it to the house," Jesse instructed.

"Are we celebrating something Father?" Elihu asked.

"We are," Jesse responded.

Elihu smiled and left to carry out his father's orders.

With their father and Elihu gone, the others could scarcely contain their curiosity. They continued working until the sun had nearly set, as was their custom, then marked their progress with stakes to resume their planting the following day.

They walked to the well just inside the exterior wall surrounding their home and washed their hands, arms, and faces before rinsing the dirt from their legs and feet.

Already they could smell the savory aroma wafting its way from the kitchen. The table was set in the courtyard. Torches and lamps were lit all around the yard. A large jug of wine waited at the center of the table.

"I thought Sukkoth was next month," Abinadab exclaimed.

Elihu returned from the trash heap with the empty bucket he'd used to dispose of the slaughtered calf's entrails.

"Elihu, what's this all about? What's going on?" Eliab asked.

"Don't know. Father hasn't told me," he replied.

Abinadab and Eliab exchanged curious glances.

Abigail and Zeruiah exited the house, their arms full with the plates they'd been preparing. A moment later their father emerged with a large plate of meat, followed by their mother who carried a large plate of bread and cheese.

"Come my sons, gather around the table. Come!"

Each of Jesse's seven eldest sons took their places at the table, with Eliab to his right.

"What are we celebrating Father?"

"I'll tell you in a moment," Jesse said before instructing his family to bow their heads. "God of our ancestors, Abraham, Isaac, and Jacob, we thank you for your provision and for blessing me with so many sons. Amen."

Eliab instructed his family to sit.

"I received a letter from King Saul himself today. Your brother David has found favor with the king. Saul has asked that he remain in his service there and inquired if I have any other sons who might be of service. General Abner has begun building an army and requires strong, brave, young men." Jesse turned to Eliab. "My son, my right hand, you will go and serve the king, serve our people, and represent our family." Jesse turned to his left. "Abinadab, Shimea, you two will also go."

Jesse was interrupted as Joab stood at the far end of the table.

"May I go as well?" Joab asked.

Irritated, Jesse waved his hand and motioned for him to sit down.

Zeruiah pulled her eldest son back down into his chair.

"Don't interrupt," she whispered.

"Mother, we want to go too," Asahel said, tugging at his mother's arm. Abishai nodded his head vigorously in agreement.

Zeruiah hushed the three boys as Jesse continued.

"My sons, you are strong, make your father proud. I have prepared this feast to strengthen you three on your way. Nethanel, Raddai, Ozem, Elihu, I need you to stay behind to help tend the fields. Perhaps a day will come when you too may go and serve, but your place is here for now."

Jesse lifted his cup from the table.

"To my sons," he said, raising the cup. "May you be strong and courageous in battle."

FIXER

1067 BC, Gibeah, Benjamin, Israel

David could hear the king's tirade from the hall where he stood waiting to be summoned. The family had just returned from northern Israel during a visit with the neighboring kingdom of Tyre in an attempt to establish some friendly commerce arrangement. It was not an infrequent occurrence during David's brief stay at the palace to hear one of the king's children being dressed down for various reasons. To a young shepherd whose upbringing had, for the most part, occurred in the fields under the tutelage of his patient grandfather and away from the watchful eyes of either parent, it was a stark contrast to what he'd expected.

Each of the king's children had apparently erred in some way, but Michal it seemed had committed the greatest infraction by way of flirting with one of the Tyrian princes. King Saul was irate.

The princes, except Jonathan, and princesses were all present and stood arrow straight along the wall as Saul berated them.

Tears ran down Michal's cheeks as the king paced in front of them.

"How much money? How much time and effort have we poured into you four, only for you to behave this way?" Saul asked rhetorically. "I might have expected as much of Michal, but Merab, Malchishua, I expect more of you two! You're certainly old enough to know how to keep your sister, your brother, and yourselves in line. I am the King of Israel, I have more important things to deal with than correcting an insolent child while entertaining the King of Tyre!"

"Michal, do you want to lose all respect of our people? How do you think you will be perceived when people see you behave in this way in the presence of Gentiles?" Saul asked, glaring at his youngest daughter.

Michal stared at the floor, trying to control her sobs.

"ANSWER ME!" Saul shouted.

"Father, I…" Michal tried to respond, "he made me laugh. I did not intend…."

"Stop making excuses!" Saul shouted. "I don't care what he did, I care what you did! You children repeatedly fail to obey my words! You shame me in the presence of my enemies! Ish-bosheth, playing with your food, Malchishua, you'd have thought we starve you here the way you ate in front of them. How much have I emphasized the importance of showing strength and dignity?"

Saul paced in front of them, his face red with anger. He seized a decorative vase and threw it hard against the opposite wall, smashing it into a thousand tiny pieces.

"Get out of my sight! ALL OF YOU!"

Ahinoam waited outside and consoled each of her children before entering the room. Saul stood with his back turned, leaning forward on his table and staring into the fireplace.Cautiously, the queen moved to his side and placed her arm around him.

"My love," she said softly, "they are just children, you accomplished what you sought out to do. I think you notice their actions far more than any of the Tyrians," Ahinoam reasoned.

"The fighting season is almost upon us again," Saul replied. "We must project strength in the presence of our neighbors. Only strength."

"I know you have not slept well since we left. It's been days my love. I've already summoned the musician. Why don't you try to catch up on some rest?"

Saul nodded.

"You're right," Saul acknowledged.

"Do you want me to send him in?" she asked.

"Yes," Saul said, turning to embrace his queen.

"I love you," Ahinoam said before kissing him. "Get some rest. I will see you in the morning."

***

Michal paced around her room. Embarrassed and frustrated, she continued to cry alone. The one man whose approval she sought was the one man whose attention and affection was always out of reach.

"I didn't ask for this," she said to herself as she sulked around the room. "I didn't ask to be a princess."

She looked out over the palace grounds from her balcony. Servants were filing out of the palace toward the gate that led to the heart of Gibeah. The Passover celebration, followed by the Feast of Unleavened Bread, was one day away. The city was filling up with people returning home to visit their families and loved ones. People decorated their homes and doorposts in preparation for the Passover.

Beautiful scarlet cloths were hung over doors to symbolize the lambs' blood that was painted over the doorposts, to distinguish Hebrew households - those who worshiped Yahweh - from the unbelieving Egyptians.

Oh, to be one of them, she thought. To live a carefree life, without the expectations of royalty.

Michal's eyes widened. She turned and went quickly to her wardrobe and found the most inconspicuous stola she owned and quickly changed. She located a hooded cloak and donned it. Pulling her hair free, she used both hands to ruffle it and pulled it forward over her shoulders. Looking in the mirror, she pulled more of her hair slightly over her face, completing the disguise. A moment later she was through the courtyard and following a small group of kitchen staff towards the gate.

Her heart pounded as she approached the gate. The servants ahead of her talked and laughed as they walked. She took a few quick steps to draw herself closer to the group as the gate was opened for them.

Seconds later, she was outside of the palace walls and among the crowded market.

The place was alive with the anticipation of the coming holiday. Smiling people greeted each other as they passed and lined up to purchase supplies to prepare to feed the extra mouths that would be filling their homes over the next several days. It seemed every vendor in the market was selling unleavened bread.

Several vendors displayed the scarlet cloths used to decorate Israelite doorposts.

Forgetting her father's scolding, Michal was exhilarated by the lively bustle of the market. She walked from shop to shop, carefully examining the wares and delicacies offered. A group of men and women were crowded around a boisterous man, cajoling onlookers to join or place bets against him at the shell game on the table before him. The man's hands moved the shells almost as quickly as he talked.

A small stage at the far side of the market hosted various performers and actors who recited lines, sang, or acted out small skits to entertain the crowd. Michal wished she'd remembered to bring a purse in her haste, for she hadn't the smallest silver coin with her to purchase anything or offer the performers for their efforts. Several other young women about her age sat nearby, watching the performers, commenting, and conversing every so often. She sat close by, hoping to overhear some of the conversation.

With rapt attention, Michal watched the performers and forgot about her father's cutting words. A play was being performed on the stage, a retelling of the story of Samson and Delilah. She'd heard of the controversial twist on the story, one which portrayed the Philistine beauty as something less than contemptible. The time passed quickly as the play unfolded. The bustling street grew quiet as people returned to their homes or retreated to the establishments that remained open but out of sight. When the final scene concluded, Michal was suddenly surprised to find the small sitting area almost empty. The few that remained in the audience stood and slowly departed.

She felt a terrible sinking feeling in her stomach as she looked down the street on either side to find the market starkly vacant. Frantically, she stood and hurried back in the direction she thought she'd come from. The streets looked so much different now than they had earlier while the shops were open, brightly lit, and filled with people. Few lamps still burned at street corners and Michal had never been into the market unaccompanied and thus had not taken the time to learn the names of the streets. She cursed herself for her foolishness as she frantically searched the streets for some familiar sign.

"Looking for something, beauty?" Michal heard from somewhere in the shadows.

"Sure is late for a pretty girl like you to be out and unaccompanied," another voice said as two figures emerged into the dim flickering streetlight.

"I'm lost," Michal confessed. "I need to get back to the palace."

"The palace eh?" one of the men said.

"What might you be doing there?" the other asked as he circled uncomfortably close.

Michal pulled the hood from her head and brushed the hair from her face.

"I'm Princess Michal, daughter of King Saul. Step back and show me the way to the palace gate at once!"

The two men laughed.

"What are you laughing at?" Michal demanded.

"My you're a lively one," one of the men said as he reached for her arm.

Michal snatched away from him.

"No princess of King Saul would be out and about all by herself at this hour," the larger of the two men responded.

"Princess Michal!" someone shouted from behind.

The men's eyes shot up to the dark shadow where the sound originated. Michal spun around, relieved someone had recognized her, though who approached them now in the darkness, she had no idea.

"I've been looking all over for you," said the dark figure.

Michal was befuddled, completely unsure of the approaching figure's identity.

"I don't know how we got separated. Please forgive me. We're expected back at the gate," said the figure as he drew closer. "Raanan! Raanan! I found her, she's over here," he shouted over his shoulder.

Michal discerned that it was a young man by the sound of his voice. At the very least, he seemed far less menacing than her present company and she welcomed the opportunity to remove herself from the current predicament. She quickly moved towards him as he stretched out his hand. She took it.

"Thank you men. She's in good hands now," the young man said to the men. "The rest of our party is just around the corner."

The men had already begun to shrink away at the mention of the king's armor bearer.

The young man quickly led her around the corner to the adjacent street.

"Where is Raanan?" Michal asked.

"Probably asleep right now," the young man responded. "He's on the day shift at the moment."

"You called for him, you said they were right around the corner!" Michal almost shouted, stopping and yanking her hand away from the stange boy..

"Keep your voice down, Princess. I said that to keep those men from following us," he said as he reached for her hand. "The palace is just around the corner. I happened to be walking by and heard you."

"Who are you? Are you one of the guards?" Michal asked.

"I wish. No, but I know all of them," the young man replied.

"How? Do you serve in the palace?"

"Yes, yes. I was headed home for Passover and heard you shouting. I recognized your voice and thought it odd to hear the princess in that part of town, so I turned the corner and there you were," he said. "I was a little surprised to see you to say the least. Now, if you don't mind, I don't think those men were the sort we want to spend our evening with."

Michal accepted his hand and followed as he quickened his pace.

"My father is going to kill me!" Michal said.

"Only if he finds out," the young man responded.

Michal hurried along next to the strange young man, wondering how on Earth he intended to get her back into the palace without her father's knowledge. She felt a mixture of relief at being found and dread at being found out. Ahead, she could see the palace walls and the gate from which she'd made her earlier departure.

They approached the gate and stood below the tall rampart.

A moment passed as they stood silently in the open and vacant street.

"Do we knock?" Michal asked.

The young man cleared his throat loudly as he looked up to the parapet above.

The silhouette of the guard appeared above them, outlined by the moonlit sky.

"Who's that?" the guard challenged. "What do you want?"

"Jacob? Is that you?" the young man called from below.

"David?"

"Yes, can you open the gate please?"

The guard disappeared from sight above them. Movement could be heard behind the gate and a small rectangular slot in the door slid open.

"What's the matter? You forget something?" another guard asked from behind the door. "You know we're not supposed to open the gate after hours. Who's that with you?"

"Look," David said. "Trust me; you really want to open the gate. It's the princess."

The man behind the opening eyed the princess questioningly.

"What are you trying to pull, David?"

Irritated, David turned to Michal. "Would you remove your hood so they can see who you are? It's the only way we're getting in at this hour."

Michal slowly removed the hood from over her head.

The guard behind the gate disappeared. David could hear the two guards speaking from behind the wall. A moment later, they could hear the sound of the huge bar being lifted from the door. The gate opened slightly, and the guard beckoned the princess inside, then pulled David aside and spoke in a hushed voice.

"What are you doing? Why were you two outside the walls together? Where is her escort?" the guard interrogated.

"Look, as you know, I just left," David answered, "by myself, I might add. I was passing through the southeast quarter when I heard her shouting. I went to check it out and there was the princess."

"And what were you doing in that part of town at this hour?" the guard asked.

"I was on my way home. I wanted to get an early start."

"Early? It's the middle of the night. Look, I've got to report this. Saul will have our skins if we don't."

Michal began to cry. Now safely inside the palace walls, the excitement had begun to fade as the repercussions of her actions began to dawn on her.

"I wouldn't be so hasty," David suggested. "The princess isn't the only one whose reputation is at stake here."

"What's that supposed to mean?"

"Look, she snuck out, sure, but on your watch. Sure, she'll get into trouble with the king, but what do you think will happen to you?" David asked. "He's going to hold someone accountable for her sneaking out unnoticed."

"And you just happened to walk by and find her, right?"

"I'm just a musician. Keep in mind that I was with the king just a short while ago. I have an alibi, the best possible alibi. There's no way this comes down on me, but I'm willing to keep my mouth shut if you are."

Michal looked up, hopeful she might yet walk away from this night with her reputation intact.

"If King Saul finds out about this later, we'll all be dead," the guard responded.

"I'm in no hurry to lose my head," David responded. "What about you, princess? Can you keep this to yourself?"

"It will go to my grave," Michal responded.

"There we have it," said David. "What do you say?"

"Go then, you escort her back. The captain will be making his rounds any minute. If we aren't both at our posts, he'll start asking questions."

"We'd better be on our way then," David said as he turned to leave.

The guard seized David's arm. "If you get caught, it's on you. We'll deny we ever saw either of you."

"I wouldn't blame you at all," David responded before turning to the princess. "Shall we?"

Michal accepted his hand and followed as he led her to the court-yard that her balcony overlooked.

"That's you right?" he said, pointing up to her room.

"Yes," the princess replied, still not sure how to feel about this young man who knew so much about her and the inner workings of the palace.

"Can you climb?"

"Can I climb?" she asked.

"Yes, can you climb? It's the only way you are getting back in that room without alerting someone."

"I used to climb trees before it became 'unlady-like,'" Michal responded.

"Good enough," David replied. "This will be no different." He moved to the wall adjacent to the balcony and began scaling the offset corner stones that formed the wall just underneath.

Clinging with both his hands and feet, David shimmied up the tiny joints and crevasses until he'd reached the parapet, then swung his leg over and onto the balcony. Looking back over the parapet, he beckoned the princess to do the same. She stood looking up at him in disbelief and shook her head.

David climbed back down.

"I'm a princess, not a monkey," she whispered impatiently.

"Alright, I get it," David responded.

"Is there another way?" Michal asked.

David thought for a moment.

"My cousins and I used to do this thing we called the 'human ladder.' You can walk up my thigh and step on my shoulder, head, and hands. It would get you close enough to grab hold of the parapet," David suggested. "I promise not to look up."

With no other option besides her father finding out about her earlier transgressions, Michal relented.

"Alright."

"I guess this is 'good night' then," David responded. "It's been a pleasure, princess."

She sighed.

"I wish I could say the same."

The princess placed one foot on David's bent knee, then stepped up onto his shoulder with the other as David pressed his back into the wall behind him. David held his palms together in front of his face as Michal stepped up onto his hands and was hoisted up. David stretched, stood straight, and pressed up until Michal reached the railing of the parapet overhead and pulled herself up.

She turned and looked back down at the audacious young man that, in all likelihood, had risked everything to help her.

"Thank you, David," she said.

Even in the darkness, she could see the broad grin spread across his face.

"Till next time," David replied, then with a bow, turned and proceeded back towards the gate.

Michal shook her head and smiled as she watched him go in the moonlight. She felt a bittersweet sensation, relief at being returned safely to her room, exhilaration at how the young man had looked at her, and disappointment, knowing that nothing could ever come of it.

MONSTER

1067 BC, Jezreel Valley, Israel

G oliath awoke to the smell of ash, as he had every morning for the past month. He thought momentarily about the previous night. Images of slaughter danced around in his head, intermingled with the spoils he'd savored over the past week.

He sat up and saw his armor bearer, Alcander, sitting beside the fire.

"Any word?" Goliath asked.

"Nothing new," Alcander responded.

Goliath stood and stretched.

"You still can't sleep," he observed.

Alcander shook his head. "Maybe a few hours. It's hard to tell anymore," Alcander responded. The same images that brought joy, even nostalgia, to Goliath's mind plagued Alcander's and robbed him of peaceful rest most nights.

"You're too sentimental for this work," Goliath chided. "Just remember that every one of the Habiru we slaughter would just as soon slit your throat or drive a tent peg through your temple while you sleep. They're all filth," Goliath muttered.

Alcander had known better than to express his thoughts about their recent activities over the preceding months. Any scruples he had about their business, he'd learned to keep to himself. They'd all been indoctrinated with a healthy dose of hate for the Habiru, but Goliath's far surpassed that of the average Philistine.

Alcander suspected this was due to how the Habiru regarded the giant and his kind. While their fellow Philistines all but worshiped him, the Habiru did not regard him with the same esteem. They'd learned that many, if not all, of the Habiru considered the race of giants to be abominations, descendants of an unholy hybrid offspring of godlike beings and mortal women. Their sires were thought to be godlike by the Israelites in that they were greater than humans, possessing a sort of transcendent understanding of things combined with immense power for miraculous intervention or devastating destruction. However, these beings lacked the same prestige assigned to the gods of the Greeks and Philistines, being mere messengers or servants of a far more supreme deity, the one the Habiru called Yahweh.

Alcander, like Goliath, had come to learn these things as a witness to various interrogations of Habiru prisoners. He was impressed when, despite their impending doom and the infliction of great pain through various creative means inflicted by the giant, they cursed their captor, refusing to pay him homage and promising his destruction at the hands of their king and his sons. Goliath was not one accustomed to scorn and had not borne it well, for this had ignited in him an insatiable hate for the enemy. This hate manifested itself in unspeakable acts of cruelty. Alcander did not enjoy the task of protecting the brute, which inevitably made him witness to such vulgar atrocities.

Exiting his tent, Goliath could see the fires of the encircled village; Endor, the Israelite squirter had called it. He'd estimated there to be approximately one hundred inhabitants. This Israelite tried to claim he was Hittite, thinking he'd avoid the fate that awaited him. There were the cowards and the valiant among any people, but this man didn't seem to possess the same vigor as many of the other Habiru they'd captured.

"This place hardly seems worth the effort," Goliath remarked, looking down at the small town. From their position on the hill, they could see far beyond the village to the highlands behind it in the east. "Such a weak people have no right to so fair a land. It belongs to those strong enough to take it and keep it. When I rule this land, you will have your reward," Goliath promised.

"It would be a great honor," Alcander replied as he stood.

The remaining sleepers among the Philistine cordon began to waken as the eastern sky lightened.

"Are you ready?" Goliath asked.

"Always," Alcander replied as he stood.

The two men began their daily routine of calisthenics, alternating between pushups, squats, sit-ups, and flutter kicks until both had achieved one thousand repetitions of each. Dripping with sweat, Goliath took a cloth from his pack and wiped the dirt from his body. Alcander prepared a medicinal oil concoction, heating it by the fire as Goliath moved through his daily routine of stretching his hips, back, and shoulders.

Taking the oil from Alcander, Goliath poured some out on his hands and massaged it into his neck and shoulder muscles, calves, and lats, working out the remaining stiffness. The medicinal oil also served to prevent chaffing where the leather straps of his armor and caligae were secured against his body.

Alcander assisted as Goliath began cinching the leather straps of his armlets. He lifted the breastplate and backing. The giant bent as Alcander placed the armor over his head and began buckling the straps on his sides. He knelt and placed the greaves around Goliath's shins, cinching the leather thongs tight around the back of his massive calves, which were almost eye level from Alcander's kneeling position.

"In any other army, your armor bearer would be a champion," Timaeus said as he strode up to their position.

Annoyed by the staff officer's presence, neither warrior acknowledged the comment.

"I guess in any other army, he might have to face you though," the captain exclaimed, rapping Alcander on the shoulder. "Not a bad tradeoff."

Alcander was silent as he worked meticulously preparing Goliath's armor for the battle that would soon commence. Taking some of the oil, he worked it into the areas where leather met muscle and skin.

The captain watched the two warriors prepare for battle, ignorant to the irrigation he was causing.

"Is there a reason you've slithered up here or are you just looking for the best place to watch the battle?" Goliath said, becoming more agitated at the man's presence with every passing moment.

"Ah, yes," he replied, clearing his throat. "Ah, Alcander, Colonel Demeter wants to see you." The captain said, finally revealing his purpose for being in their midst.

Goliath took the armor from Alcander and picked up where he'd left off as the armor bearer stood and followed the captain from their position on the cordon.

"He really doesn't like mi-mas, does he?" the captain asked when they were out of earshot.

Alcander smiled. Mi-ma was a derogatory term, shortened from mi machitis or "non-fighters". Infantrymen often used "mi-ma" when referring to support personnel and officers who conducted the planning but stayed away from the actual fighting. This captain was particularly disliked by most of the troops for the disparity in the way he regarded those in authority compared to the line troops.

"Let me give you a tip," Alcander replied. "If you want to be respected by the men, never refer to yourself as a mi-ma again. It's one thing for the men to call you that behind your back, which they do," Alcander added. "It's another entirely to act the part." As Alcander approached the colonel's tent, he turned back to the captain.

"It's not that he doesn't like mi machites. He understands the necessity for support staff. He just doesn't like you."

Upon entering the tent, Alcander was greeted by the rest of Colonel Demeter's staff.

"Good morning Alcander," the Colonel welcomed. "How is our friend?"

"Ready to be unleashed sir," Alcander replied.

"Very good," the Colonel exclaimed as he ushered Alcander from the command tent to his own private quarters. The two men stood alone in the dimly lit tent. "Can he be controlled?"

"He is excited by the prospect of ruling the land. I think he will go along with whatever he perceives as beneficial for himself. I should caution you though. I take it from comments I've heard from others that many think him to be slow or dimwitted. I believe this is a mistake."

The colonel looked at him questioningly. "Really? What would give you that idea?"

"He seldom reveals the thoughts behind his actions. In fact, he seldom speaks at all. But he is deliberate in what he says and does. He does not have the air of a fool. He says little, but what he says shows discernment and forethought. More importantly, he is disciplined. These are not the characteristics of a fool."

The colonel nodded.

"And what, if anything, does this change?" he asked.

Alcander considered the question.

"I can see you are taking a liking to him. That may serve to ingratiate you with him, but do not forget your mission. You are not here simply to massage his muscles, work out with him, and tidy his armor," the colonel said sternly. "He is an investment that must be protected. What happened at Hachmon was fortuitous but reckless. There was nothing deliberate about his behavior there. I trust you to restrain him when appropriate until we are sure he is ready. I've brought you here to remind you of this before the battle today. I shouldn't have to tell you what will happen if something unfortunate were to befall so great an investment."

"Understood," Alcander replied. "Is that all then?"

The colonel dismissed him with a wave of his hand.

Alcander exited the tent. Protect the giant, he thought. It sounded preposterous but was proving more difficult than it sounded. There had been warriors among some of the Israelite hamlets they'd sacked. Untrained, but warriors still, and Goliath was a very large target.

Alcander had been selected because of his size, speed, and handedness. He could keep up with the giant better than any man in the Philistine army and could shield the giant's blind side. However, this had proven exceedingly difficult at times and there had been several near misses. Already, Alcander bore the scars from several missiles meant for Goliath and he was on his third shield. So far, they'd only met limited resistance. When they turned their eyes south toward the Israelite heartland, things would be different.

Eventually, the real fighting men in the south would get wind of their incursion. The tribes of Benjamin and Judah had developed a reputation among the Philistines. Alcander's job would grow increasingly difficult as time went on, but there were plenty of others ready to fill the void. He, like the giant, was just another pawn.

***

Goliath was the first to notice the approaching rider. He pointed out a single trail of dust thrown up by the messenger's horse as he approached across the open ground.

"He looks like one of ours," he reported, judging by the appearance of the rider's armor.

"Looks like he's riding hard," the sentry said. "Must have some important news."

"Let the colonel know," Goliath instructed as he watched the rider approaching rapidly.

The sentry disappeared to report the new arrival.

Moments later, another captain arrived at their position on the perimeter and stood beside the two men as the single rider approached their position.

The rider gave the hand signal indicating his friendly intent. Goliath replied with a gesture indicating he could approach safely.

"Friendly approaching!" Goliath shouted, his deep voice alerting all on the line nearest him to hold their fire.

The rider kicked his horse and again resumed his approach with his hand raised held out to his sides, exposing his palms to the wary sentries. He cautiously examined the massive soldier before him as he warily reached their position. Though he was still seated atop his horse, he had to look up slightly to meet the giant eye to eye.

"Greetings," the captain said. "From where do you come?"

"I am Kallias, servant to King Achish of Gath. I have come with urgent news," the rider declared.

"Let's have it," the captain responded.

"I must speak to the colonel. I carry orders from the five kings."

The captain looked annoyed.

"I'll take you to him," the captain replied, then turned and started towards the colonel's tent. In route, the messenger informed the captain of the general nature of the message in hopes that it would ensure a speedy audience with Colonel Demeter.

Upon reaching the colonel's tent, the rider dismounted. He was an impressive figure, well built, and despite his long journey, appeared well kept and unwearied by the long ride.

The captain ushered in the messenger. Two of the colonel's guards flanked the unfamiliar visitor to escort him inside.

Waiting for a pause in the discussion as the colonel and his officers talked informally of the order of battle for the day's attack, the captain stepped forward to gain the colonel's attention.

"Colonel Demeter, sir. A messenger, an officer named Kallias of Gath, servant of King Achish, has an urgent message for you," said the captain.

"Kallias?" one of the staff officers exclaimed as he turned around. Recognizing the messenger, his face instantly conveyed his delight. "My friend! What brings you here?"

"Alexandros," the messenger exclaimed as the two officers embraced. "I didn't know you would be here. How long has it been?"

"Too long, far too long. I haven't seen you since I was assigned to this battalion, so at least four years," Alexandros replied. "Return to your post," Alexandros said to the two guards flanking Kallias.

"What message do you have for me?" the colonel interrupted the officers' small talk, appearing somewhat annoyed at the delay caused by their familiarity.

"Colonel Demeter, the Habiru are mustering near the border of blood. King Achish feels an intrusion is likely. Many of our other divisions are still at sea. The Five Kings have reached a joint resolution requesting your return to Philistia immediately."

"Well then. It seems our work here is done," the colonel said with a smile. "Ready the attack on the village," he commanded the staff officers standing nearest him. Immediately, captains and officers dispersed to join their men and Kallias was left alone with the colonel, save his two guards. Kallias could hear orders being shouted outside the tent. "We'll snuff out this little hamlet before the long march south." The colonel turned as if to leave. "Why don't you accompany me? There's bound to be a bit of a show at least."

"It's a long way back, Colonel. I really should be going. I do not mean to overstep, but the kings have requested your immediate return."

"And return we shall, immediately after we sack this village. I insist, you really must see the jewel of Philistia in action," the colonel said, referring to the elite unit he commanded.

"Yes, colonel," Kallias responded, unable to think of some pressing reason he could not stay which wouldn't offend the superior officer.

As they exited the tent, the Philistine camp was alive with the last-minute preparations for battle. Kallias could see the giant he'd encountered earlier now leading the fifty or so soldiers in his platoon towards their position on the line. For a moment, Kallias imagined the people in the village below. Terrified mothers nursing their infants, fathers clinching their farm tools, unable to comfort their crying wives and children. He pushed the thought from his mind. Their extermination was a foregone conclusion, sealed by the actions of their own leaders, Kallias thought.

The messenger mounted his horse alongside Colonel Demeter and his staff. They trotted the horses up to the front of the line and the colonel rode out in front.

"After we wipe this little excrement from the face of the earth we'll be returning south to the border of blood," he shouted so that the entire line could hear. "The enemy has provoked all of Philistia. As if the unprovoked slaying of our men at Geba was not enough, they have gathered there at the border to invade our lands. It is time to put them down and take the land our forefathers sought out and bled for so long ago. These nomads thought to take this land from us when the Egyptians spat them out, but we will accomplish what our forefathers started. There is no place for us if not this place. They have shown that they will not live in peace with us. Their leaders provoke us at every turn, massacring our people," the colonel shouted.

Kallias could tell that the colonel meant what he said. His words portrayed a genuine conviction as he continued.

"You will give no quarter to the enemy. Not a single man, woman, or child is to be spared. We have a long journey, so take only what can be carried easily."

The colonel then turned his horse towards the village and raised his right arm above his head, his sword extended high into the air.

The Philistine captains repeated the gesture all down the line.

The colonel dropped the sword in an arc, its point extending towards the village. The entire line roared to life, sprinting down the hill.

After the wave of foot soldiers passed him, the colonel looked over to his staff as they walked their horses up alongside him. Kallias took up a position near Alexandros.

"Shall we?" Alexandros asked as he nudged his horse into a canter.

Kallias could hear the screams and clanging of metal grow louder as they drew closer to the small village. He saw the giant snatch a cowering youth from the ground and sling him like a child's doll into a mud-brick wall. Kallias gasped. He looked to the colonel, then to the men on his right and left. It was as if they were watching a play or competition. For them, this was entertainment.

The giant's sword was sheathed, his javelins slung over his back. He grabbed a Hebrew man by the arm as he tried to flee from his tiny home. Kallias watched in horror as the huge menace tore the man's upper extremities free from his body while the officers to Kallias' right and left laughed and applauded. He turned to see the colonel pointing to the monster, still tearing through the village, savagely smashing, throwing, and smashing any Hebrew unfortunate enough to cross his path.

"Look at him!" the colonel said. "He loves this! The gods made him for this!"

Kallias sat silently on his horse viewing the carnage before him as the giant seized an injured man from the ground, lifting him with one arm by the man's neck. He held the man's limp body cubits off the ground. Pulling the man's face close to his own, the giant ripped off a piece of the man's flesh with his teeth and spat it on the ground, then using his free hand seized the man's lower jaw and ripped it from the man's face. There could be no doubt, the giant was savoring every excruciating kill. He was covered in gore.

As he watched in utter disbelief, Kallias made no attempt to conceal his disgust as the colonel's staff around him, including Alexandros, laughed and commented on the massacre unfolding before them. This battalion was not the same as the ones he was used to serving. These men were vicious warmongers.

Kallias drew his sword and kicked his horse. She barreled down the hill, heading straight through the wide open street of the village below towards the giant. Seeing the next victim, Kallias drove his horse between them and cut the giant off. The horse reared up in front of the giant. Goliath stopped in his tracks and glared at Kallias.

"THAT'S ENOUGH," Kallias shouted.

"GET OUT OF MY WAY!" Goliath shouted back at Kallias as he began to go around the officer's horse.

Kallias moved the mare to cut him off again and raised his sword threateningly. This was all the provocation Goliath needed. The giant kicked the officer's horse with such strength that it stumbled and nearly fell. Goliath stepped toward Kallias and slapped the sword from his grip with one hand, seizing him off the horse with his other.

"This is what the gods made me for!" he growled as he held the officer suspended in midair from his throat. The giant slowly grabbed Kallias' left arm and began to twist.

"STOP! RELEASE HIM!" Kallias heard a voice say from behind the monster just as his shoulder joints began to strain.

Goliath stopped twisting Kallias' arm, still holding him suspended in midair.

"You will release him! He is a Philistine officer! He is not our enemy!"

"He threatened me!" Goliath shouted over his shoulder.

"He does not know our ways, nor our mission. He was mistaken. Now, release him!" the officer shouted from behind.

Goliath released his grip, and Kallias dropped to the ground, gasping for breath.

"Stay out of my way!" Goliath said as he thumped Kallias's helmet, then left the two Philistine officers and headed off to find another victim.

Alexandros walked his horse over to Kallias, dismounted, and extended his hand.

"Come on," he said. "I need to tell you about what we've been doing all these months."

Kallias batted the hand away and stood on his own. He glared at the man he'd once known.

"Murdering defenseless women and children, apparently!"

Alexandros shrugged.

"Yes, I suppose so," he admitted. "But it is for a greater cause. Philistine lives will be saved by what we are doing here. This is a campaign of the mind. Every tiny village and hamlet we massacre in this way shocks and paralyzes the enemy into submission. We always allow a select few lucky ones to escape destruction and flee back to Gibeah or some other place along the way. They spread the story of the massacre, of the giant, of our strength. Every one of them we kill saves countless Philistines."

"You! You all have inflamed the Hebrews' hatred for us!" Kallias said incredulously. "This is the reason for their aggression! This is why they muster at the border! You have provoked them!"

"You're wrong! You know that war with them is imminent. Their God instructed them to wipe out the inhabitants of the land and possess it. Did you know that? That doesn't leave much room for negotiation, does it? We're merely preparing the way. How many of those shepherds and farmers down south do you suppose will want to fight when word spreads that we have a god fighting our battles? How many Philistine lives will be saved when they realize the cost of opposing us?"

"You tell me! What do you think they'll do when you leave them no alternative but to fight? Now that you've allowed these men to conduct themselves in this way, do you think they'll somehow be model Philistines when they return to their homes? Do you think you can control that monster?" Kallias exclaimed, pointing in the direction Goliath had gone.

"You saw for your own eyes the control we have over him. All of this has been orchestrated for far longer than you know. When we've subdued the Hebrews, these men will be heroes. It matters not how we win. History is written by the victors my old friend."

Kallias shook his head. "It's not right what you are doing here; the gods will not honor this."

"Ha! Then where are they? Did you see any of them intervene just now? Where is this Yahweh of theirs?" Alexandros asked mockingly, his arms spread out and looking to the sky. "I don't see Him."

"The gods enjoy the entertainment, especially when it's carried out by one of their own. Goliath is our Achilles. He is our Hercules! Did not the gods give him to us? You think they were gentle with their enemies? Come now! What about the Israelite Samson? Was he the gentle sort? Did he spare our brothers or our poor when he burned our crops and massacred our people?"

"These backwoods Israelites don't deserve this land. We either take it from them or someone else will, the Egyptians, the Assyrians, the Chaldeans. If we don't take this land now, they'll be at our doorstep later. We'll be pushed into the sea, swallowed up and lost to history like the Hittites. If we do not provide for our children, who will?"

Kallias remained silent, too angry to respond.

"Only the strong survive, my friend," Alexandros said, touching his shoulder. "You should be thankful. I will smooth this over with Colonel Demeter, but you should know that our instructions come from higher than him. Be careful what you say and do from here. I am still your friend, so I will keep this conversation between us."

Alexandros handed Kallias the reins to his horse and mounted his own.

"Come on," he said. "Return with me and let me do all the talking."

Kallias looked up the slope towards Colonel Demeter and his staff officers. Alexandros was right. They would never let him leave still breathing if they suspected an ill report on his lips. It would be better to feign a misunderstanding. Reluctantly, he saddled his horse and followed Alexandros up the hill to rejoin the other officers as the screams of the villagers could be heard behind him.

STICKS AND STONES

1067 BC, Valley of Elah, Judah, Israel

Now the Philistines gathered their armies for battle.
And they were gathered at Socoh, which belongs to Judah,
and encamped between Socoh and Azekah, in Ephes-dammim.
I Samuel 17:1

E liab was awakened by Shimea for yet another watch. Already he was regretting his decision to join the army. As the eldest in his family, it wasn't as if he'd had much choice. It would have been a disgrace to allow his younger brothers to go and do the fighting themselves while he stayed behind and Jesse hadn't sought their council before deciding who would go. He thought back on his time training with Raanan. Military service seemed so much more exciting back then. Reality was different. The waiting was excruciating. Days and weeks of monotony interspersed with hours of hurry and commotion. The weeks had turned to months since he'd last left their home outside of Bethlehem.

It would be sunrise soon, which meant they would hear the taunts yet again. Another day of listening to that monster shout at them from across the battlefield.

They started early every day before sunrise. The monster's discipline only added to the dread his stature inflicted on them. While many Israelites were still trying to sleep, this man, this freak of a man, was already awake and taunting them as he would continue to do until sunset.

Eliab could see someone walking in his direction; even in the dim moonlight, he could identify the figure by his size and mannerisms.

"Shimea told me you'd be up soon," said Raanan.

"Day number thirty-five," replied Eliab.

"Counting the days are we?" Raanan jeered. He knew his friend was not enjoying life in the service. "I bet you could go back home and swap with David. Someone's got to watch the sheep. He'd probably prefer to be here anyway."

"Don't be a jackass," Eliab replied, irritated. "You want to tell me you're enjoying this? This is what you expected military service would be?"

"I've been doing it long enough now that I'd be surprised if it were any different. I've learned to make the most of it, as should you," responded Raanan. "Besides, you could end this whole thing right now. Just stroll on up there and tell Goliath you've had enough of his mouth."

"You're the one with all the muscle. You go tell him," Eliab replied as he stoked the fire. "Besides," he said in a hushed voice, "Saul is the biggest guy in all of Israel by a long shot. Shouldn't he be the one stepping up? Or at least leading the fight? What's the point in all this waiting anyway? If we're going to fight, let's get it over with; I'm tired of sitting here."

"I'm with you on that one," Raanan said in a hushed voice. "You know, they say there are four more like him. We'd better get to fighting before they come out from whatever mountain cave they live in. You see what one of them does to the men. Can you imagine if more of them show up?"

Eliab shook his head. "Every day we sit here waiting is another day wasted. Something needs to happen soon."

Raanan nodded.

The two men sat quietly peering out into the darkness. The quiet was once again broken by the muffled sounds of shouting coming from across the open battlefield. The giant was at it again.

"I guess that's reveille," Raanan said.

Eliab laughed. He appreciated Raanan's lightheartedness. Raanan's humor helped to break the sense of dread the giant's taunts caused him. Most of the men present felt it; they could see it in each other's demeanor even if they didn't admit it out loud.

"How does he know so much about the Queen?" Eliab asked sarcastically.

"Ha!" Raanan laughed. "I wouldn't joke about that too loud," he cautioned. "I just wish I had the courage and ability to challenge that uncircumcised bastard." Raanan said as he shook his head. "Jonathan will be here in a day or two. I bet he puts a stop to this."

"Where has he been?"

"Saul sent him and some others to round up more men. Guess the king wanted him off the line and thought it would be a good idea to send Jonathan in person to do the recruiting."

Eliab nodded. "I just assumed he was here."

"Ha! No, I don't think Jonathan would have let this carry on like it has. I think Saul feels threatened by Jonathan," Raanan confided in a low voice.

"There you go again. Analyzing everyone's feelings," Eliab replied. "It's his own son, his heir, why would Saul be threatened by him?"

"Maybe I'm wrong, but there is no doubt there is not a man in this army who wouldn't follow Jonathan. It will be interesting to see how he responds when he hears that son of Rapha."

Eliab nodded, knowing his friend's intuition could be trusted.

"Well, I'm going to head back. It was good to see you. I'll stop by again when I get the chance."

"Thanks for gracing me with your presence," said Eliab as Raanan stood. Raanan jabbed him in the shoulder. "It's not every day you get to rub elbows with the royal guard," said Eliab.

"Yeah, yeah. See you around," Raanan said as he departed.

*****

David carefully followed the runner as they made their way stealthily through the lowlands toward the Israelite position at the edge of the valley. According to his brothers' most recent letter and the additional information Jesse had gathered from the runner David now followed, they would have to maneuver around the Philistine army in order to reach the Israelite main body. When the Philistine army had penetrated the border into Israelite territory belonging to the tribe of Judah, Saul and his men moved to cut them off, maneuvering into position between the Philistines and their supply lines from Gath and Ekron. Responding in kind, the Philistines had moved north to cut off Saul's army and Israel's primary supply lines resulting in a stalemate, leaving both with dwindling supplies.

The runner answered the challenge of the perimeter guard and approached cautiously. Following a brief exchange, David reached into the bag, took some of the bread and cheese, and handed it to the sentry. The man expressed his profound gratitude for the unexpected nourishment which, however brief, provided some reprieve from the monotony of watching and listening for hours on end. The runner led David to the top of the hill on the northwest side of the valley and showed him the tent where a lion's head standard was pitched.

"Captain Jehoshaphat," the runner called from outside. "David, the son of Jesse, of Judah has returned with me along with some bread and cheese for the men."

"Enter," the captain called from within.

The captain welcomed David into his tent and gratefully received the offering from Jesse. Turning to the runner, Jehoshaphat instructed him to distribute the cheese among the men, as he personally escorted David to his brothers' bivouac. According to the runner, the captain was well liked by the men and made regular visits up and down his own portion of the line, visiting regularly with the men and getting to know them. The captain remembered the three brothers from Bethlehem well as they'd stood out to him, especially the eldest. All three men were strong and well proportioned, evidence of a life of labor in the fields. The captain expressed that he expected great things from them in the coming battle.

"Come, it's time I walk the line anyway. I'll show you where they are," the captain said as he held open the loose flap that served as the door to his tent.

The captain led him down the eastern side of the hill and across the creek bed at its base, then proceeded along the line to where Eliab, Shimea, and Abinadab were camped. Coming upon the three, Shimea was the first to notice David as they approached. He jumped to his feet, excited to see the familiar face.

"David!" he exclaimed. "What are you doing here?" Shimea asked as he embraced his youngest brother.

Abinadab stood and joined David and Shimea. Eliab was lying on the ground with his face covered by the leather lining from his helmet. He lifted it momentarily to acknowledge David, then placed it back over his face and continued his rest.

"We received your letter. Father wanted me to bring you all some provisions so I accompanied the runner back here," David explained.

"When did you get home?" Shimea asked.

"Well, Saul is here with you all, so there wasn't much need for me at the palace. When he left Gibeah, I was released from service and went back to watching father's sheep. Although Joab did a great job while I was gone and is taking care of them now."

"Did you see my boy?" Shimea asked excitedly.

"He's growing like a weed. When was the last time you saw him?" David asked.

"It's been several months. I miss that little tyrant. Was he talking yet?"

"He wasn't talking when you left?" David asked.

"No."

"Well, he's making all manner of noises now. All the time. Next thing you know, he'll be gossiping like his cousins. I need to get him out of the house and into the pasture with me."

"I would appreciate that," Shimea replied.

The captain stood quietly observing several feet away, enjoying the lighthearted conversation of the two brothers.

Turning to Eliab, David asked, "how is Raanan? Have you seen him?"

"Still Raanan. I'm sure he'll make an appearance if you stick around long enough. Did you bring your harp? Maybe you can play him a lullaby," Eliab answered contemptuously.

Shimea shook his head. "Some things don't change, do they brother?"

David shook his head. "Anything else you need?"

"No, we've got plenty of supplies for now, but they're making it difficult for much to get through. Tell Father and Mother we appreciate them taking such good care of us out here. We're going to be spoiled by the time we get back home," said Shimea. "Tell my wife and baby boy I love them and look forward to seeing them."

"Will do brother. Send word if you have need of anything," said David.

"Tell them we said thanks," Abinadab exclaimed as he slapped David on the shoulder.

"I better go if I'm going to make it back before dark," David replied. "I'll be back soon. We're praying for your safety and courage for the battle."

***

It had been more than a month since they'd come here and several days since Raanan received the report that Jonathan would be arriving later in the day with several thousand men he'd recruited from Israel's northern territories, lands recently ravaged by the same Philistines that now stood opposite them on the other side of the valley between Azekah and Socoh. Jonathan would bring some much needed provisions along with the heavily armed reinforcements.

Standing atop the hill looking north of the army's position, Raanan could see Jonathan and a large entourage emerge from the wood line at the edge of the hill to their north. Jonathan was at the head of the group, walking briskly alongside his horse.

Finally, thought Raanan. The stalemate would be broken. Sending a runner to report the news to King Saul that Jonathan was a short distance off and accompanied by approximately one thousand men and a hundred or so horses and mules, as best he could tell, Raanan mounted his horse and sped off to greet the prince.

Jonathan greeted him as he dismounted.

"What's the matter Raanan?" Jonathan asked, observing his demeanor and the haste at which he'd come to greet them.

Walking closely alongside the prince, Raanan began to relate the details of the situation, keeping his voice low so that only the prince could hear.

"We're in a bad way Jonathan. There's a giant. A beast of a man they call Goliath, he is challenging the army to send out a challenger. He demanded that we send a champion to fight him. It's been going on since right after you left."

"No one has stepped up I take it?" Jonathan asked.

"The men are afraid. It's not good. He's taken the fight out of them."

Jonathan had heard reports of a giant from some of the men who'd accompanied him from the north. Though he'd never seen one, he'd heard enough from the men of Jezreel and further north to know that they were no fairytale.

"Why did no one send word to me?"

"Saul forbade it," Raanan responded. "He wanted you to focus on recruiting as many men as possible."

"Good," said Jonathan as he continued walking at a pace that was difficult for Raanan to match.

Raanan was beginning to wonder how all these men had kept up with Jonathan at this pace all the way from the northern tribes.

"Good, sir?"

"Killing one man is better than widowing and orphaning thousands, don't you think?" Jonathan asked.

"Yes sir!" Raanan replied with a smile. The prince's confidence was contagious.

***

As they approached the army, Jonathan could see Abner near the perimeter. With a subtle gesture, he indicated that Jonathan should come to his father's tent atop the hill. The prince knew instantly where this would lead. For a moment, he considered whether or not to acquiesce.

Yuval discerned the internal struggle from the familiar look on the prince's face.

"Honor thy father," the armor bearer teased.

Jonathan returned an annoyed look, then conceded a smile.

"You know me too well sometimes."

Jonathan looked up to see Malchishua approaching.

Malchishua and Yuval slapped their hands together in a tight grasp at chin level. Malchishua strained as Yuval began to apply his viselike grip. Malchishua resisted momentarily before yielding to the stronger man, then embraced him and greeted his older brother.

"Father wants you at the head-shed," Malchishua reported. "I'll take them from here brother. Well done!"

Shaking his head, Jonathan broke off from the group of reinforcements and proceeded to his father's tent, followed by Raanan.

As they entered, Raanan was stopped by Abner's hand upon his chest.

"Back to your post son," he said in a respectful but firm tone before entering the tent and closing the flap behind him.

Inside, Jonathan approached his father as he stood staring grimly over the terrain model. Several officers who'd been standing with Saul immediately made their way past Jonathan, exchanging somber greetings as they exited the tent.

"I hear your efforts were not in vain. How many have you gathered?" Saul asked, his back still turned to his son as his eyes scanned the model in front of him.

"One thousand, one hundred and four the last count we took," Jonathan replied as he joined his father's side.

"Good. Very good work my son."

"Father, this champion of theirs, he's one man…"

"And you are one man I cannot spare," Saul interrupted. "I will hear no talk of you fighting that abomination. Is that clear?"

"If not you or I, then who, Father? Who?"

"Perhaps Yuval, he is nearly the giant's equal," said one of the king's advisors.

"Yuval? You would send my armor bearer to do my job? Yuval is a strong man and a mighty warrior, but he is not God's anointed. This has never been *our* fight, do not base your decision as if it were."

Jonathan scanned each of the doubting faces in the tent.

"Where is Samuel? What does he say?"

Saul drew his sword and swung it down hard on the table next to him sinking the blade deep into the wood.

"Never mind Samuel! I won't lose the entire kingdom based on a single fight. We will all fight! Why do you think you were sent to gather those men?"

"Think how many lives may be saved, Father! You must let me fight him," Jonathan reasoned, following his father around the model towards his makeshift throne.

"I will hear no more of it!" Saul shouted. "Your selfish thirst for glory blinds you," he accused. "Do you think the Philistines who outnumber us will lay down their weapons and serve us? There is no end to this fight that does not involve the clash of armies."

Jonathan knew his father could not be convinced. He'd been able to avoid directly disobeying his father at Geba and Gibeah, but now he felt trapped.

Saul placed his hand to his head. Again, the tormenting. His mind swirled and raged.

"Tomorrow, we will fight. Abner will go over the details with you. I'm going to my tent," Saul said as he exited the tent while Abinadab held the flap open.

***

David watched the star-filled sky over Bethlehem as he worked out the melody of a song in his head when his thoughts were interrupted.

"Psss. Psssss. David."

He felt Joab elbow him and sat up. He could see the lamp approaching now.

"Someone is coming," Joab said.

"Maybe Asahel decided to join us," said David, judging by the height at which the lamp floated above the ground and the speed at which it approached. The boys waited as the lamp grew closer.

Abishai sprung to his hands and knees, then crawled towards the opposite side of the rock.

"Where're you going?" Joab asked.

"I'm going to give him a little surprise," he said as he slid down the back side of the rock to the ground.

Joab could see Abishai sneak around to the brush off to their right as the lamp grew closer. As the lamp reached the brush, they heard Asahel call out.

"David! Uncle David!"

Not a moment later, Abishai must have sprung his attack because they heard a loud roar followed by a terrified shout just before the lamp fell to the ground and went out. The next sound was Abishai's laughter, followed by some cursing from his younger brother as he climbed up the large boulder to where the boys had made their camp for the night.

"What a jerk!" Asahel exclaimed as he plopped down next to David. Abishai sat down next to him and placed his arm around the younger brother.

"I'm sorry brother. You know I couldn't resist," said Abishai, laughing and clearly still pleased with his accomplishment.

Asahel answered with his elbow to his middle brother's ribs.

"Your little cousin keeping you up?" David asked, referring to Shimea's son Jonathan.

"Not yet. You know he doesn't start crying until everyone is asleep! I came because Grandfather needs you to take some provisions to Uncle Eliab, Shimea, and Abinadab tomorrow morning. He says he wants you to leave early. It sounds like things are heating up and he wants to make sure they have some good food before battle."

"Did he want me back at the house tonight?" David asked.

"Na. He just said to leave early so you get there before... uh, what's that word?"

"You mean stand-to?"

"Yes!" Asahel exclaimed. "You'd be better off staying out here. Like I said, the little guy likes to wait till everyone is asleep," he said as he unrolled the skins he'd brought to serve as his bed for the night. "I'm sure not going back in there."

David thought for a moment, considering what he'd need to do to prepare for the morning. He would need to leave early indeed to arrive before stand-to. He looked to the horizon. The moon could not yet be seen. The sun had just set and it would take more than half the night to get there in time. If he left when the moon was on the horizon, he could make it to the Israelite battle line before stand-to. Inwardly, he wanted to be there with them, with the men he'd come to know and train with at the palace. He wanted to see the army when they were on line and ready for battle. He wanted to stand shoulder to shoulder with them as King Saul inspected them before the battle. Truthfully, he missed the feeling of importance that came with serving the king, whom he'd come to love as the encouraging father he'd never had. One day, David thought, one day he would be on the line with them. David took the skin of water sitting next to him and guzzled its contents.

"Anyone else got any extra water?" David asked.

Asahel offered his.

"Why are you drinking so much before you go to sleep?"

"It's a trick I learned from one of the guards at the palace. If I drink enough water, I'll wake up early to relieve myself, not to mention it's a long hike to the shephelah."

"That's brilliant," said Asahel, "but what if you wake up too early? And how will you know what time of night it is?"

"That's what the extra water is for," David replied. "You can tell the time of night by marking the position of certain constellations and their position in the night sky, just like the sun during the day time. You try it. Find a constellation just on the eastern horizon."

"There," Abishai pointed to his younger brother. "That's the Big Dipper."

"Perfect, now the Big Dipper is very long, so you have to pick a single star in the constellation, and that's your reference point. The sun set in the west not long ago. This time of year the days are longer. See that constellation over there?" David asked as he pointed to the east. "It's just over the horizon in the eastern sky, just as the sun is just below the horizon in the west right now. When it gets directly above us, it's about midnight. I'll need to leave before then to get to the army before sunrise. I want you to wake me when you have a full hand's breadth between the star and the horizon," David said, demonstrating with his hand held sideways and fully extended away from his body.

"Did you learn that from the guards as well?"

"No, that I learned from Saba," David said. "If he were here, he could name just about every star in the sky. He knew what time of year they would be visible and for how long. I think he knew more about stars and sheep than anyone alive." David was quiet for a moment.

"You miss him, don't you?" Joab asked.

"Yes," David replied. "He was the only adult in our family that cared anything about being a shepherd. Almost everything I know I learned from him."

Joab thought about what it would be like to have such a man in his life. The only thing his father had ever taught him was vigilance and attention to detail. He'd learned to sleep light and could perceive the subtle differences in how the door was shut on his father's return home in the middle of the night and what it conveyed about his mood. He could tell by the way a man breathed whether he was angry or jovial.

"I wish I was going with you tomorrow," Asahel said as he lay down.

"I'm sure we'll all get to serve one day," said David. "Won't that be something?"

"Yeah, if Eliab, Abinadab, and Shimea don't kill all the bad guys first," Asahel replied. "Hey David, what's General Abner like?"

"I haven't met him yet really, but everyone loves him as a leader. He's hard, but everyone trusts him. Raanan says he knows how to bring out the soldier in a man."

"Who do you think is the better fighter? Jonathan, Saul, or Abner?" Asahel asked.

David laughed. "I wouldn't know bud. I've never come close to any battles, but from what I've heard of Jonathan at Michmash, he did what no one else was willing to do. No doubt, Jonathan is a courageous warrior."

"What did Jonathan do at Michmash?" Asahel asked.

Before he could answer, Abishai sprang to his knees and recounted the story, nearly word for word as David had told it to him. David himself had gotten the story from the palace guards and since his return to Bethlehem had retold it several times already. The three brothers were awed by the story. Their thirst for war stories was unquenchable.

"Hey David," Joab finally interrupted. "Did you get to see the princesses?" Joab asked.

"Yes indeed," David replied. "Michal is the prettiest girl I've ever seen. She's about my age, a little younger, petite, with long black hair. She's got the most beautiful green eyes."

"Woohooh," exclaimed Abishai, "sounds like David's got a thing for the princess! Better watch out," he teased, "King Saul will send you to be some Philistine's tea boy if you're not careful."

At this, they all laughed. David especially.

"Well, I've got to get some sleep," David finally announced. "I'll see you when I get back from running the provisions to the front tomorrow. Good night," David said and laid his head to rest.

***

Jonathan walked among the sleeping troops, praying over them as he went. Several were already wide awake, preparing for the day. He stopped to talk with these as he went along, taking note of their names and positions. Some sharpened their swords and spear points; others honed and fletched arrows and tightened bow strings. Older men stretched their shoulders, hips, and backs. All night, Jonathan had walked among these men, some of whom might be dead just a few hours from now, their lives sacrificed for the Kingdom of God's people. He treasured every one of them. Some men he passed sleeping like babes, already clad in full armor, with shield and spear laid across their chests.

As Jonathan passed a large young man, he stood and saluted his prince. Jonathan returned the gesture.

"No need for the formalities out here. What's your name soldier?"

"Simon, your highness. Of the tribe of Benjamin."

"How old are you Simon?"

"Fifteen sir."

"You're one impressive fifteen-year-old. You're already as tall as I am."

The boy smiled. "Thank you sir."

Jonathan motioned for him to have a seat as he joined the young soldier by the small fire next to where they stood.

"Did you get any sleep last night?"

"Not much sir," the youth replied.

"What troubles you?" Jonathan asked.

"Well, if you don't mind me speaking freely sir," the soldier said in a low voice.

"Go ahead."

"It's the waiting sir. Everyone seems to be losing heart. No one knows why we're just sitting here. To what end are we staying here not doing anything?"

Jonathan had not expected such a forward question from such a young man. "Well, can I let you in on a little secret, just between you and me?"

The young man looked around. Seeing those nearest to them were fast asleep he replied in a hushed voice, "Yes sir!"

"Well then, you'll be pleased to know we won't sit here much longer. The king plans to attack soon. I can't tell you the exact time, but you need to get a good night's rest tonight and be ready for anything in the morning. You understand what I'm telling you?"

"I think so sir, but what about the giant?"

"He's one man. If the Philistines thought they could beat us, they wouldn't send him out parading around asking for a duel. They lost at Michmash and now they're scared."

"Yeah, that makes sense," the youth said. "Is it true what they say? What they say you and Yuval did at Michmash, did you really take on the Philistine army, just the two of you?"

Jonathan laughed.

"I wouldn't put it that way." He thought for a moment. "Do you remember the story of Gideon?"

"Yes! It's one of my favorites. He killed over one hundred and twenty thousand Midianites with only three hundred men. When the three hundred surprised the Midianites in the middle of the night, they were so confused and terrified that they turned on each other."

"That's right. That's right, and what about Deborah and Barak? Do you remember what happened then?" Jonathan inquired.

"A great storm swept over the Canaanites, making their heavy chariots useless in the mud. Many of the enemy drowned by the weight of their own armor in the river," another soldier responded. The man had, up till this point, been silently listening as he heard the prince speaking nearby.

"That's right," Jonathan affirmed. "It's not about the size of the army or how many there are. God likes to use the weak things of this world to defeat the things that are strong. He uses what the world considers foolish to defeat those the world considers wise. Look around you," Jonathan said, pausing. "All this, you, me, the stars above us. It was all created by the God we serve. The Philistines mock Him. They worship Dagon and Ashteroth, gods made by their own hands of their own finite imaginations or inspired by fallen angels. Even according to their own beliefs, their gods are limited. They are small. One controls the weather, one controls the crops, another warfare, and so on. The one true God, Yahweh, created it all. He knows all. He rules over all. He is not some weakling god fashioned by the hands of man. He is here among us now, He goes before us into the battle. In fact, the battle is already won. If you are right with Him, what have you to worry about? For in death, the struggles of life are no more, but joyous for those who have faith. So to die is gain for us. Knowing Him to be good, we can leave our fate to Him."

The young man thought on this for a moment. "So you don't worry at all?"

"Why should I? Will it save me in battle?"

The youth shook his head.

"I trust that God will see me through. And if He doesn't, then my work here is done. Do you remember the story of Enoch who walked with God? He was so close to God that he never experienced death. He drew so close to God that God took him. You see? It shows us that this life is not the goal. This life isn't what's important. God is the goal, to draw near to Him. Do you see?"

Simon nodded. "I think so," he replied.

"Good! I've never felt so close to Him as in battle, when I am fully reliant on Him, when chaos is all around, when all depends on Him. At home in the safety and comforts of the palace, it's easy to forget how badly we need God and how good it feels to be in His presence. Out here, on the field of battle, I am at peace."

Simon sat staring in awe at the prince. This man is true royalty, thought the young soldier. Like the prophets of old. Like Moses, Joshua, and Caleb, so was this young leader.

"Are you preaching again?" asked a voice from behind.

"Ah, God's appointed angel sent to watch over me. Yuval, come and meet this young man. Simon is his name," Jonathan said as he stood and welcomed Yuval by the fire.

"You shouldn't be roaming about. A Philistine spy would like nothing more than to put an arrow in your back," said Yuval.

"Yuval does not share my belief, or at least, he professes not to," said Jonathan.

"I have found no rhyme or reason to how this God of yours operates," said the armor bearer. "If he truly is all powerful and everything is by His design, then I will die with a curse on my lips."

"Well then," Jonathan said, turning to the young man. "When he's in this sort of mood, there's no reasoning with him."

Jonathan stood and placed a hand on Simon's shoulder.

"May God bless you and keep you, may He make His face to shine upon you and be gracious to you," he prayed. "I'll see you on the battlefield when the time comes."

The young man smiled. "Thank you. I'll be there."

"Good night soldier," Jonathan said as he and Yuval departed to check the perimeter positions.

***

David could hear the faint clatter and noise of the camp before he could see it. He was too late, he thought. He hastened his pace as he approached where he knew the sentry would be located. In the darkness he heard the challenge.

"He came from Ur!"

"Was his father named Torah?" David shouted back.

"David?" the sentry asked from his concealed position in the thick vegetation.

"Yes, my father sent me with provisions."

"Come on," the sentry replied, welcoming David. "Your brothers sure are fortunate. They get more provisions sent from home than nearly any of the other men here. You'd better hurry though. Abner has ordered everyone online a half-hour early this morning."

"Will do! Thanks!" David said as he sprinted through a stand of terebinth trees towards his brothers' bivouac. When he arrived, they were nowhere to be found. Two guards stood watch nearby with the company's personal belongings and provisions. David sprinted over to them.

"I've brought provisions for the sons of Jesse. Do you know where they are?"

One of the men recognized David from prior visits. "They'll be down the trail that way. Just follow those men there," he said, pointing to a small contingent of soldiers that David could make out from the light of several small campfires. "Your brothers should be on the far right of the Judahite line. Their stuff is just there," he said, pointing to some baggage nearby, which David recognized. "You can leave the provisions there. They won't be eating anything on the line."

David set the bag down, feeling somewhat ashamed he had not arrived earlier.

"Thank you!" he said as he set the bags down and pulled several loaves from within, then sprinted off after several men departing the area towards the line of battle. He called after them, not wanting to surprise them suddenly in the darkness.

One of the men turned around.

"Hold up men," the soldier said, stopping the others with him.

"What's the matter? What do you need?" asked the man.

"My father sent me to deliver provisions for my brothers this morning. I didn't expect the army would be called to the line so early. Can you help me find them? Here's some bread for the trouble," David said as he handed the soldier one of the loaves.

"Sure. What are their names?"

"Eliab, Abinadab, and Shimea, sons of Jesse from Bethlehem."

"Ah," said the man turning to the other three that were with him, "he's looking for Eliab, Abinadab and Shimea. This is their little brother." Turning back to David he said, "sure, I'll show you where they are. Come with us." The men picked up their pace as they turned and proceeded toward the line. They appeared to be in a hurry to get where they were going.

"You're fortunate," said the soldier before proceeding in unnecessarily crude terms to explain how one of the other men in their party had broken the lacings on his greave and had to go back to their tent to fix them. Using an expletive to emphasis nearly every noun that proceeded from his mouth, he explained that they need to get back to the line before their captain began to think they were cowards.

This was not the first time David had heard soldiers use foul language. He'd always found it somewhat humorous, but it seemed this man's very dialect was profanity. Mother would not approve, David thought to himself. The man concluded his rant by asking if David had come all the way from Bethlehem by himself.

"Yes," David replied.

"This morning?" the man asked. "In the dark?"

"Yes, why?"

The man let out a stream of expletives as he asked the other men whether they'd heard David's answer.

"We have to go everywhere, do everything, in groups of four, then you come trotting up out of the darkness having hiked from Bethlehem by yourself. That's strong kid. You weren't worried about getting captured?"

"No, not really. I know the way pretty well. I've been here many times in the daylight and the dark."

"Well, you should be. We had a couple guys go missing." The man indicated through his course speech that it was unknown whether they had deserted or "gotten snatched." "That's why we're under orders to do everything as a group of no less than four."

As they approached the line, the men slowed their pace. The clatter and noise of their armor grew quiet and David could hear someone shouting and assumed one of the Israelite officers was addressing the men. The soldier that had escorted David to the line walked up to the back of one of the soldiers on the line and rapped him on the shoulder. David did not recognize the man was Shimea till his brother turned around. The soldier pointed to David.

"David! What are you doing here?" Shimea asked, stepping out of the line. Immediately, Abinadab and Eliab turned their attention from the battlefield. Eliab shook his head and turned back to the field.

"Father sent me with provisions," David said, producing the loaves he'd pulled from the bag. "I'm sorry; I left early, hoping to catch you before you were called to the line."

Shimea accepted the loaves and handed one to the Abinadab and the other to the Israelite left of him on the line. The man thanked him and broke off a small piece, then passed the rest to the man to his left. Abinadab repeated the gesture and handed the second loaf to Eliab, who took a piece and passed the rest down the line of men.

Shimea bent down and lowered his voice. "We were called out earlier than normal this morning. Look brother, you shouldn't be here. It's not safe. I think something's going to happen today. Jonathan just arrived in camp last night. He's not the kind to put up with much of this."

"Much of what?" David asked.

"Goliath," said the soldier who'd escorted him. "You haven't seen him yet?" The man went on to describe the giant in the most articulate profanity David had ever heard.

David listened and could now tell that the speaker he'd heard shouting was a Philistine. The voice he'd heard was so loud and deep that he hadn't realized it was coming from across the field. David tried to see above the heads of the line of men in front of them.

Shimea and the soldier took David over to the line. The soldier knelt down, putting his knee out as a base for David to stand upon. Shimea helped support him and David stepped up to see over the Israelite soldiers in front of them. He could now see over the men into the valley. An empty space separated them from the Philistine line across the open field speckled with terebinth trees, from which the valley received its namesake. On the far side of the Philistines was a large stand of the ancient trees. The valley had become well known for these trees since they were the primary source of turpentine, the most common antiseptic used by both the Philistines and Israelite forces. Contrasted against the trees, David could see the Philistine army arrayed before them. In front of them was a massive mountain of a man, like none that David had ever seen. The plumed helmet that covered the top of his skull made him look even taller. His polished armor added to his intimidating appearance as he seemed to gleam even in the dim light of the early morning. He was dressed like a god of war.

"Come here and get a look at this son of a jenny. Every forsaken day it's the same thing, every morning. The king said he'll reward the man who kills him with wealth." The man's voice trailed off as David strained to hear the filth pouring out of the Philistine's mouth.

A real giant, David thought to himself.

"... I defy the ranks of Israel! Give me a man and let us fight each other," the giant shouted. "Come now, my harvester is thirsty for the blood of Yahweh's anointed! I hear he is the greatest among you. Send out your King, and I will show you the strength of a god! "

When no one stepped forward, the giant continued.

"No? Then perhaps your queen, Ahinoam, would fare better!" the giant shouted as he made an obscene gesture.

David's awe at the spectacular figure turned to contempt.

"What did he say?" David shouted. To his brothers' dismay, David's outburst caused the soldiers nearest them to turn in his direction. Still standing on the man's knee, David looked down at the kneeling soldier.

Angrily, David asked, "What did you say is the reward for removing this insult from Israel by killing this man? No uncircumcised Philistine can get away with taunting the armies of the living God!"

"You heard what will be given to the man who kills him," said one of the soldiers "Why? You think you're up to the task?" he said with a chuckle. "You know they say there are four more just like him. Are you going to kill them too?"

Several of the soldiers nearest them laughed nervously as David stepped down from the man's knee. The conversation was interrupted by more of the giant's taunting.

"Where is Jonathan?" Goliath called. "Can you hear me? Jonathan? Prince Jonathan! INSTIGATOR! You started this, now it's time for you to finish it! Will you Hebrews let your Prince hide behind you?" the giant asked as he swept his huge spear point from one side of the Israelite line to the other.

"I'm serious!" David shouted.

"Sounds like your brother is calling us out," one man said, nudging Eliab with his elbow.

Eliab could hear no more of it; it was one thing for David to make a fool of himself, but now he was insulting the entire Israelite army. They would become an embarrassment to the entire tribe if this persisted any longer.

"Why have you come down here?" Eliab asked angrily as he turned and glared at David. "Who is watching your tiny flock in the wilderness?"

David glared back at him, but before he could answer, Eliab continued.

"I know you, you're arrogant, and your heart is evil. You've come here to watch the battle. Get back home before you disgrace our father's name," Eliab said as he shoved David's chest, knocking him to the dirt.

The soldiers around them grew quiet.

David stood and brushed himself off.

"What have I done now? I was just asking a question!"

Eliab stared back at him incredulously. He looked fierce under his helmet and armor.

David turned to the soldier who'd last spoken to him. "What is the reward?"

The soldier looked at Eliab, then back to David.

"The king has promised great riches, marriage into the royal family, and freedom from taxes for the man's entire family."

David turned now to Eliab.

"Look at the bright side. You can't lose. If I kill the giant, you're free from taxes. If I die, you're less one arrogant disgrace of a brother!"

The soldiers couldn't believe the way David was talking to his older brother, whom many of them respected as a formidable soldier. It was as if Eliab's accusations had further cemented the idea in the youth's mind. They stood silent.

"What must I do to challenge this man?" David asked, looking at each of the soldiers around him.

"Get back to your damned sheep David!" Eliab said as he stepped menacingly towards him.

"Eliab," Shimea said, stepping between them and placing a hand on the elder's shoulder. This was getting out of hand. "The enemy is over there," Shimea said, pointing to the Philistines.

Eliab began to brush Shimea aside when the tension was suddenly interrupted by a low voice.

"That'll be enough."

The men turned to see their captain standing in their midst. They parted as he stepped forward. David recognized the man from his prior visits.

"David," the captain said sternly.

The youth half expected to receive some sort of punishment for causing such a disruption among the captain's ranks just prior to battle.

"Yes captain," David acknowledged.

The captain turned and took several steps in the opposite direction. When David did not follow, he paused. Turning his head slightly with his back still to David, he asked, "you coming?"

David looked at his brothers, then, without a word, hurried after their captain.

***

Gathered around the crude diagram of the valley and surrounding areas, Saul and his staff talked of the various courses of action that had been developed over the past several weeks. Movement from the tent's entrance caught Saul and Jonathan's eyes as one of the captains requested to enter.

"Jehoshaphat, captain of the tribe of Judah, requests permission to enter."

"Send him in," Abner replied.

Hearing the general's answer, the captain entered.

"Good morning General Abner."

"Good morning, what've you got?" Abner asked.

"There is a young man who wishes to challenge Goliath."

Everyone turned their attention to the captain.

"Who?" Abner inquired.

"I doubt you've ever heard of him. He's young, but strong and confident. His older brothers are within my ranks and they're all reliable men. I believe his father is a man named Jesse from Bethlehem," said the captain. "He is the only man that has come forward."

"Bring him to me," Abner replied.

Jehoshaphat turned and exited the tent.

Joash scoffed as he poured a cup of wine near the far end of the officer's tent. "Are you really entertaining this? I thought we agreed that it would be foolhardy to send any one soldier to fight Goliath. This sounds like some deranged youth who either wants to make a name for himself or has a death wish."

Jonathan was silent. He wanted to see the youth for himself.

"We'll see," was Abner's only reply.

A moment later Jehoshaphat returned with the young man.

David stepped into the tent with his staff in hand.

Saul let out a disappointed sigh.

"A shepherd," Saul said aloud.

The only part of the youth not covered by his shepherd's clothing revealed the dirty face of young boy, lacking the slightest sign of any facial hair or the lines that come with age.

Jehoshaphat leaned toward David and instructed him to remove his hood.

Given his current state of cleanliness, David had hoped to keep the hood on, but did as instructed, revealing a head full of wild, dirty red hair. It occurred to David that he'd never before presented himself to the king in such a state. Undoubtedly, he looked different than he had on the occasions when he'd played the harp at the palace, bathed, and dressed in fitting attire.

"Is it true you wish to challenge the giant?" Saul asked.

"I heard the king desired someone to slay this uncircumcised Philistine," David responded without hesitation. "Do not let anyone be frightened because of that man. I am your servant," David said as he stepped toward the king. "And I will go and fight with him."

Joash laughed, then finished his cup of wine before setting the chalice on the table beside him.

"You can't fight this Philistine," Saul replied with a dismissive wave of his hand. "You're only a youth, and he has been a warrior since his childhood. You, you're a shepherd, what do you know of battle?"

"Maybe he intends to choke the giant as he's being eaten," Joash said, laughing as he moved to pour more wine into the chalice.

Suddenly, the cup sprang from its position with a loud clang, spattering wine on the back wall of the tent.

Joash had not even seen David load the sling, much less release the shot that had struck his cup. When the surprised officer realized what had happened, David had already loaded another stone. Furious, the captain turned towards the youth.

"How dare you boy!" he shouted.

Abner stepped forward and raised his hand. "Wait! Let him speak."

"I dare say that Philistine is a larger target than your chalice," David rebuffed the captain. "I have worked as a shepherd for my father. I've defended his sheep since I was a boy. Whenever a lion or a bear has come and attacked one of my lambs, I have gone after it and struck it down to rescue the lamb from the predator's mouth. If it turned to attack me, I would take it by the chin, beat it, and kill it. I have killed both a lion and a bear, and as your servant I will kill this uncircumcised Philistine too, since he has dared to taunt the armies of the living God! The Eternal One, who saved me from the paw of the lion and the paw of the bear, will save me from the hand of this Philistine!" David declared indignantly.

The men stood silent, awestruck by the youth's audacity.

"You killed a lion and a bear with that?" Saul asked.

"More or less. I had to finish them off," David replied, "but yes."

Saul walked over and laid a chalice on the table at the far end of the tent with the open end toward the young shepherd, then walked over and stood beside him.

"Put a stone in that cup," the king instructed.

Without hesitating, David stepped forward and launched a stone at the cup. The stone smashed the inside of the cup hard and sent it toppling through the air.

"Brilliant!" Saul shouted. "Can you do that every time? Even under pressure with a moving target?"

"With respect my king," David replied. "I've never had much luck getting lions or bears to hold still."

Saul smiled at the youth's brashness.

"Are the men ready?" Saul asked as he turned to his general.

"The Judahite, Gadite, Naphtalite, and Danite divisions are on the line," Abner said. "The Benjaminite and Ephraimite divisions are positioned in reserve and the Simeonites infiltrated last night to concealed positions here, hidden on the right, eastern flank as planned," he said pointing to a spot on the diagram.

Saul took the youth by the shoulders and looked at him squarely.

"Go then, and may the Eternal One be with you!"

Abner stepped towards him. "Do you require anything for the battle?"

David reached into his bag and pulled out a few small stones and examined them. "Let me go down to the creek and choose some proper stones."

"Very well," Abner replied before turning to his amor bearer. "Get the word out, I want everyone ready."

"Wait," Saul said. "Put my armor on him," he instructed his armor bearer.

Jehoshaphat helped David remove his shepherd's cloak and hood, revealing the sunburned shoulders and arms underneath. The armor bearer lifted Saul's coat of mail and brought it over. He lifted it over David's head and lowered it onto his shoulders. Then, placing the breastplate on David's shoulders and helmet atop his head, the armor bearer went to secure Saul's sword to the youth's waist.

David stretched out his arms, burdened by the heavy weight.

"My King," said David. "Thank you for your concern, but I cannot do what is necessary burdened by the weight of this armor."

Saul realized the folly of his instruction as David's shoulders sagged under the weight. He nodded to the armor bearer. The man removed the helmet and lifted the breastplate and mail from the boy's shoulders.

"Did you really pursue a lion and a bear for the life of one sheep?" Jonathan asked.

"I am their shepherd," David responded.

"I see that," Jonathan replied. "My point is, you risked your life? You risked your life for a sheep?"

The youth thought for a moment.

"They are my father's sheep. They were entrusted to me; what good is a shepherd who doesn't look after his sheep?" David asked.

It was clear to Jonathan that the youth had never second-guessed the decision to go after the beasts. It was as if it were no decision at all. He was the shepherd and the shepherd protects the sheep. There was never a question in the youth's mind as to whether he would go after them or not.

Jonathan was beginning to like this young man.

"What is your name?"

"David, son of Jesse from Bethlehem."

"Come, I'll walk with you to the creek."

The prince and David exited the tent and proceeded down the hill towards the creek bed in silence. When they arrived, David knelt and grabbed a handful of stones from the shallow creek.

"They say the giant has four brothers," David said as he carefully selected a single circular stone and placed it in the satchel tied about his waist. Examining the creek bed through the clear, cool water, he reached and selected four more of similar size and shape, all slightly larger than a chicken's egg. Carefully turning them over in his hand one at a time, he placed them one by one into the satchel. Jonathan watched the boy's hand as he examined the rocks and saw it begin to shake. David clasped this shepherd's staff and stood, his head bowed momentarily. Jonathan saw his lips move but could not hear the words.

"I'm not stupid... and I'm not crazy," said the youth aloud. "The giant frightens me, just like anyone else, but God has delivered me before. He'll do it again."

The youth's words confirmed what Jonathan suspected. He was familiar with the surge of anxiety one felt before the coming battle and took the youth's trembling hand as proof of his sanity, rather than cowardice. Jonathan felt a kindred spirit in the young man and he too began to feel the knot forming in his stomach as the two stood for a moment, silently examining one another. David crossed the creek back to the bank. The prince placed his hand on the youth's shoulder.

"Allow me to pray with you."

***

As Jonathan and David walked to the king's tent, men along the way stared at David as he passed, not sure if the rumors circulating through the camp were true or if some other clandestine plan was afoot.

Jonathan paused at the entrance. David turned to him as Jonathan again placed a hand upon the youth's shoulder.

"I'll see you on the battlefield. I give you my word I won't be far away."

Jonathan lifted the curtain and David proceeded inside where King Saul was waiting.

Yuval ran up to accompany Jonathan as he walked purposefully away from the tent.

"What the hell is going on? Is he really going to fight Goliath?" Yuval asked.

"Yes. But win or lose, we're not sitting this one out," Jonathan said as they walked. "Be ready. I'll meet you on the line."

Yuval nodded, then sprinted off towards their tent as Jonathan proceeded to the line. He passed some men stoking a fire and lying about, unarmed; their shields and swords strewn about in the dirt. He continued walking till he was in the midst of the troops, then stopped abruptly and listened. He could hear Goliath's foul words over the rabble of the men in camp. A hush fell over the men as they noticed the prince standing in their midst. He turned and shouted to no one in particular.

"What is this? A training exercise? Arm yourselves! Get on the line! Don't you hear that?"

All around, men began donning their armor and scurrying to join the men at the line. Not one of them had ever seen or heard the prince shout before. The news spread quickly throughout the camp so that nearly everyone present was fitted and on the line of battle as David, Abner, and Saul emerged from the king's tent.

The troops parted as King Saul walked ahead of David through the wall of men.

Yuval arrived with Jonathan's helmet, shield, and spear. The two men looked each other over as was their ritual, pulling at a lacing here, readjusting a strap there. As they finished, Jonathan could see his father approaching. Saul stopped at the line. David looked up at him and then proceeded forward of the troops.

Jonathan took one step forward of the line into the vacant space between them and the enemy. He could feel his heart racing. The other officers followed suit all down the line of Israelites. The Philistine line had already begun to tighten up as they noticed gaps in the Israelite line begin to fill.

Jonathan had known this feeling before. He'd felt it when he and Yuval attacked the Philistines at Michmash. He'd felt it even earlier when they'd ambushed the Philistine patrol and charged the gates at Geba. It came when he knew contact with the enemy was imminent. His hearing became more acute, his vision sharper. Time itself seemed to slow. He could feel and hear his own heartbeat now. He felt a strong urge to urinate, the body preparing itself for the fight ahead. He knew from prior experience that the current rush of pent-up energy would find its release the moment he launched into action. The decision point, the moment just before battle, was the most uncomfortable.

This feeling was worse than before, he thought. He was not in control. He could not strike first as before. There was nothing he could do, nothing to assuage the restrained fire now burning in his veins, ready to be unleashed. It was all up to this young man standing before them now.

David stepped further ahead of the line of battle, exposed and alone on an empty stage. With no armor whatsoever, he looked scrawny in front of the armored men along the line. Armed only with a staff and the loaded pouch of his sling hanging from his right hand, the Philistine line erupted with laughter at the sight of his hairless torso and sun-reddened shoulders. There was no turning back at this point, Jonathan thought. He prayed for the audacious youth.

Across the valley, the giant could be seen wading through the enemy line with his spear in hand. As is was over a third longer than a standard spear, it loomed high above the rest. Leary of some trick to coax the champion within bowshot, his armor bearer moved ahead of him with the giant's huge shield in hand ready to protect the champion as they drew closer to the Israelite line. The shield was so large it appeared to move on its own, with only the bearer's lower legs and crested helmet exposed. Closing the distance, Goliath's eyes focused on his challenger. He would have been elated if not for the feeling that he was being mocked.

Furiously, he shouted across the open field.

"Am I a dog, that you come to me with sticks?" He wasn't going to give them the satisfaction of taking this boy seriously. He spiked his spear in the ground and sat down in the huge chair that had been placed in front of the Philistine line to accommodate his constant provocations, adding to the insult. "By the gods, curse you!" he said as he leaned back against the chair and propped his feet up. Motioning with his hand, he shouted, "Come here and I will give your flesh to the birds of the air and the beasts of field!"

David's face grew bright red with anger. The words had barely left the giant's lips when David shouted at the top of his lungs, thrusting the end of his staff toward the giant.

"You come at me with sword and spear, and with a shield, but I come to you in the name of the Lord of hosts, the God of the armies of Israel, whom you have defied! Today, the Lord will deliver you into my hand and I will strike you down and cut off your head and I will give your carcasses to the birds of the air and the wild beasts of the earth so that all the earth will know there is a God in Israel! And all who witness will know that the Lord saves not with sword and spear, for the battle is the Lord's, and He will give you into our hands."

Goliath had heard enough. He stood and stepped forward. No sooner had he straightened that David lurched into a sprint. Goliath seized a javelin from the quiver lashed to Alcander's back and pushed him out of the way. He wouldn't need a shield for this. Even grown men under pressure couldn't hit the side of a barn during battle, much less with a giant bearing down upon them.

Jonathan could not believe what he was seeing. The youth was running at the giant. Goliath hastened his pace, though he did not raise the javelin to throw it. He would beat this insolent child to death in front of both armies.

The distance was closing fast. Jonathan could see David's staff pumping to one side as he sprinted. Half a second later, the youth's right hand raised above his head and rotated rearward in a circular motion. David's stride was broken suddenly when he bounded off of his right foot. His right foot struck the ground again as his arm fully rotated behind him, the taut sling moving in an extended arc from his hand as his entire body shifted forward onto his left foot, the weight of his shepherd's staff now pulling him forward. In a blink, David's arm snapped forward of his body and released the projectile in an upward trajectory towards its mark.

Jonathan heard what sounded like a mallet splitting a watermelon.

The giant's stride stuttered and slowed, his enormous knees wavering as he stopped in the middle of the open field and the javelin dropped from his hand. Goliath collapsed to his knees. Then, like a hewn tree, he fell face forward into the dirt, sending clouds of fine dust curling into the air around him.

Jonathan didn't blink. He did not breathe. The entire Philistine and Israelite lines were silent. Already, David had reached the giant's body almost as soon as it hit the ground. He went straight for Goliath's sword and jerked the massive cleaver from its sheath. Jonathan seized Yuval's shoulder as he saw the giant's left hand move as if reaching for David. The young shepherd kicked the hand away. Then, awkward with the weight of the sword, which was nearly as long as himself, David gripped the hilt with both hands. Swinging the point of the blade around behind him as he lifted the hilt high into the air, using his entire body, David swung the sword in a large arc over his head.

The blade came down like an axe, making a loud clang as it passed through the giant's neck and struck the rocky dirt. The scene reminded Jonathan of a chicken on the butcher's chopping block. Both armies watched in awe and silence as David sawed the sword forward and back in two quick motions, freeing the giant's head from his body. The youth dropped the sword into the dirt, then stepped forward and bent down. Grabbing two handfuls of the giant's curly black hair, he straightened and brought it waist-high. Stepping onto the giant's back, he heaved the huge head high above his own, exposing their dead champion's face to the Philistine line with a victorious shout, the sound of which none who heard it would ever forget.

Jonathan's heart was pounding. It felt as though it would burst from his chest. In an instant, he thrust his sword into the air and shouted at the top of his lungs. He was sprinting towards the Philistine line of battle before he even realized what he was doing. Behind him, the entire Israelite army roared to life and sprinted forward.

The front line of Philistine troops shuddered. Men on the front stepped backwards into the men to their rear. After over a month of the same uneventful daily routine, none of the Philistines had come to the line expecting a battle. Many, relying on their champion to decide the battle, had left their weapons in their tents as they'd come to watch the spectacle. Now, with the Israelite line descending upon them, they were unprepared and terrified. The line began to crumble.

The open space where David alone had stood was flooded by a wave of Israelites. He dropped the giant's head, seized the massive sword from the ground and began sprinting towards the enemy line. Jonathan was the first to reach David's side, accompanied by Yuval and several of his men, the rest of the army not far behind.

Some of the braver and more disciplined Philistine commanders shouted at their men to hold the line. It was in vain. With their backs exposed and their attempt to flee slowed by the mass of soldiers to their rear, the front line of Philistine troops was quickly decimated. The bravest among them were the first to go, swallowed up by the tide of Israelite soldiers.

David swung the huge sword wildly, barely able to control its weight. Jonathan, working to David's left, slew one after another with Yuval taking a position to David's right. The two men worked in tandem to protect the young warrior. The Philistines at the rear of the line who'd been slow in their retreat were knocked to the ground and trampled by their fellows.

The melee along the Philistine front was so condensed that the Israelites' feet hardly touched the ground as they advanced over the enemy dead. As the throng of terror and confusion began to disperse, the Israelites sprinted after their prey until their lungs and legs burned. Gone was the disciplined shield-to-shield fighting they'd trained for. This was a massacre. After forty days of provocation and angst, the Israelite soldiers unleashed their rage upon their tormentors.

The fleeing Philistines made for easy targets as the battle quickly spread from the Philistine camp to the surrounding terrain. In their hasty retreat, the enemy shed weapons, armor, and anything else that might slow or impede their escape.

Jonathan looked back for the young hero. David, still lugging the massive sword, was covered in gore and clearly exhausted as he struggled to keep up with the quickly advancing Israelites.

"Yuval, stay with him!" Jonathan shouted before continuing his pursuit.

For miles, the Israelites chased the fleeing Philistines, slaying any stragglers unable to outrun the tide. The mass of enemy soldiers had split into two groups as they were funneled down the two main roads to Gath and Ekron. The Israelites, led by the fittest among them, continued the pursuit for well over an hour, until Jonathan could see the walls of Gath ahead of them. It wouldn't be long before those in the lead came within bowshot of the city walls and they were well within Philistine-held territory. Still, many Israelites pressed forward, knowing every enemy slain was one less that could oppose them tomorrow.

Their lines stretched thin and approaching the fortified Philistine city, Jonathan took the horn girded at his waist and blew with every bit of strength that remained in his lungs. The soldiers still ahead of him slowed and turned to see that they were alone. Breathing heavily, they watched their unburdened quarry reach the gates of the city.

Jonathan and the other senior men present rallied the Israelites into formation and began the trek back to the Valley of Elah in a more ordered fashion. A runner was sent ahead to report their progress and announce the prince's retrograde back to camp. An officer commanded the rear to watch for a counterattack from the Philistine capital as they covered the great distance back to camp. The officer's precaution was unwarranted.

Spears, shields, helmets, and other armor were stripped from the enemy dead littered along the way. As they approached the valley, the number of fallen enemy increased. Large black birds filled the sky as the midday sun burned hot on the enemy corpses. Wild dogs had already begun to congregate, chewing at the flesh of the dead. A few brave Philistine women and elderly from the surrounding countryside had already begun to gather their dead and search the bodies for their loved ones, ignoring the Israelites as they approached the Philistine camp. Some of the young Philistine women moved from face to face, rolling the bodies over here and there to get a better look.

Still about two miles from the valley, Jonathan spotted two men assisting an elderly couple, too old to move the limp bodies on their own. As they drew closer, Jonathan recognized the familiar mannerisms of his armor bearer, then noticed that the other had a huge sword wrapped in cloth tied securely to his back. Jonathan stopped as the formation of Israelites continued their march back to camp.

"Yuval, David, we need to head back to camp."

Both men looked back to the elderly couple, who bowed their heads in appreciation. The haggard pair stoically resumed their search before the two men joined the prince on the road.

As they reached the Philistine camp, the soldiers stood amidst a field of spears, swords, shields, breastplates, and empty helmets, far outnumbering the enemy dead.

"Stay with me," Jonathan instructed as he and David continued past Israelite soldiers and Philistine widows combing the dead.

No communication was necessary. They made straight for the single body which lay in the middle of the open valley. David squatted down and sat the head up straight on the stump of the severed neck, holding it erect as he peered at the once manacing face of the champion of Gath. The stone was embedded deep in the giant's forehead, just above a significantly pronounced brow.

"Lion. Bear. Giant," Jonathan said as he peered over David's shoulder.

The youth produced a knife from his belt and used it to pry the stone from the giant's skull. He stood and walked over the headless body before kneeling to wipe the excess blood from the stone on the giant's ezor. David stood and turned to Jonathan and tossed the stone.

The prince caught it and examined it before offering it back to David.

"Keep it," David said with a nod. "As a reminder of what God can do with little things."

Jonathan watched as the youth reached down, cut a large piece of cloth from the giant's garment, and wrapped the head in it. Jonathan assisted as they ungirded the huge belt and sheath from the giant's waist.

David wiped the sword clean and placed it in the sheath before slinging the belt over one shoulder. He slung the giant's massive head over the other shoulder, holding the excess of the garment in his left hand.

Jonathan looked at this young man, wearing only the ezor about his waist with the large sword secured to his back, the hilt extending diagonally above his right shoulder, the tip pointing down and extending past his left knee. Blood speckled the cloth containing the giant's head..

"Well done, David, son of Jesse."

Yuval stood observing the encounter between the two warriors. Something about the moment lingered in his mind. He felt like he'd just seen Joshua and Caleb meet for the first time. No one knew the prince better or enjoyed his confidence more than Yuval. He, like Jonathan, had felt a nearly instantaneous affection for the young man.

Jonathan turned to find that every Israelite in the vicinity was watching the two of them.

"Praise be to Yahweh! Our strength and our deliverer!" Jonathan shouted. "Today He has given us a mighty warrior. His name is David, the son of Jesse!" Taking David's right wrist, Jonathan thrust David's arm high into the air. "David!" Jonathan shouted. "The lion of Judah!"

"David, the Lion of Judah!" the army around them shouted in reply. "Blessings to David and the house of Judah!" another man exclaimed, followed by further praises from all the men around them.

Jonathan let go of David's arm and turned to him.

"Come, we have much to discuss."

The three men began walking back to the Israelite camp as the rest tended to the wounded and gathered what valuables they could from the Philistine camp. Men stopped and stood upright as David, Jonathan, and Yuval passed.

As they approached Saul's tent, Jonathan could see Raanan waiting outside, beaming as he saw David approaching. David returned a broad smile.

"You two know each other?" asked the prince.

"Yes!" Raanan exclaimed. "I'm the one who brought him to the king," Raanan responded.

Confused, Jonathan looked at David then back to Raanan.

"I thought it was Jehoshaphat who brought him forward."

"Today, yes, I'm referring to last year," Raanan explained, then lowered his voice. "When the king couldn't sleep, I recommended David because of his skill as a musician."

Jonathan stared back at Raanan, unsure what on earth the man could be referring to.

"If I may explain," David said. "I've played the harp for the king in the past. Raanan has been a close family friend for many years and knew of my interest in music, so when the king was in need of a musician, Raanan was kind enough to recommend me for the king's service."

"Wait," the prince said, shaking his head. "So you've met my father before today?" Jonathan asked.

"I've played the harp for him, yes," David responded. "But, it was usually late in the evening when the king was very tired and there are many musicians in the king's service."

"You did this often?" Jonathan asked.

"For several months, yes, your highness, before this year's fighting season," David said.

Jonathan shook his head.

"Well, I don't think he, or anyone for that matter, will be forgetting you henceforth," Jonathan said, disappointed that no one had seemed to recognize the young man despite the fact that he'd had such a close and apparently frequent audience with the king in the past. "Look, my father generally expects the formalities, but when it's just me, you can forget the 'your highness' and 'my prince' stuff, alright?"

"Yes, your..." David caught himself. "Understood."

"You're a fast learner," Jonathan said as he entered the tent while David waited outside.

A moment later, the flap that served as the door was held open, and Abner exited.

"Our champion and the deliverer of Israel," Abner said as he placed his hands on David's shoulders. "The spirit of the Lord is upon you young man." He turned and held open the tent for David to enter, then ushered David to the center of the vast tent.

"King Saul, our champion," he announced.

David stepped forward and laid the massive head before King Saul. Saul finished wiping the blood and sweat from his head and arms. He smiled broadly as he tossed the soiled towel to one side.

"Welcome! Welcome," he shouted as he approached David and took him by the shoulders. "Well done, young man, well done!" Releasing David's shoulders, Saul bent down and peered into the giant's face. "Good heavens! Would you look at this beast!"

David unslung the sword and presented it to Saul. The king took the sword and examined it before handing it to Abner.

"You've done it!" Saul shouted, still elated and relieved by the victory. "They will sing songs of this victory for millennia! You will accompany me to Gibeah. I need men like you. I'm going to make you a commander. No one in your family will ever pay taxes again."

As David waited for the mention of the royal wedding a huge smile spread across his face. To his chagrin, no mention was made.

Abner's attention was fixed upon Goliath's sword. He examined it from end to end.

"They spared no expense in crafting this piece of work," Abner said, noting the intricate design along the blade.

It was nearly the length of a man and incredibly heavy compared with any he'd wielded in the past. Nearly three times the weight of a standard sword, but balanced perfectly. The hilt, long enough for both hands of an average man to grip, was capped with an iron ball, which worked with the lengthy hilt to balance out the weight.

"This is an improvement," Abner remarked, touching the iron quillions that turned upwards towards the tip of the blade. "It could stop a blade instead of merely deflecting it."

The blade had a diamond shaped cross-section and was double edged like most Philistine swords, though the edges ran parallel the majority of its length, tapering to a point only at the very end, making it stronger, but heavier and more difficult to wield one handed, as if it weren't already.

"This thing was made for cutting and smashing rather than stabbing," Abner observed.

"There's no telling how many lives have been snuffed out by it," Jonathan said as Abner passed the weapon to him. "Though I hear he preferred his bare hands. Now... now, it will be a symbol that victory does not belong to the many or to the strong, but to those who trust in the God of Israel."

"Well said," Saul replied as Jonathan passed the weapon to him. Saul stepped back and wielded it for a moment, making several arcing swipes with the blade and taking careful note of the weight. Lying the blade on the open palm of his left hand, he turned and extended the hilt towards David. "It is customary that the victor take the spoils of the vanquished."

David took the hilt in both hands and held it with the point extending upwards away from him. Light shining through the seams of the tent gleamed off of the blade.

"The victory is the Lord's. It belongs to Him. It should be kept in His house, somewhere that it will be safe and won't fall back into the hands of the Philistines."

"Land of Goshen! He's right!" Saul exclaimed. "It should be where all can see it as a reminder of God's provision. We'll put it somewhere that all Israel can see."

Moving over to a table along the outer wall of the tent, Saul poured a cup of wine.

"Tonight, we celebrate," Saul exclaimed as he lifted the cup.

Saul sent messengers to solicit offerings of wine and food from the surrounding villages and secure casks from nearby storehouses. As the tent emptied of his staff, Saul turned to David and placed his arm around him.

"From now on young man, you will be as one of my own. You will live under my roof and eat at my table. Perhaps one day, you may even lead a division."

"It would be an honor to serve my king," David said.

"Then arrangements will be made."

Saul's arm around David, they exited the tent. Saul called one of his staff over to them.

"You will ensure a dwelling for David near my tent and assist with whatever affairs need to be addressed to facilitate his travel with us to Gibeah. Send word to his family. See to it that they do not worry for his absence."

"It will be done, my King," the officer responded.

"Thank you for your courageous deeds today David, son of Jesse," Saul said, grasping David's shoulder. He then returned to his tent, leaving David and the servant alone.

Jonathan waited while David gave instructions on how to reach his family's home near Bethlehem.

When the staff officer departed, Jonathan approached David and placed his robe over the young man's bare shoulders. He took the belt and sword from around his waist and strapped it around the youth's.

"I cannot accept this," David said. "It is far better in your hands."

Placing his hands on David's shoulders, Jonathan looked into the face of the kindred spirit before him.

"Consider it an even trade for the stone," the prince said with a smile. "My armor and my bow will also be yours. I, Jonathan, son of Saul, son of Kish, am your friend and ally from this day forward. Nothing shall come between you and I," the prince said as he held out his right hand between them with his palm toward his chest.

David clasped Jonathan's right hand in his own.

"May the Lord see that nothing does," David replied.

"The Lord is our witness," Jonathan confirmed. "We have much work to do."

ENVY

1067 BC, Gibeah, Benjamin, Israel

"Saul has struck down his thousands,
and David his ten thousands."
I Samuel 18:7

As news spread of the Philistines' defeat, offerings poured in from a grateful populace and the sun set on the Israelite camp as men ate, drank, and celebrated, telling and retelling stories of the day's battle. Saul strode through the camp walking among the men, exuberant from the recent turn of events. The Philistines had been beaten badly today.

We may actually enjoy some peace for a time, Saul thought to himself as he walked among the unburdened troops. He could feel the difference in the air. Men singing merrily, laughing, and joking. Nothing at all like the gloomy atmosphere of the previous days. He approached a loud group of soldiers crowded around a bonfire. They raised their cups to the sky.

"To David, the champion of Israel," one man shouted as the others around him chimed in.

"TO DAVID, THE CHAMPION OF ISRAEL!"

Another man noticed Saul standing nearby.

"T-t-to Saul, long live the king!"

The other men repeated the chant, though far less spirited than their earlier shouts.

Saul continued through the camp of exuberant men. Here and there he saw half-drunken men reenacting the youth's triumphant victory. One man stood over a watermelon, pretending to struggle from the weight of his sword, then swung it down slicing the melon in two. He then grabbed one of the halves and held it above his head and shouted as David had done on the battlefield. The men around him laughed and applauded the likeness of his performance.

"Where on Earth did he come from?" Saul heard them say.

"I heard he's from Judah," another replied.

"David, the Lion of Judah," another man proclaimed.

"That's right! He even looks like a lion with that wild hair of his!"

Saul laughed. David did somewhat resemble a young male lion, his wild red hair giving the appearance of a young lion's mane. Ironically, the standard of Judah bore a lion's head with a thick red mane.

"Where is our champion?" Saul heard a familiar voice from behind.

Saul turned to greet Abner.

"With Jonathan," the king replied.

"Ah, two of a kind."

Saul smiled. "Perhaps we shouldn't leave the two of them unattended. Before you know it, we'll be at war with Egypt."

"Or Greece," Abner said with a laugh. "With the right training, he will be a valuable leader. In a matter of days there won't be a village or town in all of Israel that doesn't know his name."

Saul nodded. "There can be no doubt about that. Can you imagine?"

"What's that?"

"Having his fame and popularity at such a young age?" Saul asked. "It would have ruined me."

"It didn't ruin Jonathan," Abner replied.

"No. No, it didn't."

Saul approached a pile of Philistine weapons and picked out a sword.

"We have the upper hand now," he said, examining the blade. "I'm going to make sure they never pose a threat to us again."

Abner watched as Saul surveyed the camp, listening to the men around them singing songs of praise to Yahweh, intermixed with shouts of praises and toasts to David. Though the battle was over, Abner still sensed an uneasiness about the king.

"What's on your mind cousin?" Abner asked.

"It should've been me," Saul said in a quiet voice. "I should have fought the giant."

"Don't be ridiculous. I've never once seen you use a sling my entire life."

Saul shook his head. "I should have been prepared to fight him as Israel's leaders have in the past."

"We've never had a king before you. Moses, if you recall, did not go out to fight as Joshua did. But do not compare yourself to those who came before, learn from them."

"The men will lose respect for me now. Don't you see? They expected me to go out there. It doesn't matter how David won. What matters is that he stepped forward."

Abner could see the swift turn of emotion coming over Saul again and tried to head it off.

"Cousin, surely you can't be serious. When have you seen a king do this? Give me one example. That's exactly what they wanted you to do. You are a warrior, but you are not a slinger. They wanted you! You made the decision to send David out there after you saw what he could do. It was a wise and calculated decision, neither foolish nor cowardly. That is what a leader does. If you'd sent any other man out there to fight, they'd have been killed. Our slingers are many, but none rose to the challenge. I've not seen one as skilled as David," Abner said, trying his best to reassure the king. The last thing he needed was for Saul to slip into one of his fits of rage or melancholy now.

"Perhaps you're right," Saul responded quietly.

"You are the king. It is not your place to fight every battle," Abner continued. "You're not a young man anymore. Your head is gray cousin. Duels are a young man's game. Do you think they would expect you to be fighting champions ten years from now," he asked. "Of course not. You have done what is most important. You chose your champion wisely and look at the great victory it wrought. A foolish king might have been driven by pride and gone forward to fight the giant and we'd all be serving the Philistines. A wise king thinks with his head, not his emotions. The men will respect you so long as you take care of them, lead them, and make good decisions. The last thing they need is a king who foolishly reacts to any challenge to his pride and vanity. Do not forget that you are the Lord's anointed."

Seeing Saul's demeanor somewhat lifted, Abner changed the subject. "So, what's next? Gath? Ashkelon? Ekron?"

"I want to complete the work that our forefathers failed to do. Everyday I hear complaints about the Canaanites and Philistines still living amongst our people. It's time we drive out these people from among us. We've been tolerant of their presence for long enough."

Abner nodded, simply thankful he'd successfully navigated his way around another manic episode.

"Agreed. But for now, why not give the men a furlough? Give them some rest as we plan our next move," Abner suggested.

Saul nodded in agreement as he ran his fingers over the shiny bronze plated artwork of a Philistine officer's shield, a mural of the half fish, half man image of their god, Dagon, slaying his enemies.

"Very well. I'm sure the men will appreciate the rest. I'll pass the word along."

"What drives men to place their trust in a god they themselves created," the king asked, still gazing at the bronze image.

"I think it helps them make sense of a world they can neither control or explain," Abner suggested. "When something goes wrong, they blame it on some upset deity."

"And yet Adoni has rescued us time and again, despite me," Saul said.

"Despite you?" Abner replied, slightly irritated by the regress in their conversation.

"Never mind cousin. I'm very tired," Saul said as he rubbed his face with both hands.

"I think some rest would do you well. I'll tell the guard you're not to be disturbed. Shall I send for a musician?"

"No. Given how long it's been since I slept, I think sleep will come easy tonight."

***

As the troops began their march to Gibeah, there was an energy among them Saul hadn't seen since their return from Jabesh-Gilead so many years ago. The men held their heads high and walked proudly as each city and village they passed met them along the way with praises and singing. Men caught tokens of affection thrown to them by farm girls and city women alike. Men and women played their instruments while the young women and children danced in the streets and sang ancient songs of Yahweh's provision.

Wreaths and woven flowered crowns were placed on their heads and draped around the men's necks as young women kissed their cheeks and hugged them. Old men congratulated them and passed them small gifts of appreciation. Elder women met them along the way with cakes and other treats. So many had offered them water along the route that there had been no need to stop and but for the crowds slowing their progress, they would have made the distance in record time for such a large body of men.

As they drew closer to Gibeah, it seemed the entire city had gathered to welcome them. A faint melody could be heard and grew louder and louder as they approached. Joyous singing rose above the shouts of praise and before long, it seemed the entire massive crowd was singing the same ditty. The officers took to their horses as was the formal custom of leading their troops in parade. Saul mounted his impressive stallion and held his head high as they entered while Abner quietly peeled off and stood beside the gate as he proudly watched the men pour into the city.

"Here, take mine," Jonathan said, handing his reigns to David.

David looked at him, unsure how to respond to such honors.

"You should take my horse, go on!" Jonathan insisted.

"No, thank you, but I can't," David refused.

"I'm not asking," Jonathan said with a smile.

David quickly realized the prince would not be deterred. His face flushed, he finally conceded and mounted the beautiful horse. Jonathan and Yuval walked alongside him as they entered the royal city. Entering the massive crowd, the chanting and singing could finally be heard over the general din of applause and praises.

> *Saul has struck down his thousands,*
> *and David his ten thousands!*
> *Faithful is the God of Jacob*
> *to deliver us from our enemies!*

"Do you hear that?" Jonathan asked David.

David's face turned a shade redder. He nodded.

"Yes," he responded, "but the victory is the Lord's." he said, pointing skyward.

"I'll give you that!" Jonathan shouted above the chorus.

As they slowly eased their way through the mass of people and through the gates, the chant continued, louder and louder. Jonathan could see his father up ahead, mounted on his great black steed. Saul turned in his saddle to see Jonathan walking alongside the horse, surprised to see David seated there in his place. He turned back in the saddle and held his head high as they passed through the throngs of people that lined the streets all the way to the palace.

The palace gates swung open before them. Saul and the royal guard poured into the courtyard.

The guard fell into formation as the king dismounted and handed his reigns to the groom. David could see Queen Ahinoam and the princesses, both of them as beautiful as ever, standing by, ready to embrace their father and brothers. Michal, a year younger than David and the youngest of all the king's children, beamed with delight. She looked more beautiful than David had ever seen her before. The queen bore her typical regal demeanor, clearly pleased with her husband's return, but displaying little emotion beyond a welcoming smile. Merab, attractive by any standard, possessed the restrained bearing of an older, mature sister.

The princesses greeted Saul with a low bow, then returned their father's kisses to each side of his face before bowing low again and retaking their positions. Queen Ahinoam extended her hand, which King Saul took as he stood next to her and turned to wave at the crowd. The people erupted with applause. Saul smiled, then turned and proceeded with the queen into the palace hall. The princesses remained at their positions and repeated the greetings again with Malchi-shua and Abinadab.

Jonathan ushered David forward.

"This is David, though I'm sure he needs no introduction at this point," Jonathan said as he pulled David towards the princesses.

Merab bowed slightly.

"Indeed, your reputation precedes you," she said as she extended her lightly jeweled hand for David to kiss it.

Michal's cheeks turned bright red, as she bowed and extended her hand. David took and kissed the hand whose touch had eluded him for so many months prior to this occasion. He was elated.

***

Saul watched as Ahinoam sat at the edge of their bed and tied the strings of her sleeping gown and pulled her robe over her shoulders.

"Why don't you stay with me tonight," he asked.

Ahinoam sighed. "Come now my love. You know why. It is not as though I enjoy being apart from you," she replied softly.

"I'll sleep better if you were next to me," Saul insisted.

"We both know that's not true," Ahinoam replied as she stood and consoled him. "I will summon a musician. Do not trouble yourself. You know my love for you has not wavered. Try to get some sleep. I know you must need it."

"I am very tired," Saul confirmed. "Perhaps sleep will come more easily now. At times, I slept so well in the field. There are regular interruptions, yes, but nothing like before. A tired body helps."

"I would imagine so," the queen replied. She moved over to his side of the bed and kissed him. "I hope you have a restful night," she said before leaving the king's chambers.

A short way down the corridor she addressed the sentries on duty.

The guards saluted her and one reported, "first watch and all is well."

"Good evening," she said, greeting him softly. "I need you to summon one of the king's musicians."

She noticed the guards exchange a curious look at each other before she turned to leave. "What is it?" she asked impatiently.

"My Queen, it's just that all of the musicians were sent home before we deployed to the border. I haven't seen any of them since the king's return today. I don't know if any have been summoned."

"Sent home?" The queen asked indignantly. "Who made this decision?"

"Ah, they were not needed in the king's absence. It's been months my queen," the ranking sentry answered. "Joash sent them home to avoid the expense."

"There is one, but…" the second sentry started to say.

"But wha?," the queen asked.

"David, my Queen, he returned with the army," the sentry replied.

"David?"

The guard hesitated. David would be in no condition to perform for the king tonight, having returned to a city waiting with open arms to receive him.

"Well, where is he?"

"My Queen, surely he is out amongst the people. We may not be able to find him at this hour, since he was not summoned for duty," the sentry insisted. "He may not be in the best condition to play following the long march today," he offered.

"Then I suggest you find him quickly," Ahinoam responded before departing for her chamber.

With the Queen out of earshot, the two guards turned to one another.

"What a stitcher!" the sentry exclaimed. "'I'm done with the king, now fetch someone to play him a lullaby,'" he mocked.

"Careful talking like that," his colleague scolded. "You know how sounds travels in these halls."

"He was with Jonathan, right?"

"Yes, I'll start there. I'll send someone to join you while we look for David," he said before departing.

***

A knock at the door woke Jonathan from a deep sleep. Gently pulling his arm out from under his wife's head, he stood and covered himself.

"What could they want at this hour?" she asked as she rolled over.

"No idea," Jonathan replied as he started toward the door. He peered through the opening and saw the familiar face of Raanan.

Jonathan opened the door and stepped outside.

"Raanan, Nahshon," he said, acknowledging the men. "What's going on?" he asked in a whisper.

"I'm terribly sorry to rouse you Jonathan, but your mother instructed that we summon a musician and they've all been sent home. We were hoping you knew where David might be."

Jonathan peered back at him, clearly annoyed. "You've got to be joking."

"I'm afraid not."

"Please tell me you're just trying to take him for a drink," Jonathan said as he leaned against the doorframe.

"I wish that were the case. The Queen…" Raanan tried to say as Jonathan shook his head and opened the door.

"I can't help you," he replied before closing the door behind him.

Raanan couldn't blame him. In fact, Jonathan's refusal to give up David's location made Raanan respect him all the more. Nevertheless, it left the guard in a predicament. Queen Ahinoam was ruthless when it came to the king's welfare. Ever his zealous advocate, the queen perceived any hesitancy to follow either her or Saul's orders as a sign of disloyalty and treated such with extreme measures, resulting in a high turnover among the royal guards. While her attacks had never been aimed at him directly, Raanan knew this to be the reason for his rapid assent within the ranks of the King's Guard. So far, he'd skillfully managed to stay in her good graces.

"You know she's going to have our hides, if we don't find him," the sentry said.

"What can she really say if we look all night and can't produce him?" Raanan replied.

"She's going to want to know where we looked."

Raanan shook his head in frustration.

"And she'll ask him where he was, no doubt."

There was simply no way around it. They had to continue searching even if the prince were concealing David.

"Maybe he's back at the barracks," Nahshon suggested.

"It's not where I would be if all of Gibeah was waiting to buy me a drink, but let's hope you're right," Raanan responded.

The two men walked hastily towards the barracks where David had stayed during prior occasions when his services were needed. They made their way through the courtyard between Jonathan's home and the king's when a strange sound caught their attention. It sounded like a heavy object had been dropped from the balcony of the second floor of the palace. Suddenly, they saw a dark figure move quickly behind a column.

"Hold it! Who goes there?" Raanan said in a loud, stern voice as he drew his sword.

A moment passed in silence.

"Raanan," they heard a hushed voice say from behind the column.

"Who is it? Who's there?" Raanan responded loudly.

"It's me, David," the figure said in an excited but hushed tone before stepping out from behind the column.

"David? We were just looking for you!" Raanan said as his eyes shifted upward to the balcony. "What were you doing?"

"Oh, I was, just out for a walk," David said. "Headed back to the barracks now, couldn't sleep."

"Princess Michal's room is up there," the sentry said, pointing over Raanan's head to the balcony above.

Turning his eyes to the balcony, Raanan saw a female silhouette disappear quickly from sight. A moment later, the dim candlelight that had illuminated her outline was put out.

"Boy, you don't waste any time, do you?" Raanan said as he turned back to David. Even in the darkness, Raanan could see the giddy expression on the other sentry's face.

"You said you were looking for me?" David asked, trying to change the subject.

"Yeah, and lucky for you, the queen wants you intact at the moment. Look, she sent us to find you to play for Saul. None of the other musicians are here. I'm sorry David, but we need you."

"Well," David said wryly, "anything to help an old friend."

"I bet," Nahshon replied smiling.

The three proceeded to the king's chamber. Raanan paused outside. Lighting a small lamp, he handed it to David and listened for any signs the king was still awake. He could hear Saul moving about from within and gently knocked on the door.

"Come in," the three men heard the king say from within.

"God be with you," Raanan said with a hint of sarcasm as he opened the door.

David nodded and entered.

In the dim candlelight, David could see Saul standing at the far end of the room, near a table where he often read while David played. Saul appeared to be examining one of several scrolls spread out upon the table.

"Reporting for duty my king," David said. Saul turned to see David standing just inside the door to his room.

"David," Saul said, surprised. "Are there no other musicians available?"

"I'm the only one my lord," David said. "Would you like me to get started?"

Saul considered the question. He thought of the chants earlier in the day. "David, the lion of Judah." The song stuck in his head, endlessly repeating. "Saul has slain his thousands and David has slain his ten thousands." He couldn't shake it. A moment ago he'd looked forward to some comfort and hopefully a long night's rest. Now, the very source of his most recent frustration stood before him. What sort of trick is this that fate has conspired against me, Saul thought to himself.

"Go ahead," he instructed, figuring that whatever song David played would be better than the one endlessly cycling through his mind.

Saul put out the candles near the table as David proceeded to the spot where he and the other musicians would take up their instruments to play. On previous occasions, he'd always had his own lyre. The harp left there for use by other musicians was larger, much larger than what he was accustomed to.

As Saul extinguished the last lamp, he caught the glint of his spear laying atop one of the scrolls, pinning the curled document flat upon the table. Quietly, he lifted the spear from the table and carried it over to the bed. Living in the field, one became accustomed to sleeping with his weapons and carrying them everywhere. It felt strange not to have it in close proximity. Another spear still leaned against the wall where he'd staged it many months ago during his restless nights of tormenting dreams, just one more reason for Ahinoam's decision to sleep in a separate room.

As he laid down in the darkness, physically exhausted, his mind continued to churn. The sweet sounds of the lyre began to soothe his mind with a familiar calm as he settled into the soft bed. Focusing his mind on the tunes from the lyre as each string was plucked and its sounds reverberated through the room. Just as his thoughts began to subside and he felt himself fading into restful slumber, an off-note brought him back to consciousness. He squeezed the spear in frustration and opened his eyes. Concealed by the darkness of the room and veils surrounding his bed, he could see David illuminated by the flickering of a single candle next to him on the floor, casting his shadow upward against the wall behind him, giving the appearance of a large dark silhouette standing over him.

The larger instrument appeared awkward in David's hands. Suddenly, Saul remembered his playing on prior occasions. He rarely inquired any of the musicians' names and talked to them less often. It had been impossible to know, Saul thought, that one of them was capable of slaying a giant with the unfettered confidence David displayed on the battlefield. Saul laid his head back and tried once again to focus on the notes. "Saul has slain his thousands and David his tens of thousands." Again, the annoying melody penetrated his weary mind like water seeping through the holes in a thatch roof. The notes, Saul reminded himself, focus on the notes. It had worked almost without fail on most prior occasions. Focus on the notes and sleep will come, he thought.

Again, he felt the tension of his body melt into the softness of the large bed. His mind began to still as the melody took hold. "Focus on the notes," he repeated to himself as he tried to block the invasive thoughts from entering his weary mind once again. Suddenly, another off-note as he felt his mind slipping into unconsciousness, then abruptly, the music stopped altogether. Irritated he sat up in his bed. David was standing over the table looking over the maps and scrolls. How had he gotten there so quickly? Saul wondered.

"What are you doing?" Saul shouted.

David turned around as he placed the king's crown upon his head.

"This fits much better than your armor," David exclaimed.

"Take that off!" Saul shouted as he stood from his bed and charged toward the youth. "Have you lost your mind?"

Just as he reached David, the dim candlelight reflected in the youth's eyes. Saul reeled back in terror as slitted red eyes stared back at him while the figure of the youth grew large and dark into an ominous black shadow looming over the king.

Saul shouted in terror, waking himself as he jerked upright in his bed, drenched in sweat and clenching his spear. Confused to be back upon his bed, he looked to see the dark figure near the wall on the far end of the room. He quickly rose to his knees on the bed and threw the spear with all his might. It pierced the thin veil and flew across the room, striking the shadow over David's shoulder, embedding itself in the plastered wall. David jerked rearward and stood, dropping the harp and falling back against the wall. Saul was already on his feet with the second spear from his bedside. He threw it at David's chest, hoping to pin him there to the wall. David rolled to the right against the wall, narrowly avoiding the spear as it embedded in the wall next to the first.

"My King!" David shouted. "My King, what have I done?"

Saul's sword was already in his hand as he started toward David when two guards burst through the door with swords drawn and torches in hand.

Saul stopped midway across the floor.

"What's going on?" One of the guards shouted.

"He…" Saul started to say, pointing his sword towards David. Saul looked at the table where his crown lay, then back at David, confused. "He… I…" Saul was still breathing heavily as his mind cleared and returned to reality. He shook his head. "It must have been…" He paused. Looking around the room, to the spears embedded in the wall, the bewildered guards staring at him, then back at David. "Say nothing of this to anyone. Go! Leave me! All of you!"

David quickly moved toward the door as one of the guards held it open.

"Is everything alright, my King?" the guard asked.

"I said leave me!" Saul shouted as Queen Ahinoam entered the room.

Saul sank to the floor in the middle of the large room. The Queen looked upon her distraught husband then to the spears protruding from the wall near where the musicians sat. She turned to the sentries and David.

"You will speak nothing of this," she said in a hushed but sharp tone. "Go," she commanded, then started toward her husband as the guard bowed his head and shut the door.

Standing in the empty corridor, the two sentries stared inquisitively at David.

"I'd better get back to the barracks," David said before turning to leave.

"David, wait," the guard called in a hushed voice, moving towards him. "I'll be back in a moment," he said to the other sentry and left with David towards the barracks.

When they arrived, the sentry woke Raanan and hurriedly recounted what had occurred, despite the king and queen's commands.

Raanan sat on his rack trying to process the information.

"You'd better get back to the king's room; I'll stand guard here at the barracks to make sure no one comes for you," Raanan said. "Don't speak a word to anyone else," Raanan commanded before the sentry departed.

The sentry quickly departed to the king's chamber.

"This is crazy," Raanan said as he and David sat in the darkness.

David was silent, still trying to process the events that had just unfolded. If the king wanted him dead, who was there to stop him, David thought to himself.

"Go ahead and try to get some sleep David. I'll stay awake. I don't know that there is anything else we can do right now. You'll be safe here. Maybe the king really was just dreaming. You know how he gets at night. None of us are supposed to say anything, but there is a reason Ahinoam won't sleep in the same room anymore. I know they said not to tell anyone, but," Raanan paused, "but I think that maybe we should tell Jonathan."

David leaned back against the wall beside his rack, unsure how to feel about the recent events.

Raanan watched David as he leaned back against the wall next to his bed.

Raanan feared for David if the king wished to keep tonight's events a secret. He was somewhat thankful the queen had somehow been alerted to the incident. Raanan alone knew why she'd begun sleeping in her own separate chamber many months ago. The events that had just been recounted to him reminded Raanan of that night nearly a year ago. While it came as no surprise, it was no less unsettling. He said a silent prayer for his tormented king as he sat stalwart in the dark barracks, unsure whether the greater threat lay within or without the palace walls.

***

"I want you to make him commander of an eleph" Saul said as he finished his breakfast. "We're going to put this young man's talents to work. Have him conduct raids on the Philistine border outposts and any Canaanite garrisons within our borders."

Abner was quiet. David was far younger than any other captain in their ranks and now he was being called upon to lead men in battle without any training or preparation. It was late in the morning. Saul's eyes were red and tired, his countenance wretched. Saul took a drink from the cup of wine before him, then poured the cup full again.

Reading his cousin's silence as a rebuke, Saul followed quickly with, "it is decided cousin. I know you have your reservations, but make it happen."

Abner acknowledged the order, then turned and departed the king's hall for the army's quarters outside of the city.

Seth, his armor bearer, could sense his general's frustration as he joined Abner's long strides through the courtyard towards the gate.

"Is something wrong?"

"Nothing," Abner replied. He didn't complain to his men. To him, an order from the king must be treated as if it were his very own, but he'd already begun to suspect what the king truly had in mind. Saul was reacting once again to the capricious opinions of the outspoken and now he wanted to put the promising youth, not to mention all under his command, into harm's way.

"Find David and bring him to the muster," Abner said finally. Seth peeled off to locate the young victor as Abner continued towards the gate. Approaching the gate, the keepers swung it open, revealing Joash waiting to enter. The two adversaries greeted each other as they passed. Abner cursed to himself, feeling like a reluctant pawn in a child's game.

"God help David," Abner prayed as he made his way to the training fields. "God help us all."

***

Following the muster, Abner called a meeting of the eleph commanders. The roughly two hundred elephs were led by commanders who'd risen up in the ranks, men who'd demonstrated their capacity for leading men. Nearly all of them had successfully led a me'ah, a unit of approximately onc hundred men, before achieving the command of an eleph. Each eleph was made up of roughly ten me'ahs and each me'ah was broken into two groups of fifty men or, occasionally, depending on their skillset and mission, three groups of thirty or more. The eleph commanders were typically recruited from the best performing me'ah within that unit. Though this style of merit-based promotion created stiff competition among the me'ah commanders, the leader's reputation among the men he served was firmly established well before he ever took command.

While the tribal elders did not infrequently seek the promotion of their sons, often tethering their contributions to the same, most of the commanders were men of no significant background, heritage, or means. For these, the army had been their best shot of achieving distinction and success. While it was true that David had stepped up where no one else had, these men had devoted countless hours to the men they served and had shown themselves worthy of distinction. Abner suspected that David's overnight ascent would not be well received by many.

Of the two hundred elephs, only sixteen remained on duty immediately following the battle at Elah. The rest would rotate on and off duty for the remainder of the year. The royal guard, which was separate from the regular army, maintained a more consistent presence at Gibeah.

While the victory at Elah had been overwhelming, Israel had not come away completely unscathed. Of those reported dead following the battle, one eleph commander had been killed and another severely wounded. Both men had shown valor, leading their men from the front on the road to Ekron where the Philistines had managed to form a small defensive position against the Israelite attackers who'd become widely dispersed over the long pursuit from the valley. The wounded commander's unit rotation would begin at the end of the month, while the dead commander's unit was not set to report for duty until over three months later. Abner decided that David would replace the deceased commander rather than having him replace one of the others. This would give David a full three months of training and shadowing the active commanders before taking command of his own. Abner sent word to the eleph's officers informing them of the transition. Better that they get used to the idea than begin vying among themselves who would take command.

Abner selected the best of the sixteen active commanders for David to live with and shadow for the next three months until his eleph rotated in for its month of service. Currently, he would shadow Adriel for the rest of the month, then Jehoiada, then Ahithophel. Ahithophel had been with the army since Jabesh Gilead. Not only was he from David's tribe of Judah, the men loved him. Abner could think of no one better to help bring the youth up to speed. Then there was Jonathan, who would provide some continuity throughout the youth's expedited three-month military education.

Still, one brave act did not make a man fit for command. Courage was just one of the attributes necessary for leading men. Abner feared that what the youth lacked in knowledge and experience, he would try to make up for with bravado. It was a good way to get men killed. David would need a strong and experienced soldier at his right hand when the time came for him to lead.

THE PACK

1066 BC, Gibeah, Benjamin, Israel

David watched as a blue-green-breasted bird chased a dragonfly around the courtyard before landing in a nearby almond tree. Its colors were brilliant in the mid-day sun. He was enjoying the quiet stillness of the palace courtyard during a short break between training and classes, when his meditation was broken by the sound of a familiar voice.

"Contemplating Mycenaean naval strategy?"

David turned to see Jonathan, Abinadab, and Malchishua approaching.

"What's that?"

"Shua tells me that Nathan has been boring you two with more history lessons," Jonathan said as he approached. "I know it can seem insignificant at times, but pay close attention," Jonathan advised. "You never know what strategy of some past battle you might put to good use one day."

"It's not the history so much as the language that I'm having trouble with," David admitted.

"Mmm," Jonathan gave an understanding nod.

"I suppose sheep don't talk much do they?" Malchishua teased.

"Even less than donkeys," David replied.

The princes laughed.

"Don't get discouraged. These two have been trained in Mycenaean and Egyptian for most of their lives." Jonathan turned to his brothers. "Did David tell you he speaks Moabite?"

"He did not. Holding out on us, eh?" Abinadab asked.

"It never came up," David responded.

"We were just wondering, how is it David, that you were here at the palace for all that time and no one recognized you at the valley before the battle? It's not as if you were a cook or someone who wouldn't be seen. You were playing the harp for our father in his very bed chamber. It still baffles me," Malchishua said.

"I'm sure I was just one of many," David responded.

"No. No, I don't think so. We know our father," Abinadab said, while Jonathan nodded in agreement. "Someone recruited you or at least recommended you, how else would you end up here playing for the king? It's not like we hosted tryouts."

"It was Raanan. He's been a friend of my eldest brother since before your victory at Geba; there wasn't much to it after that. I came. I played. Your father liked my songs and that was it."

Malchishua and Abinadab looked at each other, clearly unfamiliar with the name.

"Well, that just about solves that riddle," Jonathan said as he jabbed Abinadab's arm. "You two don't know who Raanan is?" Jonathan chastised his younger brothers. "He's only the most impressive-looking man in the royal guard. You two seriously don't know the names of the men that have kept you both safe all these years?"

"Oh, you mean the one with the huge biceps?" Abinadab asked.

Jonathan shook his head in disappointment as he turned back to David.

"Well, you must be pretty good then."

"For a shepherd, I suppose."

"Alright, cut it out," said the prince, slightly irritated. "You know it's not humble if you boast in your humility. There's no shame in telling the truth, but since you want to walk around it, go get your harp. I want to hear you play something."

"Alright then," David said as he stood to his feet and departed in the direction of his quarters.

"See what I mean?" Abinadab asked with David out of hearing.

"Yeah, he doesn't say much, does he?" Malchishua responded.

Jonathan nodded his head. "

You have to put yourself in his position. He's a young shepherd. He's spent more time with animals in the field than he has with people. Now, he's rubbing elbows with princes and royalty. Maybe it's just his way, or maybe he's still feeling things out. Even a foolish man is considered wise when he keeps his mouth shut, and one thing is clear; educated or not, David is no fool."

When David returned with the harp, he sat and positioned himself, resting it on his thigh. He closed his eyes and began to pull at the cords. As the three princes listened to the sweet sounds of the instrument, Jonathan sat and leaned against the trunk of a tree. Malchishua and Abinadab followed suit as they listened intently, disarmed by the soothing melody as David began to sing.

The tune was slow and light, gentle. Then David began to sing the words, a confession, a lament regarding the fleetingness of life and earthly treasures.

> *My hope is in you.*
> *Save me from all my transgressions,*
> *do not make me the scorn of fools*

David sang as the men contemplated the deep and thoughtful words.

Jonathan leaned in, listening with wonder at how such a young and cheerful young man could write such a somber song.

> *Hear my prayer, Lord,*
> *listen to my cry for help, do not be deaf to my weeping.*
> *I dwell with you as a foreigner, a stranger,*
> *as all my ancestors were.*
> *Look away from me,*
> *that I may enjoy life again before I depart and am no more.*

When he'd finished playing, David opened his eyes to see the three onlookers sitting quietly in front of him. All three appeared to be contemplating the words of his hymn.

After a moment, Malchi-shua broke the silence. "Did you write for our father?"

"You might say it was influenced by him," David responded. "Some of it I'd already put together long before I came here."

"It sounds like him," Abinadab responded. "Not like something he'd write. I don't think Father would ever express himself in those words, but it sounds like…" Abinadab considered his words for a moment, "like what his thoughts might be."

"I thought it might be a comfort to him," David responded. "I think there are times when we all wish that we had done things differently, we want God to turn away, to not see our mistakes."

"You certainly have a gift David," Jonathan said as he stood to his feet. "That song says more about my father than a thousand words could. Thank you," the prince said solemnly. "It is a rare talent to know people, to feel what they feel and be able to communicate it. It is no wonder that God put you here with us."

Abinadab and Malchishua nodded in agreement.

David bowed. "It is my pleasure," he said.

"Has Father heard it yet?" Abinadab asked.

"No, not yet. I'm happy I was able to try it out on you three. I thought I might play it the next time he calls for me."

"I'm confident he will approve," Jonathan said as he bent down and picked up a round pebble from the rock path through the courtyard. "Till then, let's put another one of your skills to work," he said as he tossed the stone towards David.

David caught the stone.

"How about a lesson?"

"Sure," David said examining the stone. "The first lesson is to choose the proper stone," he said as he held it up between his thumb and forefinger. "While the shape is good, this one is far too light."

"Here." Abinadab had picked up a heavy, round rock about half the size of his palm and tossed it to Jonathan. "David has been instructing me already," he said with a smile. "How about a wager? Your bow against my sling."

"Well, well. You must have been putting in quite a bit of practice to be that confident. I'll take you up on that one," Jonathan replied. "What's the wager?"

"Respect," replied Abinadab.

Jonathan gave a nod and the four men departed as Jonathan retrieved his bow and David stowed the harp.

A short time later the four gathered in a nearby field used for archery and slinging practice. As Jonathan walked out to meet Malchishua, David, and Abinadab, they could see his newly acquired composite bow. Narrow strips of shaved wood were glued together to make a stronger material. The stronger bow meant that it could fire heavier arrows faster than the more common bows. Jonathan had taken painstaking efforts to acquire it after discovering one belonging to a slain Philistine archer at Michmash.

"Fan-cy!" exclaimed Malchishua, drawing out the word.

Abinadab whistled as he gazed at the impressive weapon with ornate designs etched into the wood and two wolf heads at the opposite ends whose open mouths held the bowstring. "Hey David, behold Judah's taxes for all of last year!"

"How many Philistines do you think it's killed already?" Malchishua asked.

"That's what the notches here stand for," joked Abinadab as he pointed to the grip.

"That's to improve your control over the weapon when your hand gets sweaty or bloody in battle. One day when you're grown, you boys will know what that's like," Jonathan replied cooly.

"Oh-ho," exclaimed Malchishua.

"Well, let's see how that fancy piece stacks up to this sling I made," Abinadab challenged.

The men stood next to each other at the firing line and stared at the straw-stuffed dummy approximately seventy cubits away.

Jonathan strung an arrow. Raising the bow in his left hand, he drew the arrow back as his forward left arm lowered to eye level, exhaling a slow and deliberate breath as he focused on the target. His right thumb knuckle pressed to his cheek, he released the string held by his middle and forefinger at the pause between breaths. The arrow pierced the painted eye of the dummy before skidding across the dirt behind it to a tightly packed reed wall meant to stop and collect stray arrows and sling stones.

An arrow shot from most bows would sink about halfway into the firmly packed target.

"I think you missed," teased Malchishua.

"Wow," Abinadab exclaimed. "You'll get nearly twice the distance with that."

"That's what I was hoping for," Jonathan replied.

Abinadab and David collected a number of stones of the desired size, shape, and weight from a basket of sling stones staged nearby. Abinadab loaded his sling. Stretching the cords tight with both hands, he released the loaded pouch with his left hand as his right hand pulled the sling around into an arc above his head, made several rotations, then shot forward, releasing the stone. Grazing the right shoulder of the target, the dummy twisted on the tripod that held it erect.

"Ha!" Abinadab exclaimed triumphantly, pleased that he actually struck the target.

"Not bad for the investment," Malchishua chided.

"Nice shot!" David congratulated.

"Let's see what you've got, David," exclaimed Malchishua.

David dropped the loaded sling from his right hand as he lunged forward and whirled the projectile over his head and released it. The projectile struck the target's forehead and blew through the back, sending a cloud of dust and bits of hay into the air.

Abinadab shook his head. "Land of Goshen!" he exclaimed. "How much longer till I can do that?"

"Depends on how much time you want to spend practicing," David replied.

"How long have you been training with the sling David?" Jonathan asked.

"At least thirteen years."

"And how many days out of the year would you say you practiced?"

"While I was a shepherd? All of them."

"And how many hours did you spend practicing?"

"Well, it's easy to lose track of time watching sheep day in, day out. It's hard to say," David replied. "At least one hour, but on some days, I could spend the entire day hurling rocks if there were plenty of grazing in the area."

"There's your answer," Jonathan said to Abinadab. "You've been practicing for what, two months now? Only thirteen more years to go."

Abinadab held the sling out to Jonathan. "You give it a try."

Jonathan sighed as he removed the quiver from his back and handed it along with the bow to Malchishua before accepting the leather sling.

"I can tell you right now how this is going to go."

David handed the prince a stone and took several steps back and to Jonathan's left. Abinadab and Malchishua took this as a sign they should do the same.

Jonathan attempted to repeat the movements he'd seen David perform and lurched forward sending the stone high over the target and the thatch wall far behind it.

"Ha! Abinadab shouted. "I'm finally better than you at something!"

"Well, there is a first time for everything, isn't there? Everyone has his strengths and weaknesses. I'll stick to what I'm good at," Jonathan replied.

"Abner says a leader should be proficient with any weapon," Malchishua reminded them.

"Shua is right. I suppose I could do with some instruction myself," Jonathan admitted.

"But first!" Malchishua said as he held the bow out to David.

David smiled as he accepted the bow. "It's only fair I suppose."

Taking an arrow from Malchishua, David nocked the arrow and positioned his feet and body in line to the target. He raised the bow and began to pull the string rearward.

"Good heavens," David exclaimed as he eased the string back straight and looked at Jonathan. "I may have to work my way up to this."

"It's a big boy weapon," Jonathan replied. "But look, when you lift your left arm, keep it straight," Jonathan said, demonstrating. Go high, then as you come down, pull back and try to bring your right hand to your cheek. That will make it a bit easier to draw. Try to bring it down on the target, exhaling as you bring your left hand down before you release. Don't take too much time trying to aim perfectly. You'll get fatigued the longer you hold it, at least until you've practiced holding it for longer periods."

David repeated the movements as the prince had instructed. He was barely able to touch his wrist to his cheek before he released the arrow, striking the target in the thigh.

"Good show!" Jonathan exclaimed.

"At least you hit the target," Malchishua said.

The princes took turns shooting the new bow with each demonstrating a high degree of skill.

"No worries David. We'll start you training on a lighter bow, then work your way up. Besides, you won't see any other bows like this one. The standard ones used by our archers will be much easier to train with," Abinadab offered. "For now, why don't you help us with our slinging."

After several hours of practice, which saw some moderate improvement in the princes' slinging, the men started their return to the palace.

"Look at us, it's like you're already part of the family," Abinadab said as he nudged David with his elbow.

David smiled, unsure how to respond.

"Yeah, I heard that the man who slayed Goliath was supposed to have a royal marriage or something like that, right?" Malchishua asked.

"I'm already spoken for," Jonathan replied.

His younger brothers laughed, but David seemed uneasy with the conversation.

"We have another problem," Abinadab replied. "But I doubt our friend here is going to admit it."

"Ah, yes, Merab still hasn't married yet," Jonathan responded. "And I think our young friend here has stolen the heart of another."

David's face was getting redder.

"Boy, you gingers don't have much of a gambling face, do you?" Abinadab quipped.

David and the others laughed.

"I guess not," David admitted.

"We've been discussing your little dilemma," Jonathan offered, stopping before they entered the palace gates. "Obviously, it's a delicate situation. You want to marry Michal, yes?"

David looked uneasily at each of the brothers.

"Don't worry. It seems there was one member of my family who took note of your presence here even before you killed the giant. We've seen the way Michal looks at you. We've seen the way you look at her," he said with a more stern demeanor. "Let's just say that it's clear your *admiration* is mutual," Jonathan said, breaking a smile. "The truth is, we'd love nothing more than to have you as a brother-in-law and I believe the king did make a promise."

"Look, it's no big deal," Abinadab added. "It's not like Merab has shown you the least bit of attention. But Merab is the oldest and must be married off first, so do you want to marry Michal or not?"

"Yes. Most definitely," David responded.

"Then we will work on things from our end," Jonathan said. "You just keep doing what you've been doing. But here is the thing, when the time comes and you are asked about marriage to one of the princesses, you need to decline, but respectfully of course. Talk about how you're not fit to be the son-in-law of the king, that sort of thing. Too much pressure. The queen will accept that. It'll take some time, but the queen had already narrowed her selections for Merab long before you killed Goliath. It's just a matter of saving face at this point. The king made a promise that neither my mother or Merab want to keep. So the refusal has to come from you. Once Merab is married, we'll make sure you get the first shot at Michal. They're our sisters after all. We want them to be happy, but you can't just give in. You have to protest at first, for the same reason or Merab will be insulted."

"Won't the king and queen find another husband for Michal if I protest?"

"Don't worry about that," Abinadab replied. "Like he said, it's all about saving face when it comes to dealing with royalty, especially the feminine variety. We'll handle things from our side to make sure that doesn't happen."

"How long have you three been working on this?" David asked.

"What do you think?" Jonathan asked rhetorically.

"Probably since the moment you killed Goliath," Abinadab said with a smile.

The men started walking towards the gates again.

"Now, since you already know your way around the palace, why don't you acquaint yourself with your future bride," Jonathan said, nudging his young friend.

David stopped.

The three princes stopped and turned toward him.

"What do you mean?" David asked.

"Look, once you rotate out, it will be a while before you get a chance to see her again. I know there isn't really any opportunity for the two of you to get to know each other for the reason we just discussed."

"What about the guards?"

"What about them?" Jonathan asked. "How do you expect to be one of the king's elite if you can't even sneak past a few palace guards?" he asked, giving David a light jab on the shoulder.

David wondered if this was the beginning of some elaborate prank.

"Are we really having this conversation? You're suggesting I sneak past your father's guards so I can see your sister?" David asked.

"Consider it part of your training," Jonathan said wryly. "Just, don't get caught. Michal is the apple of our father's eye."

"Besides, it's not like you really need our permission now, is it?" Abinadab asked.

David's eyes shifted as he examined each of the princesses' faces. They each stared at him knowingly.

"Just don't forget that she *is* our sister," Malchishua reminded David as he put his arm around David's neck and shook him slightly.

"I know my limits," David responded as the princes split off and went their separate ways.

***

Michal sat alone in her room, reading by the candlelight as was her common ritual before she finally fell asleep. The cool night air wafted in and around her room from the open balcony. She was just becoming accustomed to having the room to herself. Merab had not long ago married Adriel of Meholah and moved to their own separate and much larger room in the palace. Michal missed the company of her sister but was happy with the marriage. Now that Merab was married, none stood between her and David.

Her reading was interrupted by a faint sound that caught her attention. She stopped and listened. All was quiet. Then another noise broke the silence similar to the sound she'd heard before and in the corner of her eye, she saw a small object skip across the stone floor as it clattered away from the balcony. When it came to rest, she noticed it was a small round stone. She stood from her bed and covered her shoulders with a cloak as she walked cautiously to the balcony.

Peering over, she saw no one in the courtyard below. Then, as her eyes scanned the shadows, a figure emerged from a darkened corner of the courtyard into the moonlight.

David smiled up at the princess and waved, tossing a small rock in his right hand and catching as if to affirm that he'd been the source of the prior two intrusions to her room. She smiled back at him. Looking around her room, she sought for some way to assist him up to the balcony. She pulled a decorative rope down from where it hung from the curtains near the balcony. As she peered over, she was disappointed to see that David was no longer visible in the courtyard below. Suddenly, she heard a muffled grunt.

She moved over to the spot and found David, hanging with just his fingertips over the stone edge wall of the balcony. Pulling himself up, he threw his elbow over the precipice and swung the same side leg up as Michal reached and pulled him over to keep him from falling. He rolled clumsily over the parapet onto the hard floor, then jumped up to his feet.

Michal pulled him behind the curtain to avoid being seen, then laughed at his outrageous performance.

"You're crazy! What would you have said if you'd fallen and broken your leg under my balcony?"

"You mean like the last time I tried to talk to you?" David asked.

"You got lucky last time. How was it they didn't catch you?"

"I suppose I'm just that sneaky," David teased. "This is a beautiful room," David said, trying to change the subject.

"Thank you. So what makes you think I won't have my guards come in and arrest you? You know we'll both be in a lot of trouble if you're caught in here. Even the champion of Israel might have a hard time explaining that to my father."

"I suppose you could call them if you like, but I'd prefer you didn't. It would be a rough way to start our marriage."

Michal's face flushed.

"That's a bit presumptuous! Of all the arrogant men in my father's service..." she said feigning anger.

Her complaint was cut short as David gently took her hand.

"I believe you know the affections I've had for you. When I heard that your father promised a royal wedding for slaying Goliath, I was assured of the victory, and I knew I couldn't let someone else steal this blessing from my hand. I'd hoped that you'd feel the same. Now please, tell me if you share my affection. If not, I will quit this endeavor to be your husband, but if so, I will pursue it with every bit of strength that is in me, no matter what price your father demands."

Her demeanor had softened during his speech. For years she had flirted with him during his time at the palace. Indeed, she'd found many opportunities to speak with him when he came to play the harp or while he waited in the halls for her father to summon him at any hour. Almost without fail, she'd teased him in some way, but now the shoe was on the other foot. His gentle words disarmed her. No man had ever been so forthcoming with his feelings.

She didn't withdraw her hand, but placed the other on top of his. "I do love you David, but when I heard about my father's promise, I feared it was Merab you would marry."

David took both of her hands in his.

"Merab never so much as looked upon me before Goliath. There was no one in your father's house that took much notice of me before the giant, except you. I have loved you since the first time you spoke to me, but the joy of seeing you only brought that much sorrow. Who was I to dream of marrying a Princess of Israel?" David said, shaking his head at the memory of it. "But then, then God delivered the giant into my hand! The thought of you was no longer accompanied by despair, but hope filled my heart and now that I know you love me as well, my heart is full with the promise of our future together."

Michal laughed at David's excitement. "You never cease to surprise me. Warriors do not talk like this," she said.

"I will never stop surprising you," David assured her with a smile. Taking one hand in both of his, he kissed the back of it and backed towards the balcony. "Until next time, my love."

A moment later, he was over the parapet.

Michal ran to the ledge and looked over. David had already disappeared into the darkness.

Her heart still pounded with the excitement of his visit and the feel of David's lips on the back of her hand as she walked over and fell backwards onto her bed with a sigh.

BRIDEPRICE

1066, Gibeah, Benjamin, Israel

Now Saul thought to make David fall by the hand of the Philistines.
I Samuel 18:25

T he king sulked. He hated when Ahinoam argued with him this early in the morning. He hadn't the patience for it, especially while he tried to enjoy a good breakfast.

"A king should make good on his promises," Ahinoam asserted.

Their six children sat around the table eating quietly while the queen peppered their father with all of the reasons their daughters should already be betrothed.

"By their age, most princesses have been spoken-for for years. We haven't so much as identified suitors for either of them. It's high time we do so! You promised your daughter's hand to the man who slew the giant."

Following through with the promise to give his daughter in marriage to the man that slew Goliath was becoming quite the thorn in his side. Could no one see his disdain for David? His very presence set the king on edge. Worst of all, his own family loved the young man.

"Father, I do not wish to speak out of turn," said Jonathan, "I know it's not my place, but there is hardly a man among your servants I would prefer for my *younger* sister."

"I second that," Abinadab offered.

"Me as well," replied Malchishua.

"Can't I just enjoy my breakfast without you all berating me? Haven't I got enough trouble without you bothering me with these trivial matters?" Saul asked loudly.

Merab bowed her head and started to cry.

"Trivial? You think our daughters' future is trivial?" Ahinoam asked.

Saul disliked seeing his eldest daughter cry almost as much as he despised the look the queen was giving him.

"Very well!" Saul said at last as he pounded his fist on the table. "Guard!" Saul shouted.

A large, armored man entered the dining room where the royal family ate their breakfast together.

"Send for David!"

The guard acknowledged the order and exited the room.

"You know this is not the way I meant," the queen said. She reached for his arm before Saul pulled away from her.

"A king should make good on his promises!" Saul shouted before returning to his meal, violently cutting the meat on his plate and shoving it in large chunks into this mouth.

The awkward silence was broken by a knock at the door.

"ENTER!" Saul shouted.

David entered and greeted the king and queen. Ahinoam smiled uneasily at the handsome young man that would soon be her son-in-law.

Saul stood.

"I made a promise to the man who slew Goliath that I would give him my daughter in marriage. Well then, here is my elder daughter, Merab! I will give her to you for a wife. Only be valiant for me and fight the Lord's battles."

Michal's eyes widened as she glanced to her mother and Merab, then to Jonathan.

Jonathan sat back in his chair and nonchalantly raised his hand to his chin, briefly raising one finger over his lips. Michal saw the gesture but didn't appear at all comforted by it.

David cleared his throat.

"Ah, thank you, my king," he said as he went to a knee and bowed his head. "But, my king, who am I, and who are my relatives, my father's clan in Israel, that I should be son-in-law to the king?"

Jonathan smiled. Perfect.

Saul was almost compelled to like the young man in spite of himself.

"A promise is a promise. And a king's word is the law," Saul said. "You will lead our men in battle. Since it is as you say, victory against the Philistines will be your brideprice. When this season for war has come to an end, you will have proven yourself and you will become my son-in-law."

What's this? Jonathan thought to himself. His father was already placing more demands on David.

David glanced up at Michal. She was staring at the table in front of her. Merab, too, stared blankly at her plate as her hand moved to grasp Michal's.

"May the Lord give me victory against the king's enemies," David replied.

"Indeed. You may go," Saul said before returning to his breakfast.

David glanced at Jonathan to see the Prince give an almost imperceptible nod of affirmation before he turned and exited the room.

Ahinoam looked at her eldest son. The two exchanged a smile before returning to their breakfast. The Queen looked at her eldest daughter in time to see her eyes turn briefly towards the guard before the door was shut. Adriel, of the king's royal guard, was one of the king's closest and most trusted men.

When he'd finished eating, Jonathan excused himself from the table and kissed his mother and sisters.

"Well then, now that that's sorted out, we've got a division-sized rehearsal starting today," Jonathan said. "I'd better be off."

As he left the room, Ahinoam noticed the prince place his hand on Adriel's shoulder and whisper something as he left the room. While no one save Merab seemed to notice the encounter, the queen detected the slightest change in the soldier's demeanor.

****

Saul sighed and rested his chin on his fist as the next litigant presented his case. Ahinoam placed her hand atop his, gently reminding him of his duty to at least give the appearance of concern for the matters being argued. Saul straightened and listened to the two lawyers as they presented their client's cases. Saul wondered if other kings had this same problem or whether it was unique to their people. It never ceased to amaze him how there were so many incongruous ways that people tried to interpret God's law.

When a soldier entered the court and engaged in a brief exchange with one of the guards, Saul perked up. The lawyers' presentations were coming to an end and he perceived the new arrival to be a messenger from one of the forward divisions. Saul stirred and cleared his throat loudly. The lawyers were experienced enough to know that they were reaching the end of the king's patience and quickly concluded.

"Thank you," Saul said to the men. "You've each represented your clients well and have given me a great deal to think about. I'll have a decision to you within the week. You're dismissed."

"King Saul," the guard announced, "a runner from David's eleph is here with news from the front."

The king and queen had heard the third in a long line of civil squabbles that had risen to their attention after numerous appeals from lower courts. News from the front was a welcomed reprieve, even for the queen.

"For Heaven's sake, come forward!" Saul shouted.

The runner stepped forward and saluted the king and queen.

"Come, come!" Saul instructed the lanky youth. "What news do you have from the front?"

The runner took his place before the king and stood at attention. This was the first time he'd reported to the king directly. He was a tall, skinny teen.

"Sir, the Wolfhounds, uh, I mean the third eleph, seventh division of Judah report continued victory over His Majesty's enemies. Your servant

David is continuing to push south along the border of blood. We met the enemy East of Ekron, West of Timnah. We received sixteen casualties: seven killed and nine wounded. Five of the men are expected to return to service within the week, three were patched up and sent home under escort to recover, one is in poor condition and was brought to Gibeah and is being treated by His Majesty's surgeon as we speak. There were fifty six confirmed enemy killed during the battle. The wounded were numerous more, but we were unable to account for them due to the speed with which we pursued the enemy."

"Who ordered you to pursue the enemy south?"

The soldier bowed.

"Commander Hushai always insists that his leaders take initiative when opportunity presents itself. David found it advantageous to pursue the fleeing enemy. We followed them all the way to another eleph, which had been moving to reinforce them and caught them off guard west of Azekah. The battle that followed was an overwhelming defeat of the Philistines there, but due to the battle's proximity to Gath, we withdrew to high ground west of Beth Shemesh."

The news was bittersweet. Yet again, David had prevailed and eluded death, but his successes were still gain to the kingdom. Despite his hatred for David, his effectiveness as a commander was undeniable.

"What is your name son?" Saul asked.

"Benaiah, son of Jehoiada the priest."

"Thank you Benaiah. My guard will see to it that you are taken care of before you return to your commander. But first, you shall take this report to Abner. He may have orders to take back to your commander. You may go."

The young man bowed and walked briskly out of the hall.

"Will you hear the next case?" Seth asked.

"No!" Saul shouted. "Have them wait!"

Ahinoam could see the frustration in Saul's demeanor.

"I can't take any more of this. I'm going to clear my head," Saul said as he stood from his throne and exited the hall.

Ahinoam calmly stood and followed after him, stopping to instruct a servant to bring some wine for the king. She entered the king's chamber to find him pacing the floor.

"May I guess what has you so upset?" She asked.

Saul looked at her, annoyed. "I'm not upset. I am bored and frustrated with these squabbles. I sit here and play parent to these adults that can't get along, while David is out fighting my battles!"

"You are concerned for your future son-in-law," Ahinoam suggested.

Saul grunted. "I suppose so," he lied.

"I've been thinking, and I wanted to speak with you about that," Ahinoam said softly.

Saul looked up in surprise. "Were you not the one who reminded me of my vow to give my daughter to David in marriage?" Saul responded.

"Yes, yes, I was. But how much better would the kingdom be served with two valiant men for our daughters. We have two, you know?"

"What are you getting at?" Saul asked, when a thought hit him. "Is one of them pregnant?"

"No! Heavens no" the queen replied. "I just think it would be better that your daughters be *happily* wed than to force them into marriages that neither would have chosen for themselves."

"I've had to read between the lines all day woman. Can you please just tell me in plain terms what you are getting at?" Saul said impatiently.

"Michal loves David; it's plain for all to see and he was smitten with her long before you ever promised him a royal marriage. While Merab would never tell a soul of her true affections, it is clear to me that she cares for your servant Adriel."

"Adriel? How do you know these things?"

Ahinoam cocked her head. "I am their mother."

"Plain for all to see? All accept me you mean?"

"Saul, you did not recognize David even though he'd played the lyre for you numerous times before he killed the giant. Your focus is out there, outside the palace walls. As queen, my focus is inside these walls."

The queen had always been the more perceptive about such matters. While Michal was captivatingly beautiful, young, and vivacious, she could be reckless and even foolish at times. Merab had always been more like her mother, a discerning erudite. Any man would be blessed to have her at his side. There was no denying that Michal was the more beautiful of the two, but Saul had always feared she would fall for some servant foolish enough to bring shame on his household. This was a far better solution. Adriel was from a noble and wealthy family, highly respected among all the tribes of Israel - no one would question the marriage given David's apprehension.

"I've been a fool," Saul replied, tempering his enthusiasm. "As always, you are right, my queen. Why shouldn't our children be happy and have the desires of their hearts? Merab will have to be married before Michal can be given to David. I trust you've already worked out the details."

"Of course," Ahinoam replied with a smile. She embraced the king and kissed him. "You have no idea how happy this makes me. Your daughters will be overjoyed, not to mention your future son-in-laws."

Saul smiled. "No one more than I," he replied.

***

The sky turned hues of red and orange on another day garrisoned at Beth-Shemesh. David watched as his men continued to drill in the fading light.

"Their improvement is astounding, isn't it?" David heard the familiar voice say from behind.

"Yes. Yes it is," David replied. "Thanks to your leadership and training."

"Thank you David" Dodo replied. "You give me the credit, but you are the commander of this eleph. You should be proud of your accomplishments. It was you who implemented many of the changes before I arrived. I heard what this lot was like before you arrived. You're not just a cocky young shepherd with a sling anymore," the old warrior said as he slapped the young commander on the back and squeezed his shoulder in a gesture of affirmation.

"It's good to have men like yourself. I don't know what I'd do without you. It was no small thing for Jonathan to send you here, and I am truly grateful."

"It has been my pleasure. Speaking of princes, Benaiah just returned with word from Gibeah."

David turned to see Dodo's face, attempting to gauge the severity of the news he was about to receive.

"Princess Merab has been given to Adriel the Meholathite. They will be married soon. I'm sorry to be the one to tell you," Dodo said in a somber tone.

David smiled. "That's a shame," he replied, turning his attention back to the men. "I suppose my lack of eagerness to return did not bode well with the queen."

"I wouldn't say that," Dodo replied playfully. "You're not quite off the hook."

He had David's full attention now.

"Saul wants you to marry his youngest daughter, Michal."

David smiled and nodded as he turned again to watch the men rehearsing maneuvers in the field below them. He shook his head.

"Does it seem to you a little thing to become the king's son-in law? Perhaps it would be if I were from a family such as Adriel's, but how am I to pay the brideprice for a princess since I am a poor man and have no reputation?"

Dodo laughed. "No reputation? Come on now David. Humility does not suit you. Nevertheless, I will communicate your concerns, but don't think that I am fooled."

"What do you mean?"

"Any one of these men would gladly take your place. I've seen Michal blossom from a little girl to the beauty she is now. You know you'd be a fool to refuse the king's offer."

David shook his head. "You know what I mean. I do not come from a noble family such that I should be the son-in-law of a king. I was a shepherd not long ago."

"And Saul, the king? Was his family noble when he was anointed? What about Gideon? Joshua? Caleb? And what's wrong with being a shepherd? You're beginning to sound like one of those high-minded types."

"I cannot, I will not, take from my father's house or from my brothers' inheritance to pay a bride price. Do you know that I have seven brothers and two sisters, not to mention all their children? I cannot burden my father with the price of a princess. I have nothing to offer. Apart from this, yes, I would be thrilled to hear these words."

"I understand, but not every bride price is paid with treasures," Dodo replied. "Why, even Jacob served Laban seven years for Rachel."

"Fourteen, if I remember correctly," David replied.

"Yes, well, that was for two daughters and Adriel has solved that problem for you. With your approval, I will communicate your concerns to the king myself. A matter such as this requires some discretion."

David wondered what he had in mind. Things functioned smoother with the old veteran around, but his faith in the old soldier was bone deep.

"I don't know what you have in mind, but I trust you won't get me in over my head."

"We'll leave tonight," Dodo replied.

***

Saul was surprised to see the familiar face of the soldier among those waiting to have his ear. Saul instructed Raanan to bring the man forward.

Dodo came forward and knelt before the king. Saul lifted him and embraced the man.

"Come, come," Saul said as he ushered Dodo away from prying ears and eyes. "How are you, my old friend?"

"I'm well my lord, no worse for wear. I have come from the border where I have been serving with David. Jonathan sent me to help provide some more *seasoned* guidance to the eleph. I must say though, he has required very little help. The men are faring exceedingly well. David is a natural leader."

Saul nodded, "Good," Saul replied. "So what news do you have from my future son-in-law?"

"I spoke to him after I received your message. When I saw how deeply it vexed him, I sought that I should communicate his concerns to you directly."

"What do you mean? What is he vexed about?"

"It is no small matter for your servant to become the son-in-law of the king my Lord. David fears he lacks sufficient means to pay Michal's bride price. He could not burden his father's house with this matter, being nearly the youngest of all his many siblings."

"I see," Saul replied, careful to conceal his elation. "I anticipated this and I have worked out a solution. Thus shall you say to David, 'The king desires no brideprice except a hundred foreskins of the Philistines, that he may be avenged of the king's enemies.'"

"One hundred Philistine foreskins?" Dodo asked. He had not anticipated this proposal and immediately regretted that he'd taken the matter upon himself.

"That's right. I'm certain David will be pleased with this prospect. I have full faith and confidence that he will accomplish this task. After all, with men like you, this is a minor feat."

A minor feat? Dodo thought to himself. They hadn't killed that many Philistines in the past five skirmishes with the Philistines; how was this supposed to be a "minor feat"? And foreskins, why not hands or something, anything else. Now, Dodo understood David's reaction. This was indeed "no small thing," as he had put it.

"Alright then, you have your message. I'll await David's payment in full. He has one month. He is not the Princess's only suitor. If the job isn't done by then, I'll assume he has refused my accommodation. Understood?"

Dodo felt like he'd just received a blow to the stomach. One hundred Philistine foreskins in one month, he thought. "Yes, my king."

"God speed to you," Saul said as he returned to the throne and instructed his court administrator to bring the next case forward.

Dodo bowed and stepped away. He was dumbstruck.

The youth, Benaiah, stood at his side patiently.

"Well?" Benaiah asked as they turned to leave. "David will be pleased, won't he?"

***

Benaiah could hear the sounds of iron scraping whetstones despite the strong eastward wind that swept through the camp. There was comparatively little banter and talk as the men prepared their minds for the task ahead.

Normally this time of night, most of them would be sleeping. When the sun went down on a night in the field, the men typically took the opportunity to catch up on much-needed sleep due to a strict ban on fires within the camp. Tonight was different.

A half-moon illuminated the surrounding countryside as sparse clouds passed quickly overhead, casting blackened patches on the ground as their shadows moved silently across the camp. Benaiah recalled David's reaction to the king's offer. He'd been elated by the prospect. There had been several raids by the Philistines into Israelite villages to the south along no man's land, the disputed border of blood that ran parallel to the coast. In the previous three days, David sent small reconnaissance teams to gather as much information about the identity of the Philistine units responsible for these incursions.

One of the reconnaissance teams, led by a captain named Ribai, had captured a Philistine messenger headed north to Gath. He was a young adolescent, similar in age to Benaiah.

"What Philistine units are responsible for the raids that occurred four days ago?" Benaiah recalled Ribai, the reconnaissance commander ask the messenger.

"A company from the 5th Division of Ashkelon," the boy replied immediately.

"Where are they stationed and what is their makeup?" The interrogator asked.

The boy hesitated, contemplating his answer.

"You need to answer quickly and truthfully boy," Ribai reminded him, "if you have any desire to live beyond this conversation. You are an enemy soldier, no different than the rest. For all we know you are part of the band that raped and pillaged our people; why should we treat you any different?"

"That's not what happened," the youth shouted. "Our people only seek back the land that was taken from them. We were here first."

"So you *were* there?"

"No, I... I didn't say that."

"Then you did not see the murdered men, the burned homes, and ravaged women and children your men left behind."

"I don't believe you," the boy insisted.

"You don't have to believe me," the interrogator countered. "We know it was the 5th Division, the same division you serve, led by Commander Andreas."

The youth looked stunned.

"We know more than you think," Ribai informed him. "That is why you need to be truthful."

"What reason do I have to believe you? Even if I tell you the truth, you'll kill me," he replied.

"The choice is yours, my young, uncircumcised friend. You could leave this camp as you arrived or you could leave here wishing you'd been born a woman. Either way, you have my word that we will not kill you, though you might wish we had if you withhold information from me," Ribai said calmly as he picked up a small knife from the table and ran his thumb perpendicular across the blade. "We won't be releasing you until our work is done. So we'll know if you lied to us."

The youth sat silent.

"You're too young to be married. That's a shame. Perhaps you will make a nice tea-boy for one of your kings, or maybe a servant in some wealthy man's home."

The youth remained unmoved.

Ribai nodded to the man on the boy's left. Instantly, the prisoner was snatched up and brought down hard on his back. The two men that held him now laid the weight of their upper bodies on the boy's arms and shoulders. Two others seized the youth's legs and pinned them to the ground.

"Last chance boy," Ridai said as he stepped between the young man's feet, pointing the knife down toward the prisoner's groin. "I've no patience for this sort of thing."

The boy stared up at his captor with wide eyes.

"Very well," Ribai said as he knelt down and touched the blade to the boy's skin.

"I'll talk! I'll tell you. I'll tell you," the boy shouted, much to Benaiah's relief.

Ribai instantly withdrew the blade. "Now that's my boy," he said as the men released the prisoner's legs and shoulders. The two men at his side lifted the boy from the dirt and sat him up.

"Thank you for being reasonable young man," Ribai encouraged his prisoner. "I do detest violence. I think you will find me a most hospitable host whenever the slightest reciprocity is shown by my guests."

The youth sat wide-eyed, astounded and confused by the interrogator's change in demeanor.

The reconnaissance commander sat down uncomfortably close to the prisoner and placed a hand on the back of the boy's head.

"Now, tell me."

Benaiah recalled the details the youth had disclosed regarding the enemy's positions, their daily routine, and nightly changing of the guard, information that would seal the fate of the boy's countrymen. Their lives had been exchanged for his manhood. The impression had been seared into the young Israelite's mind and he resolved to never be taken alive by the enemy. Benaiah wondered if this had been the captain's intention when he'd permitted the young soldier to remain present during the interrogation.

A clandestine team of reconnaissance scouts posing as shepherds were able to confirm much of what the boy had divulged over the preceding days. Confident of the enemy's makeup and identity, they prepared for the reprisal mission that followed.

"This is no ordinary mission," David explained to the men earlier that day. "We need to send a message. Any incursion into our land, any act of violence on our people, will evoke a response tenfold on those responsible for it. We must get inside their heads. They must know and fear that an attack on Israel will cost the very lives of the ones responsible. The cost must outweigh any potential gain. This is the only way that we can protect our people. There is no alternative."

"Ein breira!" The men shouted in response.

"To do this, we must act quickly and decisively," David continued. "We will be the instruments of God's hand upon those who have attacked our people. We will send a message that God's wrath awaits those who attack our people. When their comrades see, they will know without a doubt that the God of Israel delivered them into our hands."

"I won't lie to you," David continued. "King Saul has demanded a brideprice from me. You men deserve full disclosure. Saul requires of me one-hundred Philistine foreskins."

The men erupted with laughter.

"Is that all?" one man responded.

"One-hundred Philistine foreskins? Ha! I'd pay that for a one-eyed prostitute!" shouted one of the men, followed by another chorus of laughter.

As the laughter faded, David spoke solemnly.

"I would not have you men go out and risk your lives without knowing this. The truth is that we are attacking this unit for what *they* have done. We would be doing this regardless of any brideprice. I would collect them myself if necessary. You men know me. You know what is in my heart and what I believe. I believe our God has ordained this thing. As such, it may serve two purposes. When the Philistines find their brothers slain and their foreskins removed, it will send a message."

"We are set apart, chosen among the nations, are we not? Circumcision is the outward showing of what should be the inward condition of our hearts, that we belong to the Lord. We are His people. So then, when the sun rises on the Philistine camp and their brothers find them, it will be known that those who touch the sons and daughters of the God of

Israel touch the apple of His eye. They will think twice before attacking our people. They will fear His retribution."

Some quietly nodded in affirmation. There could be no doubt that this would send a strong message.

"Abiathar and I will do the dirty work. None of you need concern yourselves with the task, but even I will not begin to collect the king's fee until we have achieved our objective."

"This is not a mission for the entire eleph," Dodo said, stepping forward. "You men have been selected for your valor. Each of you has shown yourselves capable men. These missions will be far more dangerous than anything you've done before. If you choose not to participate, you may leave now, but speak nothing of what has been said here. If you choose to stay, the same rule applies. You will discuss nothing of this mission with those outside this tent."

None of the men stirred.

"Very well," Dodo continued. "The Philistine 5th Division has an outpost positioned on the east slope of a hill west of Azekah, thirty-eight stadia from our current position. There are three Philistine units of approximately fifty men each, which we know to be responsible for the raids on Socoh and Libnah. Our spies confirmed that they returned to their garrisons last night after being gone for five days. Typically, that means they will be resting and won't have any other duties for two days. They are set up in a triangle of mutually defensible positions. Two forward and one back further up the hill to the west," Dodo said as he used a long pointed stick to identify three rows of sticks and rocks resembling the enemy positions on the terrain model between himself and the men. "Ribai's team has already scouted the position and positioned men along the route. We will link up with them en route, and they will serve as guides on insertion and exfiltration. We are going to swing around the western side of the hill to approach from over the top, so our approach will be a bit longer than thirty-eight stadia."

"We will strike all three simultaneously tonight. The most important part of this mission and those that follow is that you leave no trace of our presence. We will use only the captured Philistine weapons we have provided. We must use stealth to our advantage. That means no armor. We will strike hard and fast. You are going out in three units of thirty. You will be outnumbered. Surprise is our ally. If we lose it, we will fail. The seasonal winds should aid in concealing our movement."

Squatting down beside the terrain model, David took the stick as Dodo handed it to him. "Elhanan, you will take the lead on the westernmost position. Mebunnai and Ittai, you and your men will provide support. I want as many men inside the perimeter as possible once it's secure. We can't allow any squirters to alert the other two barracks. We have to hit them hard, quickly, and quietly." David said, pointing to each position as he spoke. "These positions are within bowshot from each other and surrounded by a low wall approximately waist high on the eastern side," he said, pointing to the rectangular rows of rocks on the model. "They've not yet completed fortifications, but they have established two crude barracks at each location. They've had roughly four to six men on watch throughout the night at each position. They are typically stationed at each of the four corners of the wall, with one to two additional sentries along the eastern wall. Their focus is to the east generally as they don't seem to expect an attack from their rear, further up the hill and closer to Philistine territory."

David stood straight. "Let's assemble back here at dusk to review your plans and coordinate. We'll rehearse throughout the day, get some rest, and step off at nightfall."

The young messenger approached as the men departed the tent to begin their preparations.

David could tell the youth had something on his mind. "How did I do?" he asked the youth.

"This reminds me of something the judges would have done," Benaiah responded.

David nodded. "It is indeed."

"But, if I may…" Beniah paused.

"Go on, let's hear it," David said.

"One hundred circumcisions is quite a lot. Even performed on dead men, this will take time and this is a mission that requires haste, does it not?"

"Yes, that's why Abiathar is coming along."

"Yes, but even so, remaining there longer than necessary could be extremely dangerous. You said this needs to be fast."

"If it's taking too long, I won't do anything to jeopardize the men or the mission. I appreciate your concern," David assured.

"Well, I was thinking that I could help. You know my father is a priest. He trained me since my youth in everything related to his priestly duties. I have seen many circumcisions and I have even done them myself."

"Your father allowed you to circumcise?" Abiathar questioned angrily. "You may be a Levite, but you've not been ordained!"

"I… I practiced on goats!" Benaiah confessed. "Father insisted that if I were to perform a circumcision of one of God's people, it wouldn't be my first. Whenever we would slaughter an animal, I would practice on the animal before butchering it."

David and Abiathar laughed at the thought.

"But I've watched him perform hundreds of circumcisions on baby boys and even grown men! I tell you, I can help."

"You've already been put through the gauntlet of serving as my runner. Dodo tells me you've been diligent in your training and show great aptitude."

Abiathar turned to David. "He is a child," Abiathar said in a low voice.

"That's what many still say of me," David responded.

"Alright, I'll let you go, but I want you to stick close to Abiathar. Do you understand?"

"I will not leave his side," the youth affirmed.

"Alright then. Go and listen in on Elhanan and the others. You could learn a lot from watching them work. I want you to participate in the rehearsals as well."

"I understand! I will be ready."

The youth bowed and departed quickly after the commanders.

Abiathar shook his head in disbelief. "What sort of youth asks to go on a mission such as this?"

"What sort of commander consents to it?" David responded.

"Hmm," Abiathar grunted, shaking his head. "I always thought you were cut from a different cloth. It seems he was taken from the same fabric."

***

It didn't take Heleb long to fall asleep as they waited for their last briefing before the night's operation. Mebunnai couldn't help but marvel at the man's cool-headedness given the mission they were about to undertake. He grabbed Heleb's foot and shook it. Heleb opened his eyes and reached up as his friend took his arm and pulled him to his feet.

"Time to get dolled up, is it?" Heleb asked as Mebunnai handed him the bowl of black clay.

Mebunnai took his place in the center of the large tent with Elhanan and Ittai. The three men took turns briefing the scheme of maneuver and actions they'd rehearsed the entire day leading up to this point. By now, it was a mere formality, one last chance to clear up any confusion about the plan.

Ittai concluded the briefing with the challenge and pass for their linkup with the scouts.

Each man checked the man to his left and right to ensure they were covered head to toe in black. Given the amount of ground they'd have to cover and the time of year, it would need to be reapplied closer to the enemy positions.

A moment later, the men were ready. David gave the older leader a nod.

"Let us pray," Dodo said.

The men knelt as Abiathar began.

"Yahweh, eternal and almighty God of Israel, you have given this land into our hands that we and our children may inherit it. We come today to do the work set out for our ancestors. Let us not fail in this. Let not our hearts be fearful. Help us to be strong and courageous. Do not let us be afraid, for you, our God, are with us. To you belongs the victory and the glory which you have already predestined."

As the priest's words fell silent, David took up the prayer. "Lord, you are our shepherd. Though we walk through the valley of the shadow of death, let us fear no evil, for You are with us, Your rod and Your staff, they comfort us. Prepare the way for us in the presence of our enemies. Amen."

David lifted his head and looked at the men around him. They would be a terrifying sight for anyone in their path.

"Each of you men are dear to me. I have prayed often for you and I believe the Lord has already given us the victory. He who dwells in the shelter of the Most High will abide in the shadow of the Almighty. Our enemy hides behind low walls on the hillside, but the Lord is *our* refuge and fortress. Do not fear the night. We are the night. We are the shadow of the Almighty. Tonight, you will see it with your eyes and witness the punishment of the wicked, those who have slain and ravaged the children of Jacob. Because you have made the Lord your dwelling, no evil will befall you, for He will command His angels concerning you to guard you. We are His avengers, the ministers of God to execute wrath upon these uncircumcised men of violence."

"Ein breira!" shouted one of the men.

"Ein breira!" they responded in unison.

Dodo pulled open the flap of the tent and looked outside. The sun had set and there were no campfires in the southern portion of the camp as he'd instructed. He held the wax canvas of the tent open as the men filed out and into formation. Moments later, they were on the move.

Elhanan squinted in the darkness, trying to keep the perfect distance from the man before him and avoid disrupting their ranks. The pace was challenging but sustainable, at least for this group. The men about him were well known among their division and Elhanan, slightly surprised that he'd been selected, would die from exertion before slowing these men down.

He'd been placed in the middle of the column of twos. The trail they followed was just wide enough for two but barely so at several points. The faster runners in front set the pace with the slower runners in the rear to help prevent them from bunching up along the way. Elhanan tried to calm his nerves by focusing on his breath. Thirty minutes into the movement, they had not slowed down once to orient themselves. He'd counted the hilltops and bends to this point and knew exactly where they were. Over a third of the way there, he thought. In less than an hour, they would reach the attack position, where their final checks would occur prior to the assault.

They'd passed two pairs of reconnaissance scouts already. There would be five more before they reached the back side of the hill.

Sharar breathed heavily. "You're getting too old for this work," his wife had told him months ago before he left. Every day was a new ache. He spent more time stretching these days to maintain his physical fitness than he did actually strengthening the body. Still, none of the men around him would have guessed it. The pair of scouts they'd linked up with at the last split in the trail set the new pace. He was ready to curse them given the fact they hadn't been running for the past hour like everyone else. He was concerned they would cause the group to become too dispersed, but when the clouds parted momentarily, a quick look to his rear confirmed that his concerns were unfounded. Nearly there, he thought. Just keep the pace a little longer. Finally, the men ahead of him began to slow and stopped on an upward slope.

"This is it," the scout whispered in the darkness as the following troop slowed to a walk and the two lead scouts parted in opposite directions as the column followed suit. They stretched forming two lines abreast each other on the reverse western slope of the hill opposite of where their quarry slept, or so they hoped.

More black clay was applied to slick and sweaty bodies and faces, swords were drawn and arrows nocked. Two groups of ten archers would lead the way on this attack, performing a double envelopment of the position in order to silently eliminate any sentries on watch. An arrow that missed its target might land silently in the dirt or brush, but a stone risked alerting the entire camp. Slings were forbidden unless absolutely necessary.

David waited in position at the crest of the hill where, to his surprise, the Philistines had failed to position any rear guard. The dim light of the flickering campfires below told nothing of the deadly scheme unfolding before his eyes. Embers rose from several campfires as their fuel was stirred. A fiery branch at each location was waved in a large arc over the sapper's head, having successfully dispatched the few Philistine sentries that stood fire watch.

Without a word, the main body of men rose from their positions and descended on the sleeping camp below. The archers turned sappers held open the makeshift gates of the encampment while the main body silently flooded the enemy position and formed up along the barracks' walls.

A Philistine emerged from one of the barracks only to be seized from behind. A hand covered his mouth as a razor-sharp blade was dragged across his throat. His struggle was brief and nearly silent. His lifeless body was moved aside as the men silently crept into the long open hallway of the barracks. Moments later, the sleeping Philistines were dispatched as newly sharpened blades were brought down simultaneously in nearly complete darkness save for the moonlight pouring in through the open doorway and windows. The Israelite infiltrators muffled the sounds of struggling men in their final throws. To those waiting at the doorways of the neighboring barracks, little could be heard over the strong west wind.

Their bloody task completed, the men filed out of one barrack and into the next. Upon entering, Sharar was met by a staggering Philistine. The man, still half-asleep, pushed him out of the way without a word and exited the doorway before an Israelite seized him from behind, covering his mouth with one hand and wrapping his other arm around the man's neck, locking his grip into the elbow of the opposite arm. The man threw his head rearward, smashing the nose of his attacker before the Israelite fell to his back and wrapped his legs around the struggling Philistine's waist.

The rest of the men were already moving into the second barrack. Seconds later, the Philistine's body went limp. Elhanan rolled the man's lifeless body off to the side, recovered his sword from the ground, and drove the point into the man's bare chest for good measure. By the time he entered the room, the others had already completed their task.

As planned, the men rallied on the southern wall and performed a head count. It was nearly an hour after midnight. They had approximately three more hours to complete their task and two more positions.

The archers had already moved on to the next position further down the hill, this time enveloping the two lower positions simultaneously. This would be more difficult. They would wait for the guards to change before silently eliminating those on watch. The sappers would immediately hide the bodies and take up the dead men's positions as others infiltrated and signaled to David and the rest of the men waited further up the hill.

The southernmost position was taken first. A Philistine awoke in the first barracks and began screaming before his head was nearly removed by the Israelite nearest him.

In the next barrack, a Philistine awoke and went to the door to inspect the cause of the noise. The Israelite standing guard at the door allowed him to exit the barracks unmolested, but when the man was sufficiently out of the doorway, the Israelite seized him from behind, covering his mouth and muffling his cries for help. The Philistine bit down on a finger that had slipped into his open mouth as his attacker slid the blade across his neck.

The Israelite raiders slipped out of the barrack and into the next, still undetected.

The men rallied on the northern wall closest to the final Philistine position.

"So far so good," David whispered to Dodo.

"Let's not start celebrating yet," the old veteran whispered back.

The archers exchanged signals, giving the all-clear, and the assault force proceeded through an opening near the northwestern corner of the position and into the final Philistine position. As the first wave entered, the men were startled by the loud barking of a dog from somewhere within the camp. A moment later, a "thwack" could be heard as an arrow struck the dog, followed by a short, high-pitched whimper. The raiding force continued as they had trained and moved into position along the walls of the barracks. They could hear men beginning to stir from within. Several Philistines exited the barracks with swords drawn and were cut down immediately. The raiders now had the upper hand, having elim-inated the other two supporting positions. Suddenly, the doors of the barracks were slammed shut, barred, and barricaded from within.

The blackened Israelites were too close to the wall to be targeted by any potential archers within. The two foes were at a momentary stalemate. As rehearsed, several Israelites went to work. Taking burning wood from the fire, they ran the burning timber along the edge of the thatch roofing, setting the barrack roof ablaze. The fire was then spread to the doors of each barrack. Several new fires were built up beneath the small windows of the barrack. The men inside screamed and shouted among each other from within as the Israelites waited outside.

As the smoke began to fill the last remaining barrack, Abiathar and Benaiah, along with a small guard force, were already at work in the first barrack. Several guards held candles above as the priest and young runner performed their grizzly task. One of the men vomited but continued to hold the candle as they worked. Another held out an open leather satchel as they tossed in one foreskin after another.

"Ah!" Abiathar said, shaking his head. "These scoundrels are disgusting."

"Just imagine where they've been," one of the soldiers joked. "Make sure you don't nick yourself. You'll probably get leprosy."

"Or worse," said the soldier, holding the candle near to one of the corpses.

"What's worse than leprosy?" one of the men asked.

"That!" said the soldier, holding the candle-light over one Philistine who'd been afflicted by some terrible disease of the genitals.

The weak-stomached soldier nearly vomited again.

The soldier holding the bag contorted his face. "Land of Goshen! We did that man a favor," he exclaimed. Several of the guards laughed.

"We'd better skip that one," Abiathar told the young Levite.

Benaiah continued working, moving quickly from one man to the next. The fact that the men around him were joking about the task at hand gave him a strange mixture of feelings. How was it possible for good men to be doing what they were doing and laughing about it in the process? He wondered. He realized that death and gore had become so commonplace for these men that it no longer carried the same connotation.

***

The moon was already beginning to set on the horizon by the time the Israelites cleared the final barracks. David immediately went to work, collecting the flesh that would pay the price for his royalty. Immediately, many of his men joined him in the grizzly task as others curiously looked on.

"Well, I won't be writing home about this one," one man remarked.

David and those with him quickly caught up with Abiathar and Benaiah, much to their appreciation. The men consolidated and secured their bounty, then thoroughly washed their hands at the well that supplied the Philistine positions.

After receiving the final headcount, David praised the Lord. Not one Israelite had been killed, and there'd been only minor injuries suffered by a handful of men while taking the second to last barracks. The men formed a double stacked column and exited the position crossing back over the hill westward then north and east to friendly territory. David was the last to leave the position, counting once again the head of every Israelite as the men passed.

The pace set by those in the lead would typically have been difficult for many to sustain, but on this night, as the chill of the approaching morning set in, the men were alive with the thrill of victory and retribution. Even the heaviest among them seemed to glide along the trail as they passed over the rolling hills and terrain in the darkness, racing the coming of day.

The small clandestine force approached the division camp from the rear and flooded quietly back into friendly lines and straight into their separate command tent near the rear of the position where the division's physician waited. The sky was just beginning to lighten in the east as they began their debrief of the night's events, a practice Abner had insisted upon and drilled into in the entire Israelite army. The physician saw to their few and relatively minor wounds, the worst of which was a nearly severed finger. Dodo led the men through the exercise of retracing their steps from the moment they'd left camp to their return.

"We need to improve our breaching tactics," one man said when the briefing came to the point where the fifth and sixth Philistine barracks were taken.

"There won't always be time to smoke out the enemy. What if the wind hadn't been favorable? We got lucky tonight."

The men were quiet. He was right. It had taken them significantly longer to clear the last position. If they'd run into the same problem at any one of the previous barracks, the mission would have gone much differently.

"Any suggestions?" Dodo inquired.

"What if we could set fire to the inside of a structure?"

"How would we stop the enemy from immediately putting it out?" another responded.

"Up north, we have pine trees. When the trunk is cut, they produce a sap that burns easily and is difficult to put out. When the trees die in the forest and the bark has rotted off, the heart of the tree often remains. This part of the tree is very useful for many things, but when it burns, it sweats the sap and will drip flames. What if we made a weapon from this? We could set it on fire and drop it through a hole in the roof or throw it in through a window."

"Perhaps we could use the liquid to run under the door before setting it ablaze," another man offered.

"Sounds promising," David said. "Why don't the two of you work on this and report back to Dodo? Perhaps you could put the sap in a clay jar so that it would shatter and spread the fire when thrown."

"We would need a lot of sap," the soldier responded. "Also, it hardens over time, so we'd need to mix it with something."

"Let's talk more on this after the briefing," David concluded.

Dodo inquired again. "Any other ideas on how we could improve or speed up our breaching tactics?"

"Let's say we do find a way to produce what he says," said a large man. "The Philistines covered the windows and barricaded the doors. We need a way to make a hole in the wall or the roof. If we'd had sledge hammers and mattocks, we could have busted them in." The man spoke with a long draw, characteristic of Simeonites, many of whom were known for precision stone cutting.

Other suggestions were heard, followed by the mistakes and successes of the night's mission. The debriefing continued on into the late hours of the morning. David congratulated the men for a successful mission and Dodo dismissed them. The men were beyond tired and ready to get clean and catch up on some rest.

"What was the final count?" one of the men asked.

The others who'd started to leave the tent stopped, curious to hear the final number of enemy slain.

They all turned to the young runner who'd salted and strung the foreskins for drying during the long debriefing to prevent their rot and decay, the stench of which was already overpowering. Like the rest, the young Levite was still covered in black, though his arms were completely clean, having taken great efforts to wash the filth from his hands and arms after hanging the foreskins.

"I stopped counting at two hundred," Benaiah reported. "But it's at least that many."

The men around them erupted with shouts of excitement, elated to have been part of a nearly flawless victory over the enemy. They'd taken on and defeated a far larger fortified enemy position without a single loss of life. They, like the judges of old, had dealt a substantial blow to the enemies of Israel.

"Two-hundred!" Dodo exclaimed.

David smiled broadly as the older soldier placed his arm over his shoulder and shook him.

"So, shall we start calling you Prince David?" Dodo asked.

David shook his head. He was still covered head to toe in black grime, streaked with tan lines where sweat had run its course along his skin.

"Do I look like a prince to you?"

Dodo placed his hand on David's shoulder. "You're a great soldier and a great leader David. The men love you because it's clear that you love them. Life will start to get more comfortable for you now."

"I'm just getting married," David responded. "I have no intention of leaving the men."

"I know you don't, but some things are not within your control. Like it or not, you will be the king's son-in-law. There's no dishonor in taking the designated time to be with your new bride. Trust this old man when I tell you, you'll pay a high price for it later it if you don't."

"The men come first," David assured him. "I'll have time for my wife when I'm old. Like you."

"That's what I said," Dodo replied with a grimace. "And I've been paying for it ever since."

"I thought I'd leave before sunup tomorrow to report to Saul. The sooner we can dispose of those things, the better."

"We'll have everything in hand," Dodo assured him. "Go and claim your prize."

"Thank you," David responded. "None of this would have been possible without you."

The old soldier nodded, then turned and left the tent.

David and the men slept the remainder of day. He awoke with several hours of darkness remaining before sunrise. David saddled his horse, safely securing the brideprice that had come at such great risk to his men, then departed for Gibeah.

***

Saul sat impatiently listening to the disgruntled father argue his case. His son-in-law had sought and obtained a divorce not six months after marrying the man's oldest daughter. The man had agreed to work for him for seven years in exchange for his daughter's hand. Now, the young man was backing out of the deal. That's why you demand payment up front, Saul was thinking when one of his servants approached.

He waved the man forward, which caused the plaintiff to pause momentarily.

"Continue," Saul ordered the man as the servant approached and inclined to Saul's ear.

"David just arrived at the southern gate."

"By himself?" Saul asked as the plaintiff's words droned on.

"Yes my king. David reports that he has collected the brideprice for your daughter Michal."

Saul felt a rush of conflicted emotion. His plan had failed, but his hatred for the Philistines exceeded his disdain for the young warrior. He was both disappointed and elated. Little time had passed since his stated offer. How could he have produced such a large sum of enemy dead so quickly? Saul wondered. Bewildered, he turned to the guard.

"Excellent. Send him in," Saul instructed.

Again the plaintiff stopped his narrative.

"That's enough! I will send you both my decision!" Saul shouted. His mind had been made up before the man even began speaking. Still, he needed to maintain the appearance of neutrality.

When David appeared at the far end of the hall, Saul put his feelings for David aside, relieved as he was for a valid excuse to remove himself from the current squabble.

"David! Come forward by boy!" Saul shouted. "Now this is a suitor who makes good on his promises!"

David walked forward and knelt before the king laying the leather bag of enemy flesh before Saul.

"200, my king," David reported.

"200!" Saul shouted. "Double what was required. Come, stand David!" Saul approached and embraced the young commander. "Come," Saul said, ushering David out of the hall, "I want to hear how you accomplished this feat." Turning back to the guard, Saul instructed the man to collect the bag and follow them out of the hall.

"King Saul," the clerk interrupted. "What of the other parties? Shall they wait or come back tomorrow?"

Saul waved the man off.

"Tomorrow, have them return tomorrow," Ahinoam answered the clerk as she followed after the king and her soon-to-be son-in-law.

The guard approached the bag and knelt, opening the top to examine the contents. He instantly regretted the decision as a wave of putrid stench invaded his nostrils. He quickly cinched the bag closed and lifted it, holding it as far from his body as possible as he followed after the king.

Saul sat at a table in the center of the room and motioned for David to join him.

"Tell me everything," the king instructed.

Saul listened intently as David recounted the mission.

"It reminds me of our victory at Jabesh! Just exactly! Albeit, on a far smaller scale."

Though David had heard the story numerous times, Saul recounted the entire battle and how they'd marched throughout the night and surprised the Ammonites in their sleep around the besieged city.

"It's been nearly 28 years since then," the king said, reminiscent of his past glory. "I wasn't much older than you at the time. Can you imagine leading that many men? Without any prior preparation or training? You have trained soldiers. Imagine! Just taking men as they come to you from their farms and fields. Why, I myself had just been leading a team of oxen when I received the report that the city was besieged. Can you imagine?"

"Truly, I cannot," David answered, elated that Saul appeared to be in good spirits. "I've often marveled at the thought of it. There can be no doubt that God was with you."

"Truly. Truly He was!"

"It's why we could have faith that He would give us the victory as well, though, as you stated, on a much smaller scale."

"Oh, Michal will be elated to hear the news," Ahinoam said, trying to turn the men's attention back to more civilized matters. "It will take some months to plan the wedding. Do you think you can stay out of harm's way until then?"

"He is the commander of an eleph!" Saul said, dismissing the queen's suggestion.

"Well, if anything happens to him, you'll have to answer to Michal," she reminded the king. "And me!" she added with a scowl. "Congratulations on your victory, David. I know you will make a fine son-in-law," she said before departing the room.

"Keep doing what you are doing. I want to hear of more missions like this," the king instructed. "Our enemies must learn the price of attacking our people."

"Then, with your permission, I'd like to return to my men."

"Certainly! I won't keep you," Saul said before pausing briefly. "Are you sure you would not like to see your future bride before you return?"

"Many of my men have families they have not seen in months, my Lord. I should get back."

Saul straightened. "Go then and fight our enemies."

David bowed briefly, then departed before the king's disposition could turn sour. Pleasantly surprised by the interaction, David made his way to the garrison just outside of the palace walls, hoping to see some familiar faces before his return south.

Entering the headquarters, he was greeted by one of General Abner's advisors. He was an ancient-looking man with a limp who the men warmly referred to as Methuselah. Or was it his real name? David thought to himself. He'd never heard the man referred to as anything else.

"David! Surprised to see you here," said Methuselah. "What brings you?"

"Just stopping by to see if any of the princes or Abner are around."

"I'm afraid you just missed Abner. Abinadab and his men are on the coastline headed north. Jonathan went up to Dan and Malchishua is somewhere in between, near Jezreel, I think," Methuselah offered. "Abner has plans to leave with several elephs towards the Negev when Jonathan returns. Seems like every nation around us wants to pick a fight at the moment. I'd give anything to be your age again. I heard you were down at the border of blood, collecting skins. How's that going?"

"We're cleaning house," David remarked. "Pretty soon, we'll have them all converted, Lord willing."

"Good, good," he said in a long slow draw. "Show no mercy," the old-timer encouraged David, cursing the Philistines. "Kill every last one of them!"

David sensed the sincerity in the man's voice. There wasn't a man his age in Israel who hadn't fought in at least one battle with the Philistines. Many, if not most, of them bore a bitter hatred of any non-Israelite, but the eldest of them seemed to believe there was a special place in Sheol for the Philistine. David had heard it was best not to inquire of the man's history with the Philistines. There was good reason he still devoted his waking hours to the army rather than living out the remainder of his numbered days in peace. It was apparent that the worst of his scars were not the visible kind.

"Well, I'd best be headed back South then. We'll give them Sheol," David said before turning to leave.

He'd been excited to share his recent success with his like-minded mentor and soon-to-be brothers-in-law. It would have to wait. As he proceeded to the stables to collect his horse, he hoped that somehow he might happen upon or get a glimpse of the princess before his return to the front. If he waited till nightfall, he might gain a secret audience with her and no one would be any the wiser. He shook the idea from his head and mounted the horse.

Many of his men had not only wives but children at home. They didn't have the luxury of seeing their loved ones; he wouldn't betray them by prolonging his visit any longer than necessary. If he hurried, he would be back before nightfall.

LITTLE BEAR

1065, highlands of Ephraim, Israel

T he dark-haired boy sat up and rubbed his eyes as the night sky was beginning to turn from black to a dark shade of blue in the east. He'd always been an early riser, but this morning was different. He heard the hushed voices of his parents and saw the dim glow of candlelight flickering through the window to the room where he slept. He rose and walked to the doorway to investigate. His father and mother were in the yard. His mother handed his father a large leather satchel.

"There's two days of water and bread."

His father pulled his mother near and kissed her.

"Thank you, my love."

"I put the last of the lentils in there as well."

"I told you just the bread," her husband replied.

"You will need your strength, Dov and I will be fine," she said. She appeared to be struggling not to cry when she spoke the words. She turned her face away from him and he pulled her back into his embrace.

"I need to go now. Tell Dov I will be back soon."

"He will want to look for you."

"That's why I'm leaving before he'll have the chance."

She laid her face against his broad chest.

"If I'm not back within a month, go to Giloh. They will see that you and Dov are taken care of and you will be safer there."

She lifted her eyes to meet his.

"I don't want to hear any talk of that. Come back to us."

"I will," he said, then turned to leave.

She watched her husband until she could no longer see his dark silhouette, then sank to the ground and stared in the direction he'd left for what seemed like an eternity. The sun was already on the horizon when she returned to the house. As she crept to where her son slept, she wondered what life would be like if Huzziya didn't return, how hard they would have to work, and how Dov would learn to become a man like his father.

Saying a prayer, she asked for his protection. Her heart sank as her eyes moved to where her son should have been sleeping. She opened the curtain to confirm what her eyes and heart already suspected. The boy was gone.

***

The boy knew better than to alert his father to his presence. His mother would surely have his hide when they returned from whatever errand this was. Carefully, Dov followed his father from a distance, moving along the crest of the hillside and using the terrain to conceal himself as he'd been taught. It was difficult keeping up this way since his father was walking on much smoother, flatter ground. Before the sun rose, Dov was already drenched in sweat and exhausted. Still, it never occurred to him that he should turn back. Trying to keep his father in sight without detection had become difficult as they crossed over the hill country. His father certainly didn't seem to be taking the easy route. Where was he going? Dov had never been this way before.

His body gleamed with sweat. His legs burned from the strain of keeping up and walking farther than he had ever before. Urged on by both his curiosity and love for his father, he continued. What was the meaning of the conversation he'd heard between his mother and father that morning? He had to find out.

Eventually, after several hours of walking and long after the sun had reached its apex in the sky, he could hear a strange commotion ahead of them. When they finally crested the ridge that had obscured their view, the boy was astonished at what he saw.

He could see large groups of men gathered together in separate groups. Dov studied the groups of men in an effort to discern their activity. He crouched and laid down on the dirt behind a large rock to conceal himself.

Several groups of men to his left were hurling stones at small targets, approximately fifty cubits in front of them. Others were shooting arrows at longer distances. Still others were in formation, moving as a line with shields held in front of them, long spears protruding over each man's shoulder and thrusting forward with each step of the forward line. Another group was circled around two men appearing to demonstrate this same action. One group he found particularly intriguing was circled around two men who appeared to be wrestling in the center. They were moving very slowly and deliberately. Finally, his eyes moved again to the last assembly. The two instructors in the center of the group demonstrated various maneuvers using short wooden swords.

What was this, he thought. Never in his life had he seen so many people gathered together. Dov thought about the recent visit from his father's friend from the town called Giloh of Judah. His godfather, Ahi, as they all called him, was a soldier in Saul's army. He'd tried to convince Dov's father to join the ranks and serve with him. His father! Suddenly, Dov was reminded of his father. Where had he gone? In his amazement, Dov had lost track of him.

How long have I been watching? Dov thought to himself. Suddenly, he caught a glimpse of movement to his right. He looked and saw a large man sprinting towards him, spear in hand. Almost instantly, the man was upon him, the sharp point of his spear aimed at Dov's chest, the man's arms cocked to thrust it downward and pin him to the ground.

"Who are you boy? What are you doing here?" The man asked.

Dov stammered for a moment, frightened by the man. "I... I followed my father, he... he's down there!" Dov shouted back.

The man lowered the spear. "We could have killed you boy," the sentry shouted. "My archer might have if I hadn't stopped him."

For the first time, Dov realized that another man was now approaching from behind and carrying a large bow in one hand, an arrow with a small bronze tip positioned on the bow with his other.

"It looked like he was following that other fellow that approached on the road," the archer reported. "They let him in, so they must have recognized him." Nodding to Dov he added, "I thought he was a man from the distance."

The first sentry bent down and checked Dov for weapons.

"Get up," he instructed. "How old are you?"

"Fourteen," Dov replied.

Looking down at the tall, gangly youth, the sentry pondered momentarily what to do. "Awful tall for a fourteen-year-old," the sentry mused. "Come with me," he said finally.

Dov followed the man down the hill towards one of the groups of men. The sentry with the bow turned his attention outward, scanning the land before returning in the direction from which he'd come.

"What's your father's name," the sentry asked, glancing downward at Dov.

"Huzziya" he replied.

"The Hittite?" asked the sentry.

"Yes! Yes! You know him?" the boy responded, surprised by the sentry's response and apparent knowledge of his father.

"Know *of* him. Most every man here knows *of* him." The sentry paused, searching the various groups of men. When he found the one he was looking for, he pointed the tip of his spear. "Your father is a friend to one of our commanders. We'll start there. Those men, up ahead," he said, pointing his spear to a large group of men still several hundred cubits away, "those are his men."

"How did you recognize them from so far away?" Dov asked.

"Their commander is from the tribe of Judah. Do you see the lion there?" the sentry asked, pointing to a tall banner. "That's their standard."

Dov focused on the banner far across the field, then noticed for the first time various others. He wondered what they might represent. Apart from the lion, one bore an ox head, another a bounding hind, and another bore a wolf's head. Dov thought it fortuitous that his father's friend was apparently the commander of the group represented by a lion. The lion was significant to their people. His father had always told him it was a symbol of strength for the Hittite people.

He was now being led to a confrontation with his father. Dov was both excited and troubled. What would he say? What would he do? Dov began repeating a barely audible prayer as they walked.

"Please don't let him be angry, please don't let him be angry, please don't let him be angry…"

As they drew closer, Dov's fear of his father's wrath was replaced by excitement as he watched the men train. He'd always wanted to be a soldier. These men knew his father; he was a friend to their commander, Dov thought to himself. He realized there was much about his father he didn't know.

The men with the lion standard were training in hand-to-hand tactics. Working pairs, each man executed a striking maneuver on his counterpart, who would block, then follow up with a counter strike.

As they approached one of the pairs, the sentry asked, "Where is Ahi?"

The two men stopped their exercise and examined those around them. A moment later, one of them pointed to two men walking amongst the group.

"There!" he said.

Dov instantly recognized both men. The two walked among the troops, examining each man's form as they executed the maneuver on their counterpart, making corrections when necessary.

"Thanks," the sentry said as he and Dov approached the two instructors.

They paused as Ahi began addressing the men.

"Alright! Circle up!" Ahi shouted, waiting for the men to direct their attention towards him in the center of the group as the pairs in the middle crouched or took a knee. "If you learn these basic principles, you will substantially increase your likelihood of survival. The good thing is you don't need to know a lot of different ways to kill your enemy, so long as you can master a few simple techniques and execute them well. The next technique we'll be focusing on is the takedown."

Ahi turned and placed a hand on Dov's father.

"Many of you already know my friend here, but for those who don't, you've heard me speak of the Hittite warrior who saved my life at the battle of Jabesh. His name is Huzziya and he is to be given the same respect and attention you give me. I've persuaded him to leave his peaceful home and join our ranks. What he has to teach you will keep you alive. Understand?"

"AHU!" the men shouted in unison.

"Huzzy here is going to demonstrate," Ahi announced.

The sentry recognized the poor timing of his arrival and pulled the boy aside to avoid interrupting the commander's demonstration. Dov watched as the two men faced off and assumed a fighting stance. His father launched forward, dropping his forward knee to the ground, seizing Ahi behind his front leg and pulling it to his chest, then drove his shoulder into Ahi's abdomen as he lifted the leg, forcing the Ahi to the ground with a thud. Ahi flung his arms out as if to slap the ground as his upper body struck the dirt.

"Now! Make sure to execute the fall we instructed earlier and take it easy on your training partners. We don't need to lose anyone to injury. Not today," Ahi shouted from the ground.

Huzziya reached down and grabbed Ahi's wrist, then lifted him to his feet.

"Now he will demonstrate a bit slower. Watch as he drops his forward knee and sweeps his rear leg around. If I were to step back, he would be able to regain his fighting stance, rising to his feet again."

The two men demonstrated the point, Huzziya shooting forward and then back to his fighting stance as Ahi stepped backward out of his reach.

"As I shoot forward, I'm going to grab behind the knee and pull his leg to me, disrupting Ahi's balance," Huzziya announced in his thick Hittite accent.

Dov watched his father perform the maneuvers, which had long become second nature. The soldiers in the circle around them watched with avid amusement as Huzziya demonstrated the technique several more times.

"Alright. If there aren't any questions, you men can get to it," Ahi instructed.

When the men began practicing the maneuver on one another, the sentry approached his father and Ahithophel.

"Ahi," the sentry called, "your friend has a visitor," he announced as they approached.

The two men turned to the approaching sentry.

"Dov!" Huzziya exclaimed. "What are you doing here? Is everything alright?" he asked in a low but excited tone as he stepped towards his son.

"I.. I followed you," was all the boy could say. Dov could feel his face turning hot, the tension in his throat growing with each second his father stood silent.

Graciously, Ahithophel interrupted.

"It's good to see that courage runs strong in your family!" Ahithophel exclaimed, grasping Huzziya's shoulder. "It's good to see you Dov," Ahi exclaimed as he placed his arm around the youth, "and that you are growing into your nickname! You'll be as tall as your father in another year or so."

The boy smiled. "Yes sir," he replied. "Where is Eliam?"

"Don't change the subject son," his father said sternly. "Who is with your mother?"

"No one," Dov responded as he looked to the ground.

"Why don't you go get a drink? You've come a long way," Ahithophel said, pointing to some men drawing water from a nearby well.

Dov looked to his father, who nodded his approval before starting off towards the well.

"Well, my friend, that's one tenacious young man you have there," Ahithophel said.

Huzziya shook his head. "What am I to do with him?"

"Well, he's here now. Now that I've finally got you here, I'd hate for you to leave. Does he know the way back?"

Huzziya was silently weighing the options. The last thing he wanted was for one of these men to be burdened with escorting his son back home. How had Dov followed him for the past eight hours without being noticed? Huzziya wondered.

"What do you say we put him to work?' Ahi finally suggested. "Dov has more hand-to-hand training than most of these men. He could probably best half of the grown men here. Am I right?"

Huzziya looked around. "No," he said stoically. "Far more than half."

Ahithophel laughed. It was the deep, sincere laugh that Huzziya had missed for many years. Huzziya didn't think there was anything funny about what he'd said, but there was something about Ahithophel's laughter that always eased his spirits and, as always, broke Huzziya's composure. He smiled as he shook his head.

"His mother is going to kill me."

"No doubt about that. Why don't we have him help with the demonstrations? He can help you inspect the men as well. It'll allow me to go see how things are developing."

"I don't want him to see the battle."

"You know we need every man we can spare. Eliam is on reconnaissance and we need all the help we can get right now. Most of these men know nothing about this kind of fighting; they are farmers and shepherds nine months out of the year."

"He is only fourteen," Huzziya replied, "but I suppose we weren't much older at Jabesh."

"I understand your concern, but what other option is there? We can't very well send him back home right now. Saul could order the attack at any moment." Ahithophel paused and considered the problem momentarily. "Look, what if we have him stay in the rear? He can help provide water and aid for the wounded."

Huzziya watched as his only son returned from the well. He knew the gore and terror that his son would be exposed to, even at the rear, but at this point there was little else that could be done. The enemy's reconnaissance could intercept him or he could get lost if sent home on his own. They were a long way from home and it would be impossible for him to make it back before dark.

"Son of Baal," Huzziya cursed. After a long pause, he came to the conclusion there was no better option. "Go do what you need to do. He and I will take it from here."

242

"You don't know how much I appreciate having you here. Thank you my friend," Ahithophel said before departing.

Huzziya turned to his son.

"Well, you're here now, so we're going to make the most of it. Your mother will know where you are. She'll be worried, but there's nothing we can do about that for now. You're going to help me train these men," Huzziya said. "So, let's get to work."

"Yes, Father," Dov responded, trying to conceal a smile.

The father and son returned to the center of the group as the men finished their last drill.

"Alright then," Huzziya said loudly for all to hear. "Tell me, what's the next thing they need to know," Huzziya asked his son.

"Well, they just learned how to get the opponent to the ground, now they should learn how to keep him there or disarm him," the youth replied.

"Or kill him," Huzziya added.

"Yes, or kill him."

"Show them," Huzziya instructed.

The men around them stood to see the demonstration as Dov squared off against his father. He executed the same single leg take down his father had just demonstrated, then used his weight to flatten the older man to the ground. Dov created just enough space to press one knee into his father's diaphragm with one hand on his father's shoulder and the other on the opposite knee, effectively preventing him from rolling in either direction or alleviating the pressure on his torso.

"Do you see?" Huzziya asked, scanning the men around them. Several nodded their affirmation.

The two Hittites stood to their feet and squared off again.

"Show them again!"

For the next hour, the two Hittites continued their instruction of the most basic maneuvers used to control an opponent and maintain superior positioning in hand-to-hand combat. At the end of the hour, a new group of fifty men cycled through as the previous group made its way to more complicated team and section training stations.

The training was interrupted when several successive blasts from a shofar echoed across the valley, alerting the men to move into formation.

The two men Dov was instructing scrambled to their feet. Dov turned to see his father already at his side.

"You will stay back with the men, protecting the supplies and tending the wounded. I don't want you near the battle; is that understood?" Huzziya said sternly.

Dov nodded.

"Do you understand?"

"Yes, Father," Dov responded.

Huzziya pulled his son's head to his chest and kissed the top of his head.

"Go," his father instructed, pointing towards the tents that would serve as the aid station. "I need to get ready and join the men."

Huzziya watched as his son made his way toward the tent before joining the others already donning their armor, then proceeded to the formation. As he made his way to the front, he joined Ahithophel under the lion's head standard.

The now middle-aged commander smiled as he approached. It had been years and many gray hairs since they'd last fought together.

"Once more, my friend," Ahi said.

"Ein breira!" Huzzy responded.

"Ein breira!" Ahi and those around them shouted in unison.

***

Abner stood before them, stoically watching as the last of the men hurried into formation.

The captains sounded off down the line as each eleph reported ready for battle.

Abner called the commanders forward and brought them up to speed on the minor changes in the situation. There would be no changes to the order of battle briefed earlier in the day. There was no observed change in the enemy's positions or makeup, and the sun was moving into a favorable position. Till this point, they'd been held in reserve as Abner commanded the battle from the hilltop while Jonathan's forces fought in the valley below. Abner was confident the Philistines had not yet revealed their full strength. Reports of cavalry in the area made him especially leery of employing his reserves too soon, but now a downhill flanking maneuver from the west would be aided by the setting sun.

The captains returned to their elephs. The bugler sounded the order to march and the entire front line of the division simultaneously stepped forward. Several men vomited, before straightening back into an upright position. They moved to the west of the valley and into position cresting the ridge that had concealed them to this point. Down in the bowl that was the Jezreel valley, they could see Jonathan's forces clashing shield to shield with the enemy below.

A long horn blast filled the air and the forest of spears along the front line lowered into horizontal position. Men pissed and soiled themselves without slowing the march. A second blast set the men at a quicker pace and the Israelite line sped toward the foe. Across the battlefield, Philistines along the western side of the battlefront began to adjust to the approaching Israelites, shifting and reorienting as quickly as possible as their attackers charged down the hill.

Another blast sounded from the bugler and the swish of arrows sounded over the Israelites' heads as their archers released a volley high up and over the attacking front line. The arrows darkened the sky above their line like a cloud passing over the battlefield before raining down on the enemy line ahead of them.

No sooner had their arrows landed than a volley of enemy arrows was returned, rising high from somewhere in the Philistine rear and over the open space toward the attacking Israelite division. Huzziya and Ahithophel commanded the men to quicken their pace and the front line launched into a sprint, closing the distance between themselves and the enemy. The Philistine arrows came down on those in the rear of the formation who weren't able to keep up with the pace of those at the front, but most landed within the unoccupied space between the advancing heavy infantry and the archers in the rear.

Less than one hundred cubits away from the enemy's spearpoints the attacking Israelites slowed their pace and tightened up their formation as a second volley of arrows was loosed by the Israelite archers.

"TSAHV!"[2]Ahithophel shouted. The men instantly raised their shields overhead to protect themselves from stray friendly arrows as they advanced. From under his shield, Ahithophel peered at the front line of Philistines just ahead.

Focused on the approaching Israelites, the Philistines held their shields tightly to their front. The Israelite arrows came down hard on their exposed shoulders and helmets. He could hear the clatter of several Israelite arrows falling short of their intended target.

"PANIM!"[3] Ahi ordered. The command was echoed by the men as the men lowered their shields toward the enemy to their front, still reeling and attempting to recompose following the onslaught of arrows.

The Israelite force smashed into the Philistine's western flank. With each step, the line of spears across the Israelite front punched forward, then recoiled as the line advanced.

Infantrymen in the Philistines' third and fourth ranks launched javelins overhead at the Israelite line. Ahi raised his shield just in time to receive a javelin meant for his face. The tip of the javelin pierced the upper portion of his shield and cut his left cheek. Unable to hold the shield upright with the long javelin deeply embedded in the metal plating, Ahi allowed the forward rank to step ahead of him as a soldier from the second rank filled his place along the front. Ahi looked right and left across the line of battle. They'd broken the enemy line and were now in their midst.

Ahi piked his spear into an injured Philistine, slashing wildly at the legs of the advancing Israelites, then drew his sword and removed the man's head before attempting to dislodge the javelin from his shield.

---

[2] Hebrew for turtle

[3] Hebrew for face.

Planting the base of the shield in the dirt, he chopped down on the shaft of the javelin with his sword.

Ahi looked right and left before rejoining the line when he heard the blast of a Philistine trumpet from the rear of the Philistine line. Turning to his right, he saw Philistine cavalry approaching fast. As the columns behind him turned and braced for the attacking enemy, those to his front continued their assault, unaware of the horsemen bearing down on them.

"ECHELON RIGHT! ENEMY CAVALRY! ECHELON RIGHT!" Ahi shouted as he ran along the rear of the advancing forward echelons shouting the command.

Ahi alone stood in the gap that had formed between the advancing front and the next eleph of advancing Israelites, which had stopped to brace for the impact of the approaching horsemen.

Ahi sprinted towards their northernmost flank, shouting to alert them of the approaching cavalry, his voice failing over the din of battle. Taking several men by the rear plate of their armor, he turned them toward the approaching horsemen. The men repeated his command as the enemy horsemen smashed into the unsuspecting column and raked across its exposed back.

Ahi held his shield above his shoulder in an attempt to protect several soldiers as the blades of the horsemen slashed along the rear of the line. The enemy's blades shrieked as they raked across his shield. The still advancing line stepped forward, leaving him exposed. The inside of his shield smashed his face suddenly as a sprinting horse collided with his body, knocking him hard into the dirt. His vision blurred, ears ringing, Ahi rolled onto his side to raise himself when a Philistine javelin pierced his leg and into the dirt below him.

Ahi gasped in pain as he sat up and braced the javelin with both hands. He tried in vain to dislodge it from his thigh as he looked up to see a Philistine rider approaching fast with his spear poised to deal the final blow to the now defenseless Israelite.

For a moment, time slowed as Ahi watched the rider bearing down on him. A more perfect target never presented itself Ahi thought in the fraction of a second that passed as he saw himself through the eyes of the approaching enemy. Then suddenly, from the rear of the line to Ahithophel's left, a soldier sprang forward into the space between him and the approaching doom. The soldier knelt and simultaneously planted the butt of his spear into the dirt, raising its point toward the enemy horse, which was impaled as it drove into the planted spear, snapping the shaft as it sank deep into the animal's breast.

The horse smashed into the soldier, crushing him as its rider toppled head-first into the dirt at Ahi's feet. Ahi watched, helpless as the rear line of Israelites adjusted and filled the gap to protect the flank and backs of their advancing forward lines. A moment later, he was swallowed up by the advancing rear columns. Several men noticed the injured and exposed Israelite commander and moved to withdraw him from harm's way.

A soldier knelt down and examined Ahithophel's leg carefully. He wrapped the leg tightly above the wound as several others held him to the ground. The soldier then placed his foot on Ahithophel's leg at the ligature and wrenched the javelin free as blood spurted from the wound. Ahi clung to his consciousness through clenched teeth as the soldier knelt and packed the wound with linen cloth before binding it tightly with a leather belt. He directed four nearby Israelites to place Ahithophel atop two discarded shields and remove him to camp before disappearing to aid another wounded Israelite.

As the soldiers began hoisting him from the ground, Ahi pushed them away.

"STOP, STOP," he commanded.

The soldiers pulled back when Ahi stretched his hand upward toward them. One of the men hoisted him up on his uninjured leg. Blood poured from the puncture as he hobbled towards the crumpled soldier who'd been his salvation.

There, half covered by the Philistine warhorse, lay Huzziya.

Ahi gasped as he fell to his hands and knees in the dirt. His heart sank as he examined the broken body of his friend, searching for any sign of life that might restore his hope.

"We'll bring him sir," a soldier said as he pulled Ahithophel up from the ground, still clinging to Huzziya's body. Three others seized the commander and lifted him, pulling his arms free from the lifeless body of his friend. The men carried Ahithophel to the crest of the hill where other wounded were being staged until they could be safely taken back to camp. The leader of the small team promised to return with the body of the Hittite and they departed as a physician moved to inspect and triage the wounded.

Eventually, he was placed in the shade of an open tent alongside other wounded men further from the battlefield. Ahi sat up and examined the dressing on his wound. A slow trickle of blood ran down the side of his leg into the dirt below.

As he lay there among the wounded and dying, it seemed so odd that the battle continued only a short distance away. He remembered the soldier's promise and hoped that it was a lie meant to comfort a wounded, potentially dying man. Now was no time to remove the dead. He looked around to the other men in the tent, some wailing in agony, some weeping in despair over the loss of a limb. He resolved within himself to wait quietly for assistance.

There were several attendants moving about the dying and wounded. A Levite priest walked the rows of wounded men, praying over them, stopping now and again to kneel down and speak with some. A physician attended by two sturdy female aids triaged the wounded, stopping to treat those in the most urgent need of care. Several other more delicate women spooned water to the thirsty and washed the dirt and blood from broken and mangled limbs.

Ahithophel laid his head back against a discarded robe that had been rolled up and placed there for a pillow by one of the soldiers. He shut his eyes and attempted to pray, struggling to find the words.

"Welcome Huzziya into your presence Lord. He is my friend," he said as his eyes burned with tears. "Permit me to live and I will care for his family as my own."

Ahi opened his eyes to find the priest sitting crosslegged beside him in the dirt, quietly saying a prayer of his own. A moment later, the priest lowered his eyes to meet Ahi's. The old Levite's demeanor displayed nothing but compassion and empathy.

"You're an officer," the old man observed, offering him a drink of water to wet his dry lips.

Ahithophel nodded before accepting the cup and propping himself up on his elbows before taking a long sip.

"A good one, I gather," the priest said, examining Ahithophel's wound and blood spattered armor.

Ahi was silent.

"My name is Ahimelech. By what name are you called?"

"Ahi."

The priest looked at him quizzically.

"Ahithophel," he confessed.

"Ah!" the priest exclaimed, "surely it is providence that the siblings of foolishness and royalty should meet here this day. I love to know how people come about their names. Tell me Ahithophel, how it is you became a brother to folly."

Ahi was becoming annoyed with the priest. "Just say your prayers and move on. I'm sure there are others here who'd love to talk with you."

Ignoring Ahi's suggestion, the priest continued. "I've found that dying men tend to reflect more on the foolishness of their past rather than the good they have done. Many times we must be reminded of the good we have done. It is why our forefathers erected monuments of God's faithfulness. They are constant reminders that Yahweh is a forgiving father. He knows that we are but dust. Tell me Ahi, are you right with Him?"

"I believe I am," Ahithophel said through clenched teeth. "Though I am not pleased with Him at the moment."

"That's understandable," the priest replied. "Even Job, the most righteous of men, was broken and suffered greatly. He who created us is able to use the broken pieces to serve a greater purpose."

The priest was briefly interrupted by one of the large female aids giving instructions to several young litter bearers.

Ahithophel looked to see the team of young boys hoisting the limp body of a soldier onto their makeshift carrier before taking their positions at the four corners of the litter and lifting the body. They carried the slain man off to where the dead were being collected, to be later identified and delivered or recovered by their family or tribesmen.

Ahi recognized one of the boys in an instant.

"Do you see that dark-skinned boy in the front? The strong one?" Ahi asked the priest.

"I do," Ahimelech replied.

"That is the son of the man who died that I may live. How do I explain to him that God will bring good from this?"

"Ah," the priest responded. "It is a heavy burden you undertake if you seek to explain the all-knowing and omnipotent. We needn't explain it. It is true whether we choose to believe it or not. How can we justify when we know not the outcome? Do not presume that you must make excuses for the Almighty. He does not require that we plead his cause, but that we trust and obey."

"Trust?" Ahi asked. His face contorted as he tried desperately to maintain his composure.

"Yes my friend. At least your friend has you to look after his son, woe unto the man who falls and has no such friend."

Ahi was spent. He lay his head back against the robe as the tears came.

"I will caution you before I leave you in peace Captain," the priest said as he stood. "Sometimes the deepest wounds cannot be seen and often take the longest to heal. The loss of a friend is a grievous wound indeed, but it too will heal with the right medicine. I can only share what I have to give, but I have found healing in the service of others."

SHORT LEASH

1065 BC, Gibeah, Israel

The two men circled the arena facing each other, each calculating the other's movements. Bent low to protect their legs from an attack, each man's left arm hung low in front of him with the palm towards the opponent, ready to defend an attack against the exposed forward leg.

"Time to see how soft my sister has made you," Jonathan said as he faked a movement towards his younger opponent.

David slapped his hand away.

"Don't worry! We've been doing plenty of wrestling," David fired back as he lunged for his opponent's arm, barely missing it.

Jonathan countered by pushing David's head down and to the right, instantly wrapping his right arm around David's neck as David went to grab Jonathan's exposed left leg.

Grabbing his right wrist with his left arm and straightening his back, Jonathan tightened the choke around David's neck, pressing his forearm tight against his throat. David's back arched upwards in a vain attempt to release the pressure on his neck and spine. A moment later, he slapped the older man's thigh and the tension loosened.

After catching his breath, the two men squared off again. This time, David kept his head back and erect to avoid falling prey to another choke. He raised his arms slightly, hoping to tempt a low attack from the more experienced and stronger opponent. Jonathan's left hand shot up towards David's head. He recoiled, straightening his back as Jonathan went low for David's forward leg. As David flattened his chest on his opponent's back, he attempted to loop his left arm under Jonathan's right, when he was driven to the ground. Jonathan pressed his left shoulder into David's abdomen, flattening him on the ground as he stepped around David's legs and pressed harder into David's rib cage.

Jonathan could hear the labored breath of his opponent as he intensified the pressure and swung his right leg over David's and mounted him. David rolled to his right side in a miscalculated attempt to avoid the maneuver, when Jonathan set the choke by pressing David's upturned left shoulder into the left side of his neck while simultaneously pulling up on the right side of David's neck with his own left arm and hand, now secured firmly in the crease of his right elbow. David let out a croak as he strained to resist the submission.

A moment later, David patted Jonathan's shoulder with his free hand as silvery dots began to appear in his fading vision. Jonathan immediately released the choke and stood.

David rolled to his back and gasped for breath. His face was red from exertion. Both men were completely drenched and drained from the day's training but elated. David smiled up at his mentor. Both men and their onlookers laughed. It had been a short and decisive victory.

"Every time!" David exclaimed.

"Don't feel too bad," he heard from a bench to the side of the arena. "He's been doing that to me for over ten years now," said Abner as he stepped into the sparring arena.

"One of these days," David said, as he stood.

"You should know better than to fight on another man's terms," Abner replied.

David tilted his head slightly, not sure what the general was referring to.

"You don't let your opponent choose the terms of the battle. You pick your battles to put your strengths against the enemy's weakness. Like you did with Goliath," the general explained.

David looked down, his hands on his knees, still panting from the earlier exertions.

"I guess I never really thought about it that way," David admitted. "I knew he had a big head and I was good at slinging rocks. More than that, he'd cursed the Almighty."

"Well you'd better start using *your* head. I'm starting to question your decision-making abilities," Abner said as he raised an eyebrow. "For instance, you're down here sweating with another man while you're supposed to be on your honeymoon. Haven't you had enough training down in no-man's-land?"

"Is there such a thing?" David responded.

"Good answer," the General replied. "I take it you've been training with Dodai. Keep it up and you may yet get the better of him, eventually."

"He is coming along very well," Jonathan replied. "His swordsmanship is exceptional."

"Excellent!" Abner exclaimed. "He will need it for his new position."

David straightened. "New position?"

"Saul has decided to make you captain of the Guard," Abner explained.

David straightened, unsure what to say.

"Don't worry. You've met Seth already. You needn't be too concerned with a man like that at your side. Keep training hard and learn from him and your mentor here. Don't let the position go to your head and you'll do just fine."

"Thank you Abner, this is a great honor. I won't let you down."

"No. I don't think you will," Abner replied. "May the Lord go before you."

"Thank you General," David replied again.

Abner nodded in reply. "Carry on," he said as he departed the arena.

"Congratulations," Jonathan said. "You'll be working with the best."

"I thought you and Yuval were the best," David replied.

Jonathan smiled. "I'll let you be the judge after you've trained with Seth for a while. This will be good for you," Jonathan reassured him. "Back here at the palace, you'll get to work on your languages, which, let's be honest, could use a lot of work."

"Hey, I speak better Greek than most Philistines and I haven't heard anyone here who can speak better Moabite."

"Ha! That's not saying much. Philistine Greek is hardly proper Greek and the Moabites just speak an adulterated goat-Hebrew. You're a prince now. You're going to be dealing with a lot more than just Philistines and nomads. The men of the guard come from all over, Ammon, Edom, Crete, and Zobah. Every last one of them has earned their place, but make no mistake," Jonathan cautioned, "they are loyal to no one but my father. You'll have to be on your best behavior."

"I'm sure I don't know what you mean," David said with a smile.

"Yeah, well consider yourself warned. Breaking the rules for your men's welfare will get you a long way with the army out there, but here with the Guard, just know that everything you do is going to make its way back to my father."

"Noted. So how do I gain their trust? How do I lead them?"

"Be the best. Train hard and don't give them any slack," the prince responded. "At least not for a while. Not till they've earned it. Just as before, be humble. Don't let your past successes go to your head. The guard basically runs itself. Watch how they do things and see how you can make improvements. Seth will help."

GODFATHER

1065 BC, Giloh, Judah, Israel

The party of three traveled quietly as they trudged along in the midday sun. Huzziya's funeral had been small and somber. Ahithophel had insisted Huzziya's widow return to Giloh with him, where they would be cared for. As for himself, the veteran wondered how exactly he would provide for so many mouths now that he was a cripple. Even now, his godson led the donkey on which he sat, unable to walk as the boy and his mother trudged along.

Somehow, he would find a way to provide, and somehow, he would walk again.

As they approached the city, Ahithophel felt a pang of shame, shame that he was returning home with the assistance of the family left behind by the man who'd twice saved his life. The city guards stood at attention as he approached the gates to Giloh.

His wife, daughter-in-law, and granddaughter were among those to welcome him home. With some difficulty, he dismounted the colt.

"This is Hebat", he said, introducing the widow to her new family. "And we call this young man 'Dov' after his father." Ahithophel placed his hand on his wife's shoulder. "This is my wife, Naomi," he said, then introduced his daughter-in-law, Tirsa, and granddaughter, Bathsheba.

Peeking out from behind her mother's gown, the beautiful dark-haired girl stared silently up at the impressive and somber young man. Naomi and Tirsa embraced Hebat and Dov, kissing them and welcoming them to Giloh.

Ahithophel ambled along, ushering his new guests towards their new home inside the city. All along the streets, shows of respect and admiration for the city's most beloved warrior could be seen. Each one of them felt like a dagger to his heart as he walked beside his friend's widow and fatherless son.

When they arrived at the home, Naomi ushered the guests in and showed them to their room.

"It's not much," Naomi said apologetically.

The stoic widow thanked her sincerely and began the business of unpacking the few belongings she'd decided to bring from their home in the wilderness.

Dov floated around the house, curiously examining the new abode and its amenities. He had to admit that it was a substantial improvement from their home in the mountains, though as he looked out the open window into the city, he longed to return home. His thoughts were suddenly broken by the sound of clattering in the adjacent room. Dov moved to the doorway and saw Ahi struggling to lift himself. A line of fresh blood ran down from the wound in his leg.

Instinctively, Dov moved to his aid.

"There are bandages in the pantry," Naomi said as she moved to retrieve them, then knelt next to her husband as Dov helped to lift his leg so that the old bandages could be removed and new ones applied.

"Thank you," she said. "It will be nice having you here."

Dov nodded and stood to his feet before hoisting Ahithophel off the ground.

Back on his feet, the veteran refused any further assistance and hobbled over to the den and sat down. Naomi began showing Hebat her way around the kitchen. Dov watched as his mother took it all in. With his mother distracted, he turned his attention to the man before him and sat down at his feet.

"I want to serve as my father did," Dov said. "I want to be a soldier."

Ahithophel had expected this was coming. He turned his attention to the youth whose eyes steadily returned his gaze. The young man bore a striking resemblance to his father.

"Will you help me?" Dov asked.

WANTED

1064 BC, Gibeah, Israel

And Saul spoke to Jonathan his son and to all his servants, that they should kill David. But Jonathan, Saul's son, delighted much in David.
I Samuel 19:1

Another sleepless night, Saul thought as he kicked the blanket off of his legs and sat up. He stood and went to the balcony overlooking the palace courtyard and Gibeah below. It was a clear and beautiful night with more stars than one could count in a lifetime. King Saul breathed in the cool night air trying to clear his mind.

Still the thoughts assaulted his mind one after another like a pack of ravenous hyenas.

Ahinoam was not pleased with his recent decision to deny David the year long reprieve from military service which was typically granted to newlyweds. She was not convinced when he'd explained that service in the King's Guard was not regarded the same way as service in the Army, though Saul considered his justification particularly creative. With David close by, he could keep a closer eye on him and put a stop his growing list of military accomplishments.

His spies, mostly members of the foreign guard, were keeping a close eye on David, though his plan had partly backfired. Despite his hopes, David was spending almost as much time with the princes as he spent with the princess. On top of that, the Queen, who'd always been his avid supporter, was now at odds. Saul had never felt quite so isolated.

"Just another family member questioning your leadership. How they all love him."

The words of Samuel drifted back into memory. "The Lord has torn the kingdom of Israel from you today, and has given it to a neighbor of yours, who is better than you."

"Better than me?" Saul growled. "Did you not choose me? I did not want this. You did! You set me up!" Saul shouted into the night.

"Better than me…" Saul said again to himself.

The chorus of the people rang yet again in his ears, "Saul has slain his thousands and David his ten thousands." He could see David sitting atop Jonathan's horse, wearing the royal robe and armor as they'd entered Gibeah. He could see Jonathan, his eldest son and heir, training the young man, spending every waking moment with him, Jonathan, who'd disobeyed his order at Michmash and challenged his authority. Even Abner, his oldest friend and confidant was pleased with the decision to bring David back to the palace.

"They conspire to do you harm."

"They do conspire," Saul thought. "My own son, the heir to the throne… my neighbor!" Saul said aloud as he paced the floor of his room. "He considers himself too righteous, too holy to do the deed himself. He would use David to usurp me. To kill me!"

"Disloyal traitors. There is no one you can trust."

Saul's mind swirled with conspiracies. "Which of them has Samuel chosen to replace me? It must be Jonathan," Saul mused.

"No. No, he would be the rightful heir," Saul said as he paced the floor. "Samuel said the kingdom would be stripped from me… it must be an outsider. David has corrupted his mind. He has tricked Jonathan in some way. Surely it is David. David is the one. *He* must be eliminated," Saul continued aloud. "I must separate them. I will isolate David and strike him before he is able to strike me."

***

Rebecca awoke to a familiar scene. Her husband, the prince, was studying his own transcribed copy of the scrolls of Moses by the light of a small lamp, a kettle of hot water over the fire, and the first rays of sunlight peeking over the eastern ridge. She stoked the fire and took some of the tea leaves from a clay jar and dropped them into a cup. She was thankful for her husband's morning routine since she needn't prepare the fire or wait for the water to heat before pouring the steaming hot water onto the leaves. She left them to steep and walked over to her husband wrapping her arms around him and laying her head upon his back and shoulder as he peered at the scriptures before him.

"Good morning," she whispered.

"Good morning, my love," Jonathan replied.

"What are you reading this morning?"

Jonathan hesitated. He straightened and pulled Rebecca onto his lap. Pointing to a line in the scripture, he began to read.

"'Is anything too hard for the Lord? At the time appointed, I will return unto thee, according to the time of life, and Sarah shall have a son.'" Then turning up from the scriptures, he touched her face. "Sarah was well past the age of bearing children and Abraham was an old man when God gave them Isaac."

Rebecca sighed and stood.

Jonathan grabbed her hand and stood.

"I have to believe that God will give us children if we are patient. We must trust that His timing is better than our own," Jonathan said as he pulled her into his embrace.

She lay her head against his broad chest as he wrapped her in his arms. Even Abraham, their patriarch had done as most other men would under the circumstances; she could hardly fault her husband if he chose to do the same. It was hardly uncommon for princes and kings to have many wives.

"Any other prince would have taken another wife by now."

"Perhaps," Jonathan responded, "but there is not another prince on earth with a wife comparable to mine."

Rebecca smiled as her eyes began to well with tears.

Their embrace was interrupted by a knock at the door.

Jonathan moved to open it slightly as Rebecca concealed herself from view.

"Prince Jonathan, King Saul is calling for you, your brothers, and the commanders," the guard announced.

"Any idea what this is about?" Jonathan asked.

"I am not sure, but he specifically instructed us not to inform David, so if that tells you anything...."

Jonathan disappeared into the room to remove his robe. He donned an ephod and girdled his sword.

"What's going on?" The princess asked.

"I don't know, but don't worry, I'll update you when I return."

Jonathan kissed her and joined the guard waiting outside. As they proceeded across the courtyard and into the hall, the guard turned towards the king's chamber, away from the great hall.

"Where are you going?" Jonathan asked.

"The king wanted everyone in his private chambers."

Jonathan began to feel a knot in his stomach as they approached the king's room.

Seth opened the door as they approached and Jonathan saw his brothers and Abner already inside. Jonathan paused outside of view and leaned close to the large guard.

"What is going on?" he whispered.

"He's been up all night. I swear he hasn't slept a wink in three days. I could hear him pacing back and forth, talking to himself..."

Seth's report was interrupted by a shout from within the chamber.

"JONATHAN!" Saul called from within. "Get in here!"

The prince entered the room and Seth began to pull the heavy door shut behind him.

"You too!" Saul shouted as he motioned for one of the other guards to replace him outside.

"No one comes within 50 cubits of this room," the king commanded before the door was shut. The king's eyes were wide and red with fatigue.

Jonathan looked around the room to see the king's closest circle of advisors and guards, with the exception of David.

"There is a snake in our midst," Saul said in a low voice with his back turned to the men in the room. His knuckles were pressed into the table in front of him.

The men around the room cast glances to their right and left.

"It has come to my ears that the son of Jesse, my own son-in-law, aims to usurp my Kingdom. As you know, he has a great following among the people, so we must be shrewd in our handling of this matter. I want him eliminated. I don't care how you do it so long as it looks like an accident. I, I am the Lord's Anointed. I do not want the people to know that it was by my hand. Is that understood?" Saul asked, still with his back turned.

The room was silent.

Saul spun around, "DO YOU UNDERSTAND?" he shouted.

"Saul, from where did you receive this report?" Abner questioned.

"NEVER MIND THAT! I gave you an order. Do you want to continue to serve as general of the armies of Israel or do you want to go back to the plow?"

"We understand," Abner said. "I will see to the details so that your hands may remain clean. Is there anything else?"

"That will be all," Saul responded and moved to the balcony.

Abner motioned for the other attendants to leave ahead of him.

"I'll meet you all in the hall. Not a word of this to anyone. Wait for me there," Abner commanded in a low voice before returning to the king's chamber.

Jonathan and the others proceeded as directed to the great hall.

His brothers moved quickly to either side of him.

"What have I missed?" Abinadab asked.

"Nothing that I'm aware of," Jonathan responded.

"Surely David would never betray Father, never!" Malchishua whispered.

"I know," Jonathan responded. "Let's hear what Abner has to say," Jonathan said, careful not to voice his growing fear that their father was losing his mind.

Abner joined them almost as soon as they'd arrived.

"Are we alone?" he asked.

"The cooks and other servants will start preparing breakfast soon, but apart from the guard, there's not typically anyone stirring this early. I ordered the entries guarded," Seth responded.

"Good. I wasn't able to get anything else from Saul. Someone tell me where is this coming from. Why has no one reported this to me?" Abner demanded.

Jonathan broke the silence. "I don't think anyone knows, I spend more time with David than anyone. I tell you, the man is blameless. Unless someone can prove to me otherwise, I tell you it is a lie."

"Who would lie about this? For what reason?" Abner asked.

Jonathan turned to Seth. "Tell them what you told me."

"The king hasn't been sleeping. He didn't sleep at all last night. The men reported his behavior to me so I personally stood watch for much of the night. When I asked if he wanted me to summon David or another musician, he refused. He forbade it. I could hear him talking to himself, pacing around his room in the darkness, " Seth reported.

"Are you saying your king has gone mad?" Abner asked pointedly.

All were quiet.

"Speak candidly with me man! Certainly, I've given you no reason to distrust me," Abner insisted.

"I've had suspicions for some time now," Raanan reported. "Things got better for a while, but since David's marriage to the princess, they have grown steadily worse. When he does sleep, he talks as if he is awake. He screams and curses and thrashes around on his bed as if he's being attacked."

"Why was this not reported to me?" Abner asked.

"The king forbade it," Raanan reported. "The queen also."

Abner cursed and shook his head. He could hardly fault the faithful soldier for not disobeying a direct order from his king and queen.

"Where is David now?"

"I turned over with him late last night. I'm sure he's probably asleep."

"Does *he* know of the king's suspicions?" Abner asked.

Raanan hesitated before responding. "It's not something we talk about, but yes. There was," he hesitated for a moment, "an incident."

"An incident?" Abner asked.

"It happened before the king sent David south, shortly after he killed the giant. One night David was playing the harp. Things hadn't been so bad back then. One of my men, Korah, was on guard just outside of the king's room. They could hear David playing when, all of a sudden, they heard Saul shout, followed by a loud noise. The harp had stopped and so Korah opened the door just in time to see the king hurl a spear at David. It just barely missed him. He didn't know what to do, David had clearly been playing only moments earlier and was barely able to get to his feet in time to avoid being struck. There was another spear sticking out of the wall that Korah thought must have caused the first noise."

"The king acted embarrassed, like he didn't know what had happened. He said that he'd been asleep and didn't realize what he was doing, then ordered that no one speak of it. Korah didn't even know if he should tell me, but as the only witness, he was terrified," Raanan reported. "Shortly after that, he was sent to the line. David also. I've told no one for fear of their safety."

"Was there any indication that David had done something? Why would Saul try to kill him?" Abner asked.

"None. As far as he could tell, it was completely unprovoked," Raanan responded.

Abner pressed his fists into the table in front of him. This was getting out of hand.

"Does anyone have any reason to suspect that David has actually done anything worthy of suspicion or punishment?" Abner asked.

The men around him were silent.

"I have known David longer than anyone," Raanan responded. "I know his family; I know him. He would never."

"Does anyone have any reason to believe otherwise?" the general asked.

Jonathan looked to the faces around him. They were all in agreement.

"I will hide David in my house until I have the opportunity to speak with my father. Surely I can get to the bottom of this and persuade him," Jonathan offered.

"One of us has to try," Abner replied. "Whatever you're going to do, you'd better do it quickly. Before daylight," the general instructed. "No one else speak a word of this to anyone until I tell you otherwise. For the sake of the kingdom, if Saul tells you anything on this matter, report it immediately to Jonathan or me, even if Saul or Ahinoam forbid it. For his own good, we must know what he is planning."

All in attendance were silent. They each knew the repercussions if Saul learned they'd disobeyed a direct order from him. They each knew the danger Abner now placed himself in even as the king's closest confidant and companion.

The general gave a nod to Jonathan. Jonathan motioned for Abinadab and Shua to follow him and they disappeared into the dark corridor.

"What are you going to do?" Shua asked that they walked speedily through the hall.

"Do you remember how we used to sneak about the palace grounds when we were younger?" Jonathan asked.

"Yes, why?"

"We can't be seen warning David or going to his home. Father was ready to kill me for eating honey when I defied his orders and that was before his recent decline. We need to get word to David that it's not safe for him to leave today. He needs to report that he has fallen ill, or better yet, have Michal report it so that he doesn't expose himself. Abinadab, you go and deliver the message to his men, no details, just report that he's not well. I need to go receive the morning report in order to avoid raising any suspicion. Shua, you take the secret way to David's and make sure he knows not to leave just yet. Tell David to meet me at the hidden den at nightfall and how to get there undetected."

"Got it," replied Abinadab before breaking away.

"What about Michal? Do I let her know what's going on?" Shua asked.

"Best leave that to David, just don't tarry there long. Come join Abinadab and me after you've delivered the message."

"Right, see you then," Shua said before he too peeled off to deliver his message.

As Jonathan proceeded to the training fields he prayed for David's safety. For now, there was nothing left to do but act as though it were just another day in garrison.

When evening approached and the men were dismissed from their daily regimen of training, the princes snuck away to the hidden meeting place they'd found in their youth. It had been years since they'd used it to hide from their instructors or their mother, the queen. The den or "wolves' den" as they'd called it in their youth, was a hollow within a thick patch of vegetation in the palace garden at the foot of one of the palace walls; it required crawling on one's knees at various points along the hidden trails through the trees and shrubbery, but had remained untouched since the last time they'd used it. It had seemed much larger then. They waited expectantly for David, hoping he hadn't found difficulty navigating the narrow and hidden pathway.

"Jonathan," they heard in a whisper.

The three were surprised that David had managed to approach without detection.

"David?" Shua responded in a whisper.

"Coming in," David replied before entering the small, but well hidden sanctuary.

There was just enough light from the palace courtyard lamps that passed through the thick vegetation to identify the human contours against the light-colored stone of the palace wall.

"Nice place," David said, admiring their childhood haunt.

There was no time to mince words and little that Jonathan could do to ease the weight of the situation. The prince reported the morning's events to his young friend, leaving out no significant detail.

Distraught by the news, David sat on the dirt ground. "I don't understand," he confessed. "I know the king is not well, but what have I done? I love the king as my own father. What have I done to cause him to hate me this way?"

"You have done nothing to warrant this. As I live, I will do all that I can to persuade my father that you are blameless," Jonathan assured him. "Look, tomorrow is Wednesday. Without fail, Father goes every week to review and address the troops before the march. Go ahead of us well before light and wait near the large rocks on the southeast corner. You know the place?"

David affirmed that he did.

"You can easily conceal yourself there. Be on your guard in the morning. Stay in a secret place and hide yourself there. I will go out and stand beside my father in the field where you are and I will speak to my father about you. If I learn anything, I will tell you. If he is persuaded, I will let you know. If your life is in danger, I will help you hide until we can get you to safety."

David nodded. "I am not worthy of your kindness."

"Say nothing of it. A true friend does what is right. You have been a brother to us in our adversity. We will not abandon you now."

"That's right David," Shua affirmed. "We are with you."

"We'd better go now to avoid any suspicion. Best to stay hidden until the morning. Pray the Lord guides my words and opens my father's heart to receive them."

***

David rested in the princes' well-hidden childhood sanctuary until sunset. Abinadab surprised him when he arrived at one point with a skin of water, a loaf of bread and some cheese, along with a covering of antelope hide to carry him through the cool night. David welcomed the company, however brief, after the long day of solitude. He saved most of the water and food for the following day. Using the prince's intimate knowledge of the grounds and his own understanding of the guard schedule, they stealthily made their way along hidden paths through the garden to the outer wall. They waited concealed near the wall for Shua to distract the guards at the appointed time.

Hearing the prince enter the tower and begin conversing with the guards, Abinadab whispered "beh-hahts-lah-khah" ("blessing and success") and sprinted the short distance to the wall. Laying his back against it, he interlaced his fingers and held them low to catch David's foot and help him up and over the wall. Using the prince as a ladder, David climbed atop his shoulder and leapt up, grabbing the top edge of the wall with his fingertips. The prince reached up with his palms turned upwards and braced his arms against the wall under David's feet, providing him one last push before David swung his leg up and atop the wall, then disappeared from sight.

The fugitive quickly made his way through the darkness to the appointed place. A thick tangle of short brush and brambles surrounded the rocks and made for painful navigation through the short, but dense vegetation to a well-hidden spot that would allow the best observation of the training area. There he rolled the hide around his body and waited, thankful the young prince had the foresight and consideration to provide at least some separation from the ground and dry night air that sucked the warmth from his body.

Despite the weight of his current situation, the night's events proved exhilarating and his heart still pounded from the excitement. He was moved by the devotion of the princes who, for no benefit to themselves, had risked incurring the king's wrath to help him.

***

Jonathan rose earlier than usual after a restless night. Most of the night he'd spent in prayer, pleading for wisdom and for the life of his young friend and confidant who'd come to feel like the closest thing to a son he might ever have. He could begin to see the approach of morning and started his preparations for the day. With his armor cleaned and securely donned and tightened, he knelt by the table where his scrolls lay unfurled. He'd not eaten or drank since receiving his father's instructions concerning David.

"Lord God of all creation, I come to you humbly seeking your guidance. I know that you set my father apart to lead your people, the descendants of your servants Abraham, Isaac, and Jacob. If you have stripped the kingdom from him, if you have bestowed this weighty burden upon another, guide and bless that man. If it is me, aid me and guide me to lead your people. Bless me with wisdom to lead your people to victory over our enemies. If you have chosen David, then praise be to you for I have found him to be a righteous and trustworthy friend. I know he is prepared to fight your battles and I commit that I will serve him. Only, do not withhold this from me, that my pride might prevent me from doing what is right. Show me who you have chosen."

"Guide and bless my words today as I speak with my father. Comfort him and assuage his fear and distress that he may receive the truth of my words. Preserve the life of my friend, David, son of Jesse, give him victory in many battles yet to be fought. Charge your hosts that they protect him and go before him in battle. Give him wisdom and courage in battle. All of this I pray that your name may be exalted among the nations, for you alone are worthy of honor and praise."

Jonathan stood and picked his helmet up from the table. He glanced once more to see Rebecca still lying asleep in their bed before stepping quietly out and closing the door behind him.

***

Jonathan, his brothers, and Abner could see the king approaching the training grounds in the dim morning light. Jonathan had asked that they pray with him before approaching the king to request that he spare David's life. Now as the entourage of guards and staff approached, he prepared to appeal to the king before any further damage could be done to David's reputation. If Saul announced his demand on David's life to the whole army, there would be no turning back. So far, as only a small group of those closest to his father knew of his intentions, he might still be persuaded.

"Well, here goes," Jonathan said before stepping off to confront the king.

"Good luck," Abner replied as Jonathan headed off in the direction of his father.

"Good morning men!" Jonathan shouted, hoping to slow his father's pace.

"Good morning Son. Tell me that it is a good morning indeed!" Saul said as he stopped and turned to meet the prince. "Where is the son of Jesse?"

Good, Jonathan thought, at least I won't have to bring it up.

"If I may have a word in private Father."

Saul turned and nodded to those accompanying him. All but Joash seemed to welcome the opportunity and quickly proceeded to the training grounds.

Jonathan knelt and bowed his head in submission to his father.

"What are you doing?" Saul asked.

Jonathan's head bowed, his hand open and turned upwards, then began his plea. "My king, who among your servants cares for you more than I?"

Saul stiffened. "There is none. Now, rise my son before someone sees you!"

"My father, whose fate is more closely intertwined with thine own than mine?"

"None," Saul answered. "Now rise son, why is it that you come to me in this way?"

"I am here before you as your servant, Father. If I have not found favor in your sight then you may end my life here and now. I submit to you. If you do not trust me, then I am not worthy to be called your son and heir."

"You are worthy, you know that there is none that I trust more, now rise and tell me, what is the meaning of this?"

"I have come to plead the life of a faithful friend and servant, one who is like unto a son of the king. If you trust me, then I pray you will hear my words. Is there anyone who knows his deeds better than I? Is there anyone closer to David than I?" Jonathan asked.

Saul looked on him stoically.

"Surely you know that I love David as my own brother, as my own flesh, that I swore an oath to him. I thought that you loved him as a son.

After all, look at what he has done! I've seen you delight in him and who else does the king call upon when he is troubled? Tell me what perverse lips have corrupted the king's heart and caused him to hate his loyal servant. Tell me the name of his accuser so that I may cut out his forked tongue and bring an end to his lies."

Receiving no reply, Jonathan continued.

"As the Lord lives, I tell you, David has not sinned against you! Let not the king sin against God and his servant David, because he has not sinned against you, and his deeds have brought good to you, only good. He took his life in his hand and he struck down the Philistine, and it was the LORD that worked a great salvation for all Israel through him. You saw it! You saw it and rejoiced! Why Father? Why then will you sin against innocent blood by killing David without cause? Do you not recall your distress in the valley?"

Saul, moved by his son's submission remembered how the giant's words had taunted him. He remembered the relief he felt when the giant fell slain. He recalled how David's music had once soothed his troubled soul and for a moment, his suspicions waned.

"As the Lord lives, he shall not be put to death."

"He will not be arrested or imprisoned?" Jonathan asked. "Tell me he will not."

"He will not," Saul responded as his placed his hand atop Jonathan's head. Then, without a word, he proceeded to join the guards who waited a short distance away.

Jonathan rose and watched as his father joined them and proceeded to the training grounds. He was thankful that Abner had already begun the morning's march.

He turned to the rocks nearby, where he knew David waited in hiding. When the last of the column had disappeared around the bend, Jonathan called to him.

"David! It's safe, come on out!"

David appeared on the other side of the thick brambles and made his way through the rocks and out of the thicket.

Bowing several times before the prince as he approached, he went to kneel at Jonathan's feet when the prince seized his shoulders and lifted him.

Jonathan reported the king's words as the two soldiers stood alone on the edge of the training grounds.

"I understand if you are still uneasy given the circumstances, but my father is a man of his word," Jonathan assured.

David nodded.

"Come on, I'll go with you back to the palace to make sure no one takes your head."

David smiled. "You are too kind."

"It's the least I can do," Jonathan replied as they headed back towards the palace.

***

1063 BC, Gibeah, Israel

"And there was war again."
1 Samuel 19:8

Months passed without incident as David enjoyed the regular interaction of his new family afforded by his position as Captain of the Guard. It seemed, for a time, that even the king enjoyed the presence of the young shepherd from Bethlehem as the winter settled in and, with it, a brief period of peace and reprieve from provocation or incursion by their neighboring enemies. As the days warmed and lengthened, so awakened the hearts and passions of men for war.

At Jonathan's insistence, David was made commander of an eleph within the prince's division, as the Israelites again went out to meet the

Philistines in battle. Throughout the fighting season, David prevailed as before against the Philistines, gaining greater respect among those who served alongside him.

Saul received the reports of Jonathan and David's victories with mixed emotions as he continued to deal with civil matters and tribunals from the palace in Gibeah and frequent travel to the courts at Dan and Beersheba. Frustrated, Saul begrudged the busyness of dealing with civil squabbles while his cousin, sons, and son-in-law gain more and more glory.

Mindful of the growing bond between his sons and the young man he fears God has selected for his replacement, Saul recalls David from service on the front to once again serve as captain of the royal guard. Isolated from those who would intervene on David's behalf, Saul seeks an opportunity to bring an end to the source of his anxiety.

***

Sitting alone by the fire, Saul stared at the dancing flames as he prodded the logs with his sword. He ran a stone across the length of the blade, enjoying for a moment the calmness it brought to his troubled mind to have a thoughtless task to occupy his idle hands. It reminded him of being on the field of battle, with the men and his sons gathered round near the fire, sharing stories of battles fought, the simple joys of life brightened by the stark contrast of impending death and gore.

The scraping of the stone across the blade reverberated off the rock walls of the large open room. Shhhhhink. Shhhhhink. Shhhhink. He wiped the blade free of the tiny particles of iron that had been freed from the blade, then tested the edge on piece of parchment. He sheathed the blade and moved over to the wall where his armor hung. His spears rested in their racks upon the mantle. He lifted one from its place and sat down before the fire, holding the shaft under his left arm as he lifted the whetstone and held it to the edge of the blade.

Examining the spearhead, he noticed the dullness of the point. How long had it been since he'd sharpened it, he wondered.

"Ah, yes. You remember."

He recalled wrenching the spear from the wall where it had lodged in the mortar between the rocks. He recalled how closely it had come to ending David's life.

"You could have ended it then. No witnesses. No one to deny what happened."

He'd missed twice before, somehow unable to strike David despite the close distance, like the hand of God himself had prevented it.

"No. You were half asleep at the time. On any other day, you'd never have missed."

Saul began running the stone across the large spearhead. No, Saul thought to himself. I couldn't miss if I were awake.

"Never."

Never, Saul thought to himself.

"Call for him."

As captain of the guard, the men have come to know him now. They trust him; they'll protect him, Saul reasoned.

"They are foreigners. Gentiles. They are loyal to you only."

Some. Yes, there are some who would betray him, Saul thought, recalling several of the foreign guard members who served as his personal informants. This was the very reason that foreigners were selected for such service.

"Send for him. You know what must be done. For the kingdom. For Jonathan, Abinadab, Malchishua, and Ishbosheth. For Ahinoam."

And Michal, Saul thought. No. She loves him. They all love him, Saul thought as he stood and dropped the spear to the ground. He paced hurriedly back and forth in front of the fire, placing his fingers to his head, he tried to clear his mind.

"Am I losing my mind?" Saul said aloud. "Is it already lost?"

Saul rubbed his eyes and looked around the room. He was alone. The sparse decor of the room assured him of this. Even his clothing hung in the open. This was by design. There was nothing and nowhere for a would-be assassin to hide.

The large harp rested in its place across the room. It had been undisturbed for weeks. Saul remembered the soothing sounds of the strings. The peace that accompanied the melodies.

"Yes. Call for a musician."

***

David hadn't been asleep long when he heard the rapping at the door. He gently slid his arm out from under Michal's head and went to the door. Peering through the peephole, David recognized the man on the other side and opened the door.

"What is it Igal? Is everything alright?" David asked.

"Sorry to wake you David, but I wasn't sure what to do."

"What is it Igal?" David whispered.

"King Saul, he's called for a musician," said the man in a low voice, thick with his Zobahite accent.

David stood propped against the doorway, momentarily processing the request. Who could he call to play for the king? Why hadn't he anticipated this sooner? You fool, David scolded himself. Who else but you to find suitable musicians to play for the king?

"Are there any musicians here? Anyone that can play for him?" David asked, though he knew the answer.

"I've inquired. Apart from you, there's no one else. Apparently it's been a long time since he's asked for one."

David pushed the hair from his face. The memories of his last performance had not faded from his mind.

"What sort of mood is he in?"

"He seemed... normal. Tired perhaps, but not in a bad way," Igal responded.

David nodded. "Alright, alright," he said, placing his hand on the guard's shoulder. "I'll be there momentarily."

The Zobahite nodded and departed to return to his station outside of the king's chamber.

David opened and closed his fingers and shook his hands, warming and loosening up his wrists as he often did before playing or, more recently, physical training. His forearms were still sore from recent sparring sessions with some of the men of the guard who, like him, enjoyed the engrossing distraction of wrestling and the physical stamina it produced. He removed the ephod he wore to sleep in and donned a more appropriate vesture. Taking the lyre from the shelf in their room, David kissed his bride and departed to a solitary room. He sat and strummed a few cords as lightly as he could, trying not to wake Michal.

"A little rusty, but it will have to do," David said to himself as he stood and placed the harp under his arm.

Moments later, David was greeted by the guards standing on either side of the door to the king's chamber.

"Men," David greeted them as he approached.

"Nothing unusual to report at this time," a Hivite member of the guard reported. "Save your being called to come and play the lyre at this hour."

"Yes, well, we'll have to remedy this situation, won't we?"

"Are you ready?" Igal asked, placing his hand on the door.

"Just a moment," David responded. "Come," he said, taking a few steps away from the door.

The two guards followed him and came close.

"The last time I played for the king, it didn't go so well."

The guards looked at one another.

"What do you mean?" Igal asked.

"Forget I said anything," David said. "I better not keep him waiting any longer. Good night, in case I don't see you on my way out. Stay sharp."

Igal nodded and moved to open the heavy door.

He gave the distinct knock that signaled a guard wished to enter, then heard Saul slide the bar from the door on the opposite side.

That's new, David thought to himself.

Igal swung the door open and announced for David.

David stepped into the dark room and greeted the king, though Saul had already retreated to some dark part of the room where he could not be seen.

"Good evening, My King. Is there something that you would like for me to start with?"

"Good evening David, nothing in particular," Saul responded from somewhere in the shadows.

David moved to take his position and tried not to make any obvious glances to the marks in the wall where he'd narrowly avoided death during his last performance.

The room smelled of smoky wet ash and David could tell the flames in the fireplace that had burned without fail on prior occasions, had been recently extinguished. From the sound of Saul's voice, he was standing close by the fireplace, concealed by the darkness of the opposite side of the room. A small flickering lamp near where the musicians played provided the only light anywhere in the room.

David sat and positioned the lyre, then began to strum the cords before he was interrupted.

"It must be difficult for you," David heard from out of the darkness.

"Forgive me. What is difficult, My Lord?" David asked.

"Being here, away from your men on the line."

David rested the lyre on his thigh.

"I miss being with the men, it is true; being there to bear their burdens alongside them, but I cannot say I have it difficult. You've blessed me far too much to make that claim my king," David replied.

"They do love you, don't they? Your men? And everyone else!" Saul said, his voice growing louder.

"You honor me My Lord. I hope that they care for me as I care for them, but they are your men. I thank you for giving me the honor of serving them and for you giving me the honor of serving you and the guard here."

"Serve them? I appointed you to lead them. You serve them?" Saul repeated. "Is that how you do it? You deceive them to thinking of you as their equal?"

"No My Lord, I do not deceive them at all. The men would see through that. There truly are many men whom I serve who are far, far better than I," David replied.

A loud crack reverberated through the room as Saul slammed his spear flat on the table. David shuddered, startled by the unexpected sound. David thought he could see the glint of a weapon flash there in the darkness where he heard Saul moving.

"Don't play games with me Son of Jesse," Saul growled. "You slew the giant, you've led men in battle these many months; don't think I don't know why you're here!"

David was growing more uncomfortable with each passing second. He hoped more than ever at least one of the guards outside might enter or knock at the door and disrupt their conversation.

"I don't know what you mean My Lord. You called me to play the lyre this evening."

"You know what I mean! You think I don't know?" Saul's voice grew louder as he slammed the spear on the table again.

David stood.

"You've been sowing seeds of discord right under my nose since the moment you came here. Since the moment you stepped forward to kill the giant. I took you in, made you like one of my own, and you repay me with betrayal?"

"Never My King!" David replied nervously. "Who has told you these things? I would…"

David's words were cut short as he saw the glint of the spearpoint hurled from out of the darkness at his head. He reeled, falling back against the wall, narrowly avoiding the projectile as it struck the wall beside him.

From across the room, he could hear what he knew was the sound of another spear being taken from its mount on the wall. Instinctively, he went to grab the spear from the ground where it had landed after striking the rock wall, when he saw the second spear hurled at him through the dark room. Unconscious of the lyre still in his hand he wielded it like a shield and deflected the second spear into the wall behind him to his left as he fell to the ground. He could see the veranda to his left beyond where the spear now stuck out of the wall, embedded between the rocks. David sprang to his feet without hesitation and sprinted the short distance to the veranda, hurdling over the parapet into the night as Saul charged from out of the shadows with his sword in hand.

Saul stopped at the parapet and searched the ground below. David was nowhere to be seen.

NAIOTH

1063 BC, Gibeah, Israel

Now David fled and escaped, and he came to Samuel
at Ramah and told him all that Saul had done to him.
And he and Samuel went and lived at Naioth.
I Samuel 19:18

Michal listened as David recounted the night's events.

"Why? Why does my father want to kill you?" Michal asked. "Of all the servants in his guard, of all his officers and soldiers, why has he set his eye upon you?" she asked as she paced the floor. "Adriel comes from a far more wealthy family. If anyone were a threat to his kingship, would it not be him?"

"There must be some reason," David replied. "I fear someone has slandered me to your father, though who, I cannot guess. Who would stand to gain from my death? I pose no threat to any of his advisors! Your brothers, your family has been more welcoming to me than my own brothers. God do so to me and more if I so much as touch a hair on their heads in malice."

David now paced the floor as Michal sat upon the bed.

"I'm a prisoner in my own home! Who can protect me from your father?"

It broke the princess's heart to see David this way. She'd never seen this side of him. Always the comforter, it seemed that he never worried.

"Was it not you who faced the giant?" Michal asked as she reached for his arm.

David turned to her.

"You were not afraid then and God delivered you. Why should you fear now?" she said as she stood, wrapped her arms around his neck, and kissed him. "What was it you said before? Something like, 'flesh can't harm me.'"

"What can flesh do to me?" David responded.

"And if God is with you," she began.

"Who can be against me?" they both said in unison.

"It is God who saves," Michal added. "That's what you said before. He has spared you twice now. Twice my father has tried to kill you and twice you've evaded him. Surely God is with you."

David returned her embrace and pulled her body close to his. She gave him a long and passionate kiss as their hearts raced together. The young lovers held each other, uncertain of what tomorrow might bring. There was no clear solution to their current dilemma, but she could at least ease his mind for a short while.

***

Hours had passed since the light had gone out in David's window. With little better to do, Perez and Moshe sat and waited for daylight.

A nearby pack of wild dogs could be heard barking and fighting outside the palace walls. Perez mimicked the sound.

"Cut that out you idiot," his companion responded.

The dogs continued their raucous howling and barking.

Bored by the long and uneventful night, Perez howled again, perfectly mimicking the noise just outside the wall.

In response, the noise of the dogs grew even louder and more shrill. Perez continued teasing the animals as they grew closer and closer to their position, until he felt a heel planted abruptly into his hip.

"I said knock it off you fool, I'm trying to get some sleep," Moshe said angrily.

Perez hammered his companion's leg with a closed fist in retaliation.

"If we draw him out, we can kill him and get paid before daylight," Perez responded. "Have your bow ready."

***

Awakened by the barking outside the palace's perimeter wall, which was also a part of their home, Michal tossed in bed, unable to go back to sleep. She looked over at David. He was sound asleep. Finally, too irritated to lay there any longer, she arose to see if she could spot the offending band of animals outside. The two windows on the side of their home which was built into the palace wall overlooked the alley where most of the noise appeared to be coming from. They sounded so close, she thought she might throw some water on them from the window above the alley in order to scare them away. As she looked into the alley she could hear the sound coming from another location as the howling dogs drew closer and closer.

It sounded like there were dogs *inside* the palace walls.

She took the basin of water with her over to their bedroom window and peered into the courtyard where the sound had originated. From the darkened window, she could just make out the silhouette of a man's legs concealed in the shadows of the courtyard adjacent to their home, the rest of his body concealed by the branches of the trees overhead. The sounds were coming from his location and drawing the dogs outside closer. She quietly went to the bed and shook her sleeping husband.

"David! David!" She said in an excited whisper.

He sat upright, startled by the urgency in her voice.

"There's someone outside. It looks like he's watching our home."

David stood and went with her to the window, careful to avoid the moonlight as they peered out, concealed in the darkness of the room.

David could hear the men's faint tussling in the darkness below. While they were obscured by the branches overhead, he could see movement as one body appeared to move away from the one Michal pointed out.

"Idiots," David said aloud. "That's got to be Perez and Moshe. Your father must have sent them to lie in wait for me."

Michal's heart sank.

David put his hand to his head. "I can't fight my way out. Even if I take out those two morons, your father could have ordered every guard here to seize me… or kill me. For all we know he's instructed the guard to do just that."

Michal listened, frozen with fear as David paced the room.

"I'll send for Jonathan!" Michal said excitedly as she turned to leave. "He'll know what to do."

"No!" David said as he caught her arm. "Your brothers are still fighting at the border. I can't trouble them now and there isn't enough time even if I could!"

"What about Abner?"

"Him as well. They are all gone."

"Seth?"

"Seth was reassigned. I think your father became suspicious of him after Jonathan intervened on my behalf the last time he tried to kill me."

Michal's stomach was now in knots. "Oh David. Oh David, is there no one that can help us?"

It was Michal's turn to pace the floor.

David's mind churned, thinking of the various escape routes and hidden passages the princes had shown him before. The only problem was that he had assistance then. There was no scaling the wall without aid. He was trapped.

Michal glanced around the room instinctively as if some answer might reveal itself. She sat on a cushion and looked across the room. Two blank, unblinking eyes returned her gaze.

A sculpture of Rahab stared back at her from the corner. The stone-faced woman seemed understanding. She looked wise and undaunted by the exigency of the situation.

Hebrew tradition said she was the most beautiful woman of her age. A tax debtor, a man of Judah and descendant of the Canaanite woman, who'd owed the equivalent of several years' wages had submitted the sculpture as payment when he had no other available means to resolve the debt. Michal was sitting on her father's lap the first time she saw it and loved it. It was supposed to have been melted down, its materials used for other more practical purposes, but Saul had finally relented and given to Michal when she'd worn him down after months of pleading and asking.

It was said to have belonged to the very woman whose image it was, given to her as a gift by one of her many suitors before she converted to Hebrew and married a man of Judah following the fall of Jericho. It was impossible to know if the story was true. What was certain is that the image was incredibly beautiful and lifelike in every way, including its proportions. When Michal learned that David was a direct descendant, she'd only become more enamored with him.

Despite the Canaanite woman's past prior to her conversion, she was said to be a wise, vibrant, and resourceful woman—all qualities Michal admired. Now they shared several things in common. They each lived in luxurious homes built into their respective city walls and now she, like her predecessor, harbored a wanted man, a man of Judah no less. Suddenly Michal shot to her feet.

"I know what to do!" Michal exclaimed.

***

By the time the sun rose over Gibeah, David had covered the northeastern trek to Ramah in nearly half the time it normally took. Heart still pounding from his midnight flight from death, he carefully approached the prophet's home. Using the curtains he and the princess had fashioned into a rope, he cleared the wall without cutting his hands to bits on the shards of broken pottery meant to deter the very act he was now engaged in.

He could see the faint light of a candle from within the prophet's home.

"Up and at it early I see, old man," David whispered as he stood and started towards the corner of the house, hoping not to alert anyone within until he was ready to do so. He crept quietly towards the house when a voice froze him in his tracks.

"Not another step unless you're ready to meet the Almighty," a voice calmly said from the rooftop.

David lifted his eyes to see two men standing behind the low parapet. The younger of the two held a bow, his arm extended, arrow drawn back with the right. Its sharp iron head was pointing straight at David's.

"I was hoping to delay that meeting awhile, if it's alright by you," David managed to say in the calmest voice he could muster. He straightened. The moonlight brightened his face as he lifted it towards the men and slowly raised his open palms towards them.

"David?" Samuel replied in a low voice, before he turned and disappeared behind the walled rooftop.

Nathan slowly eased the tension on the bowstring and lowered the arrow.

"Come on," Nathan said. "I'll let you in."

***

"What time do you reckon he usually leaves?" Perez asked.

"Never this late," Moshe replied. "Something's afoot. Go tell Saul he hasn't left yet. Ask him what he wants us to do."

Perez yawned and stood to stretch his tired body, then departed to locate the king.

He returned less than a half hour later, sweaty and agitated.

"He's not happy," Perez said anxiously. "Next time, you're the one talking to him unless we take David's head with us."

"What did he say?" Moshe fired back.

"He said go and tell him the king wants to see him. Once we get him outside, kill him."

"Kill him in the light of day? The sun's nearly up!"

"That's what he said, you want to go ask him again, be my guest!"

"Son of Marduk! What if he suspects something?"

"I imagine he already does. You said he never leaves this late!"

Moshe swore again, this time in his native Amorite tongue. "Alright, I'll do the talking, you fall in behind him. I'll walk in front so he follows me. As soon as you get the chance, you slit his gullet."

"How'm I supposed to do that?"

"Grab'im from behind and drag your dagger across his pipe you idiot!"

"Do you know who you're talking about? It's not as if we're talking about some rear echelon tea boy. This is David. David the man who killed two hundred Philies for his pretty lil bride in there. David the commander of an eleph before he was out of diapers."

"You want to alert the guard? We need to do it quietly. Do you know of a better way?"

"Guard? Look around. Saul has cleared out everyone. There's not a soul here. It's his order! Why does it need to be quiet?"

Moshe straightened and looked around. By now, the sun had risen sufficiently even within the tall palace walls to reveal the absence of the normally fully staffed grounds.

"My my," Moshe mused. "Someone has been learning. Alright, let's get on with it then."

The two left the concealment of their position and strode over to the door. Moshe looked his companion over briefly as they both straightened, then reached out and rapped hard on the door. A moment later, a stocky Hivite maidservant opened the door and stared at them indignantly.

The three stood silent for a moment in awkward silence.

"Ah, King Saul requires David, we've been ordered to come and escort him."

"I've never seen you two before. Where is Seth or the other guardsmen?"

"He's been transferred," Moshe answered. "We are guardsmen. There's been a schedule rotation."

"He's sick," they heard a voice say from behind the stoic Hivite woman.

"Sick?" Perez asked.

"Ill. Not well," the Hivite responded sharply. "You do speak Hebrew don't you?"

"Ah!" Moshe said, looking to Perez.

"I'll let him know my father would like to see him as soon as he is well enough," Michal assured them before the door was slammed shut by the maidservant.

The two assassins looked at each other.

"What now?" Perez asked. "I'm not going back to Saul."

Moshe cursed. "Alright, keep watch in case he leaves."

Moshe proceeded to the king's study, where Perez had found him earlier that morning.

He was stopped by the guard.

"More trouble?" the guard asked.

"The princess says he's sick. She says he can't leave."

"What?" Moshe heard shouted from inside the large open room.

The guard stepped aside, allowing Moshe to enter. He cautiously stepped through the doorway and immediately knelt.

"My Lord, your daughter stated that David is sick and is unable to leave his bed."

Saul threw his spear at the wall and cursed at the messenger.

"Incompetent fools!" Saul shouted. "Then bring him up to me in the bed, that *I* may kill him. Since you two seem unfit for the task!"

"My Lord... the princess..."

"Go in and get him! Now!" Saul shouted, spitting with rage.

Moshe stood and hurriedly left the room.

Perez braced himself as the dispirited Moshe approached.

"That bad eh? What does he want us to do now?"

"He said to go in and get him," Moshe replied without stopping or slowing his pace.

Perez followed behind him as they approached David's home.

Moshe drew his sword.

Perez immediately followed suit.

Moshe banged on the door with his free hand. A moment later the Hivite maidservant opened the door slightly. Moshe began to push his way into the room when the heavy woman blocked and attempted to shut the door on him, smashing his left cheek. Perez joined him and the two men shoved the door open as Moshe held the point of his blade to the maidservant's throat.

"Where is he, you heifer?" Moshe demanded.

"Fools! What do you think you are doing?" the Hivite responded before Michal entered the room.

"Get out of my house! What are you idiots doing here? My father will have your heads!" Michal shouted.

"Your father sent us, princess; now tell us where your husband is!"

"I told you he's in bed! He isn't well!"

"Where is your room?" Moshe asked.

"Ill or not, David is going to kill both of you!" Michal replied.

The men began searching each room of the house.

"This will be a lot easier if you just tell us where he is!" Moshe shouted.

The princess paced worriedly as they finally proceeded up the stairs to their bedroom. The Hivite maidservant embraced her as she began to weep.

The two assassins found the door to the couple's room and slowed their movements. Moshe opened it slowly with his sword held ready to defend himself. As the door swung open, they could see the bed across the room. Seeing the red hair protruding from under a thin sheet on the bed, they cautiously approached with their swords raised.

"You think he's really sick?" Perez asked in a whisper.

Moshe thrust the point of his blade at the back of the motionless figure on the bed.

The blade stopped abruptly with a loud clang. The figure remained motionless. Moshe repeated the gesture where the figure's neck should have been. The blade skirted off and into the mattress with the shrill screech of iron on stone.

Moshe bent forward, grabbed the sheet and ripped it off of the figure laying before them.

There on the bed lay a beautifully sculpted female figure with a red goat hide covering wrapped around the head. Perez cursed as Moshe walked over to the window. He stuck his head out to examine the distance to the ground then saw the area where they'd waited the night prior. Somehow, due to the shadow cast by the moonlight, the window had remained unnoticed by them the night before. No doubt, Perez had alerted the couple to their presence.

"IDIOT!" Moshe shouted.

***

Michal stood before her father as he poured out his rage like never before. For the first time in her life, she felt the man before her was a stranger. This was not the loving father she knew. She stood now before a judge. She longed for her mother's presence.

"My own daughter! My own flesh and blood! Tell me, why have you deceived me and let my enemy go so that he has escaped?" Saul shouted as Michal burst into tears. "Do you think your tears will save you from being punished as a traitor?"

"He made me!" Michal finally shouted. "When your servants came, he feared they meant to kill him, so he said to me, let me go, help me escape or I will kill you. Why should I kill you, my wife?"

Saul paused his relentless tirade momentarily while she spoke, tears pouring from her eyes. He stared at her, weighing her demeanor and words. Was she telling the truth? If David did threaten her, he would at last have some hope of a justifiable reason to execute the man.

"He threatened you?" Saul asked.

"Yes," Michal answered as David had instructed.

"He thought my men had come to kill him?" Saul asked. "What reason would he have to think this?"

Moshe and Perez exchanged glances without moving their heads.

"I do not know Father, I don't know why he would think that you are against him. I tried to persuade him father. I did!" Michal lied, tears streaming from her eyes.

"Where was he going?" Saul asked.

"I do not know Father, truly. He wouldn't say," she pleaded. "I was so scared," she managed to eek out between sobs.

Saul opened his arms and welcomed his daughter to him.

Michal's tears were genuine, though not for the reason she put on. She embraced her father and buried her face in his chest as he pulled her close to him.

"How could I ever think that you would betray me?" Saul said.

"Never," she exclaimed.

"I was wrong to give you away to that son of Jesse," Saul said as Michal looked up at her father through reddened eyes. "But that's a mistake I'm prepared to correct. Go home. If you receive word from the son of Jesse, you must let me know immediately. Do not speak of this to anyone else. No one. Do you understand?"

Michal nodded.

Saul ushered his youngest daughter to the hallway before turning back towards the others in the room.

"You were given a simple task," Saul said coldly to the two assassins. "Your services are no longer required."

In an instant, the two men were seized from behind. Their pleas for mercy muffled by the now tightening cords around their necks.

Michal turned away in terror at the sight.

"Recab, Baanah, send men to Jesse's home in Bethlehem and the home of Samuel in Ramah. Dead or alive, bring him to me."

***

As David and Samuel approached the walled monastery further up the hill on which Ramah rested, he wondered why he'd never heard of the place before.

"Is Nathan joining us?" David asked.

"I've given him a separate errand," Samuel replied.

As they approached the gate of the monastery, the monk atop the wall gave the signal to his counterpart below and David heard the large bar hoisted from behind the door. A moment later, the gate swung open. Samuel was the first to enter. David followed. The gate closed behind them as the large wooden beam was quietly lifted and put back in place.

Just inside the gate, a scantly clad attendant led them to the bath-house. The attendant helped the old prophet remove his outer garments and sandals. There were no greetings, no embrace of colleagues happy to see each other. All were silent. David followed the prophet's lead and began removing his sandals and outer clothing. The attendant accepted these as well, then disappeared. The two men cleansed themselves, then took a clean undergarment from the shelf and tied about their waists covering only their loins.

David followed as Samuel proceeded silently up to the tabernacle and monks' quarters that flanked it. The students paid little attention to either man as they proceeded through the grounds.

The few men David observed within the walls wore very little. The student priests wore linen ephods while others wore the same tiny linen cloth tied around the waist, which hung limp over their midsection. As David continued through the monastery, he got the impression that this modest gesture was merely perfunctory. The monastery's occupants each had long hair, which looked as though it had never been cut, at least not in a very long time. The hair of their heads was braided, then braided again, and in some cases, spun into a spiral and pinned to the back of the monk's head. Their beards were nearly as long, and braided as well, except they were left to hang down at full length in front of them or, in some cases, draped over their shoulder.

The men poured over scrolls. Some reading, some writing, attentively transcribing exact replicas of the ancient texts handed down by Moses and his successors. Many simply prayed, their voices too low to hear as David strode past. Others sat silent, eyes closed, quietly meditating.

Incense burned and filled the air with a pleasing and comforting aroma. Though there was no greeting, no welcome reception, or so much as the acknowledgment of their presence, David felt at home and welcomed in the place. He'd felt this sort of peace before, alone in the wilderness under the stars.

A strange but familiar sensation washed over him. His scalp tingled from the forehead to the base of his spine as if his hair stood straight. It was a comforting sensation he'd felt only on rare occasions with his grandfather when he enjoyed the elderly man's full attention. It brought back pleasant memories of the strong but gentle voice assuring him, teaching him, guiding him. If only Obed could have seen this place, he thought.

"What is this place?" David asked in a whisper.

"This is where the next generation of Israel's prophets and priests are trained. The prophetess Deborah had the school constructed so that subsequent generations would not go without a strong and knowledgeable generation of men whose hearts were devoted to the Lord. It is where she held court during her time as Judge of Israel. It is a holy place. That is why we removed our clothing and bathed at the entrance."

"All of these men are training to be prophets?"

"Prophets or priests, yes. The tabernacle is a replica constructed so that the priests may be fully prepared for their duties when they enter the Holy of Holies."

"I had no idea such a place existed."

"You assumed I was the only prophet in all of Israel?"

"To be honest, yes," David replied.

"Most people do. It's best that way. A man may train and study for years and still fail to accurately discern the will of God. Just because one knows the word, does not make him an expert at applying it. Those who have an agenda tend to interpret his words and circumstances to fit their own desires," the prophet said. "I believe that's why God chose you David."

"I don't understand."

"You do not put yourself before others," Samuel responded. "But I must warn you. Many men of God have started out this way. Our natural state is corrupt. It requires constant renewal through prayer and meditation to remain focused on God and not our own desires. Keep Him first and everything else will be added to you. He is too great to be second place to anything else."

David took in the prophet's words. What is there to love more than God? He thought.

"I have always wondered, since that day you anointed me - why did God choose me to take Saul's place? Jonathan would make an excellent King. It doesn't seem..." David stopped. It did not seem wise to question God's justness. "It's just, what does Saul love more than the Lord?"

"Israel," Samuel said as he stopped and turned to David. "Saul loved Israel, her people, and the acceptance of men more than he desired the approval of God. Now, however, he distrusts everyone. The thing that he put in place of God has become his downfall. Be careful that you do not do the same."

The two men entered the courtyard of the Tabernacle. Samuel held his open hands out with his palms upwards, then knelt down to sit on his ankles. He bowed his head and prayed, his words too quiet to discern. David followed the gesture.

By the time Samuel rose, David's feet had fallen asleep and his knees ached. The old prophet was clearly the more experienced at kneeling and praying for long periods of time.

"We will stay here until the Lord reveals your next steps," Samuel instructed.

"Does that mean? Will you go with me?" David asked hopefully.

"That's not for me to decide. We may plan, but the Lord directs our steps. It is best to seek his guidance first rather than fitting it to our own plans."

***

It had been nearly a week since they'd arrived at the monastery. David was feeling the effects of the prolonged praying and fasting that he and the prophet had begun upon their arrival.

Samuel seemed unaffected by their voluntary deprivation. David, on the other hand, required some adjustment. While it was not his first time fasting - Obed had long ago taught him the discipline - he had to remind himself of how little was required to survive during his days in the wilderness watching sheep. He'd grown comfortable living at the palace, having all the food he wanted, whenever he wanted. Even in the field, they were typically well provided for by their own logistics, field kitchens, and offerings from the local villages. Frustrated with his own lack of discipline, he pinched the shrinking layer of excess around his waist.

How long had he been married now and living at the palace? He thought to himself. No matter, a man on the run does not have such luxuries. May as well get used to it, though he did have his doubts about fasting when he might be forced to flee at a moment's notice. Again the worry would start to set in. He needed to engage his mind in productive thought. He needed interaction.

They'd risen early each day with the students of the monastery. They began with a reading from the scrolls, followed by a prayer and time to study the texts individually before they discussed the texts as a group. David finished his solitary prayer for deliverance, then stood and stretched his legs; it was time to move to the courtyard for their discussion about the text that had been read earlier that morning.

It was unlike anything David had ever seen; so many men, so knowledgeable about the law, so fluent in its precepts, and so dedicated to its study. They discussed various scenarios, some manufactured, some derived from their individual experiences, then applied the law in an effort to ascertain the most widely acceptable outcome required by or at least consistent with the text. The answer was not always clear.

David listened attentively as the others spoke and argued their positions.

From the corner of his eye, he saw the man seated next to him lean slightly in his direction.

"They say there are *three* sides to every story," the man said quietly so as not to interrupt the discussion.

"Three?" David asked.

"Why yes," the man said, leaning back. "There's the conflicting story of the two parties, then there's the truth."

David nodded. His current predicament and hunger had left him without much of a sense of humor.

"How long have you been fasting," the man asked.

"Is it that obvious?"

"Here in this place," the man whispered, looking around as he spoke, "you learn to pick up on the signs." The man leaned in again. "I will fast with you. What are we fasting for?"

"Direction," David responded.

"Ah! I don't mean to pry, but I'm afraid you'll have to be more specific."

David let out a long exhale. "It's a long story."

The man stood up and extended his hand. "We've got time," he said looking down at David as the rest of the men in the open courtyard continued the discussion, paying them little attention.

David looked around to the others, all of which remained seated, attentive to the two men currently debating. David realized that while he'd assumed the man's conduct would be considered a disruption, not one of the others had batted an eye when he stood and spoke.

David accepted the hand and was hoisted to his feet. David followed him from the courtyard to the room where the scrolls were studied and copied. It was empty, likely due to the discussion taking place in the courtyard.

"My name is Gad," the man said as he took a seat on the floor. "What are you called?"

David thought for a second before answering. "David."

"What brings you here David?" the chipper man asked.

David considered the question for a moment. How long had this man been here? David wondered. He was not accustomed to people not knowing who he was. Besides, wasn't this a school for prophets?

"I'm trying to get away," David finally responded.

"Aren't we all," Gad responded. "Take that man for instance," he said, pointing out of the open doorway across the courtyard at a man with a mop and bucket. "No one here is assigned the task of cleaning the latrines or mopping the floor. No, we'd all do if it needed to be done, but that man will almost never be seen without a mop, broom, shovel, or some other tool in his hand. Yet, he may be the most knowledgeable man here when it comes to the law. That man is trying to get as far away from his past as he can. As far from the man he once was anyone can imagine."

"Who is he?" David asked.

"I realize it's a bit before your time, it's before my time for that matter, but have you ever heard of the judges Abijah or Joel?"

"Samuel's sons?"

"That one still is," Gad said nodding his head towards the man. "That is Joel. So, I'm afraid you're not the first man to come here trying to escape something. That much is obvious, but my question is, what do you hope to gain from being here?"

"For now, not getting killed would be nice."

"Is that why you're fasting?" Gad asked.

"I supposed," David responded.

"Look, any one of us could die at any moment David. Why is it important that *you* continue to live?" Gad asked pointedly.

"The Lord has called me to something great," David answered. "But I don't know that I am the right man for the job," David admitted. "And even now, I'm being hunted by my father-in-law who wants me dead. If God is truly with me, shouldn't things be going smoother? If He is with me, then why am I being persecuted? Why am I on the run, hiding for my very life?"

"Perhaps there is something for you to learn in this. Hardships often produce hard men. Have you considered that this too is part of a greater design or purpose?"

David thought on the young prophet's words. "I am certain that it is. I just don't understand why it has to be this way."

"Look at the bright side," the prophet said with a smile.

David looked up and stared at him.

"You met me," Gad said with a smile.

David started to laugh when their conversation was interrupted by shouting from the gate.

"Two soldiers approaching!" declared the man on guard.

David stood, his eyes widened.

"Are they here for you?" Gad asked.

"It is highly likely," David responded.

A moment later, there was a loud banging at the gate.

The two men remained silent. They could still hear someone talking from the group of students in the courtyard as if they were ignoring the sounds coming from the gate.

They heard from the gate the loud pronouncement of the intruders.

"By order of King Saul, open the gate this instance!"

The young prophet stood and turned.

"Come on," Gad said, as he proceeded past the courtyard where other students still sat and down a hall on the opposite side. David hurried to keep up, constantly checking over his shoulder to see if the soldiers had entered.

"There is a hidden passage. Not everyone knows about it," Gad said as they came to an inconspicuous spot near the far outer wall when he stopped abruptly and inserted his fingertips into a crevasse in the rock. "Let's keep it that way," he said looking up at David.

Gad struggled with the stone which barely budged despite the young man's efforts. David knelt next to him and stuck his fingers into the crevasse and began working to help wriggle the stone free. It was clear that it had not been moved in quite some time.

"If it comes to it, you can take this path to safety outside of the wall, but be careful," he warned. "It gets dark down there and when you reach the far side, the other side of the mountain is... steep."

Once removed, David could see a very narrow corridor concealed in darkness behind where the stone had been. The opening itself was barely large enough to accommodate his shoulders.

"Go ahead, get in. Just follow the tunnel. It's dark and narrow, but you can't get lost. Keep your wits about you and don't rush out the other side."

David ducked down and crawled into the hole.

"Wait!" Gad exclaimed before he disappeared from outside of the hole.

Returning a moment later, he passed a folded ephod through the opening.

"It's the best I could do," the young monk explained.

"Much appreciated," David replied. He'd not even thought about the fact that he'd have otherwise been all but naked when he emerged from the tunnel.

"I will pray for you my friend," Gad said as he began sliding the heavy stone back into place. The light inside the small passageway shrunk to nothing but an outline around the stone that concealed it. The small sliver of light darkened as Gad's shadow passed by, signaling the stark reality that the fugitive was now alone in this dark place.

***

"This is a holy place!" the gatekeeper shouted to the soldiers. "You must remove your outer garments and sandals," the monk instructed from behind the barred door. "Your weapons are not permitted."

The two soldiers looked at each other curiously.

"I'm not going in there naked," one said.

"We're here on assignment from King Saul; you let us in or we'll be back with more to break this door down."

"Do you have proof of your assignment? An order from the king?" the monk asked.

One of the men removed a sealed parchment from his belt and held it out to the small rectangular opening in the door.

The monk accepted it and read the missive.

"You may enter if you wish. But I must insist that you remove your clothes, sandals, and weapons if you do not wish to incur the wrath of the living God. Nevertheless, do as you see fit, but do not say I did not warn you," the monk cautioned before opening the door.

The soldiers stepped inside and hesitantly began removing their clothes and weapons.

"We have reason to believe that David, the son of Jesse, is here," Ezra said as he removed his sandals.

"Search the grounds; we will not hinder God's anointed here," the monk responded.

The soldiers proceeded into the open courtyard and towards the group of students they could now see kneeling and praying at the far end. The two men wearily began to approach. As they drew nearer, they could begin to make out some of what was being said. The two soldiers realized that the men were not praying, but apparently recounting a story or vision. No one in particular, but one man at a time. As each man spoke, it did not appear that he was speaking to the others, but simply telling a story, as if he were seeing it unfold before him. Several others sat nearby frantically transcribing what was being said.

"And then from the lion a second head comes forth from it that is like a bullock. And the bullock head contends with the lion. As the bullock grows from the lion, legs and a torso appear as the lion shrinks until a full bullock wrestles free from the lion's body. Then the two contend and battle each other, but neither is able to prevail. They both begin to grow weak from the battle."

The soldiers looked at each other in wonder. What kind of place is this? Ezra thought to himself.

Another man immediately in front of them began speaking.

"A large single-horned creature with folds in his flesh approaches from the north and east. It attacks the bullock. They struggle, but the bullock is overcome and he gores the bullock with his great horn. The creature then turns its attack towards the lion. The lion has grown tired and weak. Another creature emerges from beyond where the single-horned animal came. It is a winged and powerful lion. He swoops down upon and prevails over the horned creature that destroyed the bullock and devours it. The winged lion then turns south against the weakened lion; the two struggle until the first is sapped of all its strength. It appears withered and gaunt. The winged lion seizes the weakened lion in its jaws and carries it away from whence it came."

The man stopped abruptly as if awakening from a dream.

Suddenly, one of the guards fell to his knees as if struck from behind. He then lifted his head and looked about him in terror. Ezra went to lift the man, when those around him forbade it.

"Do not touch him!" several of the men commanded sharply.

"Speak!" declared one of the long-haired men around them. "Tell what you see!"

Ezra turned and looked about him, confused.

"Speak!" the scantly clad men around them shouted impatiently. "What do you see?"

The soldier began slowly. "I, I see a… a bear. A large bear. It… it is destroying everything in its path and consuming everything. It moves towards the setting sun. From over the horizon, there… there is something there, from the setting sun… there is another creature, a flying…"

Ezra looked on in bewilderment. What on earth had come over his companion?

"Mannaseh! To your feet man! What's the matter with you?" Ezra said as he grabbed the man's arm and tried to lift him.

"Do not touch him," a monk shouted.

"Leave him!" Several others shouted in unison, but it was too late.

Ezra's sight turned to darkness. Stunned and terrified, he stumbled and fell to the dirt. He felt around in the darkness and called for Joseph, but no one answered. Suddenly, he could see light to his left and turned to see the setting sun. A terrifying winged creature with four heads appeared about to descend upon him. Ezra shouted in terror and fell on his back to the dirt, writhing and kicking as he tried to escape the approaching monster.

The monks nearest him seized him and held him firm.

"What do you see?" they shouted.

Ezra shouted in terror at the beast.

"Speak man!" the monks shouted.

Ezra screamed and turned away from the terrifying creature.

Joseph seized a nearby water pail and cast the water into Ezra's face before the monks could intervene.

Ezra awoke from the terrifying prophecy, gasping for breath. He looked to his right and left to see the wet and nearly naked men holding him firm. Looking up, he saw Joseph staring back at him, wide-eyed and awestruck. Ezra shook himself free of the monks and stood, dripping water.

Without a word, both men fled back to the gate and hurriedly dressed. A monk opened the gate slightly as they pushed their way through the opening.

The crowd of men watched as the frightened soldiers departed.

"Behold!" said Samuel, who was seated among them, "not everyone is suited for the gift of prophecy."

***

"David," Gad called from inside the hall. "They're gone! It seems the Lord had other plans for your visitors." Gad said as he, with the help of a second student began to wriggle the large stone free. This was all the signal David needed. He pushed hard against the stone and shimmied through the small passage out into the open hall.

"Ah!" David exclaimed. "It's good to be out of that forsaken hole," David said as he stretched. "What happened? Did you get the names of the men?"

As Gad retold the events that had just unfolded before their eyes, David was sorry he hadn't witnessed the event.

"Did they know I was here?"

"I don't know. They sure left in a hurry."

"You don't know?" David asked.

"I'm a student prophet, not a fortune teller or mind reader," Gad replied.

David was uneasy. It had been a harrowing experience despite the pleasantly unexpected outcome.

"Not to worry. We'll see them coming. If more return, you'll know what to do now."

David nodded. "I still need someone to move the stone back even if I can get it out by myself."

"I'll stick with you. Day and night, I will be like your shadow."

"Thank you," David responded. It was good to know he had more than one ally in this place.

***

The following afternoon, the students were once again interrupted by the warning from the gatekeeper.

"Two soldiers approaching," the man shouted from the wall.

Again, the announcement was shortly followed by the banging of hard metal against the door.

Gad and another student helped David into the escape tunnel and disappeared to watch a similar scene play out similar to the day before. Gad recounted the events to David.

David shook his head in awe and appreciation.

"God has seen me through again. I do not deserve His mercy," David said, humbled and awestruck yet again by the Lord's provision. "There will be more. I want to stay where I can see them."

"I know a place," the second student said.

***

David awoke with a start. He sat upon the straw mattress trying desperately to recall the fleeting glimpses of the foreboding dream that had awakened him. Beads of sweat covered his body. He closed his eyes and tried to recall it. The bright morning sun in his eyes, the crowd's taunts, the sound of knocking - no, something else. What was it? David wondered. It was a familiar sound, a slow pounding, or banging. A hammer on nail, David concluded. Yes, that was it.

David searched for the parchment to record his memories when he was interrupted by another sound. The same familiar announcement alerted the students of their visitors for the third day in a row.

David stood and quickly took to the hiding place on the roof he'd been shown the day before overlooking the courtyard, this time accompanied by his friend and prophet in training. The two lay on the roof side by side watching the scene unfold through the narrow holes created for water to drain from the roof. He was surprised to see Recab and Baanah enter the courtyard, but given the events of the previous two days, it made sense that Saul would send the more senior men. He watched as a nearly identical scene played out just like the ones that had been described.

One at a time, each man sank to the ground, then prophesied or at least, attempted to before the fearful visions overtook them. They, like the two before them, fled in terror and confusion.

"We are taught to describe what we see in as much detail as possible. When the spirit of the Lord comes on you, it can be…" Gad paused, tilting he head side to side, "overwhelming," he concluded. "It's a harrowing experience even if you're prepared for it. I imagine if you believed what you saw was actually happening to you, if you didn't realize it was a vision from the Lord, it would be very terrifying."

"Do you all have any idea what they mean?"

"We're working on it. Unfortunately, much prophesy is not understood until hindsight," Gad admitted.

"Why do you think God gives these visions if not to warn or guide us?"

"I think sometimes it's to warn or guide, as with Pharoah's visions interpreted by Joseph. Other times, it serves to let us know He is in control. Did it ever occur to you that nothing surprises God?" Gad asked.

"What do you mean?"

"He knows how the story ends. Nothing takes Him by surprise. Even if we fail to interpret the vision beforehand, we sometimes see the events play out and we can see them fall in line with prophesy."

"You think it's for assurance?" David asked.

"Precisely!" Gad responded excitedly. "No matter how bad things get, no matter the severity of our mistakes, He still reigns. Our failings do not surprise Him. He knows that we are dust. He can still work all things for the good of those who respond to His calling."

"You know for a prophet, you sound a lot like a rabbi," David replied.

Gad laughed. It was true, he acknowledged. He was much more outspoken than most of the quiet and introspective students here.

"Come on," Gad said. "I think it's safe to head back down."

***

Saul seized a lamp stand and threw it angrily across the room at Recab who narrowly avoided it.

"Did you not listen to the reports of the men before you?" he shouted angrily. "What did you think would happen?"

Saul paced the floor. Everyone was on edge.

"Imbeciles! Fools!" Saul shouted and wiped his arm across the table between them sending maps, weights, writing utensils, and ink flying. "I will have his head on a pike, or I will have every one of yours if he has escaped!"

Michal sat, nervously observing her father unravel in his own throne room.

"I am the King of Israel, and yet I must go and find this dog myself! So help me!" he growled angrily. "Prepare my horse!" he shouted. "Raanan!"

"Yes y Lord," Raanan responded as he rounded the corner near the entrance to the room.

"My armor!"

"Yes My Lord," Raanan said as he followed Saul from the room.

Ahinoam embraced Michal as she broke into quiet sobs.

Ahinoam summoned her maidservant. There were few men who held enough sway to quell her husband's tirades. Right now, she needed them more than ever.

***

"I can't stay here," David said. "My presence puts you all in danger. Saul will not stop."

"But you've seen what God has done. He has intervened on your behalf every time," Gad reminded.

"What about my family? What's stopping Saul from using them to get to me? If I stay here, it is certain that he will do just that!"

"Nathan is with them. You needn't worry about their safety," Samuel assured. "They have gone to Hebron until further instruction."

The city of refuge. Certainly, Saul would not attempt to harm them there, David thought.

"Why didn't you tell me?" David asked.

"I did not wish to add to your worries until I received confirmation that they'd safely arrived at the city," Samuel replied.

"Thank you," David responded. "There is only one man, perhaps two, that have enough influence over the king to persuade him that I am not a threat."

"How do you intend to get to Jonathan without Saul's men finding out?" Gad asked.

"Before I left, I instructed Michal to send word to him. I only hope that he has returned."

"I will go," Gad volunteered. "I will find him for you and arrange the meeting."

"I cannot ask you to do this," David cautioned.

"You didn't."

"Gad will leave today and seek out Jonathan. When he has found him, he will bring word to you at Jebus," Samuel instructed.

"Jebus?" David asked.

"The Jebusites boast in their fortifications and for good reason. It is against their custom to refuse sanctuary. Still, you probably shouldn't make yourself known. When you leave here, go there and wait until you receive word from Gad."

"Jebus is no small village. How will I find you?" Gad asked.

"I will go to the western gate every day at noon. I will meet you there."

"Hadran alakh my friend," said Gad, before he turned to leave.

"David," Samuel said solemnly as he placed his hands on David's shoulders. "Your path has not been an easy one I know. The way ahead is full of perils. Remember what you have learned here. When the way is hard and uncertain, trust in the Lord. Acknowledge Him in everything and He will be your guide."

There was something different about the way the old man looked at David that gave David pause. How old he looked now compared to when David had first seen him so many years ago in the field outside Bethlehem. He wondered if he'd ever see the old man again.

"I will not forget all that you have done for me," David said placing his hands on the prophet's bony shoulders. "How can I ever repay you?"

"My treasure is in heaven, but for your people's sake, do not repeat the mistakes of those who came before you. Lead them to do what is right and seek the Eternal. That will be payment enough."

***

The king and his entourage of foreign guards arrived at the well in Secu before the sun had fully risen. Secu, a village barely separable from the sprawl of the larger city of Ramah, was the first stop for any traveler visiting the prophet's hometown. Women and young adolescents from the city had already gathered to draw water before the heat of the day settled in.

A servant boy brought a ladle of water and handed it up to Saul as his horse guzzled from a bucket.

Recab nudged his horse alongside Saul's.

"My lord, do you want us to cordon the prophet's home or go straight to the school?"

Saul took a long pull from the ladle of water and handed it back to the servant.

"Hear me!" Saul said loudly to the group of mostly women and young boys tasked with collecting water. "Where can I find Samuel and David?"

The crowd was silent.

"Did I not speak clearly? I asked where are Samuel and David? I know they have come here. That fugitive son of Jesse is hiding near this place, now tell me where he is or I will show you what happens to those who aid my enemies!"

Again, the crowd was silent.

Saul seized his spear which he'd piked into the ground next to his large and intimidating steed.

Fearful of what might happen next, the woman closest broke her silence.

"My Lord! Please! Look, they are at Naioth in Ramah! Go and see," she exclaimed. "It's just there!" she said, pointing to the distant fortifications on the hill that marked the monastery.

Saul kicked his horse. "Come," Saul shouted. "My enemy is within my grasp!"

The procession followed suit and tried to keep up as Saul drove his already tired horse hard towards the city. They drove on through the gates of Ramah and up the hill towards the monastery.

As they approached the gate of the school, Saul glared up at the guard atop the wall.

"You dare obstruct your king? I know the son of Jesse lies within these walls!" Saul shouted to the man. "Open this gate at once!"

A moment later the gate swung open. Saul piked his spear into the ground and dismounted, unable, due to the size of the gate, to ride his horse straight through.

"My lord, we must warn you. This is a holy place," said one of the gatekeepers as Saul passed with Recab, Baanah, and Raanan at his heels.

Saul approached the open courtyard where the monks sat and prayed, searching the faces of the men inside.

Saul stopped suddenly as his eyes locked upon Samuel, seated in front of the others in the assembly.

"Samuel!" Saul called. "I've come here for the son of Jesse! You're hiding him!"

"You will get more than you bargained for son of Kish!" Samuel shouted back. "You dishonor the Lord in your haste."

At his words Saul looked at the other men in the place and seeing their raiment, he began to strip away his armor as he dropped to his knees.

Astonished by the sight, the entourage of guards began to follow suit, handing their armor off to the attendants as Saul began speaking with his face to the sky above.

Recognizing the prophetic words, the scribes in attendance stood and rushed closer to Saul as he stripped away the last of his undergarments and fell to his elbows, his face to the ground.

Samuel stood and walked over to the man he'd anointed so many years earlier, the memory was still vivid in his mind.

Saul continued prophesying with his face to the ground as Samuel listened. He knelt and held his hand over Saul's head. The veiny and wrinkled hand hovered over the once black hair, now completely white. The prophet's eyes welled. He strained and held back a flood of tears as he looked on the broken and aged man before him that had once held such promise. He withdrew his hand as Saul continued to prophesy before them.

Samuel looked up to the spot on the roof to his left. As he'd hoped and instructed, there was no one there to be seen. Reassured by the knowledge David would be safe while Saul remained, the prophet felt a pang of sorrow, knowing that he'd seen God's anointed for the last time.

***

David felt his way through the dark passage. It seemed to go on and on. He cursed not having brought a torch, but the number of soldiers that had shown up this time and the fact that Saul was with them was sufficient to convince David that his stay in Ramah had come to an end. He squeezed through the narrow corridor, slid over slippery wet rocks and through crevasses he could only fit through by exhaling. It seemed he was going uphill at times and downward at others. It was so dark in the passage it was almost impossible to tell. Fear began to set in. He breathed hard as he sped up, feeling his way through the tunnel, one hand on the rock wall to his left, the other stretched out in front of him.

He could feel his heart racing and his mind beginning to wander. What if there were multiple routes? What if he took a wrong turn? What if the passage has collapsed and it ends up being a dead end? What if the passage collapses behind me? Who would ever know?

In his haste, his foot struck a rock and he fell forward striking his head as he went. He lay there in the darkness for a moment panting heavily. The weight of impending doom felt like the mountain collapsing around him, pressing him down, holding him there.

There in the oppressive darkness, he heard the words of his grandfather, reassuring him in the darkness.

"Have I not commanded you? Be strong and courageous. Do not be afraid. Do not be discouraged, for the Lord your God will be with you wherever you go."

The very words spoken to Joshua as he and the people of Israel prepared to enter the promised land. David whispered the words aloud.

"Be strong and courageous. Do not be afraid. Do not be discouraged, for the Lord your God will be with you wherever you go. Be strong and courageous. Do not be afraid. Do not be discouraged, for the Lord your God will be with you wherever you go. Be strong and courageous. Do not be afraid. Do not be discouraged, for the Lord your God will be with you wherever you go."

David continued to repeat the words aloud as he stood and continued to make his way through the darkness feeling in front of him as he went. He could neither tell the distance he'd gone nor the amount of time he'd been in the dark, damp passage, though it seemed like an eternity. The space narrowed and expanded, then compressed again in some places until he was on his hands and knees crawling until finally he began to hear something above his own breath. He stopped and listened, unable to make out the sound. As he continued, it grew louder and louder. Was it the chirp of a bird? David wondered. He hurried on.

Finally, he began to see a glint of light against a rock ahead of him. As he approached it, he could see more light pouring in through the opposite end of the passage. He pressed on and sped his pace until finally he reached the opening in the rock. He stopped abruptly before reaching the end and approached the ledge cautiously. Peering down, he could see a sheer rock face and the valley below him. It was midday. He hadn't been in the tunnel for very long at all.

"Some brave warrior you are," he said to himself recalling the fear that had gripped him just moments earlier.

He searched for any sign of his pursuers. No one was to be seen down the mountain slope below. Still, to make the trip past Gibeah in broad daylight would be suicide. Best to wait until dark. He sat down at the mouth of the tunnel and unfurled the scroll that had been given to him by Samuel. It was the law given to Moses outlining what would be expected of a King if Israel should choose to select one.

He must not acquire many horses for himself
or cause the people to return to Egypt in
order to acquire many horses, since the Lord

has said to you, 'You shall never return that
way again.' And he shall not acquire many wives
for himself, lest his heart turn away, nor shall he
acquire for himself excessive silver and gold. And
when he sits on the throne of his kingdom, he shall
write for himself in a book a copy of this law, approved
by the Levitical priests.

That does not sound like much fun, David thought to himself.

And it shall be with him, and he shall read in it all
the days of his life, that he may learn to fear the
Lord his God by keeping all the words of this law
and these statutes, and doing them, that his heart
may not be lifted up above his brothers, and that he
may not turn aside from the commandment, either
to the right hand or to the left, so that he may continue
long in his kingdom, he and his children, in Israel.

David remembered Jonathan's habit of beginning each day by reading the scriptures and praying. It would be good to see him again. Certainly he will sort this out, David assured himself.

David was already sweating profusely from the midday heat. He rolled the scroll and placed it back in the leather tube that protected it before lying down. It was going to be a long night. Might as well get some sleep now.

He awoke hours later with only an hour of daylight left.

He began making his way down the face of the rock, clinging to whatever holds he could find until finally, his foot landed upon somewhat flat ground.

"Thank you God," he whispered.

Hopping from rock to rock, David quickly made his way down to the path that led south to Gibeah and beyond to Jebus. Jonathan and the rest of the army were out east. Anyone down south towards Gibeah would recognize him since the slaying of Goliath. He pulled the hood up over his easily recognizable mane of wavy red hair and prayed as he went.

"God, please help Gad to find Jonathan quickly. Protect me in Jebus and protect your servants in Naioth."

It suddenly occurred to David that there could be no one better for the task at hand. Who better to send in search of the prince than a seer and prophet?

**

Yuval ordered another cup of wine from the innkeeper and eyed the woman across the room. They'd been trading punches with the Philistines for the past month. He was happy to be away from the line, even for a moment while Jonathan responded to the Queen's request for his presence. He intended to fit as much enjoyment into his brief respite as possible.

The woman at the end of the bar returned his gaze and smiled.

Yuval stood and moved closer to her.

"You're Jonathan's armor bearer aren't you?" she asked.

He was used to being referred to as someone else's accessory.

"That's what they say," he replied as he ordered her a drink.

"Yuval is it?"

"That's right."

She leaned in closer to him. "I was hoping I would find you here."

Yuval straightened. "Is that so?" he asked, intrigued. He was used to some level of fame for their actions at Geba, though it was a rare occasion that someone actually knew his name.

She leaned in close to Yuval's left ear and whispered, "I want to show you something." She turned and walked away from the bar.

Yuval gave a wink to the innkeeper, flipped him a coin, then stood and followed.

She proceeded to a darkened corner of the room where, to Yuval's dismay, another man waited. The man dropped several coins into her hand.

"This is what I wanted to show you," she said to Yuval as she planted a kiss on his cheek, then turned to leave.

Disappointed and irritated, Yuval's hand moved instinctively to the dagger he kept on his side.

"You don't need that," the man said in an urgent but hushed voice.

"You've got some nerve," Yuval replied.

"I'm sorry to have employed such means of finding you," said the hooded man, "but a mutual friend told me this was the best place to look."

"Yeah, who is that? I want to know who to punch the next time I see him."

The man looked behind Yuval to ensure they were still alone. Confident none of the other patrons were paying them any attention, the man leaned slightly forward into the dim light revealing his face.

"The servant of your master," Gad replied. "David."

***

It had been two days since David arrived in Jebus. He'd walked the exterior walls of the city every day since. Samuel had been correct in his assessment. The city seemed impregnable. Not only was it located on a hill with steep approaches on both the east and the west, but the strong, thick walls, ramparts and internal water source made it ideal to defend. But where did its water come from? David wondered.

After waiting for over an hour at the Western gate, David observed several water carriers laden with jugs to be delivered to the city's inhabitants. Not wishing to draw attention to himself, he began walking in the direction he'd seen them coming from. Spotting one inhabitant laden with jugs of water, he proceeded in the opposite direction until he saw another, then another, till at last he reached the eastern wall. In the shade of a fruit vender David watched inconspicuously as the city's inhabitants approached a heavily fortified tower along the perimeter wall that surrounded the city.

Carriers approached with empty jugs and passed them to a man stationed at the base of the tower, then paid a small fee. Within a few moments, their jugs were returned, this time much heavier and clearly full of water. But how? David wondered. He proceeded to a shop in the souk where he could purchase a water jug or skin.

The vendor eyed him as he looked at the various sizes.

"Can I help you?" the man asked in Canaanite.

"Yes, ah, how much for one of these?" David responded, increasingly thankful of his grandfather's dealing and trading with non-Hebrew herdsmen.

"Hebrew?" the man asked as he straightened.

"Moabite," David replied.

"Ah! Your accent sounded Hebrew at first. We don't see many of their kind in here. It is forbidden for their people to associate with uncircumcised. You know that's what they call us?"

"That's what I hear."

"Disgusting practice. Can you imagine?" the vendor asked rhetorically as he shook his head. "Ah!"

"It certainly sounds painful," David acknowledged. "So, how much for one of these?" David asked, hoping to change the subject.

"This is a gerah jug. We call them that because that's what it costs to fill it. It holds a kab. This one here," the man said, placing his hand on the medium-sized containers, "is a two-gerah jug. It holds an omer, two kabs. And this one," he said leaning over the table and pointing to the larger vessels, "is called a four-gerah jug. It holds a hin or about four kabs or two omers."

"You have to pay to fill them?" David asked.

"That's right. One gerah, two-gerah, and four-gerah," the man said pointing to the vessels. "The prices are listed on the front of the table."

"I'll be honest with you. I've heard of paying someone to fetch water, but I've never been to a city where you had to pay for the water itself," David said.

"You see these fortifications?" the man asked pointing up to the wall.

"So I noticed. Very impressive," David responded.

"They don't build themselves. Citizens pay for the water so they don't have to walk miles to fill them up outside of the city. The city officials use the money to strengthen the fortifications. How else do you think we've managed to stay here without submitting to the Hebrews or the Philistines?" the man asked proudly. "The Hebrew Joshua took one look at these walls and went right around us. Ha!" The man laughed. "Look up there," the man pointed in a hushed voice now. He came around the table and put an arm around David.

David looked to where the man pointed high up on the city wall.

Now in a whisper, the man leaned in. "Half of the men on the wall are deaf, blind, or lame."

"Nooo," David responded.

The vendor leaned back, crossed his arms, and nodded.

You're kidding," David said.

Again the vendor leaned in and lowered his voice.

"Outsiders don't know the difference. They just think the wall is heavily manned. Besides, it keeps them from having to beg in the streets, while the city pays them a fraction of what it would cost to pay a full-time soldier."

"Brilliant," David said. Part of him thought the concept extremely complacent, though he had to admit, the audacity of the deception was both effective and beneficial. "I guess it's no wonder your people have managed to thrive here for so long," David said, stroking the man's zeal for his city.

"There is not an army anywhere that could take this city. We could put infants in those towers and not have to worry," the vendor boasted.

"So," David paused, scratching his head. "I still don't understand. Where does the water come from?"

"I've already told you more than you should know," the man waved and went back behind his table.

"A reservoir?" David asked.

"Ha!" the proud vender laughed. "Any hamlet has a reservoir. Look at these streets. A reservoir would not last one week if the city was cut off."

"A spring then?"

"You didn't hear it from me."

"Hear what?" David asked as he handed the vendor payment for a two-gerah jug and slung the vessel over his shoulder. "Thank you for your hospitality."

The vendor gave him an accepting nod.

"How long are you here for?"

"I'm not certain. I'm waiting for someone."

"What is your occupation?" the vendor asked.

"I'm, well, to be honest, I'm between jobs at the moment."

"You should stay awhile," the vendor said. "There is much to do here. Maybe you could learn something."

"I may do that," David responded as he turned to leave.

***

Resting in the shade of the closest watering hole, David eyed each pedestrian as they entered the western gate. The sundial in the center of the street near the gate told that noon had long come and gone. Still, what else was there to do? So he waited.

Finally, the familiar face of the bearded man appeared among the new entrants. David could not conceal his smile. He started to stand, then caught himself and sat back down. He watched as Gad looked wearily around the unfamiliar street. The others entering behind him paid little attention as they proceeded about their way. Gad's eyes finally came to the establishment where David waited, hidden in a shady corner.

As Gad started in the direction of the tavern, David remained seated.

The prophet walked past him up to the bar where he poured himself a drink of water.

"Long journey?" David asked from behind him.

Gad spun around to see David seated in the corner. He raised his eyes to heaven. "Thank you God," he said as he proceeded over to the table where David sat.

"I found Yuval, just as you said. He was not happy with the method I employed to find him"

"Good!" David said, falling back against his chair. "So Michal was able to get word to Jonathan."

"Yuval passed the message along to him at the palace and then brought word back to me. Jonathan will meet you at the rocks near the training field tonight. He said we should go and hide in the rocks there. He and Yuval will come and meet us there an hour past midnight."

"Excellent, he isn't wasting any time," David replied, relieved.

***

As David and Gad made their way through the night from Jebus to Gibeah, Gad began to question his decision to follow the future king. All he could think about were the things he could not see lurking in the darkness. This was not the young monk's idea of fun.

"Should we be using these game trails?" he asked David. "What about lions?"

David almost laughed, but then realized his new companion was quite serious.

"There won't be any lions around here, trust me. We're more likely to get ambushed by one of Saul's guardsmen on the main road than we are to get attacked by a lion on these goat paths. Besides, where's that courage you talked about back at the monastery?"

Gad huffed.

By the time they arrived at the rocks, it was nearly midnight. It had not been an easy hike and the sweat from their exertions now cooled and chilled their still bodies in the night air.

"You know, the monks back at the monastery pride themselves on living an austere lifestyle," Gad said shivering in the cool night air. "But now I'm starting to think that what they consider austere is maybe not so bad."

"Why is that?"

"Well, I was always warm, and I knew that no matter how sparse our meals might be, we always had food to eat."

"Here," David said, handing the prophet some dried venison.

"Thank you," Gad said before offering a short prayer of thanks.

David could see movement in the open field ahead of him. Two dark shadows appeared to float over the ground headed in their direction from the palace until David could make out the broad-shouldered Yuval and the slightly taller, leaner Jonathan, both covered in dark hooded cloaks.

When they'd reached the edge of the rocks, David could hear a muffled discussion and the figure he knew to be Yuval trotted off back towards the palace and stopped a short ways off. Confident they had not been followed, Yuval returned.

David emerged from the hiding place, Gad rose along with him. As David approached, Jonathan pulled back the hood from over his head. David sank to his knees at the sight of his trusted mentor, companion, and protector. Gad knelt beside him as David bowed his head low to the ground.

"What is the meaning of all this?" Jonathan asked.

"What have I done? What is my guilt? And what is my sin before your father, that he seeks my life?" David asked.

"What are you talking about?" Jonathan asked. "Far from it! Come to the palace with me, I will show you, I spoke with my father. He would not lie to me."

"If I go with you, I will surely die."

"You shall not die. Look, my father does nothing either great or small without disclosing it to me. And why should my father hide this from me? It is not so."

"Your father knows well that I have found favor in your eyes, and he thinks, 'Do not let Jonathan know this, lest he be grieved.' But truly, as the Lord lives and as your soul lives, there is but a step between me and death. I tell you, he sent men to lie in wait for me. Have you not spoken with Michal? I had to flee out of the window of my own home."

"Michal is away. What are you talking about?"

"You see? He must have sent her away so that there would be no one left at the palace to help me. He pursued me to Ramah. He sent three groups of men to find me there, then he came himself."

"Whatever you say, I will do for you. What do you want me to do to prove to you that you are safe from my father?"

"Behold," David said pointing up to the setting moon. "Tomorrow is the new moon, and I should not fail to sit at table with the king. But let me go, that I may hide myself in the field till the third day at evening. If your father misses me at all, then say, 'David earnestly asked leave of me to run to Bethlehem his city, for there is a yearly sacrifice there for all the clan.' If he says, 'Good!' it will be well with your servant, but if he is angry, then know that harm is determined by him. Therefore deal kindly with your servant, for you have brought your servant into a covenant of the Lord with you. But if there is guilt in me, kill me yourself, for why should you bring me to your father?"

"Far be it from you! If I knew that it was determined by my father that harm should come to you, would I not tell you?"

"Who will tell me if your father answers you roughly? You cannot come to me without endangering yourself."

Jonathan thought for a moment. "Come, let us go out into the field," he said pointing to the far end of the field near the shooting line. "The Lord, the God of Israel, be witness! When I have sounded out my father, about this time tomorrow, or the third day, behold, if he is well disposed toward you David, shall I not then send and disclose it to you? But should it please my father to do you harm, the Lord do so to Jonathan and more also if I do not disclose it to you and send you away, that you may go in safety. May the Lord be with you, as he has been with my father."

Jonathan stopped and turned towards David. "You must do this however." David stopped and turned toward him. "If I am still alive when you come into your kingdom, show me the steadfast love of the Lord, that I may not die; and do not cut off your steadfast love from my house forever, when the Lord cuts off every one of the enemies of David from the face of the earth. May the Lord take vengeance on David's enemies. Swear these things to me David."

"You have my word."

"As you say, tomorrow is the new moon, my father will be back and will expect my brothers and me there and you will be missed, because your seat will be empty. On the third day go down quickly to the place where you hid yourself when the matter was in hand, and remain beside the stone heap. And I will shoot three arrows to the side of it, as though I shot at a mark. And behold, I will send the boy, saying, 'Go, find the arrows.' If I say to the boy, 'Look, the arrows are on this side of you, take them,' then you are to come, for, as the Lord lives, it is safe for you and there is no danger. But if I say to the youth, 'Look, the arrows are beyond you,' then go, for the Lord has sent you away. And as for the matter of which you and I have spoken, behold, the Lord is between you and me forever."

"So be it," David said. "We will await your word."

***

Saul arrived back at the palace the following day. Jonathan sought out and informed his brothers of the situation when they arrived at the palace for the new moon feasts. Given his prior instructions not long ago, Abinadab and Malchishua were easily convinced of David's claims. Jonathan alone remained convinced that his father was not beyond reach. Ahinoam and Michal had still not returned from the coast as Jonathan had hoped. The fact that Saul had not called them home for the new moon celebrations did not bode well. His mother always had a cooling effect upon the king and Jonathan despised the concubines that clung to his father in the Queen's absence.

Even after his return to the palace, Saul seemed to be avoiding Jonathan leading up to the evening's gathering. Even Abner was unclear about where Saul had been in the days leading up to the new moon celebration. He, being the closest of Saul's advisors, seemed the most withdrawn about Saul's condition. The princes gathered around the great hall and took up their seats as wine was poured. The princess, Eve, and Sarah, the wife of Abner, gave their best efforts to ease the tensions in the room by engaging in small talk when finally the door at the end of the hall swung open and the guard called the attention of those on duty. Everyone stood customarily for Saul's entrance as he proceeded without a word to his place at the end of the table opposite Jonathan.

Saul leaned his spear against the table and sat down. The royal family sat as they each tried not to look upon the king, still dressed in full armor. Abinadab and Shua eyed Jonathan cautiously.

Abner looked at the spear leaned against the table next to him and then to Saul.

Saul gazed absently at the empty space where David sat next to Ishbosheth.

Abner leaned close, "Is everything alright cousin?"

Saul continued to gaze wild-eyed at the empty seat.

"Saul," Abner said slightly louder as he touched the king's arm.

"What?" Saul said as if coming out of the trance. "Yes, cousin?"

"I asked if everything is alright."

"Yes," Saul replied and leaned back against his throne. He grabbed the chalice in front of him and took a long drink of wine then raised his hand impatiently for the cup bearer who nervously filled the king's vessel.

As Jonathan watched Saul at the end of the table throughout the meal, he could hardly recognize the man seated opposite of him. The king was gaunt and uneasy. Apart from the terse answers he gave in response to the prodding of his family, he sat silent at the end of the table. At the end of the evening, his plate had not been touched.

Finally, as the evening drew to an end, Ishbosheth was the first to ask leave of the king.

"Yes, yes," Saul replied. "All of you, take your leave as you wish," Saul said as he stood from the table.

Everyone stood as the king rose.

"As you were," he said, waving his hand. "I want to see everyone back here again tomorrow," he declared. "Everyone!" Saul repeated as he turned and left the room.

Abinadab and Malchishua departed soon after.

As they sat, Eve placed her hand atop Jonathan's as he eyed the empty seat across the table. David's claims seemed more and more likely the longer Jonathan observed his father. He turned to meet the empathetic gaze of Eve, his wife, seated to his right.

"Maybe tomorrow will be better," Eve whispered.

Jonathan nodded quietly, then acknowledged Abner and Sarah before he rose to leave.

Abner watched the young prince from across the table. It was a rare occasion to see despair in Jonathan's eyes.

"There's still hope," Sarah whispered in his ear.

"Yes," Abner replied.

Sarah stroked the back of his head with her fingertips. "Isn't that what you're always telling the men?"

"It breaks my heart to see him this way."

"I know," she affirmed, "but that's why they need you now more than ever. You have to be the steady hand you have always been. He will listen to you if you stay close to him."

Abner turned to face his wife, now well past fifty years of age, but as graceful and beautiful as ever.

"If he'll let me," Abner replied.

***

The following evening, Jonathan and his brothers greeted each other as they assembled again in the palace hall. Jonathan moved to Abner's side of the table and embraced his uncle.

"We need to talk," Jonathan whispered.

Abner gave a somber, understanding nod.

"Tonight."

"Meet me in the study. Second watch," Abner replied.

Jonathan nodded and moved back to his side of the table opposite Saul.

Once again, wine was poured as the princes arrived and filled the table along with Saul's closest staff. The door at the far end opened and the guard again announced the king's presence. The royal family stood as Saul entered with his young and beautiful concubine Rizpah clinging to his arm. To Jonathan's dismay, the king did not dismiss her as he proceeded to take his seat at the head of the table. Raanan followed close behind.

Saul nodded to the guard and a seat was immediately produced for Rizpah, who admirably disguised her elation with a respectable amount of stoicism.

Eve placed her hand on Jonathan's thigh as he tried to conceal his frustration.

Abner eyed the armor-bearer suspiciously as he stood behind the king. Saul ignored the gesture and signaled to the servants for the first course of the evening to be served. With the king comfortably seated, the palace servants flooded from the kitchen to fill the table with the evening's meal.

Abner leaned in towards Saul, though the king failed to acknowledge him.

"Saul," Abner said trying to gain his attention.

Again, the king ignored him.

"Cousin," Abner tried again.

Saul slowly moved his eyes to meet his general's.

"Inviting your concubine is your prerogative, but why is your armor-bearer here?" Abner asked in a hushed voice.

"Assurance," Saul responded.

"For what cousin? We are all family here."

"We will see," Saul responded.

As the servants returned to the kitchen, the room was filled with an uneasy tension and quiet that couldn't be ignored.

"Why has not the son of Jesse come to the meal, either yesterday or today?" Saul asked loudly, breaking the silence.

Jonathan cleared his throat before responding. "David earnestly asked leave of me to go to Bethlehem."

"And you granted him leave?" Saul asked. "The Captain of my Guard. You granted him leave without consulting me?"

"There are plenty in your gaurd who have served you far longer than David. Besides, David has a large family and hasn't seen them in quite some time," Jonathan answered. "He said, 'let me go, for our clan holds a sacrifice in the city, and my brother has commanded me to be there. So now, if I have found favor in your eyes, let me get away and see my brothers.'" Jonathan said as he felt his father's glare bearing down on him from across the table. "So for this reason he has not come to the king's table."

"You son of a perverse and rebellious woman!" Saul shouted as he stood from the table. "Do I not know that you have chosen the son of Jesse to your own shame, and to the shame of your mother's nakedness?" Saul shouted as he seized his spear and hammered the spike hard on the stone floor before pointing the tip at Jonathan. "For as long as the son of Jesse lives on the earth, neither you nor your kingdom shall be established! Therefore send and bring him to me, for he shall surely die!"

Jonathan was done lying. The facade now gone, he leaned forward with his hands open towards his father.

"Why?" Jonathan shouted. "Why should he be put to death? What has he done?" he shouted back.

Saul repositioned his grip on the spear and cocked to throw it across the long table as Abner rose in an attempt to stop him. Jonathan ducked to the left under the table as the spear passed where his chest had been. In an instant, Jonathan was on his feet.

Abner took hold of Saul's shoulder. "Saul! What are you doing?"

Saul's foreign armor bearer took hold of Abner's arm in a miscalculated move to protect the king. One look from the general was enough to bring the man to his senses. He released Abner's arm and stepped back.

Jonathan and Saul stared at each other indignantly across the table. Jonathan's face burned with rage.

"That's twice you've threatened to kill me because of your foolish pride!" Jonathan shouted.

"And I will not fail the third time!" Saul shouted back as he pounded his fists on the table.

Jonathan took Eve by the hand and led her from the room without another word.

Abinadab and Malchishua stood and quietly followed.

Ishbosheth alone, too afraid to challenge his father, remained seated at the table.

"You need to pull yourself together, Cousin," Abner said quietly, his hand still resting on the king's shoulder.

Saul knocked his hand away and glared back at him.

"Know your place, General," Saul said before returning to his seat.

"My place?" Abner asked still standing. "My place is right here, at your right hand, as it has always been. Have I ever led you astray Cousin? Have I ever once given you cause to doubt my allegiance?"

Saul leaned forward, glaring across the table at where Jonathan had been.

Sarah stood next to the general and took his hand.

"Abner," she said softly.

Abner examined the wild and resentful look in the king's eyes and face before concluding that it was no use trying to change his mind at present. The pair turned and left Saul, his concubine and youngest prince sitting in silence at the table.

***

Jonathan rose the next morning early after a sleepless night. He secured the sword and scabbard belt around his waist and grabbed the bow from its stand along with a quiver of arrows and proceeded quietly out the door while Eve slept undisturbed. He proceeded out of the palace gate which led to the market stopping only to let the guard know he was departing alone. Passing through the market, he turned quickly down an alley and peeked back around the corner to see the two men following from a distance.

"How many?" Yuval asked from behind.

"Just two," Jonathan replied as he pulled the hooded robe off his back and traded it for a dark brown one Yuval had been wearing. Yuval took the sword and scabbard belt and buckled it around his waist, then accepted the bow and quiver Jonathan had been carrying.

Yuval nudged a dark figure sprawled out on the ground next to where he'd been waiting.

"Come on. It's time to earn your keep," Yuval said to the urchin.

The boy sat up and rubbed his eyes before standing to his feet.

"Here," Yuval said as he held out a skin of water to the lad.

The boy took several long sips of water from the skin and passed it back to Yuval wiping the moisture from his face with the top of his forearm, then shouldered a long rug that had been rolled up and tied with a leather cord.

"Alright, come on," Jonathan instructed the boy as Yuval stepped out into the street and proceeded in the same direction Jonathan had been traveling earlier.

The prince and the young boy turned around the corner of the shop and waited till the two men passed in pursuit of the disguised Yuval, then proceeded in the direction of training fields. The boy shuffled a few steps behind Jonathan trying to keep up as they exited Gibeah's eastern gate.

"Did Yuval explain the job to you?" the prince asked.

"Yes, Your Majesty."

Jonathan shook his head. "Did Yuval tell you to call me that?"

"Yes, Your Majesty."

"That's not necessary. It's just Jonathan. Do you understand?"

"Yes, Your Majesty."

The prince looked down at the boy as they walked.

A broad smile spread across the boy's face.

Jonathan laughed. He understood now why Yuval had selected the youth, a kindred spirit no doubt.

Alright, it's very simple. All you have to do is run and find the arrows that I shoot, got it?"

"Got it," the boy replied.

"What is your name?"

"Eliel," the boy replied.

"And your father's house?"

"Is anyone's guess," the boy replied.

"Eliel it is then," Jonathan replied.

As they approached the stone heap beside the archery field, Jonathan eyed the rocks without turning his head. Seeing no one, he looked behind to make sure they had not been followed.

Jonathan stopped near the shooting line and took the rug from the boy's shoulder.

Laying it on the ground, he loosened the leather cord and unrolled the rug on the ground. His unstrung bow and quiver of arrows lay before him on the rug. Resting the strung end on the rug, he used his weight to pull down on the unstrung end of the bow and hooked the looped end around the wolf's mouth at the end.

Laying the bow flat on the rug, he straightened and windmilled his arms several times to wake the muscles. He then pulled each arm one at a time across his chest and behind his head, stretching the back and shoulder muscles. He lifted the quiver and slung it over his right shoulder with the feathered end of the arrows sticking up several inches above it, then tightened and adjusted the strap around his chest.

Removing an arrow, he nocked it pointed toward the sky, then pulled the string rearward as he lowered the arrowhead towards his target, exhaling as he slowed his downward movement.

The arrow sprung forward, soared through the air, and struck the target at fifty cubits ahead of them and to the left. It was lodged dead center in the straw man's chest. The boy started towards it.

"Wait," the prince instructed. "Not yet," he said tapping the remaining arrows in his quiver. Jonathan again looked around and back towards the city to make sure they were alone.

He pulled the string back again and loosed an arrow at a target positioned twice the distance to the right of the first, striking it dead center once again.

The boy eyed the next target about another fifty cubits further and to the right. Jonathan drew down on the target, then raised the tip of the arrow several handbreadths before releasing the string. The arrow made a long arc through the sky and struck the target dead center again.

The boy's eyes widened. The target beyond this was another 50 cubits still. A distance of two hundred cubits from where they stood. The grass around it bowed and waved with the morning breeze as the heat of the rising sun began to warm the atmosphere.

Jonathan waited for the breeze to cease as he pulled the next arrow back as far as his arm would allow. Raising the tip skyward he loosed the fourth arrow. He made a high arc through the sky as the boy waited with anticipation for it to strike the target. It came down and struck the target, protruding at a high angle from the target's chest with the feathered end pointing toward the sky.

"Alright, you can go ahead and start collecting the arrows," Jonathan said as he pulled another arrow. "Start with the closest ones over to the left."

The boy jolted off towards the closest target on the left side of the field as Jonathan sent several more arrows towards the furthest straw men at the end of the range to the right near an outcropping of rocks and brambles.

As the boy went from target to target collecting the arrows, Jonathan again eyed the area, looking for any prying eyes or visitors. They were alone.

Jonathan called out to the boy from the furthest target. "How many do you have?"

"Four!" the boy shouted holding the arrows above his head.

"There should be three more!" Jonathan shouted.

The boy looked around the targets, making several circles.

"Is not the arrow beyond you?" Jonathan shouted, his voice strained.

The boy turned and looked frantically through the grass.

Jonathan looked around again. It was still early. No one could be seen in the distance entering or leaving the city, but it wouldn't be that way for long.

"Hurry up!" Jonathan called out. "Be quick!"

The boy searched frantically and finally came upon the final arrow and held it triumphantly over his head. "Seven!" the boy shouted.

"Very good! Do not stay! Come on back!"

The boy sprinted through the tall grass back to the prince and held out the arrows. Jonathan placed them in the quiver and laid it back on the rug next to the bow he'd already unstrung. He rolled up the weapon and retied the leather string, then laid it upon Eliel's shoulder.

"Go and carry them to the city," he instructed. "I'll meet you where I found you and Yuval this morning."

Pulling several coins from the purse tucked in his belt, Jonathan placed them in the boy's hands.

Eliel thanked him and departed towards the city.

Now alone, Jonathan looked back towards the furthest target then to the heap of stones and thicket to the right side of the archery field. A moment later, the dejected figure of his friend and protege appeared in the distance as he emerged from the rocks.

Jonathan walked speedily towards him.

David staggered towards the prince and dropped to his knees on the ground before he bowed to his face in the dirt.

Jonathan looked around again, then ran over to where David knelt in the dirt.

He bowed again as Jonathan approached and again as Jonathan reached him.

"Stand up my friend," Jonathan said, lifting him from the ground. "This is no behavior for a prince," he said, taking David by the shoulders.

"I love the king as my own father," David said as his voice croaked with sorrow. "Why does he hate me?"

Jonathan pulled David's head to his chest to him, kissing the top of his head. He placed his forehead to the top of David's as he too began to weep for his friend.

"I made a covenant to look after you, didn't I?" Jonathan asked. "I will not forsake our friendship nor the words that I swore to you. You *will* come into your kingdom, my friend. The Lord will not fail to see that it is done. Now go in peace, because we have sworn both of us in the name of the Lord, saying 'The Lord shall be between me and you, and between my offspring and your offspring, forever,' and I will not forget my oath. I will find you and bring aid to you when I am able. Name the men you would have me send to you and it will be done."

"It is too much," David said. "Any man who follows me must give up everything. He would have to hate his own father, mother, and children to follow me."

"Then I will leave the decision to them, but to any who would go, I will aid them," Jonathan promised. "Come on now, surely there are men you trust. Let them decide their fate. Name those you trust the most, and I will see to it they alone know where to find you."

David again refused, but Jonathan pressed him.

"Do I not know that Samuel has anointed you king? It is only right that the men should follow you. You are God's anointed, not I. I must decrease, and you must increase. You know that I will send men, whether you name them or not."

Reluctantly, David acquiesced. "Dodo. Elhanan. Hushai. Ira and Gareb. Heleb."

"That's a fine start," Jonathan acknowledged. "I will see it is done. Go and wait for them at the well west of Nob. The forest is thick there. Whoever will go will be there before sunset."

Moved by Jonathan's promise, David knelt at his feet.

"May the God of our fathers protect you my friend and may I go down to Sheol if I should ever raise a hand against you or your descendants," David vowed and kissed Jonathan's hand.

Jonathan placed his hand on David's shoulder.

"May He go with you and give you peace my friend," the prince said.

David stood and disappeared into the rocks and thick brush.

FUGITIVES

1063 BC, Nob, Benjamin, Israel

Then David came to Nob, to Ahimelech the priest.
I Samuel 21:1

Gad watched with envy as David slept effortlessly on the ground in the shade of the rock crevasse that concealed them outside of Nob. He tried again in vain to close his eyes and rest, but the thought of being discovered was too great and sleep would not come. Giving up the endeavor, he moved to the opening where he could see the position of the sun and the well outside the priests' village of Nob.

The priests would be finishing up their daily rituals right about now as the sun would soon be setting.

He watched children and women come and go from the well as the sun set. Not one military-aged male visited the well during the hours preceding sunset. Gad began to wonder how they would be able to identify David's men in the darkness.

He finally became impatient and moved back down to where David lay.

"See anyone yet?" David asked, his face still covered by the garment he'd draped over his head.

"No. Just women and children," Gad replied.

"They'll be here soon," David assured him. He sat up and stretched and stood to his feet stretching his back and shoulders.

"How will we know it's them?"

"Don't worry. I'll know it's them when I see them."

David went and laid down on the rock where Gad had been. Gad laid down and propped himself up next to David where they could both observe the well. A priest from the city came out and hung a lamp on a pole next to the well for any travelers to find their way in the darkness. A short while later, night descended on the priests' village.

The two men watched as a single traveler strode up to the well and drew some water, illuminated only by the flicker of the single lamp hung near the well.

"Here we are," David said in a whisper. "That's who we're waiting for."

David placed both hands to his mouth and made a strikingly authentic owl call. The man appeared not to react as he refilled the bladder strung over his shoulder and placed the bucket back next to the well. A moment later, he disappeared back into the darkness.

Several quiet moments passed.

"Did he hear you?" Gad asked.

Suddenly the screech of an owl sounded from within the crevasse. Gad spun around, startled.

"No worries," David comforted the prophet.

"Hushai?" David called out in a hushed voice.

"David?" they heard from somewhere in the darkness.

David stood and moved toward the voice.

"Shalom my friend," David said, recognizing the lanky silhouette that emerged in the darkness.

The tall man pulled him into an embrace and squeezed him tightly.

"I'm glad we found you. We came as quickly as we could. Unfortunately, that means we weren't able to bring anything with us save our swords and the clothes on our backs."

"That's more than I can say for myself. I'm just glad to see you. Who all is with you?" David asked.

"It is just me, Ira and Gareb. Jair and Elhanan were going to try and gather a few others. They will join us soon or meet us at the caves."

David nodded, pleased and moved by the faithfulness of the few men who were prepared to give up everything in order to follow him.

"I take it we have Gareb to thank for the screech owl," David said.

"Who else?" Hushai replied, shaking his head.

"This is Gad, seer in training. He has helped me evade capture thus far."

"Seer?" Hushai asked. "So you can tell us when and where Saul will be coming from?"

"If I see anything, I'll let you know," Gad replied sarcastically.

"Alright, we've got a long way to go. Does everyone have water?" David asked.

"Ira is refilling the skins now," Hushai said pointing towards the well. "Gareb is just behind on lookout. We have no food with us. Do you think it's worth trying to get something from the town here?"

"It's worth trying," David responded. "I know the priest here, but I'd better go alone." David handed Hushai the jug he'd obtained from Jebus. "Can you take care of this and I'll see what assistance I can get from the priest."

Hushai accepted the jug. "We'll fill up the waters and wait for you here."

***

David crept quietly towards the small village. The only guards were positioned on opposite ends at the gates. Its relatively small perimeter wall was easily climbed. He moved to the corner of the modest priestly homes until he'd reached the tabernacle. A small group of worshipers, mourners, and repentant souls knelt and prayed before the tabernacle where sermons were held. Ahimelech moved among them praying over each, stopping to exchange a few words with some.

David waited for the priest to turn in his direction before stepping around the corner so that he might be noticed. When the priest eyed him curiously, David momentarily removed the hood from his head long enough for the priest to recognize him, then placed it back.

Ahimelech began to move towards him when an outstretched hand caught his arm.

David could hear the kneeling man say something to the priest before Ahimelech patted him on the shoulder and dismissed him in his haste to move towards David. The kneeling man turned, irritated by the perceived slight, to see what it was that had required the priest's attention such that his own concerns were so quickly put off.

As Ahimelech moved towards him, David saw the kneeling man's face in the lamplight. Recognizing the man, David immediately stepped back behind the concealment of the column where he stood.

David cursed his luck that he should be seen, of all people, by the man kneeling before the tabernacle. He'd never had much interaction with the man, but knew his reputation among the shepherds in Saul's service whom he frequently rubbed elbows. Perhaps he hadn't recognized him in the dim candlelight, David hoped. Ahimelech interrupted his thoughts as he rounded the column.

The priest took David's elbow and guided him a few steps further away from the other attendants. David could feel the elder man's hand trembling on his arm.

"David, what's going on? Why are you alone and no one with you? I didn't know anyone was coming," the priest said in a hushed voice.

"Not to worry old friend, the king has charged me with a matter and said to me, 'Let no one know anything of the matter about which I send you, and with which I have charged you,' so I have made an appointment with the young men for such and such a place. Now then, what do you have on hand? Can you give me five loaves of bread, or whatever is here?"

"I have no common bread on hand, but there is holy bread - if the young men have kept themselves from women."

"Truly women have been kept from us as always when I go on an expedition. The vessels of the young men are holy even when it is an ordinary journey. How much more today will their vessels be holy?"

Ahimelech eyed him hesitantly. "All of them?" He asked.

"For such a mission as this, there are but a few of us."

Ahimelech nodded and gestured with his hands. "Ok, stay here," he said. A few moments later, he returned with a sack full of bread, trying his best to look inconspicuous.

"This is all we have that I can give you at the moment."

"Thank you, you don't know how much we appreciate this," David said, then paused hesitantly.

"What is it?" Ahimelech asked.

"This is somewhat embarrassing, but I must ask, have you not here a spear or a sword at hand? I have brought neither my sword nor my other weapons with me, because the king's business required haste."

Ahimelech thought for a moment, then his eyes brightened.

"Yes, yes, of course, the sword of Goliath the Philistine, whom you struck down in the Valley of Elah, look," he said, extending his hand towards the sanctuary, "it is here wrapped in a cloth behind the ephod. If you will take that, take it, for there is none but that one here."

David's eyes brightened. God provides, he thought to himself.

"Truly, there is none like that one. Give it to me," he said.

ON THE RUN

1063 BC, Judah, Israel

"Perhaps I missed the briefing," Ira said with typical sarcasm, "but where exactly are we headed?"

"Adullam," Hushai replied.

"Never heard of it. What's there?"

"It's more what's not there that's important," Hushai replied.

"Ok, what's not there?" Ira asked.

"Anyone friendly with the royalty," Hushai responded. "There's not much apart from outlaws, gentiles, and prostitutes."

"This whole thing just got a lot more interesting!" Gereb replied loudly, clapping and rubbing his hands together.

Elhanan stopped and turned around. "What don't you understand about keeping quiet?"

"Keeping quiet," Ira replied.

Gereb continued in a whisper, undeterred by Elhanan's irritation. "Here I was thinking we were going to be wandering the wilderness like Moses and Aaron."

"I wouldn't get your hopes up too much," Hushai cautioned.

"Too late!" Gereb replied, jabbing Ira's shoulder as they walked.

Ira shook his head as he trudged, looking down at the feet of Jair in front of him. There was little else to see in the fading moonlight and Jair was not one he wanted to trip over or run into in the darkness.

Suddenly the feet stopped abruptly.

Ira looked up to see Jair frozen in his tracks. He motioned for the others to get down.

They sprawled onto the ground, trying not to create a silhouette against the night sky as Jair watched a group of men on horseback several stadia ahead of them on the road below. Even in the dim moonlight, the glint of their helmets and armor could be seen. The helmets lacked the feathered crests of the Philistines.

"Looks like about twelve," Jair whispered. "Israelite."

A moment later, mounted patrol split, with one band headed south in the same direction they'd been heading and the second headed straight towards the small band of fugitives.

Elhanan searched the ground with his hands till he felt a large rock in the dirt.

"David," Hushai whispered, "you go down to that crevasse and conceal yourself," he said pointing to a dark void in the earth on the northern slope of the hill. "If they continue coming this way, we'll head south and draw them away from you.

"No, it would be better that I be caught instead of all of you."

"They have no reason to suspect anything of us. Chances are no one even knows we're gone yet."

"Ok, but it's too dangerous for us to continue traveling together. You all continue south to Adullam and set up camp at the cave. I'll find a way to get to you. If I'm not there by the new moon... well, I'm probably dead."

"Where will you go?"

"Where they least expect to find me," David said, nodding towards the west.

"What? Philistia?" Jair asked. "You're joking."

Hushai shook his head. "It's too dangerous."

"I'll be fine. They won't be looking for me at the border. I'll see you all before the new moon," Daivd said before backing down the slope and moving quickly around to their north. A moment later, he disappeared from sight behind a rock.

As the patrol followed the contour of the hill, it appeared to be headed directly to where David had hidden himself.

"Alright, come on," Hushai said as he stood and started south along the ridgeline, silhouetting himself along the moonlit sky. Ira, Gereb, Jair, Gad, and Elhanan followed.

A moment later, the patrol turned abruptly in their direction and appeared to increase its pace.

"Well, they've seen us. What do we do now?" Gad asked.

"Just do what we do," Ira instructed. "Try your best to look like one of us."

"Let me do the talking," Hushai said as the patrol closed in.

Within minutes, the patrol had covered the distance between them and slowed to a stop as the mounted soldiers formed a semicircle around the small band.

"By order of King Saul, identify yourselves," one of the soldiers commanded.

"Easy there men," Hushai said with his hands raised. "I am Captain Hushai of the southern division. These are my men."

"What are you doing out here? Your unit was recalled."

"I was given special orders," Hushai replied. "Same as you. I suspected we'd cross paths at some point. We've been tracking the fugitive from Benjamin. We followed him here and lost track of him about the same time we saw you all."

"Where are your orders?" the captain asked.

"I could ask you the same."

"Jair, is that you?" one of the mounted men interrupted.

"Seth? I thought you were assigned palace duty, babysitting princesses."

Seth laughed. "That's about right."

"It's good to see you," Jair responded.

"Why don't you have any weapons or provisions?" the captain inquired, interrupting their banter.

"Now, what would you do if you were a fugitive and saw armed men approaching?" Hushai asked, choosing not to reveal the blade hidden under his cloak. "Do you really think David is going to stay put if he sees you coming, jingling around with your armor and weapons like a Moabite merchant? We heard you all coming long before we saw you."

The leader of the patrol sat quietly on his horse, clearly irritated.

Gereb looked up at the soldier closest to him. The man's spear was pointed at his chest. Gereb smiled and gave him a wink. The soldier remained stone-faced. Elhanan clinched the fist-sized rock in his hand and eyed the soldier nearest his father.

"Look, we think he was headed south further into Judea, but who knows what he did if he saw your patrol. He's probably hunkered down somewhere, waiting for you all to leave. Why don't you all post a watch on the reverse slope of that hill over there," he said, motioning to their east. "See if he pokes his head out after a while? If he did see you coming, he probably went that way."

The captain didn't seem pleased with being told how to do his job.

"How can I know you aren't aiding him? Are you not of Judah also?"

"One fugitive does not make outlaws of our whole tribe. If you want to take us in for questioning, be my guest," Hushai replied. "But you'll be the one to explain how you let David slip through my fingers."

The captain grunted, then turned his horse towards Seth and pulled alongside him.

Hushai watched as the two leaned towards each other and spoke quietly.

The captain turned his horse abruptly back towards Hushai.

"We are headed to Bethlehem to post a watch near his home. If you see or hear of his whereabouts, send word."

The captain kicked his horse and steered it in the direction of the hill to their east. His men followed after.

"Good to see you old friend," Seth said before following after.

"Likewise," Jair responded.

Hushai and the others waited until the patrol disappeared from sight, then turned to look for David, to see if he would emerge and rejoin them. No sign of him could be detected.

"You think he's headed to Philistine territory?" Ira asked.

The older soldier exhaled. "That is what I fear," Hushai responded.

"Sometimes I think he's got more sand than he does sense," Jair pronounced.

"He is God's anointed," Gad replied. "He will be alright, as for us...."

"Don't we get some sort of divine protection for looking after him?" Gareb asked.

"I can't say for certain and I'm not in a hurry to test the theory," Gad replied.

ATROCITIES

1063 BC, Nob, Benjamin, Israel

Now Saul heard that David was discovered, and the men
who were with him. Saul was sitting at Gibeah under the
tamarisk tree on the height with his spear in his hand,
and all his servants were standing about him.
I Samuel 22:6

The Israelite army assembled at the hill near Gibeah before the sun was fully visible on the eastern horizon. It was already turning out to be a hot fall day, and the men prayed the assembly would be short.

Eliam could see Saul's silhouette against the lightening blue sky to the west under the tamarisk tree at the top of the hill while the men assembled in columns behind him further down the eastern slope. Saul sat on the dilapidated remains of an ancient stone wall and leaned forward with his head pressed against the spear in his hand as it rested on the butt spike in the dirt between his legs.

Obviously absent was the captain of Saul's guard. The contingent of foreign soldiers stood ahead and to the left of the divisions of tribes. Raanan, David's apparent interim replacement, stood ahead of them and reported their numbers.

Eliam could hear the men grumbling behind him.

"What's this about anyway?"

"He's lost his mind," one man whispered.

"He's gone paranoid, thinks we're conspiring against him," another suggested.

Eliam turned and silenced the men. "Shut your mouth you fools," he reprimanded. "If I can hear you, who knows who else will? Now keep your mouth shut."

Joash received the report from the commanders at the head of the assembly, then turned and proceeded up the hill to Saul. The men watched carefully for Saul's reaction to the report. There were several men missing, each of them known associates of the fugitive captain.

Saul stood and turned to face the men below him on the hill, resting his spear across his shoulders, he strode down towards the Benjaminite division.

"Hear now, people of Benjamin!" Saul shouted at the column of Benjaminite officers at the front of the division and assembled to the left of Eliam's legion of men from Judah. "Will the son of Jesse give every one of you fields and vineyards, will he make of you all commanders of thousands and commanders of hundreds that all of you have conspired against me?" he shouted.

"No one discloses to me when my son makes a covenant with the son of Jesse!" Saul continued as he walked between the columns of men. "None of you is sorry for me or discloses to me that my son has stirred up my servant against me, to lie in wait, as he does this day," he shouted as he spun on his heals and stabbed the spear into the ground.

Saul was spewing spittle with every word as he shouted angrily at the men. "So none of you know where he is or how he escaped! You are all blind, ignorant fools! Is that it?"

"Not so my King!" Eliam heard someone say among the small group of officials. Eliam's eyes searched the group of men for the source of David's betrayer.

"Who said that?" Saul shouted, turning to the voice and walking with great strides in that direction. "WHO SAID THAT?" Saul nearly screamed as he strode up the hill towards the sound of the voice.

"I did My King! It was I."

Saul continued towards the voice pushing men out of his way as he plowed through the ranks towards the voice.

Coming to the man, Saul demanded, "What is your name?"

"Doeg sire, your faithful servant. I knew not of David, eh, the son of Jesse's betrayal when I saw him. I saw the son of Jesse coming to Nob, to Abimelech the son of Ahitub, and he inquired of the Lord for him and gave him provisions and gave him the sword of Goliath the Philistine."

Saul spun around and marched back towards the head of the column.

"You," he said pointing to Eliam, "Man of Judah! Bring me the son of Ahitub, and all his father's house!" Saul turned and proceeded up the hill, then stopped and turned to Eliam again. "And all the priests! Every last priest at Nob!" he shouted, then turned again and walked back up to his perch under the tree.

Eliam turned his men over to their officers and called for his horse. A moment later, he was gone.

The men stared at Doeg, the Edomite traitor now standing at the front of the large assembly.

***

Hours later, the midday sun glared down on the men still standing in formation as Eliam returned to report that the priests and family of Ahitub were on their way as directed.

"What is the meaning of this? Have they been like this the whole time?" Eliam asked.

"Saul has been on the warpath; he's been berating the men this entire time. Where is Abner? Or Jonathan?"

"They're both in the field," Eliam replied and cursed under his breath. "I sure wish one of them were here."

"What's he going to do when the priests get here?" one officer asked.

"I suppose he'll interrogate them as he did all of us earlier."

"He wants to make an example out of someone," the man replied.

"What do you mean by that?" another officer asked.

"ELIAM!"

Their discussion was interrupted. Saul had spotted him from atop the hill.

"Have you completed your task? Where are the priests?" Saul demanded.

"They should be arriving any moment sir."

"Very well! You may join the formation. There has been enough conspiring for one day!"

"Yes my King," Eliam acknowledged and stood at attention in the front of the column.

A short while later, priests began appearing at the front of the formation. Eliam instructed them to wait as he inquired whether everyone was present.

Ahitub turned and looked at the vast group of priests and descendants behind him.

"I can't be sure," the old priest replied. "But I instructed them to not delay. I gathered all that I could find and left instructions for the rest."

As more priests and Levites trickled in behind them, Eliam took his position abreast his officers.

"Is Abimelech present?" Joash inquired.

"Here I am," the man said as he stepped abreast his father. "What is the meaning of this General?"

"The king will address you momentarily," Joash replied.

Joash turned and proceeded up the hill. A moment later Saul stood and turned towards the priests. Eliam thought he saw Joash take hold of Saul's arm before Saul shook loose and shot a fierce glare at the advisor. Saul then proceeded as he had earlier down the hill and towards Ahimelech the priest.

"Hear now, son of Ahitub."

"Here I am, my lord," Ahimelech answered.

"Why have you conspired against me, you and the son of Jesse, in that you have given him bread and a sword and have inquired of God for him, so that he has risen against me, to lie in wait, as he does today?"

Ahimelech looked to his father then back at the king, "My Lord, and who among all your servants is so faithful as David who is the king's son-in-law and captain over your bodyguard and honored in your house? Is today the first time that I have inquired of God for him? No! Let not the king impute anything to his servant or to all the house of my father, for your servant has known nothing of all this, much or little."

As Saul stared angrily at the man before him, a strange sense of familiarity came over him. A vivid memory flooded his mind. This hill, these men. They'd been here before. Saul turned back and looked up the hill to the small dilapidated ruin where he'd sat with these men, now well over thirty years ago. The musicians, the priests, the hill... the prophecy. The great wolf, the lion.... Saul turned slowly back to the priest.

"You knew," Saul said in a low voice to Ahitub. "The prophecy. You both were there. You knew. You knew and still you aided the usurper. You want it to be true."

Ahimelech stood mute. Ahitub glared back at the king with a look of defiant acknowledgment.

The word of God does not return void," the elder priest replied.

"You shall surely die, Ahimelech, you and all your father's house!" Saul shouted.

"Our sentence was pronounced long ago to our father Eli for the sins of his sons," Ahitub responded. "But hear me, Son of Kish, you contend with the Almighty. His word will come to pass whether you submit to it or not. The son of Jesse..."

"SILENCE!" Saul shouted, cutting off the priest mid-sentence. He turned to Raanan. "Kill them! Kill the priests of the Lord, because their hand also is with David, and they knew that he fled and did not disclose it to me!"

Raanan looked to the commanders standing at the front of the formation, then back to the king.

"Don't look to them! I am your King, you obey me! Kill them!"

Raanan stepped back and knelt before the king with his head bowed.

Saul was livid. "You!" he shouted, pointing at his contingent of guardsmen. "Kill them!"

Many of the men followed after Raanan and knelt as he had. The rest stood mute, unsure of the predicament that was unfolding before them.

Saul turned to his officials. Doeg stood among them.

Saul pointed to the Edomite.

"You! Turn and strike the priests!" Saul commanded as he drew his own sword and held the hilt out towards the man.

Doeg stepped toward the king and accepted the sword, then turned his attention toward the priests and walked over to Ahimelech. The priest's male family members stood behind him in disbelief.

Doeg looked back at the king.

"Kill them all," Saul demanded.

"This is madness!" shouted Ahitub as he staggered forward. "You cannot stop prophecy. It is the will of God! You only hasten your own demise!"

"KILL THEM NOW!" Saul shouted.

Doeg turned immediately and jabbed the sword into Ahimelech's belly.

Ahimelech wailed and grabbed the blade with both hands as he sank to his knees. Doeg snatched the sword rearwards slicing the priest's hands, as his entrails spilled onto the ground.

Ahitub dropped to his knees and gasped as he bent over his dying son, shielding his body.

Doeg drove the sword down into the ancient priest's back as the man wailed in pain.

Several of Ahimelech's family moved to his aid when Doeg began swinging the sword wildly, striking down the family of priests one at a time.

Several started to flee. Saul commanded that they be seized. When Eliam and the other captains did not move, he seized a man by his breastplate and ordered him to go after the fleeing men. The terrified man obeyed.

Eliam couldn't believe his eyes. He felt paralyzed. Many of the priests had begun to kneel and pray as Doeg made his way through their ranks. When he was finished, he mounted Eliam's horse and pursued the few priests who had managed to outrun the soldiers on foot, striking them down like sheep.

"Now we shall see who among you is loyal to God's anointed. Which of you will carry out my orders?" Saul shouted.

Most of the men in the formation stood silent. Several stepped forward. Of those from his company, Eliam could have predicted. Men who loved killing above all else.

Saul seized several officer helmets and placed them on the heads of the men who'd followed his command to go after the fleeing priests. When Doeg returned, Saul wrenched Eliam's crested helmet from his hands and handed it to the Edomite.

"Take these men to Nob. Kill everything."

***

Abiathar returned from Naioth with strange and exciting news. He could hardly wait to tell his father and grandfather all he had learned during his visit. His grandfather was right. It appeared that prophesy was unfolding right before their eyes. Proceeding through the small main gate at Nob, he made his way straight to the tabernacle. To his surprise, the place was unoccupied. He thought it odd that he'd not encountered anyone apart from a few small children in the street, but he discovered the place of worship and priests' quarters unoccupied, he felt a shiver run down his back.

With haste, Abiathar ran to his father's home where he found his mother and grandmother preparing a meal in anticipation of their husbands' return that evening. He breathed a sigh of relief.

"Abiathar! You're back," his grandmother announced and kissed his check. "What's the matter? How was your trip?"

"Where is everyone?" he inquired as the women went on about the kitchen.

"It was very strange," his mother reported. "A soldier came and reported that all the priests were needed at Gibeah this morning. So they all left. They've been gone all day."

"Did the soldier say what it was about?"

"No, just that King Saul required that all the priests report to him on the hill, Gibeah Elohim. Your father suggested that perhaps he wanted them to pray blessings over the army or something to that extent."

Abiathar sat and brushed his hair from his face as his grandmother brought him a cup of water.

"You said he called 'all the priests'?" Abiathar asked.

"That's what he said."

"I must have just missed them on my return from Ramah. They must have gone west of Gibeah when I took the eastern route," Abiathar said as he stood. He let out an irritated sigh. "Well, I'd best join them then. Sure wish the prophets at Naioth could have given me some foresight. It would have saved me a lot of walking."

His mother smiled as he kissed her and his grandmother.

"I'll see you later," Abiathar said as he exited the home.

Departing through the gate, Abiathar hastened his pace, eager to join the other priests for whatever business they'd been called to. Gibeah Elohim, or "the hill" as it was called, was north of Gibeah. He could proceed through the city or go west around it to arrive at his destination. Choosing the more direct route, Abiathar proceeded through the gates of Gibeah and through the royal city to the northern gate.

He proceeded quickly through the city when suddenly, he was caught by the arm.

"Come with me," the soldier instructed as he pulled Abiathar aside amidst the crowded streets of the city and into a vacant alleyway.

"Come on," the soldier commanded as they rounded a corner. Safely concealed within the alley, the soldier looked behind the priest to ensure they'd not been followed. "You're Abiathar are you not?"

"I am, what is going on? What is the meaning of this?"

"It's not safe for you," the soldier replied, removing his breast and back plate. "Stay here. I need to find us some cloaks so that we won't be recognized."

The soldier knelt to unfasten the greaves from his shins.

"I am Eliam, son of Ahithophel of Giloh. I was a commander of the legion of Judah," the soldier continued as he dropped the last of his armor atop his breast plate and stashed it under some rubbish along the alley. "I recognized you in the street. I've just been relieved of my command," the soldier informed him. The soldier then took a somber demeanor as he contemplated his words. "I don't know how else to tell you this, but the king has executed your father's house. All of the priests of Nob, he has slain just now, north of the city, at the hill. I am sorry, but you are in danger. The king stripped my command when I would not lift my sword against your father."

Abiathar did not know what to say or whether the soldier's words could be trusted.

"I do not know you, how can I trust you?" the young priest asked. "How do I know what you are saying is so?"

"I have no reason to lie to you, I can only tell you that if Saul or his men find you, you will be murdered. He's just sent a contingent of men to your city to kill everyone left. You must get as far from this place as possible."

"But my family, my eema and savta," Abiathar said. "I must go! I must get them out of the city," Abiathar said as he turned to leave.

Eliam seized his arm.

"You won't make it! Doeg and his men left on horseback; they are likely already there!"

"I don't care! I must go," the priest said as he snatched his arm free.

"Let me obtain some cloaks to disguise ourselves first. You are no good to your eema dead. Stay here. I'll only take a moment."

Eliam left Abiathar alone in the alley and disappeared into the adjacent market dressed only in the wool undergarment the soldiers wore as a layer between their armor and leather skirts. He returned moments later with the cloaks he'd obtained and handed one to Abiathar. Both men donned the cloaks and quickly headed towards the southern gate.

Once outside of the city, Abiathar all but sprinted the distance to Nob. It wasn't long, however, before they could see the smoke of the village rising above the horizon. As they approached, they ascended the final hill that obscured their view of the village. Reaching the crest, Doeg's contingent of murderers could be seen setting aflame the city gates as the last of them mounted their horses just outside the small perimeter wall. Thick black smoke billowed from homes within.

The priest paused at the top of the hill and wailed at the sight of his home engulfed in flame. Abiathar's lungs still heaving from exertion, Eliam tackled the priest and pulled him below the defilade of the hill so that they would not be spotted by the soldiers. The priest tried to pull free Eliam's grasp but found it no use as he was pulled from the highway to some nearby shrubbery.

"You're no good to your family dead, do you hear me?" Eliam scolded. "You must keep your head right now. Do not be a fool. You must survive. Who will avenge them if you're struck down now?"

The priest continued to pull away, struggling to reach the top of the hill, when suddenly Eliam could hear the approach of Doeg's mounted band. He pulled the priest to the ground and covered his mouth as the men topped the hill and rode past on their way back North to Gibeah. When Abiathar stopped struggling, Eliam released his grip. The two men watched as the mounted contingent proceeded in the opposite direction. Perceiving they'd reached a sufficient distance, Abiathar sprung to his feet and ran as fast as he could to the burning village.

Reaching the short wall, he climbed over and ran to his father's home, passing a slain elderly woman lying dead in the street. Coughing and eyes burning from the smoke, he reached the threshold and entered. The door had been knocked free from the hinges and laid partially atop his grandmother. He lifted it from her body and seeing the dark red stain upon her breast, moved to search for his mother.

"Eema!" he shouted between coughs as tears involuntarily shed from his eyes and snot spewed from his smoke-filled nostrils. Choking, he sank to the floor and nearly vomited. The heat was unbearable. Eliam lifted him and pulled him from the dwelling, then disappeared back into the smoke pouring from the open doorway as the priest struggled to catch his breath.

A moment later, he emerged with the limp body of a woman, her midsection damp and crimson with her own blood. Eliam laid her at the priest's feet and returned to the dwelling. Abiathar sank to his knees and lifted his mother's head to his chest. An involuntary wail escaped his lungs as his body trembled with sorrow. Eliam stood over them holding the elderly woman gingerly in his arms.

"Can you lift her?" Eliam asked. "We need to get out of here," he said coughing and struggling to breathe.

Bent now over his mother's body, Abiathar took a deep breath before lifting his head back into the smoke. Summoning his strength, he lifted his mother's body and the two men retreated for the nearby plot of land which held the bones of Abiathar's ancestors.

The priest laid the body of his mother and grandmother side by side on the rock-hewn bench inside a shallow cave. Kissing them both on the forehead, he exited and assisted Eliam in rolling a large round stone back into place covering the mouth of the cave.

His face lined with the streaks his tears left as they rolled down his soot-covered cheeks, Abiathar turned to his new friend.

"Thank you," the priest said. "I owe you my life."

"You owe me nothing," Eliam responded.

"Where does one go from here?" Abiathar asked rhetorically as he watched the rising smoke from his village ascending into the evening sky.

"If it's any consolation, you are not the only one looking for somewhere to hide."

"David?"

"He will need a man of God by his side. Now more than ever," Eliam replied. "He's already got some good men with him. It's a small group, but it is sure to grow. I could help you find them."

"How do you know where to find him?" the priest asked.

"I don't," Eliam responded, "but know someone who does."

"Who?"

AFTERWORD

*Therefore, my beloved brothers, be steadfast, immovable, always abounding in the work of the Lord, knowing that **in the Lord your labor is not in vain.***
1 Corinthians 15:58

I hope you have enjoyed this second book of the *Anointed* Series. As of the date of this publication, it is my hope to have book three ready for publication by the spring of 2026. However, without the Lord's hand, that may be an impossible endeavor. I would appreciate it if you would pray that the Lord guide me as I work towards completing the series. Please pray that the Holy Spirit give me divine insight into the thoughts, deeds, words, and passions of the true men whose names fill these pages.

Iron sharpeneth iron;
so a man sharpeneth the
countenance of his friend.
Proverbs 27:17

Because I have seen the great and wonderful things that my Lord and Savior has done and was always willing to do in and through me, I have chosen to follow His lead by writing this book. At the age of 21, as a new officer in the Marine Corps, another close friend and fellow Marine officer, Christopher Young, inspired me to read the books of Samuel and Kings. I am ashamed to say that while I professed myself to be a believer, I had never read the Bible from cover to cover. Because I had grown up in church, I thought I knew all of the stories contained within it.

Reading 1 and 2 Samuel set my life on a new course. I realized how little I truly knew of the life of David. Being the third of four brothers, the trio of Joab, Abishai, and Asahel specifically stood out to me. These were men I'd never heard of in church. I thought to myself, *What else have I been missing?*

The stories of these men and others contained in the books of 1 and 2 Samuel sparked my first endeavor to read the Bible from cover to cover. As I proceeded to do so, my life began to conform to the higher calling which I'd so long confessed to believe in, but failed to live out. Slowly, my personal struggles with sin, shame, and self-doubt faded as my actions and behavior conformed to my beliefs. I am proof of the life-changing power of scripture.

I have prayed that I would be a conduit through which God would reveal truth about the lives of these great men and women who, like us, were flawed. Their faith faltered, they made mistakes, but never once did God abandon those who were willing to repent and turn to Him. While the names and characters change throughout history, the characteristics of God never do. He is merciful. He is kind. He is GOOD.

I have written this book because I wholeheartedly believe in the truth of the events contained in scripture. Though I have taken license to add stories and experiences so that I might flesh out the individuals, using many of my own experiences, it has been my goal to never once deviate from scripture. I hope the reader will forgive me if I have failed in this. While I have used extra-Biblical sources to help inform my knowledge of the events, people, times, and places, when or wherever those sources contradicted the Bible, the Word prevailed. My primary goal is to inspire the reader to search the scripture for themselves and discover what lies there, waiting to be discovered between the lines on the pages. Thank you for your interest. Thank you for your time. Thank you for your prayers. Keep digging!

*The Lord bless you and keep you; the Lord make his face
to shine upon you and be gracious to you; the Lord lift
up his countenance upon you and give you peace.*
Numbers 6:24-26

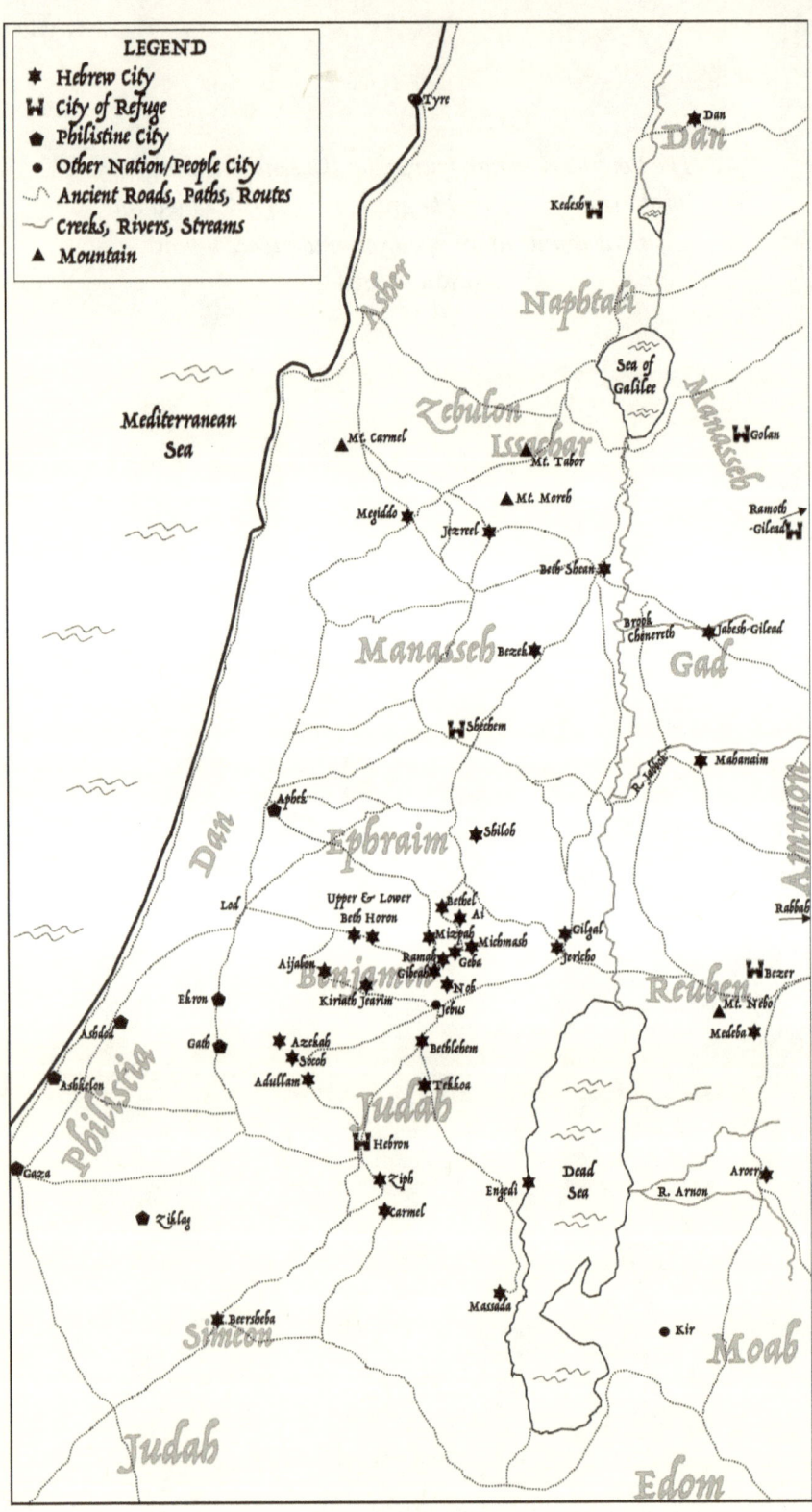

LEGEND
★ Hebrew City
ᚼ City of Refuge
⬠ Philistine City
● Other Nation/People City
〜 Ancient Roads, Paths, Routes
〜 Creeks, Rivers, Streams
▲ Mountain

Mediterranean
Sea

Sea of
Galilee

Dead
Sea

Tyre
Dan
Kedesh
Naphtali
Golan
Mt. Carmel
Zebulon
Issachar
Mt. Tabor
Ramoth
-Gilead
Manasseh
Mt. Moreh
Megiddo
Jezreel
Beth Shean
Brook
Chenereth
Jabesh-Gilead
Gad
Manasseh
Bezek
Shechem
Mahanaim
Ammon
Apbek
Ephraim
Shiloh
Rabbab
Lod
Upper & Lower
Beth Horon
Bethel
Ai
Mizpah
Michmash
Gilgal
Jericho
Aijalon
Benjamin
Ramah
Geba
Gibeah
Nob
Bezer
Reuben
Mt. Nebo
Kiriath Jearim
Jebus
Medeba
Ekron
Ashdod
Gath
Azekah
Socoh
Bethlehem
Ashkelon
Philistia
Adullam
Tekoa
Judah
Hebron
Gaza
Ziph
Engedi
R. Arnon
Aroer
Ziklag
Carmel
Massada
Kir
Moab
Beersheba
Simeon
Judah
Edom